A reason to fear

Amelia took the envelope and walked back to the house, where she built the stove to a fierce blaze. When the room felt cozy and safe, she settled herself in the big armchair to open the envelope.

It was a muddy photocopy of an old newspaper clipping. The headline read, "CANDIDATE AND FAMILY SLAIN."

Amelia crushed the stapled pages in her fist. Seeing the article, her first instinct was still to run—hard and fast. It's what she had always done before.

But her circumstances were different now. She had promised Gramps that she would put his prairie right. She had made a commitment.

She untangled her feet from the afghan and walked over to the wood stove. She wrestled the fire door open and ripped the stapled pages apart so they would burn faster. A white index card fluttered to the floor.

Amelia flung the copied news story into the fire. Then she looked down at the index card. In the same slashing blue print as the first one, her enemy had written, "TIME TO FINISH THE JOB."

She tossed it in after the article, and the flames took the card eagerly. Even as it blackened and began to burn, the words remained clear. They stared out at her, a brutal promise.

"FINISH" was the last word to fade.

WALKING RAIN

Susan Wade

Bantam Books
New York • Toronto • London • Sydney • Auckland

WALKING RAIN

A Bantam Fanfare Book / August 1996

FANFARE and the portrayal of a boxed "ff" are trademarks of
Bantam Books,
a division of Bantam Doubleday Dell Publishing Group, Inc.

ISBN 0-553-56865-5

Published simultaneously in the United States and Canada

*Bantam Books are published by Bantam Books, a division of
Bantam Doubleday Dell Publishing Group, Inc. Its trademark,
consisting of the words "Bantam Books" and the portrayal of a
rooster, is Registered in U.S. Patent and Trademark Office and in
other countries. Marca Registrada. Bantam Books, 1540
Broadway, New York, New York 10036.*

PRINTED IN THE UNITED STATES OF AMERICA

RAD   0 9 8 7 6 5 4 3 2 1

For my father, Houston Russell Wade,
who gave me the word processor.
Having a wonderful time, Dad.
Wish you were here.

Acknowledgments

Annie Dillard says there comes a point in writing a book when it is no longer possible to work on it; one can only sit up with it, as with a dying friend. This book has had its share of critical moments, some of which would certainly have proved fatal if not for the patient ministrations of my writing community. I owe a profound debt to Susan Rogers Cooper—who actually put the first outline on paper for me—and to Bill Spencer, who provided much-needed humor and sage advice for getting through the rough spots. Most of all, my thanks to the Trashy Paperback Writers, who are an essential part of my writing life: Fred Askew, Jodi Berls, Dinah Chenven, and Mary Willis. May your wordcounts ever increase!

Others who generously contributed advice or know-how are: beekeepers Robert and Mary Bost, Johnny Cox, and other members of the Williamson County Area Beekeepers Association; potter Judy Wilkens Conroy; Daryl Wade of the Austin Fire Department and Greg Ament of the Dog Canyon Fire Department; "Cowboy" Roy Henry; and Stephen McNally. (Any exaggerations or errors of fact are my responsibility.) I'm grateful to Lynne Lively (and the entire Lively clan) and to writing buddies Jennifer Evans, Chris Kelly, Carrie Richerson, Hendle Rumbaut and Michael Ambrose for their friendship and help. Special thanks to Shawna McCarthy and Wendy McCurdy for their patience, and for their faith in a first novel with so many eccentricities.

New Mexico's state slogan is the "Land of Enchantment," which should serve as a warning. Like those who venture into enchanted lands in old fairy tales, travelers who cross the border into New Mexico may never return or, if they do, may never be quite the same. That's certainly true of me. Although I returned to my native Austin years ago, the spell New Mexico cast on me has never faded. So one final acknowledgment: If there is any power of place in this book, that *tierra encantada* deserves the credit.

Part 1

HICKORY WIND-
LATE WINTER

Alianza de Oro

En el corazón azul
de la montaña
le conocí a mi amor
por primera vez.
Me dijo: Es el verano.
Le dijé: Es verdad.
Esa es toda la leyenda
de acquella alianza de oro.

Ya es invierno.
Mi corazón ha muerto
al fin del año pasado.
Mi sangre está aguada.
Siempre siento el frío.
Pero en el corazón azul
De la montaña, para mi,
Es siempre el verano.

—EMILIO VAZZA, *Canciones
del Viejo*

Alliance of Gold (Lovematch)

In the blue heart
of the mountain
I met my love
for the first time.
She said: It is summer.
I said: That is true.
That is all of the legend
of our marriage.

Now it is winter.
My heart has died
the end of last year.
My blood thins.
Always I feel the cold.
But in the blue heart
of the mountain, for me,
It is always summer.

—tr. HENDLE RUMBAUT and
　　LAWRENCE SCHIMEL

New Mexico

She drove up U.S. 54 from Interstate 10 because that was the way she had always come to the ranch. Her old pickup had held up well on the long drive from the East Coast, but now it rattled and jounced along the battered road. Amelia checked the rearview mirror often, making certain her potter's wheel was still securely lashed to the bed of the truck. It was her habit to watch her back.

She'd reached El Paso late in the afternoon, and stopped there to put gas in the truck. Between that stop and all the Juarez traffic, it was getting on toward evening by the time she left the city and, with it, the interstate. Now the mountains of the Tularosa basin rose on either side of the two-lane road: the soaring ridge of the Sacramentos to her east, the Organ Mountains, drier, more distant, to her west. The eastern range was heavily snowed, peaks gleaming pink in the fading light, and the evening sky was winter-brilliant. Narrow bands of cloud glowed like flamingo feathers above the Organs.

She had forgotten the crystalline stillness of the air here, forgotten the sunny chill of a New Mexico winter. How had that happened? Maybe that was the price she'd paid for forgetting the things she had to forget. Part of the price.

The sun flamed on the horizon, looking as if it would flow down the mountains to melt the world, and then it sank. Its light faded quickly from the sky; already the stars were taking their turn at ruling the deep blue reaches. Amelia rolled down her window, even though the temperature outside was plunging toward freezing. The desert smelled pungent and strong, and there was a hint of pine and piñon on the wind.

It was the wind that whipped tears to her eyes. Certainly the wind; she was not a woman who wept. But she was suddenly swept by a brilliant ache of homesickness—here, now, when she was very near the only home left to her—it caught at her violently. So violently that she almost turned the truck around and went away again.

To need something so much frightened her.

But she was tired, and she had only decided to come here when she could no longer face starting over somewhere new. She'd been rootless for too long.

So the truck spun on, winding north in the star-studded darkness, past the ghostly dunes of White Sands, north and then eventually east, to a narrower road, one that ran deep into the wrinkled land at the foot of the Sacramentos.

She made her way to the Crossroads by feel, and turned left without thinking. It was unsettling to be in a place so instantly familiar. The stars had come full out; the desert was bright beneath them. An ancient seabed, the Tularosa basin was now four thousand feet above sea level, and the air was thin, rarified, so the starlight streamed through it undiminished. Amelia could see the beacon of the observatory to the south, high on the mountain, gleaming like a fallen star itself.

And then she was there, bumping the truck off the road next to the dirt lane that led to the house. The gate was closed. A new gate, one of those metal-barred affairs. Amelia left the truck idling when she got out, not sure it would start again if she turned it off after such a long run. But when she tried to open the gate, she found it padlocked. Her grandfather never did that.

She climbed up on the gate and looked toward the ranch house, sprawling among the cottonwood trees beyond the fields. No lights. No smoke from the chimney pipe. The windows were dark vacant blanks against the pale adobe walls of the house. She could see the looming windmill, its blades turning slowly in silhouette, but nothing else moved.

So maybe the ranch hadn't been leased to someone else. Maybe her uncle hadn't decided she was dead and sold the place off. Maybe none of the things she'd been afraid of had happened.

She should have been relieved. But the homesickness was back, wilder than ever, and she realized that some part of her had expected her grandfather to be there waiting for her.

He was dead. Bound to be. He'd been seventy-six the last time she and her kid brother had come for the summer, and that was more than a dozen years ago. But one thing she had no doubt about—that Gramps had kept his word and left the property to her. She knew he had, as surely as she knew the pattern the cottonwoods' shadow would paint on the house in summer. This place was part of her.

She went back and cut off the truck. The silence was a living one, even in February. The rustle of a mouse in its nest and the faraway cry of a hunting night bird gathered on the wind. Amelia shivered. She put on her down vest, then took her backpack and her cooler out of the truck. Nobody would bother her things, not out here. Gramps used to say they could go a week without seeing another soul on this road.

He'd been exaggerating, of course. Something he was prone to. Amelia dropped the cooler over the fence, then swung herself over the gate. She picked up the cooler and started down the lane toward the house. The smell of the desert seemed even more sharply familiar now, thick with memories. She remembered racing Michael down this road on bikes—Gramps taking the two of them to collect native grasses by the old railroad tracks—Gramma baking biscuits in the cool of the morning. So many memories. A cascade of them.

They were falling around her like rain. Amelia bowed her head and walked up the road into it.

Chapter One

Paul Cameron Boucher was a native of Baton Rouge. The son of a geologist and a music teacher, he loved jazz, fossil collecting, and gardening. He had studied piano since childhood and was a gifted amateur. His first passion was ragtime. His second was soccer, which he played with such abandon that his mother couldn't bear to attend his matches. Boucher moved to Houston during the boom of the early eighties and, in 1983, at the age of twenty-eight, was already a senior lending officer for a major commercial bank. He was also gay.

Paul Boucher was beaten to death by a "posse club" on the evening of May 16, 1983.

Members of the club were cruising the Montrose district in a late-model blue Chevy pickup truck that balmy Friday night. They spotted Boucher walking with a companion about half a block from Shepherd Drive. His companion later reported that the driver of the Chevy asked for directions to the Pink Flamingo Bar & Grille, a well-known nightspot. When Boucher—always friendly—paused to answer, the group piled out of their truck and began beating him. They had come prepared. They used baseball bats and at least one two-by-four spiked with ten-penny nails.

His companion was also attacked, but was farther from the truck and managed to escape. His injuries required hospitalization and even-

tual reconstructive surgery, but he survived to stand witness.

In 1983, rumors of a new "gay plague" were escalating, gays were coming out of the closet in enormous numbers, and the Texas Gay Political Caucus had recently formed. Aggressive voter-registration drives were making the Texas caucus—and others like it—into a tangible political force for the first time in U.S. history.

A record-setting heat wave hit Houston in early May, one that continued unabated through the summer.

—Molly Cates, "Blood Relatives,"
Lone Star Monthly, April 1986

New Mexico

The house Amelia had come home to was set on the flats at the root of the Sacramentos, part of a property that ran back into the foothills and canyons. Surrounded by tall cottonwoods, the Rawlins house had been built more than a hundred years before of adobe bricks. Over the years, the thick walls had been covered with so many layers of sand-colored stucco, they now canted inward as they rose to the red tile roof.

The outline of the house was embellished by arches and crenellations with rounded edges, as if they had been built of snow and were just beginning to melt. The end of the log beams that supported the roof protruded about a foot from the exterior walls. A matching stucco wall enclosed the yard in a graceful line that tied the house to the earth.

Inside, Amelia lay awake in the darkness before dawn and listened to the deep humming *whuf* of the windmill turning. Awake, even though it had been late by the time she managed to fall asleep. Her grandparents' house still smelled of cinnamon and beeswax, just the way it always had. A little musty too; not surprising since it had been locked up tight for God only knew how long.

But she had found the spare key behind the loose tile by the front door, and the linens in the cupboard where Gramma always kept them. She made up the bed in her old room. The mattress was different, a futon instead of an innerspring. Gramps must have replaced it at some point. But the furniture was the same—a plain cherry wood bed and chest of drawers that Gramps had built himself, a bedside table, and a cedar-lined wardrobe. She had hung her clothes inside it the night before, and that simple act had brought more memories.

It was the memories, the familiarity, that had kept her from sleep; Amelia recognized that. Here, in a place that might be home, she could not be certain of her dreams.

The house was cold; the thick walls had always tended to hold a chill. She curled herself under the faded wool blankets for a little while, storing up her body heat for the dash to get dressed. Why hadn't she checked for firewood before she went to bed? She should have lit the wood stove in the living room last night, no matter how tired she was.

She flung back the covers, ran to the wardrobe, and retrieved her clothes. The wood-block floor was cold, and the faint odor of cedar rose from her jeans and shirt as she dressed. She pulled her boots on last, then found her down vest. At least until she got a fire going, she'd need it.

Thank heaven the solar converters were working, and she had power. She'd turned on the main switch to the pump last night too, so she had running water. Well water, sharp and icy as the devil's heart, Gramma always used to say. Amelia washed her face, brushed her teeth, and raked a comb through her brown-blond hair. It was getting long, chin-length now, so the curls tended to tangle more. She'd have to cut it soon. But first she had to find some firewood, have some breakfast, and get the truck through that gate. If she wanted grocery money, she'd better get the wheel set up and a kiln built in a hurry.

Firewood was in the bin by the kitchen door, just where they'd always kept it. The wood was rotting, but it would do.

"Thanks, Gramps," she said. The sky was getting lighter, and she could make out the pale glimmer of the mountains. Lots of snow up there this year.

Amelia cranked open one of the living room windows before she opened the vent on the stove. She knew the stove would smoke from being cold, even if the chimney pipe wasn't blocked by bird nests. The wood crumbled easily into kindling, and she held back some of the more solid chunks until she had a healthy blaze going. The metal of the stove clanged as heat expanded it, and she fed in more wood. She hadn't realized how cold her fingers were until the fire warmed them.

The stove was only smoking a little, so the chimney must be clear. She decided to get the house good and warm, and went back out for another armload of wood. The sun was rising now over the Sacramentos, dripping pale honey light on the snowy peaks. She could smell the pine forests, and they tugged at her. Maybe this afternoon she should drive up and cut some firewood.

"First things first," Gramps murmured next to her. "You need some food in your belly before you can do diddly."

Amelia turned her head. He was smiling at her, warmth in his eyes, and he looked almost the same as she remembered him: a few more wrinkles, maybe, and maybe a little more scalp and a little less hair. His mustache was white now, but she recognized the red plaid shirt he was wearing. She glanced down. Her shadow stretched long and blue on the brick patio. The growing light of dawn shone straight through him.

He had waited for her after all.

That was her first thought, bringing with it a feeling that rushed through her and seemed to end as a spot of heat in her chest. Something inside her eased: the craving she'd had without recognizing it, the crying need to come home to someone who loved her. Someone of her blood. She took one step toward him and pulled in breath to speak, without knowing what she needed to say.

"Eat your breakfast before you go off half-cocked, girl," he said, the same no-more-arguments tone she remembered from childhood. And then he was gone, without leaving so much as a shimmer in the clear morning air.

Amelia stood there a moment longer, the wood getting heavy in her arms, and watched the spot where Gramps had been. He must still be here, somewhere. She wasn't alone after all.

She whispered, "Yes, Gramps," and went inside to eat.

She checked the propane level in the storage tank and turned on the gas line to the house, then fixed herself a breakfast of coffee and oatmeal—both instant—and washed up after. She opened a couple of more windows in the house to air it out. With all the curtains pulled back to let the sun in, and the stove going, the house would warm nicely by the afternoon.

Next she walked around to the three outbuildings, all of which were locked. Gramps's workshop was closest to the house, built of the same stucco-covered adobe brick. She recognized the weathered metal double doors of the tractor shed, but the structure was bigger than she remembered, the size of a small barn. The third building was set off down near the creek. It was new. No telling what it was for, though. Gramps had always been building things and making gadgets.

Unlike the one on the gate, the padlocks on the outbuildings didn't look new. Amelia went into the kitchen and rummaged through the junk drawer until she found Gramps's spare set of keys. There were at least twenty keys on the ring, some probably going back thirty-five years. She didn't think he ever threw one away. Workshop first. She could get a crowbar there, in case she had to break the lock on the gate to bring the truck in.

She was trying the third key in the workshop

lock when she heard an engine. The sound was a loud purr in the clear silence of the desert air, but the house blocked her view of the road. Amelia walked around and stood next to the biggest of the bare cottonwood trees. The ranch gate was ajar, and a car was coming up the lane toward the house. A forest green Jaguar. She made sure her sleeve was down over the scar on her forearm, then stuffed the ring of keys in the pocket of her down vest and waited.

The car pulled up in front of her. The man who got out was tall and lean, with a deep tan and sleek blond hair. In his sports jacket, starched white shirt, and pressed jeans, he reminded her of a gallery owner she had once met in Atlanta.

"Well," he said, smiling as he looked her over. "Spence said he saw lights out here last night, but I figured he was imagining things. Couldn't see why anybody'd bother this place, especially since word's gotten around it's haunted." His voice had a pleasant pitch, warm and carefully schooled, like a radio announcer's. Gently, he added, "You're trespassing, you know."

Amelia's shoulders were tense, but she held her voice level. "Don't think I am, actually. But *you* might be. I didn't get your name?"

He threw back his head and laughed. "Oh, a *feisty* trespasser," he said. "Or maybe—a squatter?" He was looking at her baggy jeans—the ones she'd been wearing since Memphis—and the tangled froth of her hair, which was blowing in her eyes.

Amelia took her right hand out of her vest pocket and shoved her hair back so she could meet his look straight on. "No," she said, keeping her tone pleasant. "Your name?"

He smiled again. When he did, a dimple creased his cheek. "Sorry. I'm Nick Atkinson. Now, I know this place looks abandoned, but it's not. You—"

"No," she said again. "It's obvious someone's taken good care of it. I was glad to see it hadn't been left to rot."

The man leaned back against the car. He looked

so relaxed and graceful that he made Amelia feel even scruffier. "Mind telling me who you are?"

"Who's asking?" she said.

"Now, girl, don't be contrary," Gramps said. She turned her head abruptly. He was beside her and a step behind, looking at her in combined exasperation and affection, and at the sight of him, her heartbeat steadied. "That's the fella from the savings and loan—he's the trustee, since Terry Grayson died. Just tell him who you are and get on with things. You got more important things to do than fuss with him."

"What is it?" the man asked.

Amelia looked back at him. "You're—" She had been about to say "Gramps's trustee," but hesitated. "You're the trustee for this place?" she asked instead.

The man straightened from where he had been leaning on the car, and his blue eyes narrowed. "I'm the trustee for the Rawlins estate, yes. If you have business here, I'd appreciate your telling me what it is. Otherwise, I'm afraid I have to ask you to leave the property now."

"Melia," Gramps said. "Get on with it before he pitches you out on your fanny. He don't look like much, but he's a tough cookie."

"Right," she said. She faced Atkinson squarely. "I own the place." She still couldn't bring herself to tell him her name. Old habits die hard. "I'm Hector Rawlins's granddaughter. I've come back here to live."

She ended up inviting Nick Atkinson in for coffee, which he ended up not drinking. Sunlight flooded the kitchen through the open curtains, and the rosy Mexican tiles had grown warm where the sunshine touched them. Amelia made a point of getting Gramma's good cups and napkins from the cupboard and drawer where they were stored. She had to wash the cups and dry them first, but she hoped he noticed her familiarity with the kitchen.

"How long've you been here?" he asked as she set the coffee—more instant—in front of him.

She waited a beat, considering the question. Then she said, "Last night."

"That your pickup by the gate?"

She nodded.

He took a sip of the coffee and grimaced. "Got any cream?"

She opened the cabinet and found a jar of powdered creamer. The expiration date was next year's. He dumped some into his cup, sipped again, and pulled another face. His distaste for it amused her, which helped her relax a little. She sat down at the end of the table near him and warmed her hands around her cup.

"What have you got under the tarp? In the truck?"

"You ask a lot of questions," she said.

He set his cup down, and leaned toward her. "Miss—it's my job to ask questions. I'm the trustee. Surely you can understand that my first responsibility is to protect the place."

"Tell me about the will," she said.

Atkinson straightened, and gave her a worried look. "Miss, I can't tell you anything until I'm sure you have a right to know it. Look—do you have any ID?"

Amelia drank some coffee, watching him steadily. "The will's gone through probate already," she said, stalling. Surely it had been probated by now. And her driver's license was in the name she'd been living under for the past twelve years. She doubted Atkinson would turn the Rawlins ranch over to Amy Castle. She needed time to think this through. "It'll be a matter of public record. Why make me go to the courthouse and look it up?"

"Do you think I'm enjoying this?" He seemed distressed by the possibility. "I have to ask you for identification. It's my responsibility as Mr. Rawlins's trustee."

"He's dead," Amelia pointed out.

"That's the whole point, isn't it? I'm supposed to look after his interests because he's unable to," Atkinson said. He leaned back in his chair, watching her closely. "Look, don't you have any friends in the area who could put you up for a while? Somebody who knows you're here and might help?"

The obvious sympathy in his voice tightened her

spine, but she held herself still, fingers around her coffee cup, face neutral. So far, he was the only person who knew she was back, except for her nosy neighbor. Atkinson had said earlier that "Spence" was the one who noticed her lights last night. That would be Spencer Reed, whose property adjoined theirs to the north. She remembered the man because Gramps had argued with him constantly.

"Mmm," she said, giving it an affirmative sound. "More coffee?"

He pushed his cup away from him. "No, thanks. Look, Miss—Rawlins. I hate for us to get off on the wrong foot like this. Mr. Rawlins was our customer for forty years, and I want you to do business with us, too. But I do have to make certain that you are who you say you are."

He had called her "Rawlins," not "Caswell." Either Gramps hadn't told him much—and hadn't used her legal name in his will—or Atkinson was more discreet than he looked. Too much to try to figure out. She'd expected to have a few days to gather a little information before tackling the issue of her legal standing. But she'd forgotten the way news traveled in the basin.

She stood up. "Why don't you give me your card," she suggested, "and I'll come into town tomorrow morning. We can talk some more, and you can tell me what it'll take to dissolve the trust."

He remained seated, and his eyebrows drew together at the word "dissolve," but he didn't say anything right away. "And meantime, I leave you with the run of the place?"

"It must be obvious that I won't do any damage here," Amelia said.

"No," he said. He sounded regretful. "I'm sorry, but I can't do that. You could be anybody."

She sighed. "Would you come into the other room, please?"

"Why?"

"There's something you should see," she said, walking through the arched doorway. The stove had warmed the room, and with the sunshine coming in the windows, the place looked bright and welcoming. The photographs were mounted along the hallway off the living room, a gallery of formal portraits made by Gittings, one of Houston's finest photography studios.

The first was of her parents, the second of her older brother, Daniel. A family portrait came next, the one taken when her mother announced for the Texas governor's race, shortly before she was killed.

Next to the group picture was Amelia's, and beside her—wasn't he always beside her?—was Michael. She avoided the eyes of the people in the pictures.

In her own portrait, she was seated, leaning toward the camera, a small marble table next to her chair. The girl in the picture wore a bronze taffeta party dress with short, off-the-shoulder sleeves, and sat with one bare arm posed gracefully along the table. It was the sight of the arm—her left arm, with its smooth golden flesh unmarked, unblemished—that trapped Amelia, even though she hadn't looked at the girl's face. So young, she was so impossibly young, that girl, and so very oblivious of her future. Amelia couldn't stop herself from touching her own forearm. Even through the cloth of her shirt, the rippled shape of the scar was pronounced.

She drew back from the gallery of accusing faces, and glanced at Nick Atkinson. He paused at the group portrait, then moved on and studied the picture of Amelia.

He looked at the portrait, then at her, and she could tell that he recognized her.

"Good enough for a temporary ID?" she said.

He was still watching her, and she thought there was pity in his eyes. She looked away.

"I still shouldn't—" he said.

The phone rang, and Amelia started. "What—"

Atkinson turned back toward her. "That might be my office calling," he said. "Do you mind?"

She shook her head. Why would they have left the phone turned on with nobody living here?

The phone was wall-mounted, not far from the kitchen door. Amelia followed as far as the living room as he went to answer it.

"Atkinson here," he said.

"Mr. Atkinson? Judge Fuller called and said he needs to talk to you right away—" a woman said. Her voice was high, and clearly audible in the silence of the room.

"Fine," Atkinson said quickly, and glanced over his shoulder at Amelia. "I'm just about to leave here—I can call him from the car phone. Thanks for letting me know, Tanya."

He listened for a moment to something Amelia didn't catch, then added, "Okay, fine. Bye now." After he hung up, he turned and came over to Amelia. He surprised her by taking her hand and holding it in both of his.

It made her very uncomfortable. He was tall—well over six feet—and seemed to loom over her. She could smell his after-shave, something subtle and citrusy.

"Miss Rawlins, I just wanted to say I'm real sorry about all this. I know things can't have been easy for you after your family—" He broke off because Amelia pulled away from him abruptly.

She went over to the window and stared out at the mountains. They were cool and blue and distant, and Amelia wished she were there instead of here.

"I'm sorry," Atkinson said again. "Look—all right. Go ahead and stay here tonight, and come see me in the morning. We'll see what we can work out, okay?"

He left shortly afterward. Amelia had to ask again for his business card and remind him to give her the key to the lock on the gate. The card was a creamy ivory with raised black lettering. It gave his title as President of Tamarisco Savings and Loan, with a business address of Plaza Antigua, la Ciudad de Tamarisco. She hadn't realized he was president of the S&L; he seemed too young for that. Seeing his title made her even more nervous about talking to him tomorrow.

But then, everything about him made her nervous. He was too tall, too well dressed. She walked out into the front yard and watched from behind the arched entryway until his car disappeared down the road. Protected from the wind, the yard was warm and still in the bright sun. It was nearly nine.

He had asked if she had any friends here. The skin on her back prickled, and she unzipped the down vest and shrugged out of it.

"Gramps?" she said tentatively, and looked around. The yard remained empty. When she was alone here, in the place where she'd spent so much time with her grandfather, having him talk to her seemed natural. But Atkinson's presence had made Gramps's visitations feel crazier.

She shoved the business card into her jeans pocket and went to get the keys to her truck. Nick Atkinson had a point. Time to make sure somebody she trusted knew she was home.

She decided to wait until later to move her potter's wheel off the truck, and checked the fuel gauge. Another habit, even though she'd driven only eighty miles since the fill-up. Leaving the new gate locked behind her, she drove back to the Crossroads, then turned east, toward the mountains.

Highway 82 had a bad reputation even when she was a child. The road rose over four thousand feet in about fifteen miles, and in places its grade was so steep that it wasn't unusual for truckers to have their brakes overheat. She only had to go a little over halfway up the mountain, though, to an apple orchard near High Rolls, owned by Gramps's friend Mary Zuniga. Even after twelve years, Amelia doubted Mary had gone anywhere.

She was one-quarter Apache, entitled to live on the Mescalero reservation. Mescalero was the lushest piece of land in New Mexico, nestled in a series of valleys inside the Lincoln National Forest, thickly wooded with aspens and maples as well as pine, but high enough to get good skiing weather. Gramps always said settling the Mescaleros there was practically the only time in history that the Bureau of Indian Affairs created a reservation in the spot where the tribe had actually lived.

Years ago, the tribe had built a resort there called the Inn of the Mountain Gods, one of the most successful in New Mexico.

Mary didn't care to be an innkeeper, she had once told Amelia, the wrinkles around her eyes crinkling up. Innkeeping required too much brown-nosing to suit her. Instead, she had her orchard about forty or fifty miles south of the reservation, down the hill from Cloudcroft.

The air got steadily colder as the truck labored up the mountain; colder and thinner, and the truck's engine began to chug. The curves were sharp, and the land next to her alternated between sheer rocky drops and a claustrophobic bulk overhead. In places the terrain opened and she could see Sierra Blanca, the grandmother of all these mountains, shining white and regal to the north.

Fortunately there was little snow at this elevation, and none on the road. The land leveled some and became less arid, and then Amelia saw the sign to Dog Canyon off to her right. Green winter grass edged a streambed sixty feet below the road, and fat horses grazed alongside it. Three more sweeping curves, and she was there.

Today the apple stand on the road that fronted the Indian Reds Orchard was empty. There was a hand-lettered sign hooked onto the weathered gray timbers of the stall. The sign said "Pruning," but looked as if it had been there for years.

Amelia parked the truck behind the stand. When she got out, the air was cold and sharply sweet around her, and she turned back to the truck and pulled on her vest. The apple trees were bare, with all the silvery and dark gray variegations of their bark revealed. She walked in among them, taking pleasure in the squat, sturdy shape of the trunks.

She walked for several minutes, not feeling rushed to find Mary. Just being here made her feel more peaceful. The mountain had always done that for her. And Mary's orchard brought a particular serenity. She and Michael used to earn pocket money by working for

Mary sometimes, odd jobs like loading the cider press and filling jars. Coming back here was like touching another time. Another lifetime, really. One that had hardly seemed real to her for the past twelve years.

After a few minutes, she came to a high point where several of the oldest apple trees had been removed. The open space gave a clear view of the basin below. Dun and olive desert lapped along the white sands of the old missile range. The sands gleamed snowy and pure, in vivid contrast to the deep blue-violet of the mountains on the far side of the basin.

She'd been standing there for less than five minutes when Mary found her, stepping up beside her to look out over the basin.

Amelia looked closely at her grandfather's old friend, searching for changes. She found none. Mary's hair was still dark, glossy and thick in its braid, and although the broad shield of her face had its share of wrinkles, there seemed to be no more than Amelia remembered. She had no idea how old Mary was. Fifty? No, more like sixty.

"Hello, Mary."

"Look at you, all grown up." Mary was carrying a small hacksaw in one brown hand, and the battered corduroy pants she was wearing might have been the same pair she'd worn to Gramma's funeral, nineteen years ago. "Hell of a view here, huh? Maybe I should charge for it."

"Maybe you should," Amelia agreed. "Cut a road through the center of the orchard, sell cider from a stand right here. Of course you'd have to put a big trash barrel over yonder, and get a Porta Potti in."

Mary laughed. She had a big laugh that started deep in her chest and rumbled out. "Right," she said, and touched Amelia's arm, a firm, brief touch. "You want some cider, Melia? I got a pressing that's a good age."

"Sure," Amelia said. She had forgotten how easy Mary was to be around.

It took them about five minutes to reach the house behind the orchard, a big sprawl of log cabin that had been added on to so often that its original shape was completely obscured. Pines rose raggedly along the hill behind the house, and Amelia could see mounds of shadowed snow beneath them.

"Want to sit out?" Mary asked. "Or is it too cold for you?" It was sunny next to the house, which cut the wind. In spite of the temperature, the dry, chilly air wasn't unpleasant.

"Porch is fine with me," Amelia said. "It's new. Looks nice."

"Yeah, I like it," Mary said as she opened a raw pine cupboard and pulled out a couple of tin cups. She filled them from an old gallon jar full of cloudy cider that stood on a rickety table next to the door. "Been a while, huh? But your grandfather always said you'd be back." She handed Amelia a cup. "Skoal."

Amelia echoed the toast and lifted her cup. The flavor of the cider burst across her tongue. Another thing she had forgotten—how strong Mary's cider was.

"Sit," Mary said.

There were several Adirondack chairs on the deck. Amelia picked one with a footrest. Mary sat next to her, and they drank their cider in silence for a moment.

After a little while, Amelia realized Mary wasn't going to ask her anything. The muscles in her stomach relaxed. She said, "I got in last night. Somebody's taken good care of the house."

Mary nodded. "That bank fella. Your grandfather left him in charge of the place after his lawyer friend passed on. No telling why." Her aversion was plain, though whether it was for Atkinson in particular or bankers in general, Amelia didn't know.

"No," she agreed, "no telling." She swallowed. "When did Gramps die, Mary?"

Mary looked up, squinting. All the wrinkles around her eyes pleated. "That'd be three years ago," she said, "come spring. He didn't show up with his bees for the pollination like he was supposed to. I called the sheriff. They found him out by the hives."

She paused and took a drink. "The county agent thought at first the hive must've been invaded by some

Africanized, and he got stung or something. Your grandfather—he never wore one of them bee-suits."

"No," Amelia whispered. "He never did." She could remember how gentle his bony hands had been as he brushed a stinger out of her arm. *"Bees don't want to hurt you,"* he said. *"They just got to protect the hive. They'll leave you be if you handle 'em right. Next time, you wear a plain shirt, like I told you."*

Mary went on. "But it wasn't the bees. Doctor said his heart just gave out."

"Only three years ago," Amelia said. She looked at the brilliant blue arch of the sky. What if she'd defied the old threats and come back sooner? Lived with him on the ranch, just the two of them?

Maybe it would have worked out. Made him happy.

But it had never been just the two of them. After Gramma died, it had always been the three of them during the summers: Gramps and her and Michael. Their older brother Daniel never liked the ranch much. She sat up straight, swinging her legs down from the footrest.

"Nick Atkinson asked me a bunch of questions," she said. "He even asked me what was under the tarp in my truck. Got any idea why?"

Mary looked at her without speaking for a minute. "Not really. Except—he's the managing type, likes to be in charge of everything and everybody."

"I see."

"Just want to let you know I'm sorry about your family," Mary said quietly. "Most folks who knew about it figured you were dead too, since you never came back here. Especially after so long. But your grandfather never doubted for a second, even before you sent him that first card. Think you should know that."

Amelia looked into the cider cup. "Thank you," she said. She drained the last of her drink, and set the empty cup on the footrest with a faint metallic chime.

"Maybe it was the blood bond," Mary said. "Maybe that's how he knew. Or it might be he just loved you too much to give up."

Amelia stood. "I should be getting back. There's a lot to do. Thanks for the cider. For everything, Mary."

Mary got up too. "You're always welcome here," she said. The words sounded formal and meaningful.

Amelia looked down at her boots. "That means a lot, Mary. Thank you. Um, have you got any idea where I could sell my pottery? I haven't got a studio set up yet, but it shouldn't take long. And I brought a portfolio with me from—back east."

Mary thought for a minute, then slowly shook her head. "There are a few galleries in Ciudad Tamarisco," she said, "but I don't know any of the owners very much. Bunch of Santa Fe slummers, they got no use for locals. There's the gallery at the Inn, but they got a rule about only selling Indian work."

"Well, that lets me out," Amelia said. "Say, how about telling me where I could cut some firewood without getting in trouble?"

Mary looked at her. "You're kidding, right? You got any idea how much wood I cut out of here every year? You got a truck?"

"Sure."

"Then drive it around to the back, and I'll help you load."

For a moment, Amelia was afraid she wouldn't be able to speak. She had grown unaccustomed to generosity. And everybody up here went through wood at a fierce rate during the winter. She cleared her throat. "Are you sure you can spare it, Mary?" she asked.

Mary grinned. "You've been gone a while, girl. I got radiant heat now, thanks to your grandfather. Come on, let's load. The woodpile's this way."

"I'm obliged to you," Amelia said. The words came automatically. Unsettled, she was falling back on her grandfather's way of talking.

"Well," Mary said as she headed toward the back, "if you start his pollinating business back up, I'll be obliged to *you*. These days we have to hire people from outta state, and what with how small most of the orchards up here are, and travel expenses, you wouldn't believe what they charge us."

"Guess it's something to think about," Amelia said, wondering how long her money was going to hold out.

Chapter Two

On Saturday afternoon, May 25, 1983, Houston's outraged gay community staged a peaceful March for Justice in response to Paul Boucher's murder. Sixteen thousand people marched through the heart of Montrose and down Shepherd Drive toward the center of town. They gathered to demonstrate in front of police headquarters before continuing to Bell Park for a candlelight vigil that lasted until 11:12 P.M., the time at which Paul Boucher had been pronounced dead eight days before.

Mayor Marian Rawlins-Caswell came to the park to speak to the marchers. She praised them for their nonviolent protest and for their refusal to be drawn into confrontations with the groups of counterdemonstrators who surrounded them. At that point in the mayor's speech, protesters fielded by the KKK and several bands of local skinheads booed her.

A heavy police guard kept the peace during the hours-long vigil, despite the fact that emotions were running at fever pitch. Mayor Rawlins-Caswell promised a full investigation of the incident—including the allegations that a passing police cruiser had ignored initial pleas for help from Boucher's companion—along with unstinting efforts to arrest and prosecute the bashers. She proclaimed the bashing an atrocity that would not be tolerated in the City of Houston.

Their vigil concluded, the marchers extin-

guished their candles and went home. Thwarted in their efforts to escalate the demonstration into a riot, the counterdemonstrators also dispersed.

The investigation the mayor had promised went forward with all the force of her office behind it.

—MOLLY CATES, "Blood Relatives,"
Lone Star Monthly, April 1986

New Mexico

Amelia came back down the mountain with half a cord of wood wedged into the back of her truck. One problem solved, anyway. The press of everything she needed to do made her shoulders tighten as she drove. Set up a studio, build a kiln, mix glazes from materials she'd brought with her from North Carolina. Find a place to sell her finished work. Start preparing ground for a garden. Fix up a shed to keep some goats, for milk. Check on Gramps's prairie—after three years, it might well need a controlled burn to clear out invasions of creosote or juniper.

She had always wondered why Gramps didn't plan to deed the ranch to the Nature Conservancy, which would have protected his prized ten acres of restored grassland—twenty years' worth of work—for good. But her grandfather was an obstinate man, who liked doing things his own way. She had realized during her summers here that he thrived on his confrontations with area cattle ranchers like Spencer Reed, who resented Gramps for trying to get the Bureau of Land Management to enforce its own grazing limits. Maybe Gramps had wanted her to carry on the tradition.

Amelia wheeled the truck in and jumped out to open the gate, using the key Atkinson had given her. Some low clouds were piling over the Organs, headed east. Looked like she might be in for some snow. She pulled the truck through and went back to relock the gate.

First thing she had to do was get the wheel unloaded and stored out of the weather. The tarp would keep it dry, but she didn't want the motor exposed to too much cold. She parked as close to the kitchen door as she could, and started tossing the wood off the back of the truck. Later she'd probably regret not stacking it, but she needed to get the wheel unloaded.

She finished dumping the wood and backed the truck up to the wide door of Gramps's workshop, leaving enough leeway for her to fit between. It took her eight tries before she found the workshop key on Gramps's key ring. Lights came on inside as soon as she opened the door. The solar converters were still working.

The place was changed, but not unrecognizable. Gramps's woodworking equipment was neatly shrouded in plastic dustcovers, and an impressive collection of hand tools hung from hooks on the wall over the eight-foot workbench. The bench ran the length of a niche that had been formed by partitioning off a section of the shop. Amelia opened the door to the sectioned space and found a toilet, washbasin, and shower. Gramps had added a few creature comforts since she'd been here last.

She found his block-and-tackle set and hooked it to the doorway beam, which had been specially reinforced to hold it. The wheel only weighed about a hundred and eighty pounds, but she wasn't exactly Godzilla and she couldn't risk dropping it.

She unstrapped the tarp. First she removed the polymer splash guard—little more than a curved tray—from around the wheel head; then she disconnected the wired foot pedal and power cord. The flat grooved disk of the wheel head rose from a polymer wedge that encased the motor and swept back to form a saddle for the potter to sit on. A single bulky piece, awkward to wrestle inside. Amelia slid the wheel to the back of the truck and rigged a web of slings around the polymer base, knotting the lines in front of the wheel head. Then she backed the truck right up to the shop, edging it past an old metal pole next to the door.

She clambered over the sides of the truck into the bed, and ran the line through the block. To hoist the wheel, she had to stand in the doorway.

She positioned herself and started raising the wheel. Had to be careful not to overbalance—there—she hauled on the line. The strain on her arms was more than she expected, and the muscles under her shoulder blades burned. She swore.

But the wheel came up gently. She moved slowly, struggling to keep it from swaying. Then she belayed the line and went to pull the truck out from underneath.

She was rushing a little too much because she was tired. As she pulled forward, she clipped the pole with the bumper. The screech of dueling metal was hideous.

Amelia was cursing herself as she jumped out. The old truck had a simple blade bumper, and she'd caught the top edge. It was twisted straight back about six inches now, the upper edge pointed and sharp as a knife blade. *Crap.* One more thing to worry about fixing.

She undid the line and lowered the wheel, sweating hard. Her boots slipped once, but she caught herself on the doorjamb, and didn't lose her grip on the line. And then the wheel was down, undamaged.

A gritty wind swirled in off the basin, licking at the sweat on her face. With it, the wing-beat sound of the windmill rose, a deep sound that traveled along her bones. Amelia shivered. Getting late, getting cold. She put her shoulder against the base of the wheel and shoved it the rest of the way inside the shop without undoing the lines around it. She unhooked the pulley and put it back where it belonged before unloading the clay, tools, and glaze materials she'd brought with her.

Then she locked the shop doors and went back to the house to stack wood.

It was almost sunset by the time she got the wood stacked in the brick bin behind the kitchen. The only thing left in her truck was the steamer trunk that held her clothes. She dragged it off the back of the truck and into the kitchen. Then she carried two armloads of wood inside, closed the windows she'd left open, and built up the fire. Next she washed up and fixed herself a supper of Cup-A-Soup and peanut butter. She'd have to get some groceries while she was in town tomorrow.

The shelves in the living room were full of familiar books: Gramma's copies of Kipling, Dickens, and Frost, and Gramps's library of grassland restoration guides and beekeeping lore. Amelia pulled down a copy of *The Prince and the Pauper*, and read a little as she ate. The tattered red binding and the smell of the old paper reminded her sharply of Gramma and her clear-voiced readings after summertime suppers when Amelia was small.

After she finished eating, she fixed herself coffee, then dug her battered wallet out of her pack and counted her money. $328 U.S. and another $40 Canadian. Maybe she should have changed it in El Paso, in spite of the bad rate they'd offered. She wasn't sure whether merchants in Tamarisco would even accept it, and she was going to have to buy groceries and garden seed and fire brick for a kiln. Not to mention fuel for the truck—as spread out as things were here, she'd be doing a lot of driving.

And those expenses were only the beginning—until she found a deposit where she could dig her own clay, she'd have to buy that, too, and she wanted to get some goats. There simply wasn't enough to get started on, and she thought bitterly about the back wages Jefferson Crawford's cousin had refused to pay her after Jeff died. Jeff paid her stipend for working at his production pottery each quarter. She had wanted to save her money anyway, and Jefferson had always dealt straight with her. But when he died and his cousin inherited the business, Mason Crawford had said he couldn't pay any expenses until the estate was settled and the will had gone through probate.

Amelia rubbed her hands over her face. No use worrying about it now. Her last two months' wages were history, and she'd have to make do with what she had. Unless . . . She hadn't seen Gramps's will yet. Maybe there'd been a little money left after he died. It sure would help, although she felt guilty even thinking about it.

She flicked off the kitchen light, and stood at the window gazing out at the night. No stars tonight, only darkness and clouds and a fierce wind that howled around the house. Wrapping her arms around herself, Amelia listened. Her family had rarely spent much time at the ranch in winter, and the wailing wind sounded lost and lonely.

Since Nick Atkinson had left that morning, she hadn't seen Gramps even once. Was he angry with her for not coming home sooner? Thinking about it made her chest ache. She'd sent him brief notes a few times, and once a birthday card from New York, but had only written when she was traveling. She'd been too scared to mail anything from any of the places she was actually living— Tennessee, Vermont, Maine, and later North Carolina. Too scared that the Wolfen were still looking for her. She had to talk to Gramps about it next time she got the chance. Explain. Maybe he'd forgive her.

In the morning she'd ask Nick Atkinson about the trust. And she'd find out about the money, no matter how much it bothered her.

Then when she got back here, she'd drive up toward the hills and spend a little time in the place Gramps had loved more than any other in the world: his restored prairie, what Gramma always called Hector's Folly.

If she could call him back to anywhere, that would be the place.

She woke to a blue-bright morning, and knew instantly it meant snow. There was a light crisp crust of white on the world, only a couple of inches. Nothing that would keep her from driving. The stove had kept the house from getting too cold, with its slow-burning, sweet-smelling applewood. She owed Mary one, Amelia thought, as she restoked the fire.

Her wardrobe was so limited that she checked the wardrobe and chest of drawers in Gramps's room, but they were empty. Apparently the caretaker had used that room and cleared it out. So she was stuck with whatever she could scavenge from the trunk. It was too cold for her to wear her only dress, bought for her one formal gallery showing, and the rest of her wardrobe consisted of jeans and cutoffs and work shirts. Potters didn't have lots of reasons to dress up.

After putting a roasting pan filled with water on the stove to heat, she decided on a pair of jeans that still had some color to them, a black cotton dress shirt, and a buckskin jacket that she'd bought at a garage sale years before. The leather was old and soft. Her boots were black, and she had a turquoise-and-silver bolo she could wear to dress things up a little. She washed in front of the stove, even dunking her hair in the basin and scrubbing it with the castile soap. Gramma's towels were getting threadbare, but they still smelled like cinnamon from the sachets she kept in the cupboards.

Amelia pulled a ladder-backed kitchen chair over by the wood stove and hung her shirt and jeans on it to warm, then huddled next to it under a blanket until her teeth stopped chattering. She dressed carefully, even giving her boots a swab with the clammy towel she'd used to dry her hair. Her hair was still tangled and damp, so she combed it by the stove until it was dry, as she ate breakfast in the company of Kipling.

The refrigerator was pulled out from the wall a little, unplugged, its interior stripped and the door propped open. Amelia remembered to plug it in and close the door before she left, hoping the solar converters could still handle the power drain.

Then, when she couldn't put it off any longer, she climbed in the truck and drove into Tamarisco.

Tamarisco was an old town, and most of its adobe buildings predated New Mexico's statehood. It had become a thriving artist's colony toward the end of the last century, and now sprouted galleries and bed-and-breakfasts like some far-ranging offshoot of Santa Fe. Amelia could remember her grandfather complaining about the influx of artsy invaders. Today the low, flat-roofed buildings looked like a cluster of spice cakes frosted with white sugar icing.

Each year at Christmas, all the residents and merchants lined their walks, roofs, and walls with *luminarias,* lighting the entire town against the dark. Amelia could remember her first Christmas in New Mexico, a family trip to visit Gramps and Gramma when she was eight. Michael had only been two then, Daniel sixteen. She had pressed her face against the cold glass of the car window and watched the glowing golden lights until her breath had frosted the pane with a kaleidoscopic pattern of ice crystals. Papa'd had to use the ice scraper so she could see again.

The Tamarisco Savings and Loan was on the main square or plaza, which sported a circle of beautifully shaped pear trees surrounding a stone fountain. The fountain was silent today, the trees bare and frozen, but activity downtown was high. Trucks and cars inched through the narrow streets toward feed stores and banks, and parking places were at a premium. Amelia found one at the end of a cross street and hiked back toward the center of town, her breath pluming in the cold air. Men with weathered faces stepped aside and touched their hats to her as she walked past, and several women nodded and spoke. Amelia nodded back, keeping her eyes trained on the pavement in front of her.

She found the savings and loan without trouble, a two-story adobe structure painted white, with heavily carved wooden double doors in the Spanish style. Directly inside the doors was a reception area furnished with a spare Scandinavian-style console. Glass-fronted offices lined either side of the room, occupied by busy people. Upholstered chairs and a sofa in soft shades of cream and yellow were grouped near the front windows. The teller counter ran along two thirds of the back wall, with the vault open behind it. To one side, a rustic carved staircase led to the second floor.

An attractive red-haired woman who looked to be in her midfifties sat at the reception console. "Good morning," the woman said, her voice smooth and professional, her eyes assessing. "May I help you?"

Amelia recognized the voice instantly. This must be Tanya. She said, "I'm here to see Nick Atkinson. He's expecting me."

"And you are?"

Amelia had planned for this on the drive in and didn't hesitate. "Amelia Rawlins," she said.

"Please have a seat," Tanya said tonelessly. "I'll let Mr. Atkinson know you're here."

Amelia glanced at the overstuffed sofa and chairs. She stepped back to the waiting area, but didn't sit. Instead, she turned and looked out at the plaza. The clouds were beginning to break up.

"Mr. Atkinson will be with you shortly," Tanya said.

Amelia thanked her and walked over to the window. A few pigeons were scratching around the lee side of the fountain, where the snow was thinnest. Their feathers were puffed up against the cold, and Amelia wondered if they were complaining to each other about the weather.

She heard footsteps on the stairs and turned to see Atkinson coming down. Today he was wearing a navy blue suit that made his hair seem an even brighter blond. Amelia felt like a vagabond in comparison.

"Ms. Rawlins," he said warmly as he crossed to greet her. He put out his hand. "Good to see you again. Come on up to my office, please."

Amelia shook his hand, but drew away quickly, and turned toward the stairs. He led her up them, making small talk about the late snowstorm, and ushered her into his office. His desk was Scandinavian, with austere lines, no visible drawers, and a surface area of about six square yards. In front of the desk were two straight-backed antique armchairs. At least she wouldn't drown in one of these.

"Have a seat, have a seat," he said, waiting politely beside the desk. "Would you care for some coffee?"

"No, thanks." She sat. It would have been nice to have something to do with her hands, but she was jittery enough already. She glanced around his office. The walls were covered with a variety of news photographs—Atkinson at ribbon-cutting ceremonies, with political figures, on the podium at some fancy-dress function. There were a number of plaques scattered among the photos too. One of them was dated this month, from the Tamarisco Jaycees, naming Nicholas L. Atkinson Outstanding Young Businessman of the Year.

Atkinson seated himself and gave her one of his high-voltage smiles. That blue suit really set off his eyes. "Well, you can imagine, having you turn up yesterday has been a real surprise. When I talked to Senator Caswell after your grandfather's death, he said he didn't have any reason to believe you were still alive. He seemed to think your grandfather was—excuse me—a little obsessive about leaving the ranch to you."

"What did my uncle have to do with the estate?" she asked, trying for the cool note her mother's voice had always had during political negotiations. "I realize he's an influential man, but he wasn't even related to Gramps, except by marriage."

Atkinson leaned his arms on the desk in front of him. "I didn't mean to imply that your uncle tried to interfere with Mr. Rawlins's disposition of the property," he said earnestly. "I contacted the senator before filing for probate. It seemed like the best chance of getting in touch with you, before registering the property in your name. But because of what the senator told me, I more or less expected the Rawlins property to stay in trust for the time specified, and then go to the secondary beneficiary."

The secondary beneficiary was probably Michael. Amelia swallowed. "That's understandable," she said. "But I haven't had any contact with my uncle. Would you tell me more about the terms of my grandfather's will, please?"

"Miss—do you mind if I call you Amelia?"

The question caught her off guard, and Amelia shook her head.

"Amelia, then. And call me Nick." He spread his hands in an apologetic gesture. "I'm afraid a more formal identification process is required."

"What do you mean?"

"As I mentioned yesterday, we have to confirm your identity. Would Monday morning be a convenient time for you to come to the sheriff's office in Alamogordo with me?"

"The *sheriff's* office? Why there?" Amelia said. Her voice was getting strained. She took a deep breath. "I'm not a criminal."

"Oh, no, of course you aren't." Atkinson got up and came around the desk to take the chair next to her. "Look, we're only going to the sheriff's office because that's where the fingerprinting equipment is. We just need to get your fingerprints and take some pictures. Then the experts at the FBI can compare them with the ones on file for Amelia Caswell."

"I *am* Amelia Rawlins Caswell." Amelia was aware of the faint tremor along her arms. The tendons in her wrists were standing out, and she tried to relax. This was nothing but high-stakes poker, and her mother had always said that in poker a cool head was more important than a good hand.

"Of course. And this is nothing to worry about," Atkinson said. "But you do understand why I have to do this, don't you? I'm charged with holding this estate in trust for the true beneficiary, and I have to be very careful about checking the background of anyone making a claim. I can't, in good faith, accept anything less than an absolute verification of identity before filing to dissolve the trust."

"And that means fingerprints?" Amelia said. Her pulse was racing.

"Fingerprinting is easiest. Oh, and you need to write up an account of your whereabouts for the past— what is it—about twelve years? You do understand, don't you? We can't take chances on false claimants."

"I'm not a false claimant," Amelia said. She kept her tone calm and met his eyes. "You know who I am. All I want is to live in the house my grandfather left me."

"Believe me, the last thing I want is to make more trouble for you, Amelia. The only thing is, I can't do anything to help you, because then my objectivity as a trustee might be brought into question. You see, if I helped you get control of the property, and later it turned out that you had no legitimate claim, the bank examiners might think your claim was something you and I cooked up between us."

"I—I hadn't realized." Now what was she going to do?

He had that worried look again. "Don't you have friends you can stay with for a few weeks? It shouldn't take long at all to hear back from Washington."

Amelia's heart lurched so hard she could feel it in the pit of her stomach. If he sent her fingerprints to Washington—

"Publicity would be—unpleasant for me," she said slowly. "You must realize that, Mr. Atkinson."

"Please. Call me Nick." He drew his chair a little closer.

Her heart had settled into a drumbeat rhythm, slamming steadily against her ribs. "If you ask the FBI to verify my fingerprints, how long will it take for the fact that I've turned up here to hit the nightly news?"

"Mmmm," he said. "I hadn't thought about that. I guess your being alive could be newsworthy. But— this is all a matter of public record. Once you dissolve the trust, people are bound to hear about it."

"All I want is to live on my property in peace," she said. Ten minutes in this office, and she was already feeling desperate. How could she ever get all this sorted out? "Is a little privacy too much to ask?"

"Well . . ." Atkinson looked down, as if thinking, then seemed to reach a decision. "I shouldn't do this, but the place needs a caretaker anyway—the last two only lasted a month. They kept imagining things out there. Not used to being so isolated, I guess. If you're willing to take the job of caretaker—"

"Okay," Amelia said. "At least for now. Until I make up my mind about being fingerprinted."

"But you do understand that until your identity is legally established, you can't dispose of any of the ranch's assets?"

Amelia's chin came up. "I don't know what you're getting at. My intention is to live on the ranch, not sell it."

"Yes, well—just as an example—you couldn't dispose of any of the farm equipment out there. Or grant land-use rights to anyone else—"

"I told you, I don't want to sell anything," she said impatiently. "I'll stay on at the ranch as caretaker for now, and we can talk more about—about verifying my identity later. What about operating expenses? The place needs some work."

He gave a small wave. "Unless you're talking about a major expenditure, it'll be fine. Any reasonable amount, just send the receipts to Tanya. And the estate paid the last caretaker a hundred and fifty dollars a month. There's no reason you shouldn't make the same."

"That's nice of you," she said. "Sounds fine to me."

"Good, then it's a deal." He smiled at her again. "Anything else I can do for you? Like taking you to dinner tonight, maybe?"

"I've already got plans, but thanks anyway," she said automatically. Over the past six years or so, she'd gotten in the habit of putting men off. "I would like to go over the terms of my grandfather's will, though," she said. "Just to be sure I understand what's involved."

There was a brief pause. "It really would be better," he said slowly, "if you retained an attorney—someone to represent you in pursuing this claim. I want to help you, Amelia, but I'm limited as to what I can reasonably do. You have to remember, it's my job to put the interests of the estate first."

"I don't have the money for a lawyer," Amelia said flatly.

Atkinson sighed. "Of course. Look, let me check with my attorney and see what he says about this. If he doesn't see any problem with it, I'll send you a copy of the will, okay?"

Was he putting her off? Or was she just being paranoid? Jeff Crawford had always said she would have been too suspicious to let the good Samaritan help her if she'd been the one he found bleeding in the road. She looked at Atkinson and couldn't be sure of anything except that he made her nervous.

Being the caretaker at the ranch wasn't exactly ideal, but it was much better than having to pick up and leave. And it sounded like there was at least *some* money left; no banker would make such a fuss about a trust that had no assets. Relief flooded her at the thought, but Amelia stanched it with the image of hordes of news teams surrounding the ranch house.

She nodded at him. "I appreciate all this, Mr. Atkinson," she said, and took her leave.

When she left the savings and loan, the sun was out and had already burned away most of last night's dusting of snow. A few melting crescents remained in the shadows of buildings, but the day had grown brighter and warmer. As Amelia was walking back to her truck, an arrangement in one of the shop windows caught her eye. Wildflower books with beautifully photographed covers stood on a low shelf; below was an inverted galvanized bucket surrounded by scattered packets of wildflower seed. She hesitated, looking at the colorful packages, and couldn't shake the image of her grandfather's face.

The shopkeeper was a vividly dressed woman in her forties who cheerfully accepted Canadian dollars at the official exchange rate. "Get 'em all the time," she said, handing Amelia her change. "You want a bag for this?"

"That's okay," Amelia said, stuffing the seed cannister in her pocket. It had cost her $12.36 American. But she wanted to do right by Gramps, and nothing would please him more than adding some perennials to his prairie.

At the shop door, she hesitated. "Excuse me, but—"

The shopkeeper looked up from her register. "Yes?"

"Could you tell me which of the galleries handle the most ceramics? I'm looking for one to represent me."

The woman pursed her brightly painted lips. "Well—the three best galleries are Ojos, down on Brown Street, and Corazón Azul and Taggerty's in the Mercado. They all specialize in N.A. work, of course—"

"I see. Well, thanks again." Amelia walked out the door and headed for her truck. She'd bring her portfolio in and try her luck with the galleries later in the week. Right now she needed some groceries. She remembered where Gramps had shopped, the same market Gramma had gone to before she died, an ancient Piggly-Wiggly off the east end of Market Street.

It wasn't a Piggly-Wiggly anymore, but Amelia thought she recognized a face or two inside. She bought staples in bulk: flour, yeast, sugar, salt, shortening, pinto beans, rice, cornmeal, some canned milk. She splurged on some cheese and bacon, and the lure of the fresh broccoli and green beans was too much to resist. She added peanut butter, margarine, dried soup, oatmeal, and a dozen eggs, and went to the checkout stand.

A sign above the register read, "We Do Business On a Cash Basis." Watching while the cashier scanned her purchases was nerve-racking. The total was $89.36.

As she pulled back onto the highway, she was thinking about money, angry at herself for not asking Atkinson when she'd get paid. But the flat, smooth road was a sedative.

The desert beside the highway was dun and olive drab, mile upon mile of creosote bushes and bare dirt with occasional splashes of unmelted snow. The fencing of range land and overgrazing that were common during the nineteenth century had allowed creosote and salt-brush to invade the grasslands, and now the rosy soil lay exposed between the clumps of brush, completely unprotected from the eroding forces of wind and rain.

Her thoughts turned to the Folly. Gramps's restoration project had never been a big deal to her; she was always more interested in going into politics, like her mother. But Michael had caught Gramps's fever for the prairie project, and he had cajoled and pestered her into working on it with them more times than she could count. He had been so excited about the number of native grasses they'd found and restored.

The last summer they'd spent here, Michael found a new variety of side-oats along the old railroad tracks. He was meticulous in tending the stand of grass and harvesting some of the seed for planting. Gramps declared it the official hundredth grass restored to the prairie. It had been the proudest moment of Michael's life.

His whole life. Three months later, her brother was in a coma, with permanent brain damage. Amelia shifted on the high seat of the truck, then lifted her foot off the gas pedal when she realized how hard she'd been pushing the old beast.

Knee-deep grass had once covered this territory, sustaining huge herds of buffalo and deer.

Her vision of what-had-been was sudden and real. And for the first time, Amelia understood her grandfather's obsession with reestablishing it. With restoring life where less and less now survived.

Steering the truck with one hand, she pulled the seed canister out of her coat pocket and looked at the colorful label. It pictured a fairly standard semiarid mix; she recognized poppies, coreopsis, black-eyed Susans, and firewheels. Not the same as finding a lost species of grass for the Folly, but it felt like the right kind of gesture. She would drive up to Gramps's prairie and plant these today, before she did anything else. As a memorial to him.

And to Michael.

She opened up the tractor shed to hunt for a hand-held cultivator. When she found one, she tossed the claw tool in the truck. The ranch road that led back toward the hills ran alongside the narrow streambed. Cottonwood, ash, and honey mesquite grew by the stream, and piles of rock tumbled by floods made a ragged profile along the banks. The road was badly rutted, but the sun had already dried most of the mud from the snowfall into a brown crust. Amelia eased the truck along the gullies and washes at a walking pace.

She was looking forward to seeing the Folly again; her eyes were ready to see something besides creosote. The Folly was a drift of grasses and flowers in the summertime, with different heights, different shades of green, and different shapes and colors to their seed stalks—celery, wheaten, or russet. It was a nest of variety with the shape of sameness; its own small world. The fields would look different in the winter, with all their colors blanched and dried to monotony, but she would find the same variety when she looked closer. She might even take a few extra minutes to hunt for Michael's special side-oats. See if she could recognize them.

About two miles from the ranch house, the road took a sharp turn into the mouth of a broad canyon. Sycamore trees grew thick along the stream here where the road tapered out, and Gramps had always said there was an underground spring there, too. She backed the truck and turned it around so she could pull straight out when she was ready to leave.

The day had grown almost warm, pushing sixty, she guessed, and the sun was bright. She got out of the truck and took the cultivator out of the back. A pile of ruddy igneous boulders lay at the base of the ridge, looking like crumbs the mountain had shaken off.

Up the basin a ways, one of their neighbors had found petroglyphs on rocks like these when Amelia was thirteen. She and Michael had scrambled over this rock pile for weeks. They had never found anything remotely resembling a petroglyph here. But the shape of these rocks was familiar, and she climbed up and over instead of walking around, balancing the cultivator on her shoulder.

Her boots skidded a little as she reached the top. She caught herself against one of the big boulders, and leaned the cultivator on it. Already she was looking eagerly at the horseshoe-shaped tract of the Folly, a fertile plateau butted up against the base of the mountain.

It took a minute for her to register what she was seeing. But after that first frozen instant, her eyes tracked the evenness of the pale stalks that covered the plain. The plants were about twenty inches tall, and a uniform pale green. Uniform because they weren't grass—they were oats. Oat hay.

Somebody had plowed up Gramps's prairie and planted crops.

Chapter Three

The Houston Independent School District's 1982–83 school year ended on May 22. A week later, The Houston Patriot *noted in a follow-up article on the March for Justice that Mayor Rawlins-Caswell's two younger children were being sent to their grandparents' home in New Mexico for the summer, implying that she feared for their safety. With what the mayor referred to as "typical journalistic myopia," the paper failed to mention that her younger children routinely spent summers with their grandfather.*

—MOLLY CATES, "Blood Relatives,"
Lone Star Monthly, April 1986

New Mexico

She came down off the rock pile in a mad scramble, swinging the cultivator before she even reached level ground. The immature stalks of oat hay separated from the plants with a satisfying scrunch.

Amelia yelled as she laid about her with the cultivator, murdering the invaders of her grandfather's prairie. She had no idea what curses she screamed even as they left her mouth.

She had torn and trampled an area about ten feet in diameter when the hills echoed with a shotgun blast. Amelia whirled.

Spencer Reed had the shotgun in his hands and was maybe thirty feet away from her, approaching along the western boundary of the Folly beside the cliff.

"That was a warning," he said, his voice clear and cool. Amelia could barely make out his words over the ringing in her ears. "Next one won't be. You gone loco? Get out of my field."

Her hand clenched on the handle of the cultivator, and a splinter gouged into her middle finger.

"What do you mean 'my field'?" she yelled at him. "This is Rawlins property and you know it, Spencer Reed."

He stopped about fifteen feet away and squinted at her. His skin was brown and weathered, and it sagged along his jawline, but when he lifted his hat and settled it more firmly on his head, she saw that his hair was still black. He wore it slicked straight back from his high forehead. "Who's that?" he said. "How'd you know my name?"

She wanted to spit at him and swear, or stab the cultivator straight through his black heart. But that dignity and self-assurance he'd always had were still there. The same qualities that used to drive Gramps crazy.

"I inherited this property," she said carefully. "You're not only trespassing, you've plowed under a valuable resource—"

Reed made a sound of disgust. "Resource? What kind of talk is that? Nothing here but a bunch of weeds. And good land going to waste."

"You knew about the restoration project," she said. She was shaking. "You and Gramps used to fight about it all the time when you'd graze your cattle over here. It took him twenty years of work to bring this prairie back. How long did it take you to plow it under?"

For a moment, she didn't think he would answer. Then he said, "Five hours, since you ask." His black eyes glinted with satisfaction. "I know you. You're that girl of Marian's, used to run wild out here in the summers."

Amelia bit back an instinctive, "Yes, sir," and tried to cling to her anger. Fury was the only barrier to despair. A tarry pit of desolation opened in her stomach every time she looked at the oats. She stabbed the clawed prongs of the cultivator into the dirt.

"How could you destroy his life's work?" she said. "It's stealing. You're a thief." But her anger was going soft in the shocky aftermath of the adrenaline surge, turning rubbery and useless.

"I've got a proper lease to work this land," he said. "So we'll have no talk of stealing." He lowered the shotgun a little, inspecting her with a sharp stare. "I remember you all right. You used to be all over this place, you and that little monkey-brother of yours. I could've sworn all Marian's brats were dead."

His tone was detached. Her fury bloomed fresh and hot at his casual dismissal of the attack. "If you did get a lease to this land, I'll revoke it," she said. "And if you didn't, I'll kill you." She jerked the cultivator loose, flinging clumps of reddish earth in Reed's direction, and stalked toward her truck.

"Not very ladylike, are you?" he said to her back.

Amelia turned and fixed him with a stare that would have frozen rain. "Gramps was right," she said. "You *are* a worthless son of a bitch."

Her hands were still shaking on the steering wheel when she pulled up to the house. She sat there for a minute, trying to calm herself. What had happened to her? She despised violence, repudiated it in any form. But she had just threatened murder, and meant it.

Amelia leaned her forehead against the steering wheel of the truck. The plastic was getting old and had begun to crack; she could feel gritty pieces of it grind against her skin. Maybe her mind was disintegrating, too.

She had come here longing for security. Safety. A return to the world she'd inhabited before her family was murdered: the safety of childhood. A paradise where evil didn't exist.

A fool's paradise. It was stupid and dangerous to believe in such a certain world. She had been lulled into trusting this place by her own longing for things that didn't exist. Had never existed, in spite of her idealized memories of the past.

"Give over," Gramps said. "You didn't actually kill the S.O.B. or anything."

Amelia was still leaning against the wheel. She turned her head without lifting it. He was sitting next to her in the cab of the old pickup, looking as solid and real as he ever had.

"I missed you," she blurted out. "All the time I stayed away, I missed you." Her voice shook.

"Hell, I know that." He grinned at her. "That's why I kept the place for you. Even when you was getting too big for your britches, and going all political on me, I knew your heart was really right here. Some of us just got to wander a while before we recognize what we want."

"Gramps—" She stopped and cleared her throat. The splinter she'd gotten in her finger was making the skin swell and itch. She picked at it nervously. "You know what Spence did to the Folly?"

His expression changed, turning remote, and he looked away from her, off toward the cool blue rise of the Organs to their west. After a minute, he said, "It would've been better if you'd made it home last year."

"I'll put it right," she said. She could hardly get the words out. "I swear it, Gramps. The prairie will be just like you and Michael always wanted it to be. I'll see to it."

His white hair was sticking up in tufts at the back, the way it used to after he took a nap on Sundays. For a second, Amelia wondered what dreamtime she had summoned him from. He swung back around to face her. "Michael," he said, and frowned. "Michael never came back to see his side-oats growing."

There was a plaintive note in his voice, and for the first time, he sounded old to Amelia. Old and confused.

She swallowed hard. "He couldn't, Gramps. He wanted to, but he—he couldn't come. But I'm here now. I'll tend the prairie, I promise."

The lines in his face smoothed, and he nodded, accepting her word. He was still nodding as he vanished.

It took a while for Amelia to settle again that afternoon. It wasn't until she changed her clothes and started spading up the old vegetable garden behind the kitchen that she really felt calm. Digging the garden might not have had top priority, but it was the kind of work she needed.

The soil had packed down from so many summers of hard rain, but, once lifted and turned, its richness was apparent. Amelia found grubs and fat earthworms still in the soil, along with traces of straw from the compost heap. With a good garden, she could grow a fair bit of her food. Next year she might even try plowing a field and planting it in beans. If the rains came right, an acre could yield a hundred pounds of pintos.

The place remained quiet, with only the occasional chitter of a field sparrow that had wintered over and the mild voice of the wind to distract her. She wanted to avoid thinking about the Folly but couldn't stop herself. Her mind insisted on turning over what she knew—and didn't know—about the situation here. What Reed had said about having a lease on the land. What Nick Atkinson had said about her not being able to convey land-use rights to someone else until the trust was dissolved. She had assumed he meant on a permanent basis, but maybe he'd been thinking about leases. And could she do anything at all if a lease had already been granted?

By sunset, she had double-dug about half of the existing beds—a plot about ten by twenty feet. Too early to plant anything; besides, she'd have to get on with more pressing things tomorrow. She needed to go back into town with her portfolio, and hit the galleries.

She'd been earning her living as a potter for nearly ten years, working at one production pottery after another, ranging up and down the eastern seaboard. It was hard to imagine spending her days any other way; she already missed the shifting patterns of shaping, firing, glazing, and firing again, each stage its own transformation of the raw clay.

She'd stayed at the last pottery the longest. Crawford's Pottery in North Carolina—she'd worked there for nearly four years. The town of Cooperton was small and quiet, but close enough to the mountain resorts to get steady tourist trade in the summer, and Amelia had gotten along better with Jefferson Crawford than with any of the other potters she'd worked for over the years. Probably because Jeff was an intensely private person who respected her privacy, as well. He'd died last month, and the cousin who inherited had no interest in continuing the pottery. He'd also charged her full market price for the used equipment she already thought of as hers.

She should have walked away from the deal, she thought now, as she pushed the spade into the soil. Gotten a better price somewhere else. But she'd needed the continuity of keeping that wheel: Its idiosyncracies were bonded into her muscle memory. She was already losing the studio, surrounded by scraggly pines and smoke blue hills; losing her best friend, Jeff Crawford, with his laconic humor and cynical commentary on the lives of the tourists who trooped through the showroom on Wednesdays and Saturdays. She had stayed there long enough to take root, and hadn't even realized it.

Amelia wiped the blade of the spade carefully and put it away in the tractor shed before going in and washing up. Her life had suffered another transformation, with as little say about its new shape as clay had. No use brooding, though; the change was already on her. She had to force herself to fix a real dinner—only the thought of grocery money going to waste really persuaded her—but once the stir-fry of broccoli, green beans, and rice was done, she ate like a starved animal. It wasn't until she finished that she realized she'd never stopped for lunch. She would have to be more careful about that. Jeff used to nag about meals, and keep her on schedule.

She washed the dishes and left them to drain, then spent a few minutes going through Gramps's books. She looked for worn copies among the books on grassland restoration, and pulled out ten or so. These she carried into the kitchen and looked over while she drank her coffee.

Skimming through, Amelia was surprised at how much she remembered, and at how much more there was to know. Gramps used to set controlled burns to keep down invading brush. It had been one of the most exciting parts of the prairie work for her and Michael, although they had seldom been at the ranch during the winter when most of the fires were set. But she hadn't had any idea how complex the planned burns were, or of the effects they had on the soil.

She set the book on burns aside and turned to an illustrated guide to prairie grasses. An appendix included a list of commercial seed sources, two of which were circled in pencil, with the scribbled notation "good seed" in Gramps's handwriting. Amelia felt better just looking at the familiar writing, with its clear vertical lines. Gramps would help her; she'd have some guidance, no matter how overwhelming the project seemed. She read through several more books before bedtime, skipping around to get a feel for what the restoration would involve.

Later, she remembered to look for the hot-water heater. She didn't want to take any more ice-water spit baths. It took her twenty minutes to realize that she couldn't find a heater because it was gone. Gramps had installed a solar water heater on the roof instead. Its tank had been drained, and the line from the pump shut off. All it took was ten minutes with a pair of pliers to start it refilling. But the sun was already down, so she'd have to wait another day for running hot water.

She decided she could put off making the gallery rounds one more day. The managers would probably be grateful to her for holding off until she'd had a hot shower.

That meant she could spend tomorrow working on the studio and planning a kiln. Maybe a solar kiln? Although she half remembered reading somewhere that solars had severe size constraints, and she'd need to be able to fire in large batches.

Amelia's thoughts were on clay as she got ready for bed, a dreamy contemplation of latent shapes and unexposed forms. Beneath her feet, the wood-block floor was already getting cold. She built up the fire in the wood stove and decided to pile more blankets on her narrow bed to defend against tomorrow morning's chill.

She went down the passage toward Gramps's room, averting her eyes from Michael's closed door. She was reluctant to give his memory too much attention here, in this place where ghosts could walk.

The bed in her grandparents' room was still covered with the wedding-ring quilt Gramma had made before they were married. Except for cleaning, it probably hadn't been removed from this bed since their wedding night. Feeling a little guilty, Amelia gathered it tenderly up and carried it into her room.

It folded twice across her bed, with width to spare. Cuddled into it, Amelia plunged into unconsciousness like a stone dropping into a well. And only distantly did she hear her grandmother's voice, singing a soft, familiar lullaby.

She woke abruptly in dead-dark stillness, choking on a cry. The details of her dream were already blurring, but she could still see Michael, calling to her beseechingly, his face in shadows. She had been trying to grasp his shoulders, to pull him back from some danger, but couldn't seem to hold onto him. When at last she seized him and dragged him back from that inchoate dream threat, he had turned toward her with a sound like a wounded bird—a sharp, panicked skrill—and she had seen his face. He had two dark wet holes where his eyes should have been.

Amelia was drenched in sweat, but the instant she pushed the covers back, it seemed to freeze on her body. She lay there for a moment, waiting for her heart to calm, not looking at the shaped shadows that lurked in the doorway. Then the cry—the wounded-bird sound—came again.

She jerked upright, listening, trying to replay the

sound and understand it. Was it a bird? An injured mouse or rabbit? But the sound, like the dream, was already shifting in her memory, and she could not stabilize it.

The silence of the house had an ominous quality. In their absence, Amelia couldn't furnish the sounds that should have been there, but she noticed the lack. She got up. The floor was icy, and she wished for a pair of sheepskin slippers like the ones she used to have. She cloaked herself in Gramma's quilt, and, swathed in its protective armor, made her way past the threatening shadows at her bedroom door.

She was reluctant to turn on the lights. The idea of exposing herself to someone who watched from outside was too chilling. The old upholstered armchair by the side windows in the living room seemed a good place to wait and listen. Amelia gathered her feet up under her, tucking the quilt in to block drafts. The sound hadn't repeated.

She waited there in the darkness, listening, very aware of the seclusion of the ranch house. No defenses. She hadn't even considered looking for Gramps's shotgun or getting shells for it. She wasn't capable of shooting anyone. The killing she'd already done would haunt her for the rest of her life.

Gradually, normal night sounds reasserted themselves: the faint whistle of wind along the tiles of the roof, rustling grasses, faint half-heard chirrupings from the attic. The deep WHUF-*whuf-whuf* of the windmill. It sounded like the wingbeats of some huge bird. An owl, maybe. Amelia was warm in the embrace of the big chair, but was still too jittery to rest, when a warm whisper slipped across her mind.

"Everything's all right, honey-girl. Gramps will take care of us."

Honey-girl. Nobody but you ever called me that, Gramma.

"Of course not. That's because you're *my* honey-girl. Now stop fretting. Gramps and I are here. Sleep tight, Melia."

Night, Gramma. It was Amelia's last thought before she slipped into sleep.

When she woke to bright sunshine, she walked around the outside of the house to check on things. A pair of footprints were scuffed in the soft ground outside her bedroom window.

The idea that someone had been out there spying on her last night was terrifying, but she tried to calm down and think clearly. Maybe Spencer Reed had come snooping around. He and Gramps had feuded for years, and he obviously didn't want to give up the Folly.

Amelia decided to call Nick Atkinson. She had to find out about Reed's claim that he had a lease on the Folly—how could Gramps have left the terms of the trust vague enough to allow such a thing? And she had to admit that she was looking forward to hearing a friendly voice.

Tanya answered on the third ring. "Tamarisco Savings and Loan. May I help you?"

"Nick Atkinson, please," Amelia said.

"May I say who's calling?"

"This is Amelia—Amelia Rawlins. I'm calling from the ranch."

"I'm sorry," Tanya said. "Mr. Atkinson is out just now. May I give him a message?"

"I need to ask him about a lease Spencer Reed says he has on part of the property. Please have him call me as soon as he can. The number is—"

"We have the number, Miss Rawlins," Tanya said, "but please remember that Mr. Atkinson is a very busy man. I'll see that he gets your message." She hung up.

Amelia listened to the blank hum of the open line for a second, then put the receiver back in its cradle. Sounded like the only way she could be sure of talking to Atkinson was to drive into town and camp in his front office.

Which could be arranged.

She spent the day unpacking the tools and materials she'd brought with her from North Carolina. Gramps's workshop was going to make a wonderful studio.

But the best part of the day was the hot shower she took at the end of it.

By the following morning, Amelia knew she couldn't put off the gallery visits any more. She pulled her portfolio out of the trunk. The portfolio case had been a gift from Jefferson three Christmases ago, just before she'd gone to New York for her only real show. It was a gorgeous slab of honey-toned leather with a heavy brass zipper. Just holding it gave her confidence.

She wore her black dress shirt and leather jacket again, along with the turquoise bolo, and tried not to get too nervous on the long drive into town. To distract herself, she tried to place the names of the other ranches on the way. Spencer Reed's place was north, instead of south, so she didn't have to drive past it. But there were several other small places along their strip of road. The one almost straight across from her place had belonged to the Veracruz family when she was young, but she remembered her grandfather saying that Mr. Veracruz had sold out. Amelia looked along the ranch road toward the house, which she saw needed paint. A dark-haired woman wearing a red jacket was walking toward the highway from the house. When she saw Amelia watching her, she lifted her arm and waved.

Amelia barely had a chance to wave back before the truck was past. Next came the Billings ranch, off to the west, a big sprawl that spread halfway to the missile range, and several miles later, another one she couldn't place until she saw the double "L" on the gate. The Lucksingers.

The morning was bright. Amelia had her window partway down, and the desert air smelled like incense. That distinctive, sharp sweetness that she'd never known anywhere else.

She stopped for gas at a small store at the edge of town. The older Hispanic man behind the counter smiled at her when she came in and said, "Somebody gave your truck a smack?" He nodded toward the window.

Amelia glanced back, thinking at first that he

was talking about the twisted bumper. Then she realized he was referring to the big red lipstick mark Jeff had painted on the driver's door. It stood out sharply against the faded powder blue paint; Jeff always said it meant the door was sealed with a kiss.

"*Un beso grande,*" she told the man, which made him laugh.

After that, he spoke to her in Spanish as he collected her money and offered her change.

The brief exchange made her feel good, but filling the truck had cost thirty dollars. Only about two hundred bucks left.

"Time to get some work," she said to herself as she got back in and headed for the *mercado* area. It was a bricked-over avenue planted with a double row of Spanish oak trees and tamarisks down the center. Massive stone planters lay between the trees, but were empty this time of year. Amelia pulled the truck into a metered spot and dropped in a dime. Tamarisco hadn't raised the price since the meters were first installed.

Taggerty's was closed. A notice in the window announced that the gallery staff were on a buying trip to Santa Fe, and would return on the fifth of March. The second *mercado* gallery the gift shop lady had told her about was at the end of the avenue, charmingly placed, with honeysuckle vines on either side of its double doors. In the summer, it probably looked like a haven of green to pale Northern tourists unaccustomed to the blast of the New Mexico sun. The upper doors had an inlaid mosaic of turquoise tile, in the shape of a heart. Of course—Corazón Azul.

Amelia tugged at the door, and it opened smoothly, breaking the blue heart in half. She stepped inside. No one was in the front showroom. The place was spacious, without the cluttered look that too many galleries succumbed to. The ceilings were fifteen feet high, in the *bodegas con palitos* style, with unpeeled sticks filling the space between the huge beams.

The rough, blue-white plaster walls had several deep-cut niches, lighted to showcase certain pieces. Above the arches were diamond-shaped patterns of terracotta and turquoise tile. The floors were also tile—rosy Saltillo tile—topped with hand-woven rugs.

Distressed pine antiques—tables and sideboards and even chairs—were used for displaying the artwork. Amelia saw folk art, sand paintings, photographs. The pie safe on her right had a pierced-tin door. It made a perfect backdrop for a burnished black-on-black earthenware pot decorated with a traditional Pueblo feather pattern. Amelia recognized the exquisite craftsmanship before she saw the name on the inscribed placard. Maria Martinez.

She took a deep breath, tucked her portfolio more securely under her arm, and turned. A lean young man in a gray linen suit came out of a door at the back of the room. His gaze flicked over her in thorough, instantaneous assessment, pausing briefly at the turquoise bolo—it was a beautiful chunk of Kingston—but the battered condition of her boots decided him.

"Yes?" he said.

The inflection of his voice reminded Amelia of Jefferson's when he made up those outrageous histories about their tourists. So much so that she smiled without meaning to.

The man's shoulders straightened and he looked at her with more attention. "Help you with something?"

It was still a long way from a talking-to-a-customer voice, but he sounded much more interested. Amelia was disconcerted by the sudden shift, and wondered what she had done. She touched the portfolio tucked under her left arm and said, "I was hoping to speak to the owner. I'm a ceramist—"

The man was already shaking his head. "Sorry, it's off-season. We don't acquisition now."

Amelia forced herself to continue the push, despising the whole process. "My work's been shown at O'Hara's and at Geometrix in New York," she said. "I had work in a major ceramics show at Arman's."

He raised one eyebrow. "Then what on earth are you doing out here? No, never mind. Sorry, but like I said, we aren't at an accession stage just now. Thanks for coming in."

Jefferson could have outmaneuvered this man in a heartbeat. He would have made some remark about the Martinez piece and had the guy engaged in an aesthetic discussion before he knew what hit him. Jeff would have gotten him talking and learned so much about the man's aspirations for the gallery that the deal would have ended up sealing itself. Amelia stood there tongue-tied, and watched him turn away from her.

She had her hand on the door when she noticed the mosaic again. "I meant to compliment you on the gallery name."

He had paused near one of the displays off to her right, and now looked back at her. "It means 'Blue Heart,' " he said.

She smiled. "Yes, of course. I was talking about the source, though." She could almost hear Papa's voice as she quoted, " *'Pero en el corazón azul de la montaña, para mí, es siempre el verano.'* " That poem had been one of his favorites.

The young man had a blank look on his face. "Excuse me, I don't speak much Spanish."

Amelia hesitated, taken aback. "I'm sorry, I thought it must be from the poem by Emilio Vazza."

"You know Vazza?" The voice came from her left, and Amelia turned, startled. A slight Hispanic man with white hair and a magnificent nose was standing to her left.

After a second, she said, *"Canciónes del Viejo* was one of my father's favorites. He used to read to me from it when I was small. He especially loved 'Alianza de Oro'."

"A man of taste," he said, smiling. "My own favorite as well, as you may suppose from the name of the gallery. But where are my manners? I am Frederico Jarmél, and you are—"

"Amelia Caswell," she said, for the first time in twelve years. But she used the name without hesitation. Her father's memory was too close at that moment for her to deny his name. "Although my professional name was—is Amy Castle."

"Come, Miss Caswell," Sr. Jarmél said. "You

must have a coffee with me. We will talk together a little of poetry—and of that portfolio you are holding so tightly, yes?"

Amelia hadn't realized that it was Saturday. The savings and loan was closed when she walked over to ask Atkinson about the lease. Predictable. It was a bad news day all around.

Pulling the truck onto the highway, she thought about what Sr. Jarmél had said. He had looked at her portfolio with close attention, making astute observations about the glazes on each piece. He had complimented her on the craft of the work and expressed a lucid appreciation for the explorations of form in her lotus bowl series. All with the strictest of courtesies, the most impeccable attentions of a good host.

And then he had closed the portfolio, set it aside, and said, "Lovely work, Miss Caswell. Your father must be very proud. But you are not native American, are you? Not even a little?"

Amelia had met his gaze and shaken her head. And he had sighed, and shrugged, an expressive gesture of regret and helplessness.

"You perhaps noticed the certificate in the window? No? It is a small thing, the seal of the Bureau of Indian Affairs. And yet not a small thing, for without it, I should quickly be bankrupt. My dear," and here he had leaned forward and lightly touched her hand, "I cannot recall the last time we made a sale to someone living in this area. All of it goes to tourists, every single piece. And vacationers in New Mexico wish to return home with genuine native American crafts."

Amelia hesitated for a moment, then asked, "Even for utilitarian things, a set of dishes or a platter for Aunt Betty? I've worked in production pottery for years—"

But he was shaking his head again. "The B.I.A. has done an effective job of publicizing the plight of native craftsmen, whose designs and traditional artwork have been imitated for years. Now buyers are very wary of anything not 'authentic.' And if a gallery—or even a gift shop—carries nonnative work, the Bureau pulls their certification. Maybe in Santa Fe you could sell dishware. The residents there have money to spend on such things. But here—"

Amelia laughed. "You mean because I'm not native American, I can't even *try* to sell my work?"

"I'm very sorry to tell you this, but you must be aware of the difficulties you face. Could you not continue to market your work in the New York galleries?"

"Geometrix is out of business, and O'Hara's has been sold," she told him. In fact, the galleries were more interested in promoting an artist as a personality than in individual works. Amelia couldn't risk that kind of publicity.

"I am very sorry, my dear," he said. "I wish there were something I could do."

She stood, and he followed suit. "Thank you, Señor Jarmél," she said. "You've been very kind to take so much time with me."

"Not at all," he protested. "It was my pleasure. So few people know Vazza's work. You must come again for coffee, or perhaps to lunch."

He had escorted her to the door and taken his leave with the same exquisite courtesy. Which did nothing to soften the blow.

Out on the highway, Amelia held the truck to fifty and soothed herself with the subtle tones of the wintering desert. Sunlight drenched the expanse of dun and sierra soil, sparsely blanketed with gray-green creosote and silvery sage. The colors made her think of glazes, beautiful old matte glazes; celadons and pale whispery grays. The sort of glazes she had spent endless hours trying to reproduce, with some occasional success. But even if she managed to find an outlet here for production pieces, she wouldn't have any time to spare for glaze experiments.

Amelia looked out at the desert and wondered what the hell she was going to do.

Chapter Four

The H.P.D.'s internal investigation of the Boucher incident revealed that officers in a passing cruiser had refused to respond to calls for help from the victim's companion because they had dismissed the altercation as a "faggot slap-fight." The department's senior officials were inclined to hand out superficial reprimands to the officers involved, and divert attention from any accountability for Boucher's death with a high-profile hunt for his attackers.

Mayor Rawlins-Caswell's response to the Internal Affairs report was swift and decisive. She took the report public and demanded the resignation of Harold "Bubba" Walters, who had been Houston's Chief of Police for twenty-four years. Walters announced his resignation on June 14. At the same press conference, the mayor announced her appointee to the post and introduced him.

Chief Hiram Williamson was a criminal justice professional with strong credentials and an impeccable service record. A much-decorated veteran of the Korean conflict, he had been determinedly recruited from his previous post as assistant police chief with the City of Detroit.

He was also Houston's first black Chief of Police.

—MOLLY CATES, "Blood Relatives,"
Lone Star Monthly, April 1986

New Mexico

When she reached the Crossroads, a dark blue Jeep was pulling away from the P.O. boxes. Seeing it reminded her of the copy of the will Atkinson might have sent, and she pulled over to check. The Rawlins box was third from the end, the one listing so hard to port that it leaned against its neighbor like a drunk sailor. She'd have to get some cement and reset it.

She didn't really expect to find any mail since it had only been a couple of days since her talk with Atkinson, but there was a business-sized envelope in the box. Not from Atkinson, though; at least, she didn't think so. It was a cheap white paper envelope, the kind bought from a drugstore, not the expensive ivory stock his business cards were printed on.

She turned it over and frowned. The letter was addressed to Amelia Caswell. No one here would call her by that name. Gramps was stubborn about his family name carrying on, and had had no patience with the formal compounding of "Rawlins-Caswell." He had always introduced her and Michael as Rawlinses, and that's how everybody in the basin referred to them. The Rawlins kids. Or in Spencer Reed's case, the Rawlins brats.

Amelia slid a finger under the flap of the envelope and tore it open. The paper inside was also white, but it wasn't plain. It had a letterhead of sorts. A grainy black photocopy of an insignia she recognized: a crudely drawn wolf's head superimposed on a swastika. Amelia felt as if every drop of her blood had congealed in her stomach.

There were only a few words written on the paper. Ugly words, but they scarcely registered on her. It was the insignia that registered, the writing. Slanted block letters printed in blue ballpoint. Whoever had written them had pressed down so hard that the pen had torn through the paper in places. Her fingers skimmed over the raised lines on the back of the sheet in the same automatic way they sometimes touch-read the scar on her arm. The whorls of shiny flesh where she had been branded with a wolf's head superimposed on a swastika.

She looked at the blurred letterhead again, and the knot in her stomach clenched. Amelia doubled over and vomited, clinging to the rough post of one of the mailboxes for support.

She had expected to face a lot of memories here. But not this one. This one belonged in Houston. She had left it buried in the wreckage of the kitchen where her family had died.

A shadow fell across the gritty dirt in front of her, and a man's voice said, "You okay?"

Amelia sucked in air and aspirated stomach bile. She started to cough, and the man laid a hand on her shoulder.

She jerked away, ready to run, but she had no breath and doubled over again.

"Sorry," he said, backing off a step. "Didn't mean to startle you." His voice was deep. Amelia mastered the coughing fit and spat, then swiped at her mouth before straightening and turning to look at him.

He was on the tall side of medium, a little under six feet, and was built like a runner, lean and well-muscled. The hair under his slate blue cap was tangled around his face and collar, a deep glossy brown the shade of coffee beans, but his skin was that sunburned tan fair-skinned people who are outdoors all the time get. It took her a second to realize that the blue pants and white shirt were a uniform. The mail carrier. He was just the mail carrier.

"You look shaky," he said, and put his hand on her elbow. His grip was solid without being confining, offering support and nothing else.

Amelia took a cautious breath and pulled her arm away. "I'm all right now."

He released her immediately, but stood there frowning at her. His eyes were a clear, light gray. "You sure?"

"Sure," she said.

He glanced at the letter and envelope clenched in her fist. "Bad news?"

It struck her funny, and Amelia laughed. "You could say that." But laughing set off another fit of coughing.

As soon as the worst of this spell passed, the mailman took her arm and walked her over so she could sit in his Jeep. He stood beside the open door. A big blond dog stuck his head over the seat and nuzzled her ear.

"Tucker," the man said. His voice was firm but not loud. The dog immediately lay down in the space behind the driver's seat, nose on paws. The man reached past her and pulled a thermos from under the seat. "It's tea," he said as he poured some into the thermos cup and handed it to her.

Amelia set down the letter to take the cup in both hands and sipped cautiously, watching him the whole time. He stood there patiently. The tea was hot and very sweet, and it diluted the sour tang in her mouth. Her mother's prescription for an upset stomach had always been dry toast and sweet hot tea. With the first sip, her throat relaxed. She coughed again, but this time the searing tickle was gone. Maybe hot tea really did have curative powers. Or maybe her body was just conditioned to respond to it.

She drank the rest and handed the cup back to him.

"Better? You want some more?" he asked.

"Much better, thanks, but no more."

"Okay," he said and put the thermos away.

Amelia noticed that the sun was past zenith. If she didn't get back to the house soon, the whole day would end up wasted. There was a light breeze, and the air was cool, but the sunshine warmed her. She didn't want to move.

"I better get going," she said, and forced herself to get out.

The man took a step back, not crowding her. "Um," he said. "Don't mean to be rude, but I came back because I didn't recognize your truck. You the new caretaker at the Rawlins place?"

Amelia's legs felt shaky. She smoothed the letter

out mechanically. "Yes and no," she said without looking at him. She folded the paper and stuck it back in the envelope. "I'm Amelia Rawlins."

He was silent so long that she did look up then, to find him studying her closely. She wondered if he was going to say something about the different name on the envelope.

"Of course," he said. "I should have recognized you from your picture. Your grandfather always said you'd be back someday."

"You knew Gramps?" She found herself relaxing a little.

He gave a faint smile. "Everybody knew Mr. Rawlins, ma'am. He was a fine man. If you don't mind me saying so, he'll rest easier for you being here."

"If he rests at all," Amelia said without thinking.

The man gave a big barking laugh that surprised her because his voice was so quiet. "That's right," he said after a second or two. "Mr. Rawlins wasn't exactly the layabout kind."

She kept watching him. "Now that you know who I am," she said, "mind telling me who you are? Besides the mail carrier, I mean?"

The sunburned cheeks got redder. "Beg pardon, ma'am. I'm Frank Burkhalter."

"Thank you for the tea, Mr. Burkhalter."

"Burk," he said. "Everybody just calls me Burk, Ms. Rawlins."

He actually said it *"Miz* Rawlins." People in the south had found a solution to the "Miss" or "Mrs." dilemma years ago. *All in the pronunciation,* she thought. Then she glanced back down at the letter, and couldn't distract herself from its contents any more. She realized she was shivering. "Right. Well, thank you."

"Ms. Rawlins—" He broke off.

"Yes?"

"If there's some kind of trouble, I'd be pleased to help."

She didn't answer him.

After a minute, he said, "Folks around here thought a lot of your grandfather, ma'am."

She kept her eyes on the plain white envelope. The address was typed, she realized, not hand-printed like the words inside. A normal first-class stamp with a blurred cancellation mark. She handed it to him, curious to see what his reaction would be. "Can you tell me where this came from?"

He squinted at the postmark. "Looks like it was canceled here. That means it was mailed locally, unless the office on the other end missed canceling it and someone here noticed. If it's important, I could take it back to the station with me and ask around."

Amelia rubbed a hand across her mouth and tried to think. All she wanted right then was to wrap herself in her grandmother's quilt, curl up in the big chair by the window, and sleep.

Burk handed the envelope back to her. His voice was quieter than ever as he asked, "Is something wrong?"

Her exhaustion was suddenly so great that she couldn't stand there any longer. She removed the letter and gave him the empty envelope. "Yeah, sort of. If you can tell me for sure where this came from, I'd be obliged to you, Mr. Burkhalter." She turned toward the truck.

"Burk," he said to her back. "I'll see what I can find out. You sure you're okay to drive, Ms. Rawlins?"

"Yes," she said and got behind the wheel. She smacked the door shut and started the truck, then realized she was being rude. She leaned out the window and looked back.

He was standing there with the envelope in his hand, watching her. The dog—Tucker—sat next to him, his big tail gently stirring the dust along the shoulder of the road. The dog was watching her, too.

"Nice meeting you, Mr. Burkhalter," Amelia said. She pulled away before he answered.

She had a hard moment when she reached the drive to the ranch. Beneath her weariness, under the reactive exhaustion, part of her was clamoring to just keep driving. To stay behind the wheel of the pickup until she found some sleepy town a thousand miles from here. Some nameless place where no one had ever heard of Amelia Rawlins or Melia Caswell or even Amy Castle, and wouldn't care if they had.

But another part of her knew that wouldn't help. None of the anonymous places had really kept the memories at bay. Except maybe Cooperton, and that was because, after a while, it hadn't been anonymous any more. She'd made a home for herself there, without really meaning to. Gotten settled, started caring about people.

Then death had blown through and swept it all away again. And she hadn't even realized that Jefferson and the handful of regulars at the TipTop Café had become her family until Jeff was gone, and her place there gone with him. No town was safe from death. She should have known that.

At least Gramps wouldn't die and leave her. He might not be the most reliable of companions these days, but he had a real advantage when it came to this mortality business. She sat there for a moment, unmindful of the small chunks of cracked plastic that her fingers were gouging from the steering wheel. Then she dragged herself out of the truck and unlocked the gate.

When she pulled up to the house, she looked around carefully before getting out of the truck, but the place was quiet. Even the windmill was still. As she unlocked the kitchen door, Amelia wondered how many other people had known where Gramps kept the spare key. Even sliding the deadbolt home, she felt no real sense of security. She would have to change the locks.

More "have-to's" were piling up all the time. She hung the leather jacket over a chair and drank a big glass of water before she surrendered to her body's demands and took a nap.

She slept for over an hour, with the sort of limp dreamlessness that for her always signaled complete exhaustion. When she woke, her mind was clearer, and she felt more detached from the terror that had caught her by the mailbox. It had been tangible, if insubstantial, like a shadow linked to the letter. The shadow was still here.

But her body's insistence on sleep had at least granted her some distance from it.

There was something here at the ranch that mattered to her, a bridge that reached back to the best part of her past, and she wouldn't relinquish it. At the same time, she'd have to be on her guard. The Wolfen were here.

Amelia retrieved the letter from the pocket of her leather jacket and spread the creased paper open on the kitchen table. This time she let the letters form into words, allowing the sense of them to register, weighing them as dispassionately as she could.

We don't put up with white niggers around here, the slashing blue print said. *We know who you are. To bad them bootboys in Houston missed you when they exterminated the rest of that faggot-loving scum. But don't worry. The Wolf's Mouth is everywhere and you just walked right back into it. One night soon, we'll finish the job. Heil Wolfen*

So, she thought. A threat, and a greeting of sorts. We're here, we recognize you. We still hate you. And we are prepared to act on our hatred.

Amelia was very aware of the stillness of the house. The wind had dropped, and with it had gone the throb of the windmill.

She took a deep breath and laid her hand flat on the paper with the blue-slashed words. "They hate me," she said. Speaking it aloud steadied her, somehow.

After all these years, they had found her. For her, the price of coming home might be death.

Well, so be it. Maybe she'd been meant to die twelve years ago. Maybe it would have been better for everyone if she had.

She understood the letter was only the beginning. Still, there was a strange bubble of some unaccustomed feeling in her chest. Acceptance? Certainty?

She wasn't sure. She only knew that running wouldn't work any more. She didn't have the strength.

Whatever being here brought, she would rather deal with it than move on.

Amelia went into the small alcove off the living room that had served as her grandfather's office. The drawers of his battered oak desk were unlocked and empty of everything but some scattered mouse droppings and a random paper clip. The dusty vacant smell of them made her sad, but she brushed away the dust in the center drawer and stuck the letter in it.

Then she washed up, made herself a thick cheese sandwich, and carried it out to the workshop. More than ever now, she needed to lose herself in clay.

It didn't take much time for her to set up a temporary pottery studio, although the result was pretty minimalist. She staple-gunned an old canvas tarp to one of the workbenches so she'd have a place to wedge the clay and do any hand-building. It was a simple matter to unwind the loops of rope she had left around the wheel, reattach the power line and the control pedal, and press the splash guards into place.

There was room enough on the main workbench for pots to dry, as long as she didn't go into production mode. It would be crazy to do much anyway, since she hadn't even started on the kiln yet.

But right now she needed this work. She had to feel the clay come to life under her hands, its wet coolness sliding under her fingers, shaping to her vision, growing, becoming.

Amelia got a bucket from the toolshed and filled it at the sink. She'd brought clay with her, five hundred pounds of her favorite gray stoneware. The top of the cardboard box cracked open with a sharp sound, and Amelia wriggled one of the snugly packed twenty-five pound bags out. It was the size of a breadbox and shaped like an oversized brick. When she opened the plastic bag and folded it back, the wet river-bottom smell of the clay hit her.

Instantly, she thought of Jefferson's studio, with its marshy smell and bare concrete floors. The place had low, wide windows that they always left open in the summertime, with battered screens that did little to keep the bugs out.

Jeff would have been hunched at his wheel, sweat flattening his thinning brown hair. His was an enormous old kick-wheel built of heavy steel and slab concrete. The wheel had been motorized and clattered when it ran.

Amelia sliced off the top of the clay with a wire loop. She'd have to go easy on her supply.

She closed her eyes and sank her fingers into the clay, relishing its slick elasticity. This stoneware fired almost as white as porcelain, but it had more backbone to it and wasn't as buttery and hard to manage on the wheel.

Amelia opened her eyes, moved to the bench she had prepared, and began wedging the clay. The process was designed to remove any air bubbles, which wasn't really necessary in this case. A fresh block like this was solid. But she wanted to work the clay in her hands. Wedging clay was a lot like kneading bread. To work the clay, she kept the motion of her wrists a little flatter and made a more shallow fold after each rocking push.

The work pulled her into its rhythms like a tide, and Amelia let it take her. When the clay was smooth and malleable under her hands, she moved to the wheel. It took her a minute or two to locate the box of batts: large flat plates of plywood with holes that fit over the screwheads on top of the wheel head. She fitted one onto the wheel, snugging it into place with a couple of smears of clay and some water.

She wet a small sea sponge and swabbed the center of the batt with it. The sponge would help keep the clay moist as she worked. Then she pulled a teardrop-shaped rib from her box of tools and spread an old towel in her lap.

Turning on the wheel made little sound; unlike Jefferson's converted kick-wheel, this one ran with a quiet electric hum. Amelia slapped the clay into the center of the batt so it adhered to the damp spot, then wet her hands in the bucket.

It was pure pleasure to move her foot on the pedal and cup the clay in her hands. The lump had looked fairly regular, but once it was moving, its lack of symmetry was obvious. Amelia's wet hands curved around it, bracing and shaping the lump until it centered into a smooth, balanced mass.

She dampened her hands again before coning the clay, lifting it into an even round tower, spinning on the batt. She curved her fingers over the spinning clay and pressed it back into the rounded-breast shape that was the starting point for thrown pots.

If she had been doing production work, she would have begun with an exact end in mind and measured the dimensions of the pot as she worked. But this wasn't going to be a production piece. This was what Jefferson called "heartwork," the pieces created out of love. For these pieces, Amelia liked to play with the clay before deciding on a shape.

She pressed the moist sponge into the center of the spinning clay. Under the firm pressure of her fingers, the clay flowed into a ring shape with a flat layer of clay at the bottom. In a continuous motion, Amelia pulled the opening wider until she had a fat ring about five inches in diameter.

With one hand inside the ring of clay and the other outside, she set the wheel spinning faster and made the first pull. The clay rose under her fingers, growing into an even-walled cylinder about six inches tall. She automatically angled the walls inward, then dropped the speed of the wheel and sat back to examine the pot.

Gramps was sitting on a sawhorse about ten feet away, watching her. He had on the same red plaid shirt as before.

"Gramps. I didn't know you were here."

"Didn't want you to," he said. "I was watching what you're doing there. This what you do for a living?"

She nodded. "I'm a potter. Not exactly what you expected, is it? Well, me either."

He got up and moved over to stand next to her. "Oh, I'm not surprised. You always did like making mud pies."

"Did I? Well, I am an earth sign." Amelia looked back at the pot. What she liked best about it was the slight flare of the base before the walls slanted inward. She moistened her hands and the sponge and increased the wheel speed. This time, she intensified the flare at the base of the pot, pulling more clay up and out, holding the walls even. Then she drew the walls back in and shaped a narrow neck.

"That's how I knew you belonged here," Gramps said. "You couldn't wait to get your fingers into the earth. Used to pester Rosalie half to death to let you help in the garden."

The pot now had a vaguely Persian look. With her last pull, Amelia emphasized the roundness of the base and narrowed the neck to a straight column barely two fingers wide. She said, "Gramma loved it when I helped her in the garden."

"Sure, she did."

That made her look up, but he wasn't being sarcastic. He was watching her hands on the clay. She used the sponge to form a lip for the bottle, then angled the rib to slice away the edge at the bottom for a clean foot.

"Do you remember when I first promised to leave you this place?" he asked.

She thought about it, then shook her head. "I just always knew you had, Gramps."

"You were only about three and a half. You and your mother came and stayed for nearly two months that summer. We had a wonderful time, you and me. I'd take you out to the fields with me, let you ride in my lap to drive the tractor. Carried you on my shoulders near about everywhere. You were brown as a berry by the end of June, and just a-chattering about everything around you. And every other word out of your mouth was 'why.' And you weren't about to take 'Just because' for an answer.

"When it was time for you to go home, Marian was explaining it to you, reminding you about the airplane ride and all that, so's you'd know what to expect. And you were fit to be tied, because you didn't want to go back to Houston."

"I never wanted to go home at the end of the summer," Amelia said. "Well, I did and I didn't, at the same time. You know what I mean." She held both ends of the wire loop flat against the wheel and sliced straight through the very bottom of the pot so it wouldn't stick to the batt after it was dry.

"I know," he said. "But you had no two minds of it this particular time. You gave your mother so much grief. 'But *why* do we have to go back?' Until she finally just threw her hands up and told you it was because Houston was your home."

"Did it work?" Amelia asked. She was only half listening to the story, but she liked the sound of his voice. She had always loved working in the shop with Gramps, having him talk to her while their hands were busy with something else.

"You kidding?" Gramps said. "You looked up at Marian just as serious as all get-out, and you said, 'Oh, no, Mama. I live *here* now.'" He gave a wheezy laugh. "I will *never* forget the look on her face. It was every parent's dream come true."

Amelia looked up from the pot. "What do you mean?"

"Seeing her trying to cope with a little girl who was just like her. Too smart for your own good, both of you."

She smiled at him. "Lucky we had you around to keep us in line, huh Gramps?"

His face got suddenly serious. "Lucky for me," he said, and then he was gone.

The lights in the workshop flickered once. The wheel must have drained the batteries faster than the converters could recharge them. Amelia sighed, then used the edge of a scraper to break the suction between the batt and the wheel. She carried the stoneware bottle— still on the batt—over to the workbench.

It wouldn't be the same, working alone.

She turned off the wheel and cleaned her tools and the wheel head carefully, using the water in the bucket. But she couldn't dump the bucket inside, because there were no traps installed in the drains. Clay clogged pipes faster than you could spit. She'd have to wash it outside at the old hand pump near the garden.

As she carried the silty water outside, the wind picked up. It was late afternoon and still bright, but the wind was already turning night-cold. The windmill was moaning again. Something about the sound made her hurry. Her hands were freezing as she carried the clean bucket back to the workshop.

The bottle glistened like wet cement in the flickering light of the workshop, its sides smooth and even. Having Gramps leave so suddenly was bothering her more than it should have.

After a few minutes, she realized why. If she had done this bottle a month ago, Jefferson would have been examining it, too, asking what kind of glaze she planned to use. Amelia looked at the piece and tried to picture it finished, the kind of image that always seemed to come in a flash when Jeff asked. Nothing.

"So, what kind of glaze do you think it needs, Jeff?" she said. She waited a long moment for an answer that didn't come. A silly notion anyway, thinking he might turn up here.

Amelia rubbed her frozen hands on her jeans, then closed and padlocked the studio door.

She was heading for the house when a station wagon pulled up by the gate and stopped.

Chapter Five

Houston's 1983 Gay Pride Parade took place on Saturday, June 21, a day when the heat index soared to a record 109 degrees. The mayor later jokingly commented to reporters that it was "certainly the longest day of my year." She, Chief Williamson, and four city council members marched together at the head of the parade. Its route covered ten miles, from a starting point at the corner of Shepherd and Memorial, moving downtown toward City Hall.

Police protection for the parade was massive, and although a strong turnout from the KKK and several reactionary groups fostered a tense atmosphere, any provocation offered by the counterdemonstrators was quickly subdued.

When the parade reached City Hall, Mayor Rawlins-Caswell again took the podium, this time to announce that the city was initiating routine foot patrols in the Montrose district. Pairs of plainclothes officers would pose as gay couples in order to police the area more effectively. Bashers and harassers were on notice that they risked immediate arrest and would face jail sentences.

Chief Williamson announced that the department was also planning to open a storefront substation in the district. Its goal was to increase police presence in the community and promote cooperation between Montrose residents and the police force.

Two brown-shirted hecklers began shouting racist epithets at the new police chief. They were immediately arrested for disorderly conduct and jailed. A.C.L.U. attorneys had them released within hours, threatening suit on grounds of infringement of their Fifth Amendment rights.

That night, the temperature at 11:12 P.M. still hovered at 90 degrees, with humidity of 96 percent.

The Sunday Houston Record ran a sidebar with its report on the parade and the arrests, estimating the cost of police overtime required by the event at over $30,000.

—MOLLY CATES, "Blood Relatives,"
Lone Star Monthly, April 1986

New Mexico

Amelia relaxed a little. She didn't expect the Wolfen to drive up in a station wagon, but she turned on the outside floodlights over the patio anyway. A woman wearing jeans and a dark green sweater got out of the old car. "Hi," she called as she slid over the fence and started toward the house. She was carrying a basket in one hand.

As she came closer, Amelia got over her initial scare. This woman obviously wasn't a threat.

"Are you Amelia? I'm Caroline Garrity—your neighbor across the way." Her voice had the deep true tones of a church bell, and she looked the way she sounded: a serene Madonna-like face, with an incongruous sprinkle of freckles. Her hair was dark, worn knotted up on the back of her head.

She came up to Amelia and offered her hand. Amelia shook it, and found herself looking down several inches into a pair of big, dark eyes. "Nice to meet you," she said automatically.

"You okay? Burk said you were feeling sick earlier, asked me to come by and check on you."

"Burk? Oh—you mean Mr.—the mailman."

Caroline Garrity grinned. "Who lets nothing keep him from his appointed rounds—or me from mine, apparently. I brought you something to settle your stomach—mind if I step inside for a sec?"

"Not at all," Amelia murmured, though she did. Not that she disliked this woman—not at all—she just wasn't interested in getting on visiting terms with the people around here. Better for her to keep to herself.

But manners were manners. She held the door open and let Caroline Garrity precede her into the kitchen.

"It's a little cool in here," she said. "I'll build up the fire—"

"Not on my account," Caroline said briskly, as she set the basket on the table. "I can't stay but a sec—" She folded back the red-checked cloth lining the basket and pointed to a mason jar of green-gold liquid. "Chamomile tea, settles your stomach. And this"—she indicated a smaller jar of something darker and thicker—"is an infusion of peppermint and parsley. Take it by the spoonful. Had any fever?"

"No—" Amelia was off balance. "I was just—I got bad news earlier. I was upset is all."

Caroline looked at her assessingly.

"Really," Amelia said.

"If you're sure."

"I'm fine. But I'm a little confused—is Mr. Burkhalter—you said something about your rounds. Do you work for the post office, too?"

Caroline smiled. There was something about the way her eyes crinkled at the corners that reminded Amelia of her mother. "No, nothing like that. I have a medical practice—osteopathic—in town. It was just a joke about Burk wheedling me into making house calls."

Amelia was appalled. That man—a complete stranger—had sent a doctor out here without even asking her first. "He shouldn't have—I didn't realize," she said. "A house call—how much do I owe—"

"Don't be silly. It's on my way home, and Burk's an old friend. He's Mark's godfather—Mark's my son—you may've seen him around?" Caroline raised her eyebrows.

Amelia shook her head.

"Anyway, I was glad for a reason to stop by, once Burk said you were sick. You and I are neighbors, after all—and we're pretty isolated out here."

Amelia didn't want to think about that. "Neighbors?" she said quickly. "You must be the ones who have the old Veracruz place, then."

"That's right. We—that is, Mark's father and I—bought it a couple of years ago, when he was teaching at the university in Alamogordo, but—" She broke off. "I'm glad you've decided to live here. This place has only had caretakers since we came—and they were only here off and on. It's worried me."

"I should have come back a long time ago," Amelia said.

She found her hand taken in another firm clasp. "So long as you're here now," Caroline said with a smile. "Sure you're feeling okay? Call if you need anything—we're in the book. Night."

Amelia followed her to the door and said, "Thanks very much, Mrs.—I mean—is it *Dr.* Garrity?"

"No sweat—and just call me Caroline, please." Then she was off, whistling a Bach sonata as she walked back out to the highway.

The sweet sound kept Amelia at the door listening. It was getting on toward dark now, and she shivered as the wind stirred. Then she remembered the slashing print of the letter—*ONE NIGHT SOON*—and quickly slammed the door shut. She was shuddering as she turned the lock, her stomach jumping, but she left Dr. Garrity's jars in their basket. Somehow, she didn't think they would solve her problem.

Her sleep that night was disturbed by dreams of a huge white wolf that hunted her across the tumbled red rocks of the canyon.

*   *   *

The following morning was Sunday, and Amelia was restless. She did some work around the house—dusting with Gramma's homemade beeswax and lemon oil polish, washing laundry, baking some bread for the week to come. But something itched at her, and it wasn't until around nine when she went out to hang the wet wash on the line that she realized what it was. She could hear the church bells ringing, a faint clear sound that seemed to hang in the morning air. Gramma had always held to the Sabbath as a day of rest, and Sunday morning at the ranch always meant going to Mass.

Her own family had never attended church; religion had been a source of subdued conflict in their home, even though both her parents had been reared as Catholics. Papa's experiences as a young man had made him reject his religious upbringing. Before they married, he had extracted a promise from his wife that she wouldn't "indoctrinate" their children. Amelia's mother had kept the promise, but she hadn't tried to hold her parents to it. And their Sundays started with Mass at the Mission, a graceful adobe church over a hundred years old.

Amelia had always enjoyed the services held in the cool dimness of the chapel. She loved the deep, ingrained smell of incense and candle wax, and the way the music seemed to swell from the very walls. She loved the smoothness of the dark wood of the pews, and she was entranced by the glorious colors of the stained glass windows on either side of the altar. In one of them, the cobalt blue shadow of Christ was so deep and brilliant that after she stared at it, she felt blinded to other colors. During her first year as a potter's apprentice, she had driven her teacher crazy by dunking every pot she got her hands on in cobalt glaze.

Amelia sighed and reached into the laundry basket for another pillowcase. The wind rose as she pinned it to the line, making the white cotton snap, as bright as a flag in the sunshine.

She couldn't afford to observe the Sabbath as a day of rest. She finished hanging out the laundry, then went inside and sat down at the kitchen table to make a list of other things she needed to do.

Unfortunately, most of the things at the top of the list—buying new locks for the house, getting a copy of Gramps's will, revoking Reed's lease on the Folly—would have to wait for tomorrow, when the courthouse was open and Nick Atkinson would be in his office. And the number one item—earning a living—was still a big question mark. She doubted any of the stores in town would hire someone who'd never done anything but make pots.

Amelia got up and went to look out the east windows in the living room. The mountains filled them entirely, the taller peaks big and misty blue beyond the rock-and-desert tones of the lower hills. She shouldn't be wasting gas, not when she was so low on cash, she knew that. But she had been thinking of her family, and now their voices were too much with her.

So she went anyway, still looking up as she started the truck and drove out.

She followed the hairpin and S curves of Highway 82 all the way to the top this time, feeling the chill of true winter seep into the truck as she gained altitude. As she passed into the alpine zone where pine forests surrounded the road, the wind began to hum through the trees, sounding like a distant Gregorian chant. She didn't even have to consider where she was going; Dog Canyon had always been her favorite place on the mountain.

Dog Canyon was really a large valley, one of the sloping shoulders of the mountain range. The canyon ran from the Sunspot Observatory road down to Highway 82 just below High Rolls. This time of year, Amelia didn't trust the road through the canyon, because it was unpaved. But she could park on the Sunspot road by the valley's mouth and walk down.

She'd often wondered why it was called Dog Canyon. It was an alpine valley, with a large spring-fed stream that coursed down one edge to join the narrow river below Mary's orchard. There were aspens and maples in the meadow of the valley, and wild strawberries grew there in the springtime, so thick on the ground you could hardly avoid stepping on them. Pine forest closed in around the meadow, with enormous old-growth trees clustered on the steep slopes. About midway down the valley, a huge fallen pine lay across the stream gorge, next to a small clearing well away from the road. That spot had always been her favorite campsite.

She'd passed a few other trucks and cars on the main highway up to Cloudcroft, but saw no one on the Sunspot road. She pulled the truck onto the shoulder just past the canyon cutoff and parked. The air was cold on her face and at her throat. Amelia buttoned her shirt higher and stuck her hands in her vest pockets as she hiked downhill. The air was cider-sharp, and heavily spiced with dampness and pine. She opened her mouth to drink it all in. Her bones and blood ran all the way to the core of the earth here.

She felt as if she could walk straight into the center of one of the huge pines and stay there. She felt as if she were a tree herself, rooted deep into this earth.

A fallen trunk lay just inside the forested slopes about a quarter of mile from the main road. She sat down there, content merely to breathe this air as she worked her fingers through the fibrous bark of the decomposing pine. It was impossible for her to distinguish the sound of the stream next to her from the whisper of the wind among the pines.

Amelia let the sound sink into her chest with her breath, as her fingers sank into the tree trunk. That's when the clamoring voices from the past finally stilled.

She carried that stillness back down the mountain with her: a silence, an emptied thoughtless state she found only in this place and in the rarest moments of her clay work. So it was without any conscious impulse that she turned the steering wheel into Mary's driveway on the way down the mountain.

She followed the lane around the orchard to the back of the house. A late-model Ford pickup with gleaming dark blue paint was parked behind Mary's Jeep.

Amelia didn't recognize the pickup and hesitated, but Mary and her visitor were on the deck and had seen her.

Amelia got out of the truck and slammed the door hard enough to make it stick. The contrast between the two trucks was so drastic—hers with oxidized paint, its twisted bumper, and the big red kiss mark, the other with glossy dark paint and gleaming chrome—that she was grinning as she went up the steps. Mary's visitor was a stocky man wearing neat jeans with a rattlesnake belt and a blue-and-green plaid shirt. His hair was darker than the black felt of his Stetson. As Amelia approached, he stood up and removed the hat.

"You're looking cheerful, Melia," Mary said. "Good to see it. Don't think you know my cousin Willy."

"No, ma'am, I don't believe so," Amelia said.

"Willy Lachte. This is Melia Rawlins, Willy—Hector Rawlins's granddaughter."

"It's a pleasure," Willy said, nodding at her.

When Amelia put out her hand, he took it immediately. There were callouses and muscle behind his grip, and she figured him for a rancher. Someone who worked horses a lot, anyway.

"Nice to meet you, Mr. Lachte," she said. "You live hereabouts?" It could pass for polite talk, but she wanted to make sure she wasn't interrupting a rare family visit.

"Mescalero," he said.

"Willy's general manager at the Inn," Mary put in. "The hotel part. We were just about to have dinner, Melia—come on inside. I've got beans with ham hocks, fresh applesauce, and skillet cornbread."

Amelia tried to excuse herself, saying she didn't want to interrupt their visit. Mary wouldn't allow it, and ushered them inside.

The big dining table was buried under the spread she had prepared. In addition to beans, applesauce, and cornbread, there were a green salad, new potatoes roasted in olive oil with strips of poblano pepper, and the tenderest, juiciest ham Amelia had ever tasted. And apple cobbler for dessert.

Amelia ate almost enough to satisfy her hostess.

Willy Lachte seemed to approve of the heartiness of her appetite as well, and was generally so pleasant and easygoing that Amelia forgot to be nervous.

"How're things at the ranch?" he asked her. "Has the agent taken good care of things?"

"Yes, everything's fine. Well—" Amelia fiddled with her fork, then realized what she was doing and set it down. "The buildings are all in good repair, but Gramps's prairie got leased out or something—I still haven't gotten the details. Anyway, Spencer Reed is growing crops there right now. I've got to get the lease back. And then try to replant the prairie."

"That's terrible," Willy said. "I know it's a prime piece of land, but Hector put his whole heart into that prairie."

Mary was frowning. "Wouldn't think your grandfather's will would allow for leasing it. Especially not for cultivation."

"Me either," Amelia said, "but since I don't even have a copy of the will yet—"

"I do," Mary said.

"You *do*?"

"Sure. Hector left a copy with me. Just for insurance, he said. And I forgot all about it, till you said that."

Amelia closed her eyes for a moment as relief flooded her. It would be so much easier to talk to Atkinson if she could go over the will first. "Thank God," she said.

"Hang on a second, I'll see if I can find it." Mary got up and headed through the living room toward her office. Her boot heels made a martial beat on the floorboards.

"Sounds like that trustee messed up bad," Willy said. "Mary said it's some banker in Tamarisco?"

"That's right," Amelia said. She hesitated, then added, "He's been real decent to me. And he may not have really done anything wrong. For all I know, he's allowed to do whatever he thinks is best about leases or anything else that comes up."

"Maybe so, but your grandfather would hate this." He was relaxed, leaning back in his chair, but he was watching her closely. "Mary's worried about you. She was asking—" He stopped as Mary came back through the living room.

"Found it," Mary said. "I'd stuck it in the back of the safe. Here you go." She set a business-size envelope on the table and began gathering up the dessert dishes.

Amelia started to get up to help, but Mary pressed her back into the chair. "Go ahead and look at it."

The envelope was very thick, printed on thick gray paper with Terrance Grayson's name and return address printed on it. It had been sealed, and Mary's name was written on the front in Gramps's spidery vertical handwriting. Amelia ran her fingers over the neat letters and struggled against the impulse to lift the paper to her nose to see if it smelled like him. She had a sudden sharp longing for his physical presence: the smell of pipe tobacco and Aqua Velva, and the feel of his hands as they guided hers on the steering wheel of the tractor.

She put the envelope in the pocket of her jacket and stood up. "I'll look at it later." She collected some dishes and followed Mary to the kitchen.

Mary had remodeled her kitchen since Amelia had last seen it; she was loading a dishwasher. "Don't bother," she said when Amelia started to prerinse some plates. "This machine does everything. It's wonderful."

They worked together easily, without talking, and had the dishwasher loaded in no time. Mary sent Amelia back to the dining room while she put away the food.

Willy was reading the Alamogordo paper, but he put it down when he saw her. "Mary was telling me you're a potter," he said. "You planning to set up a studio here?"

Amelia sat down. "I want to. Once I work out a few snags."

"What kind of snags?"

She glanced at him, but his face was friendly. "Just the normal snags of trying to get started somewhere new," she said. "You know the kind of thing."

"You need studio space?" he asked.

"Not really. Gramps's workshop will work. I just have to save up some money to build a kiln. Unless I can scrounge some old firebrick that's going cheap."

"I'll ask around," Mary said from the kitchen door. "See if somebody knows about any." She set a plump paper bag down in front of Amelia. "A *zueti*."

"*Zueti?*" Amelia said.

"Arabic," Mary said. She looked very pleased with herself. "For 'a little something to take home with you for a snack.' "

"Thank you, Mary. I'll enjoy it."

"So if you get some brick and build the kiln, you're okay?" Willy said. "Found a gallery to sell your work?"

Amelia realized this was how normal people must feel when they went home to spend time with their parents.

"Not yet," she said. She stood and shrugged into her jacket, giving him a quick smile. "That's one of the snags."

As soon as she unlocked the door and walked into the house, Amelia knew that something was out of place. It took her a little while to put her finger on it, but then she realized that books had been pulled off the living room shelves and rearranged.

At least she thought they'd been moved. Unless she was imagining things? She walked through the rest of the house—except Michael's room—looking for other things that had been shifted.

She didn't find anything else she could be sure of, but as she looked at the clothes hanging in her wardrobe, she had a horrifying image of black-gloved hands fingering the fabric. Or pulling back Gramma's quilt from her bed—or picking up the photograph of her mother on Gramps's nightstand—

Her throat was knotted, and her eyes were burning. She thought she had come to terms with this, but she was so *scared*—

She went into the bathroom and splashed water on her face.

She pulled the towel off the rack and dried her face. Then she looked up and saw the words scrawled on the bathroom mirror.

Slanted block letters straggled across the glass in stark blood red: *1 NIGHT WE'LL COME.*

They'd drawn a swastika underneath.

As soon as she stopped shaking, she started packing.

She dragged the steamer trunk out from behind the bed and stuffed clothes into it, all the while trying to think how long it would take her to get the wheel back on the truck.

But when she threw her leather jacket on top of everything else, the envelope Mary had given her fell out of the pocket.

Amelia picked it up and sat on her bed. She wanted to stick it back in the trunk and forget it, but Gramps's familiar script was on the front, as distinctive as his voice. In a way, this was his last communication with her. The last one she could be sure wasn't a figment of her own imagination, anyway.

She opened the envelope and took out the will. It was on legal paper, folded in quarters, with a blue paper backing that was folded over an inch on the top and stapled. Along one side was written, "Last Will and Testament of Hector A. Rawlins."

She unfolded the will, determined to read once through it quickly and then go.

I, Hector A. Rawlins, being of sound mind and memory and above the age of eighteen, knowledgeable of all my properties and affairs, and having in mind the persons who are objects of my affection, do make and publish this, my last Will and Testament, hereby revoking any and all prior Wills that may have been made by me. I make the following dispositions of my property and affairs:

I. I direct that my mortal remains shall be dis-

*posed of by cremation without embalming, casket, or
ornamental urn. There shall be no headstone nor memorial other than the land I love. I direct that my ashes be
scattered over the native grasslands of the Rawlins Ranch
above the Crossroads where I have resided for all my life.*

Amelia folded the papers up again and set them
on the bedside table. It had never even occurred to her to
ask where Gramps was buried. She had known instinc-
tively that he was at the Folly.

"You need a nice drink of water," came
Gramma's whisper.

Obediently, Amelia went to the kitchen and got
one, and, as usual, Gramma was right. The cold water
eased the tightness in Amelia's throat and stopped the
burning sensation in her eyes.

"Thanks, Gramma," she said.

"I love you, sweetie," came the whisper. And
then her grandmother's presence was gone again.

Was she losing her mind? Maybe she'd gone
around the bend completely. But she didn't want to be
rational; not when the ghosts were so much comfort to
her.

She went back to the bedroom. The next clause
of the will was a standard one instructing the executor to
pay any just debts from the estate. Then came the bequests.

*As my wife predeceased me and my only daugh-
ter and my oldest grandson were tragically murdered,
and as my youngest grandson is well provided for, I
choose to make this Last Will and Testament in convey-
ance of all my properties to my beloved granddaughter,
Amelia Rawlins Caswell, to provide and care for her
safety and well-being.*

*I leave my estate in Trust for the maximum pe-
riod allowable under the laws of the State of New Mexico. The beneficiary of this Trust shall be my beloved
granddaughter, Amelia, and the Trust shall continue until
such time as she appears to claim the Trust, Corpus and
all Accumulated Income, in Fee Simple Ownership as the
sole Beneficiary of this, my Will.*

Should she not have appeared to claim the Trust

*Assets at any point throughout the maximum allowable
time period such Trust may Extend under Law, then this
Trust shall Lapse and all Trust Assets shall be delivered in
Fee Simple Ownership to the New Mexico Grasslands
Project of the Nature Conservancy, or to any successor
organization that may be carrying forth the preservation
and restoration of native New Mexican grasslands.*

*The dual intents of this Will are to first provide
for my beloved granddaughter, Amelia, and secondly to
preserve the grasslands on my property and in New Mexico generally, and this Will shall be construed in all in-
stances so as to serve these respective purposes.*

Amelia cleared her throat and said, "Good for
you, Gramps." She scanned the rest of the will, which
named Terrance Grayson sole executor and trustee of the
estate, listed two alternate trustees (Atkinson's savings
and loan being the first), and outlined provisions for a
generous compensation to the trustee. The final clause
revoked bequests to any party who contested the will.

Then Amelia carefully refolded the papers and
returned them to their envelope. The trustee had been
granted conservatorship of the estate without any over-
sight from the court, so by and large, Nick Atkinson was
free to do whatever he thought best with the assets of the
property. But Gramps had made it clear that he wanted
the Folly preserved. He was counting on her to see that it
happened.

She would stay. She would make Nick revoke
Spencer Reed's lease on the Folly, no matter what it took.

Amelia was falling.

She grabbed something to steady herself and
then she was outside herself in the dream, watching as a
tall man with sleek black hair bent over a childlike figure.
His face was turned away from her, so she couldn't see
who he was. But the child—she looked closer and saw
that it was a doll, a little-girl doll with tumbled light
brown curls and lifelike eyes with real lashes.

The man lifted the doll, and it tilted, the wide
frightened eyes closing, then opening again to stare at

Amelia. Two drops of blood spilled from the doll's gray eyes and ran down her plastic cheeks like bright tears.

The dream left Amelia huddling into Gramma's quilt again, curled up in the big armchair in the living room. The silent, paralyzing darkness of the final hours of the night eventually gave way to a burst of birdsong and a flare of brilliance in the eastern sky. Sunrise.

Amelia watched it. The muscles of her jaw ached from clenching. She had been grinding her teeth in her sleep again last night. That was something the years in Cooperton had finally eased, but it looked like the cure had been temporary.

The sun was well up when she finally summoned the strength to move. The fire in the woodstove had died down, leaving the house an icy box. The routine of re-building the fire helped unlock her frozen muscles.

She put on a pot of real coffee. A luxury, after so many weeks of drinking instant. The smell as it brewed was wonderful. Three steaming cups put some heart back in her, and by the time she'd taken a hot shower, Amelia had made up her mind to drive into Tamarisco and talk to Nick Atkinson.

The drive was completely familiar now, and the whisper-tones of the desert soothed her as she drove. In spite of her early morning paralysis, Amelia beat most of the traffic into town.

Atkinson was talking to a young woman at the reception desk of the savings and loan when she arrived.

"Morning, Mr. Atkinson," Amelia said from behind him.

He turned her way, a delighted look on his face. "Amelia!" he said. "How nice to see you. Come on in."

"Sorry to come without an appointment, but I never heard back from you when I called."

He gave the employee a nod and quickly ushered Amelia upstairs. "You called me? I'm so sorry—I never got the message. That's a call I would have enjoyed returning."

"Maybe not," Amelia said. "There's a problem at the ranch I need to talk to you about."

"I'm sorry I can't offer you any coffee this morning—Tanya's been sick, so nothing's running right around here."

"That's okay." Amelia followed him to his office. He gestured her to a seat in one of the armchairs.

He seemed as friendly as ever. "Now, what's up?" he asked, settling himself behind his desk.

Before she could answer, the phone on his desk rang.

"Excuse me just a second, would you?" he asked as he picked up the phone. "Nick Atkinson."

She half listened to his side of the conversation while planning how to approach this. Her palms were damp.

"George, you know I'm on half a dozen boards already—what are you trying to do—" Atkinson broke off. He was leaning back in his chair, laughing. "All right, George. Since it's you asking. Good. Yes, let's do that. See you then."

He hung up the phone and turned back toward her. "I apologize," he said. "The county commissioner—that's why Shawn put the call through. Now, what were you saying?"

She cleared her throat. It was hard to rock the boat when he'd been so nice to her, but she had to pursue this. "It's about the ranch," she said. "How did Spencer Reed get a lease to cultivate my grandfather's restored prairie?"

He leaned forward, his expression concerned. "I'm afraid I don't understand. Mr. Reed was very eager to lease a small parcel that adjoined his property. As I recall, he made a very good offer—especially considering that the land was lying fallow. I promise you, all the trust investments have shown a good return."

"I see," Amelia said. He was a banker, what had she expected? He probably thought the higher the return on investment the trust earned, the better job he was doing. "That's fine as long as you keep my grandfather's purpose in establishing the trust in mind. But letting Reed plow up Gramps's prairie and plant crops doesn't exactly support the preservation of native grasslands."

Atkinson made no immediate reply. After a moment, he said, "His prairie?"

"The restored prairie referred to in the will," she said. "That's the section of land you leased."

"Oh, no! How awful—I'm so sorry, Amelia. I had no idea—I didn't realize that parcel of land was anything special."

"That's not very responsible trust management," Amelia said.

He smiled at her ruefully. "You're absolutely right, I'm afraid," he said. "I can't tell you how sorry I am. I've always prided myself on being an excellent trustee."

She couldn't stand it when people said things like that. As if because his pride was at stake, she shouldn't blame him. "The main thing is to revoke Reed's lease, so I can replant."

"Well, let's take a look. You realize that Mr. Reed has legal rights here—that the lease is a binding contract?"

"When does it run out?" Amelia kept her voice even with an effort. But getting thrown off the ranch wouldn't do anything for Gramps's prairie.

Another apologetic smile. "I'll have to check." He got up and went to the bank of oiled teak filing cabinets along one wall. After a minute or two of rummaging, he located the file.

He glanced over it, then returned it to the drawer. "It runs through the end of April," he said, still standing. "There's a standard renewal clause, but the lessor is entitled to cancel. Is the beginning of May early enough for you to plant?"

"Guess it'll have to be," Amelia said. "I'd like a copy of that lease, though."

He turned back to her, and said gently, "Amelia, you're putting me in an awkward position. Until your identity is legally established, I really shouldn't be discussing the trust or any of its holdings with you. You have to realize I'm already bending the rules."

Amelia felt like pounding her fist on the desk. She got to her feet instead. "And *you* have to realize how important this is—my grandfather worked twenty years on that prairie."

"I understand," he said.

She doubted it. "So you'll cancel the lease as of May first."

"Yes, of course." He gave her another of his appealing smiles. "I'm so sorry this is even necessary. It must have been a terrible shock for you."

She had herself under control now, and spoke dryly. "Not half the shock it would be to my grandfather. Oh—it would help if you'd have Reed disc his crop stubble under." She knew it was a common practice for such leases, and it would make replanting the grasses easier if she didn't have to do it. "And the grass seed—for replanting—I'd like to bill that to the trust."

Atkinson nodded. "Yes, of course."

She turned to go, then remembered how low she was on cash. *Damn it—asking him for something was the last thing she wanted to do right now.* She took a breath. "Mr. Atkinson?"

"Please. Won't you call me Nick? Or are you too mad at me about this to call me anything?"

"Nick, then," she said impatiently. "I was wondering when—that is, when you usually paid your other caretakers."

He looked confused for a second. "Oh—on the first of the month, I think. That would be—" he glanced over at his desk calendar, "—next Tuesday. I'll have Tanya cut a check for you for February. A prorated amount, you understand. You can pick it up any time after noon on the first."

"Thank you," Amelia said. "Is it—would it be possible for me to be paid in cash?"

He raised an eyebrow. "Well, I guess we can work something out, if that's what you want." He moved closer to her. "Are you doing all right out there, all on your own? It's pretty isolated."

Having won her point, Amelia decided it was time to get out of there before she lost it again.

"I'm used to it," she said.

"Well, if you're sure." He walked her to the door of his office. "And Amelia? Thanks for letting me know about the problem with the lease—I can't fix something I don't know about. You'll call me if you need anything else, won't you?"

She was tempted to ask if he'd call her back next time, but shrugged instead. What counted was getting the prairie back, like she'd promised Gramps. "Sure."

This time, his smile could have stopped traffic. "Not that I'm promising to wait for you to call *me*."

She managed to get down the stairs and out the door without pausing for a victory dance, then couldn't remember if she'd even said good-bye to him.

Elation carried her into Ojos, the last gallery the woman at the gift shop had recommended. Amelia had brought her portfolio into town in a sort of grim determination to get all of her disagreeable errands out of the way at once. But knowing she'd taken steps to keep her promise to Gramps gave her a real boost.

It didn't last through her talk with the manager at Ojos.

Elenor de la Cruz was in her early thirties—a few years older than Amelia—with a quick smile and rapid-fire way of talking. Her gallery was pristine and carefully appointed, if not much to Amelia's taste. Bared duct work crisscrossed the ceiling, and copper pipes ran across the brick walls, which were painted cherry red.

The artwork de la Cruz carried was all Native American, and she refused to even look at Amelia's portfolio.

"I don't mean to be brutal about this," de la Cruz said, with her quick smile. "But there's really no point."

"Could you suggest any other galleries or shops I might try?" Amelia asked her.

De la Cruz rattled off a list, maybe half a dozen gift shops, and Amelia jotted the names down.

"That's about all in the area, really," Ms. de la Cruz said. She smiled again. "Good luck."

Amelia was back to grim determination by the third turndown, but she hit every single gallery and shop de la Cruz had mentioned and several more she found listed in the phone book. No luck. By noon, she was hungry, exhausted, and completely demoralized.

She made one more stop, this one at the hardware store, for new deadbolts for both the doors of the ranch house and a new padlock for the gate. Then she climbed into the truck and headed home.

Chapter Six

*Footage of Houston's 1983 Gay Pride
Parade, with the mayor, her council coalition,
and the new chief of police marching at its head
made the national news. Most of the airtime
was devoted to the arrest—and rapid release—
of the racist hecklers among the counterdemonstrators.*

*But when Mayor Rawlins-Caswell intro-
duced stiff antihate-crime and gay rights ordinances in mid-July, her actions went largely
unreported in the national media.*

*The record-breaking nineteenth consecu-
tive day of 100-degree-plus temperatures in
South Texas was covered by all three major net-
works.*

—MOLLY CATES, "Blood Relatives,"
Lone Star Monthly, April 1986

New Mexico

On her way out of town, the weathered
green-and-brown sign of Peterson's Feed &
Seed caught Amelia's eye. She had a vague
memory of accompanying Gramps there as a
youngster, and she pulled in. Maybe she could find out
about native grass seed and save herself another trip to
town later.

The parking lot was filled with pickup trucks,
some of them as venerable as Amelia's. The building was
a large box of graying pine adorned with a tacked-on

veranda. The porch had a rickety galvanized roof supported by unshaved cedar posts. She stood in the doorway for a minute, letting her eyes get accustomed to the interior gloom.

The wooden floors were dark with a silky veneer of ancient grime, and three of the walls were sheathed in raw wood shelves full of bottles and sacks and cans. In front of her lay a long wooden counter that separated the customers from the stacks of hundred-pound feed sacks and man-tall metal seed bins at the back of the building. The air was hazed golden with a mix of hay and seed chaff that made her throat tickle.

Amelia moved inside slowly, not really looking around. She was having second thoughts about coming in, but a man behind the counter had seen her and was looking intently at her.

He had a high forehead as crinkled as a washboard, and his gray hair was mussed. His washed-out blue eyes appraised her. "Help you, ma'am?"

Amelia cleared her throat. "Thank you," she said. "I just wanted to ask if you carried any native grass seed."

"Native grass seed?" The voice was a whisky-wrecked rasp, but he could still pump volume into it.

"Well—yes. I—I think I used to come here with my grandfather. He bought native seed here, I think."

The man snapped his fingers. "That's it! I knew you looked familiar. You're—you must be Hector's granddaughter." His face sobered. "You're the living image of your mother, you know."

A bunch of men—maybe a half dozen—had been grouped at the end of the counter. They all turned to look at her, curving naturally into a half-circle to her right. Something about their position and the hazy light made her teeth clench. She felt as if a belt had been cinched punishingly tight around her chest.

The man—Peterson himself, she realized—came quickly around the counter and took her arm. "You all right, Miz Rawlins?" His raspy voice sounded kind now. He smelled of tobacco.

He was between her and the other men, blocking

them from sight, and his interposed bulk deflected the torrent of darkness that was flooding her.

Amelia drew herself away from Peterson's hand and retreated a couple of steps toward the door. "Yes, sir, I'm fine. Thank you."

"Sorry if I startled you, Miz Rawlins." His faded blue eyes scanned her anxiously. "I was just trying to place why you looked so danged familiar."

"I understand," Amelia said. All she wanted to do was get out of there—preferably without being rude. "Seems I remember Gramps coming here for some of his prairie seed—d'you still carry it?"

"Hector used to order his seed from a couple of places," Peterson said. "One in Santa Fe, as I recall, and another in Las Cruces. He ordered through me sometimes, so's to get a wholesale discount. Wasn't ever any call for me to carry the stuff myself."

"I see," Amelia said. She was still feeling strange. "Well, thank you, Mr. Peterson—I won't take any more of your—"

"I'd be glad to do the same for you, ma'am," Peterson interrupted. "The Rawlins account is still open."

This abrupt benevolence was too much for Amelia. Besides, she didn't know what kind of seed she needed or how much to order. "That's real kind of you, Mr. Peterson. I'm not actually ready to order yet, just wanted to find out about sources—"

"For a spring planting, you should check the germination requirements," he said. "Some seed needs to winter over before it'll sprout. And if you want to order through me, I'd recommend placing the order six weeks ahead. Haven't done this in four or five years—it might take them a while to fill the order."

"Thank you." There was a faint buzzing in her ears.

Peterson leaned closer to her, and the smell of tobacco became overpowering. "I should tell you about the folks took over the Veracruz place, ma'am. You watch out for 'em now. That woman's a butcher—don't you trust her."

"Mr. Peterson!" one of the stock clerks called from behind the counter.

Peterson turned his head.

"What's the hundred-pound price on this super-yield alfalfa?"

"Mind what I told you," Peterson said, and went to the back.

Amelia was speechless. She turned away quickly.

"Miss?" The voice was low-pitched, barely above a whisper, and came from right next to her.

"Didn't mean to give you a start," the stock clerk said. "Just wanted to explain—Mr. Peterson hasn't been quite right since his boy died last year. Gets a little wound up about the Garritys sometimes, but—don't let it worry you none. About your neighbors, I mean." He was watching her anxiously.

Amelia said, "I see," although she didn't really.

"Mr. Peterson's heart's in the right place, miss. It's just his boy dying like that—"

"Bobby—" Peterson called, and the clerk turned, then glanced back at her uncertainly.

"Thanks," she said. Amelia escaped before anyone else could speak to her. The air outside was crisp and fresh, and she opened her window as she pulled onto the highway.

The old truck picked up speed as if it were grateful to escape, too. A cool wind swept in around her, clearing the thick sweet smell of hay from her lungs, and the pooling shadows from her mind. She didn't have to think of those things, not now. Because the air was fresh and bright, not dim and hazy, and she could breathe again.

The gate was standing open when she got to the ranch. Seeing it sharpened the hollow feeling in her stomach, and Amelia drove the dirt lane to the house at a bone-rattling pace.

Mary's Jeep was parked by the kitchen door. Of course, she'd always had keys to the place.

"Thank God," Amelia said. She pulled up next to the Jeep and went into the kitchen.

Mary was standing by the stove, stirring a pot. "Good," she said, looking up as Amelia came in. "This is just about ready. Why don't you wash up, then we'll eat."

Amelia's stomach growled loudly.

Mary grinned. "That's one vote yes, anyway."

"Let's call it two." She set her portfolio on the kitchen table and went to wash her hands.

When she came back, Mary was watching the empty space in front of the stove with a faint smile on her lips. "Your grandmother is pleased with me for bringing you good food to eat," she said.

Amelia looked toward the stove, too. "Can you see her?"

"No. But I can feel her pleasure," Mary said serenely, and dished up a steaming portion of stew.

It was delicious. She ate two large bowlsful, with thick slabs of homemade bread, and then attacked the apple cobbler Mary had brought for dessert. They talked very little as they ate, but it was a comfortable silence. After Amelia finished the last bite of cobbler, she cleared the table and refilled both their coffee cups.

"You must really be desperate to feed me to come all this way to do it," she said. "Not that I'm complaining."

Mary smiled. "Got something to talk to you about."

Amelia took a sip of coffee. "What's that?"

"Don't know how you're set for money. Your grandfather wanted to leave you well off."

Amelia swallowed hard. "He left everything here to me. Not that I know what that means in terms of money, exactly. But—" She stopped.

"You got to get things settled before you know how you stand," Mary finished for her. "Might take a little while, I know. Got Willy and me talking about your grandfather's bee business some more."

"You said something about it that first day."

"You might not be interested," Mary said. "Maybe your potting is working out fine."

"No dice. I hit every gallery and shop in Tamarisco this morning, and got nothing. *Nada.*"

Mary nodded. "I was afraid of that. That's why Willy and me talked about the bees. The orchard owners really need somebody local to do the pollinating—last year, the guy the Esquivels hired in from California missed the bloom days he promised them by a week, because his truck broke down. They got a crummy fruit set. Had to borrow money to keep going this year."

"I used to tag along sometimes when Gramps took care of his bees," Amelia said, "but I really don't know much about them, Mary. Especially the pollinating part. Most of the spring buildup was done by the time I got here in the summer."

"I can tell you what I know from the orchard end of things. And there's your grandfather's journals—he always kept real careful track of his bees."

Amelia hesitated. "His equipment—the hives and all that stuff are probably around here somewhere. But there'd be other things I'd have to buy, like the bees themselves. I just don't know, Mary. I don't see how I could do it."

Mary got up and retrieved her jacket from a chair in the living room. For an instant, Amelia thought she'd offended her, but Mary came back and sat down, opening one of the big pockets of the parka with a rip of Velcro.

"We thought of that," she said. She took a bank's cash envelope out of her pocket and laid it on the scrubbed pine table in front of Amelia. "We want to stake you for the start-up. You don't have to pay me back cash, just give me my pick of spring pollinating dates, like your grandfather used to. What I'd normally pay for the hive rental can go against the loan."

Amelia got up. "More coffee, Mary?"

"Not for me, thanks."

Amelia refilled her own cup, turned off the pot, and sat back down at the table. "This is awfully generous of you," she said. "I—" She cleared her throat and started over. "I don't know how to thank you."

"Just make sure I get a good set of fruit every year. And don't get stung."

Amelia raised her eyebrows. "Well, I'll do my best not to. Maybe you could talk to the bees about that part."

Mary smiled. "Oh, I'm not the bee-talker here. That's gonna be your job."

She went home shortly after that, leaving behind a large pot of venison stew, half a pan of apple cobbler, and twenty crisp hundred-dollar bills. Before she left, Amelia gave her the spare set of keys that had come with the new locks.

And the first thing Amelia did after Mary drove off was put the new padlock on the gate and change out the deadbolts on the ranch house doors.

The third outbuilding was a new honey house, Amelia discovered. Her grandfather's hives—including a bewildering array of tools, materials, and extraction equipment—were stored in the building.

She counted the main hive frames. There were more than a hundred of them. Amelia couldn't imagine taking care of a hundred hives of bees by herself, working on restoring the Folly, and still making time for her pottery. She wished Gramps would turn up again so she could ask him about how many bees to start with and what she could do now to start getting ready for them. It was still freezing at night, although it was nearly March. Too cold to be keeping bees yet, surely.

She hadn't seen Gramps since she'd gotten the copy of his will from Mary. The will had made her grandfather's death seem more real to her, and his absence since then worried her.

But with the pollinating business to think about, she needed him more than ever. She needed to tell him that she'd made the first step in keeping her promise to him, by getting Nick Atkinson to revoke Reed's lease.

She needed Gramps around to reinforce the reasons she was remaining here.

The windmill was turning at a brisk pace in the north wind, a steady WHUF-whuf-whuf that made her jittery. She stood in the dusty lane next to the house, letting the sunshine soak into her and the wind tangle her hair.

Without considering, she started talking.

"Gramps, I just want to thank you for trusting the ranch to me, and for not giving up on me when I was gone so long. Soon as I got your will, I went and talked to Nick Atkinson and made him yank Spencer Reed's lease on the Folly. Now, it can't be canceled until the end of next month, but, once it is, I'm going to order some blue grama and Indian grass—just the staple grasses to start— and reseed it."

She paused and waited a minute or two, but there was no sound except the whistle of the wind and the whuf of the windmill.

"Mac Peterson said he'd give me a credit account and order the seed for the prairie at discount. And Mary Zuniga and her cousin Willy are staking me to start your pollinating business back up, so I'm trying to get the hives ready for that. I could sure use your help on it, Gramps. Gramps?"

She turned and looked around behind her, but there was no sign of him.

"What makes you think you want to keep bees!"

The voice sounded directly in her ear. He was standing right next to her when she swung around again, his cheeks red.

"I've got to make a living somehow," she said.

"And you think beekeeping's easy? It's harder than it looks."

"Gramps," she said, "you kept bees for fifty years. I figured you'd help me out."

"It's hard work, Melia," her grandfather said snappishly. "You could get hurt."

"I'll be careful," Amelia assured him. "Now, where should I set up the hives? How do I start getting them ready? And who should I order my bees from?"

Gramps was scowling. "You are stubborn as a damn mule, Amelia Rawlins."

She smiled at him. "Well, at least I come by it honestly. Come on, explain what I should do with all this stuff." She turned toward the honey house.

"Just like your mother," he muttered behind her. But he came along.

He stayed with her all that afternoon, answering her questions about the honey extraction equipment and giving her a staggering amount of information about the care and feeding of honeybees.

How much she didn't know—and needed to—should have been overwhelming. Instead, her time with Gramps lifted her spirits and gave her the strength to go back to the dark house at dusk.

Gramps was saying something about checking his seed stores before she ordered any additional seed for the Folly, as she walked up to the kitchen door. It was around six, and a lucid twilight filled the arch of sky, like a bowl of faint blue smoke. The cold air traced the bones of Amelia's face—the tip of her nose and chin, the angle of her cheekbones—with ghostly, chilling fingers.

"Seed stores?" Amelia said, unlocking the kitchen door and turning on the light. She stamped her feet on the mud mat before going in, and turned to see Gramps do the same. Seems old habits die harder than we do, she thought, and grinned.

But as she turned on the kitchen light, he vanished. The house seemed much lonelier without his cheerful voice to fill the silence.

She spent the evening reading one of his beekeeping books.

Gramps had told her to start getting the hives set up and to go ahead and order her bees. It would take at least three or four weeks for them to arrive. "I'll be around to help, of course," he'd said.

With advice, Amelia thought. But his steady, practiced hands couldn't do the physical work.

She rose well before dawn and got herself washed and dressed and fed. Then she walked out to the honey house as the stars faded and color seeped into the sky. The world was wide and still and lovely, only the deep humming of the windmill disturbing the predawn peace. The air was chilly, but this morning there was a change: a scarce-perceived, incremental shift in the quality of the early light, a hint of restless stirring in the wind.

"Nearly spring," Amelia whispered. When she unlocked the door of the honey house, Gramps was perched on a stool next to the chest-high stainless steel extractor.

"Good morning, sleepyhead," he said, just the way he used to when she was a kid.

"Morning, Gramps," she said, and settled in to work.

She started setting up the hives in a sheltered field east of the honey house, close to the stream. The honey mesquite trees that grew thick along the banks would be a major food source for the bees, Gramps said, and would offer some shade.

The bee boxes were about a foot deep, white wooden boxes open on the top and bottom. Frames—like small wooden window frames—hung from a rail along the inside edge. Instead of windowpanes, the frames held sheets of wax honeycomb. This was where the queen would lay eggs and the hive would raise brood.

The hives could be three or four stories high eventually. As the hives grew, Gramps said, she would have to add extra boxes—supers—where the bees would store most of the honey.

Amelia's shoulders were aching by the time she finished placing thirty-six hives onto shallow bases.

There were more empty hives stored in the tractor shed, but Amelia wasn't sure how many bees she could manage, or even how many she could afford to buy. Gramps didn't respond to the questions she asked him then; he kept staring off down the road beside the wash. Toward the Folly.

"What is it?" she asked, but he didn't answer. Amelia hesitated for a second, then said, "I'll get to it soon, Gramps. I promise. We can start planting May one. That's only a couple of months."

Instead of answering her, he disappeared. It was unsettling not to have him around to oversee what she was doing, but there was no help for it.

She spent the rest of the day alone, carefully cutting formed wax foundation from prepared rolls and wiring it into the frames.

The next morning was sunny, with light brisk winds blowing from the north. Around ten o'clock, Frank Burkhalter drove up to the ranch. When she heard the engine at the gate, Amelia ran up from the field behind the honey house. Once she saw who it was, she relaxed some.

Before the Jeep came to a full stop, Burkhalter's yellow lab jumped out of the back and wriggled under the fence to Amelia. His big tail was wagging so hard that his whole body wobbled, and Amelia laughed. But he didn't jump up or even push his head under her hand. She liked a dog with good manners.

"Hey, big guy," she said and gave his ruff a shake. At that, he leaned up against her, so she scratched him behind the ears, and he gave a little groan.

Burk got out. It was warmer today, and he had on the blue walking shorts mail carriers wore in the summer. He had great legs. The muscles in his calves were clearly defined, like a cyclist's. Amelia looked at him, wondering if he might sit for her sometime—he would make a good subject.

He said, "Tucker, you shameless hound. Hope you don't mind, ma'am?" He looked worried, and she noticed again how light his eyes looked in his sunburned face.

"Not at all," she said, still rubbing the dog's floppy ears. They were downy-soft under her fingers, and his body was warm and solid against her knee.

Burk held a white envelope, which he was turning over and over in his big hands.

"Is this a special delivery?" Amelia asked, looking at it.

He glanced down, and the nervous motion of his fingers stilled. "I thought it might be another threat. Couldn't see just leaving it in your box."

Amelia held her hand out, and Burk surrendered the envelope. It was the same plain paper, addressed to Melia Caswell with a fading typewriter ribbon.

"I noticed it when I was casing the mail for my route," he said after a minute. "So I asked the clerk whether it had come from one of the big trucks or had been picked up by the parcel driver from one of the local boxes. She's pretty certain it originated locally. I asked about the other one, too, but no one remembered anything special about it."

Amelia tapped the envelope against her thigh, and massaged Tucker's neck with her other hand.

"If this is some kind of threat—" Burk said, and broke off. "That's a federal crime, using the U.S. mail to threaten someone." When she didn't answer, he added, "Have you thought about talking to the sheriff?"

Amelia tensed. Why was everyone trying to get her into the sheriff's office? Then she forced herself to relax. He was only trying to help her. "I appreciate your checking on where it came from. And thanks for bringing it straight out to me."

"Your place isn't that far off my route," he said. He was still looking at the envelope. "You sure you'll be okay?"

Tucker lifted his head to lick Amelia's fingers. Automatically, she started rubbing his neck again. "Things are just fine, Mr. Burkhalter."

Burk hesitated, then said, "I'd like to help. You sure there's nothing I can do for you?"

She shook her head, not trusting her voice.

"Well. Better be going, then. Give a holler if you need anything. Anything at all, Ms. Rawlins. Come along now, Tucker."

Tucker didn't budge. He hid his big blond head behind Amelia's knee.

Burk said, "Tucker," again, his voice stern.

The dog kept his head tucked behind her leg and whined.

Amelia squatted down and swung her arm over Tucker's neck. "I like you too," she said. She thumped on his chest a couple of times and let him lick her face.

Then Burk gave a short, sharp whistle. Tucker went back to the Jeep. He jumped into the back, then hung his head through the passenger window and stared out at them mournfully.

Burk watched with raised eyebrows. "I believe you've made a conquest."

Amelia smiled.

"Well, afternoon, ma'am," Burk said, touching his hat. He got behind the wheel and pulled away.

She tapped the envelope against her thigh again. Its weight and menace had tripled, now that Tucker's firm shoulder wasn't braced against her leg anymore.

Her fear seemed to build in proportion to the distance between her and the Jeep. When the road was empty, and even the dust the Jeep had stirred up began to settle, she said, "Guess it's mutual."

She took the envelope and walked back to the house, where she built the stove to a fierce blaze. When the room felt cozy and safe, she settled herself in the big armchair to open the envelope.

It was a muddy photocopy of an old newspaper clipping. At the top of the column was a small inset of a family portrait—the same one that hung in the hall. Much larger above it was the blurred news photo of a police helicopter hovering above her family's front lawn. The headline read, "CANDIDATE AND FAMILY SLAIN." In much smaller type, the subheading added, "Child Survives Attack—Doctors Fear Brain Damage".

Amelia crushed the stapled pages in her fist. She had been so badly hurt that she had missed the media circus that followed her family's deaths. Even after she recovered, safely hidden at the House, she'd avoided the news. In some ways, looking at this newspaper report was worse than her own memories.

Maybe because these words meant everything she remembered was real. Verified. Journalists' words had too much power—the power to take a nightmare and turn it into history.

Seeing the article, her first instinct was still to run—hard and fast—anywhere away from this place. It's what she had always done before.

But her circumstances were different now. She had promised Gramps that she would put his prairie right. She had made a commitment.

She untangled her feet from the afghan and walked over to the wood stove. She wrestled the fire door open and ripped the stapled pages apart so they would burn faster. A white index card fluttered to the floor.

Amelia flung the copied news story into the fire, taking pleasure in the way the flames crisped the words out of existence. Then she looked down at the index card. In the same slashing blue print as the first one, her enemy had written *TIME TO FINISH THE JOB*.

She tossed it in after the article, and the flames took the card eagerly. Even as it blackened and began to burn, the words remained clear. They stared out at her, a brutal promise.

FINISH was the last word to fade.

Part 2

GHOST RAIN-
SPRINGTIME

Now days are dragon-ridden, the nightmare
Rides upon sleep: a drunken soldiery
Can leave the mother, murdered at her door,
To crawl in her own blood, and go scot-free;
The night can sweat with terror as before . . .

—William Butler Yeats,
    "Nineteen Hundred and Nineteen"

Chapter Seven

During the month of July, 1983, thirty-nine skinheads, posse members, and rednecks (unaffiliated with any particular group) were arrested for assault and attempted assault in Houston's Montrose district. In August, the plainclothes patrols made seventeen such arrests. By September, when the mayor's two younger children had returned home and were back in school, the number of bashing-related arrests in Montrose dropped to five.

—MOLLY CATES, "Blood Relatives,"
Lone Star Monthly, April 1986

New Mexico

Amelia was cleaning house.

The spring scirocco had blown for two weeks straight, in undulating curtains of thick brown dust. "What's left of West Texas coming through," Gramps said when it started. "Happens every year this time."

The dust worked its way into every crevice in the house. The wooden floors were gritty with it, the windows masked in it. Amelia could taste it, feel it grind between her teeth. She found herself breathing shallowly all the time, then rinsing her mouth at the sink. But even the well water tasted muddy.

The two goats she had bought with part of Mary's loan were huddled miserably in their enclosure, angling their bony behinds toward the wind. Amelia washed them carefully before she milked, and cleaned the milking room constantly, but there was no winning against the dust. At least she'd had no more threats since the storm started.

But she was at the edge of sanity by the end of the second week, thoroughly sick of the blinding fog of grit, the taste and smell and sight of it, crazy with the incessant *WHUF-whuf-whuf, WHUF-whuf-whuf* of the windmill.

So, sometime after midnight on the second Monday of the spring gale, when the wind dropped and the grating sound of the windmill's spinning blades stopped, Amelia woke instantly.

She expected the wind to rise again and the torture to resume, but it was over. As abruptly as it had begun, the scirocco had blown away again, leaving the house shrouded in grime.

Gramma was agitated by the mess the wind had made of her house. Amelia herself was frustrated by the intrusive grit, and put off doing other chores—except for feeding and milking the goats—until she had the place cleaned up again. Which was harder than she expected. The dust was fine and had worked its way deep into everything.

She swept and vacuumed and swept again; she scrubbed all the windows in her bedroom, her grandparents' room, and in the main part of the house; she carried furniture cushions and rugs out of doors and pounded the dust out of them in clouds. She damp-mopped the floors and wiped down the walls.

And, finally, four days after the winds dropped, she could walk across the living room floor without feeling grit under her boots. Losing herself in the constant work had been a relief; staying busy helped her bury the old memories and forget the fresh fears stemming from the threatening letters.

But Gramma was still a fluttering, anxious presence. Michael's room needed cleaning too; so far, Amelia had avoided opening his door. Her bad dreams about him had been resurrected with a vengeance since she'd been back at the ranch, all her old guilt renewed by the pervasiveness of his memory here.

But by Friday afternoon, there was nothing left to clean except Michael's room. Amelia made a fresh pot of coffee, taking pleasure in the kitchen's newly washed and rearranged cupboards. She was sitting at the table trying to gather the resolve to open her kid brother's door when the phone rang.

She'd grown accustomed to the silences in the house, punctuated only by the small sounds of the desert surrounding it and the low wing-beat of the windmill. Startled by the shrill sound, she didn't answer until the fourth ring.

"Hello?" she said.

"Thank God," Frank Burkhalter said, laughing. "I was afraid you'd be outside working and wouldn't hear the phone. You've got this place in a panic—can you come into town right away?"

"Excuse me?" Amelia said. "What are you talking about?"

"Ms. Rawlins," Burk said, "listen to this." There was a pause. Then Amelia heard it, a faint buzzing that rose, then subsided, then rose again.

"Hear that?" Burk said. He sounded cheerful—still on the verge of laughter, in fact. "Ma'am, your bees have arrived."

"Oh," Amelia said. "They sure came quick."

"Can you come down to the post office right away to pick 'em up? The postmaster's working himself into a frenzy, and everybody's mighty nervous."

Amelia walked across the kitchen, stretching the phone cord behind her, and turned off the coffeepot. "I'll be right there," she said.

It actually took her half an hour. She spent five minutes clearing out the bed of the truck and locating the tarpaulin. She was getting low on gas, too, and figured she better stop to fuel up before she had half a million bees riding shotgun. The friendly older man who ran the independent gas and grocery at the edge of town was named Jorge Valdez. Amelia had gotten into the habit of chatting with him when she stopped for gas, and had to excuse herself this time, explaining she had to pick up some bees from the post office.

Still, she made pretty good time to the Tamarisco post office. She thought about pulling up to the loading dock in the rear yard, then decided against it, instead parking near the main doors of the low tan brick building. Best to be respectful, no matter how much they wanted to be rid of the bees. Jefferson had been the one to show her that there was a ritual—a certain order—to be observed when conducting business in a small town. One you ignored at your peril, he always said.

The instant she opened the door, she heard the bees. Their humming wasn't loud, but it echoed out clearly into the entry where the post office boxes stood. Amelia walked through the double doors to the main counter and joined the short line in front of it.

There was only one clerk at the counter, a stocky, balding man. Although he was casting occasional nervous glances toward the back room, he never looked up so she could catch his eye.

She'd been there three or four minutes when Burk walked past the doorway into the back room and spotted her.

"Ms. Rawlins!" he said. The clerk looked up at Amelia for the first time. Burk said to him, "This is the lady who's picking up the bees."

"Praise the Lord," the other man said, before turning back to his customer.

Burk motioned Amelia to the end of the counter and swung the panel up so she could come in. "Where are you parked?" he said.

"Out front," she told him. "Didn't want to break any rules."

He grinned. "Sounds like you've had dealings with the U.S.P.S. before," he said. "The postmaster won't object to anything that gets rid of these bees. They're back here."

She followed him through the back room, which was a maze of white plastic mail cartons stacked head-high, conveyor belts, and grubby canvas carts piled with parcels. The humming of the bees intensified as she and Burk moved toward the open doors of the dock, and seconds later Amelia spotted a large stack of oddly shaped wooden crates set just inside.

"Looks like you didn't let them very far in," Amelia said.

"You got it. The shipping cartons meet postal regulations, so the postmaster couldn't refuse delivery. But that doesn't mean he didn't want to."

She had ordered thirty-six three-pound boxes, with queens. They'd been shipped in rectangular wooden crates about six by eight by fifteen inches, which were nailed to wood strips in groups of three. The boxes were staggered about a foot apart along the wooden "legs," so they looked a little like a bookshelf turned sideways. Shipping labels were pasted on top. Amelia squinted through the fine mesh that covered the two broadest sides of a crate. Inside, under the massed bodies of her bees, she could see a feeding can and the smaller queen cage.

"Can't believe they ship them without anything but this mesh wall," she said. "Can they sting through it?"

"That's exactly what the postmaster asked. Can't say I've tested it. Give you a hand getting them out to your truck?"

"Sure, thanks. Just let me pull the truck around." Amelia cut back through the mail cartons and out the parcel door to the parking lot. When she pulled into the yard and started backing up to the loading dock, Burk signaled her in.

Burk picked up one of the sets of crates and headed for the truck as she went up the steps. When she picked up a set herself, she was surprised at what it weighed. Close to twenty-five pounds. Each box contained only three pounds of bees, but there were three boxes in the set, and the wood crate and the syrup in the feeding cans added up. The bees shifted and buzzed as she picked up the crate.

"Busy little guys, aren't they?" Burk grabbed

two more and carried them out the loading dock doors. "It's okay to just set 'em in the bed?" he called back.

"Sure," Amelia said. The weather was cool without being cold, so she didn't have to worry about the bees getting overheated or chilled. Later in the season, she might have to wet down the hives to keep them cool when she moved them. She grabbed another set of crates herself, prepared this time for the movement of the bees inside.

Burk was arranging the first few crates. He reached down and took the one Amelia had brought out. She backed away and went for more.

They had the truck loaded in ten minutes. The crates took up more than half the bed of the truck. Amelia closed the tailgate, then said, "Thanks, Mr. Burkhalter."

He cocked an eyebrow. "Any time, *Ms*. Rawlins."

Amelia hesitated, then shook hands with him. His grip was steady, his skin warm and callused. She was abruptly reminded of the way her mother used to grade the handshakes of her colleagues. Burk's palm met hers firmly—not flinching away or being held apart like he was afraid to touch her. Mom always said that was important; it meant the person was stable, steadfast.

"You're pretty cheerful about the invasion of the killer bees," she said as she turned toward the truck.

Burk opened the door and held it until she was seated. Then he closed it carefully and smiled at her. "Oh, it's the most fun I've had this month." The sunburned skin around his eyes crinkled, and she noticed again how light a gray they were. "Seeing the postmaster rattled is worth any amount of fuss."

She laughed, surprising herself. It felt good to laugh; she hadn't been doing much of that lately.

His hand was still on the door handle. "You going to be able to manage all right with these critters? You've never done this before, have you?"

"Used to help my grandfather some," she said. "It'll be okay."

He paused, then gave her a slow smile. "Now,

I'm not questioning your skill or anything like that," he said. "But handling bugs is pretty icky—you going to be able to stand it?"

"You must never have seen a potter at work—it's incredibly messy. I've developed a strong stomach."

"You're a potter? I didn't know that."

"It's what I've always done—but I haven't found a gallery here yet." She felt like she was babbling, but couldn't seem to stop.

"And that letter—you had any trouble at the ranch?" He moved his hand onto the window frame and leaned in toward her.

"Not unless you count the goats. I never milked so much in my life."

"Yeah, I heard you'd bought a pair from the Granberds. That's the thing with milk goats—it's either feast or famine."

"Then I'm definitely in the feast stage," Amelia said. "I've been making cheese—it's the only way I could use up all the milk." She *was* babbling, talking about herself like this.

"Well, that'll help even out the famine stage a little."

"Yeah. Except it takes time. Between dealing with the goats and the milk and getting ready for the bees, there's no time left for my pottery. Know anyone who wants to buy five gallons of goat's milk a week?"

"Not offhand. But I'll be glad to see what I can find out."

Amelia bit her lip. She wasn't in the habit of discussing her problems with strangers. So why had she brought it up? "I didn't mean for you to—"

"A real shame if the ranch is keeping you away from your regular work. Pottery—that sounds interesting."

"Well, since I haven't got a place to sell pots anyway—at least milking the goats helps feed me. What you might call a direct benefit. Everything's fine, really."

"Practical of you." He gave her a smile, then stepped away from the truck, smoothing his tangled dark hair back with one hand. "You take care, now, Ms. Rawlins. I'll ask around about that goat milk."

She nodded to him and pulled out fast, before she could say anything else. Why had she let him rattle her that way? He'd thought she was asking him for help, and she never did that.

Amelia shook her head, furious with herself, and punched the accelerator. Then she remembered her cargo, and slowed the truck again. Today, at least, she needed to make it home in one piece.

She got back to the ranch around three. Michael's room would have to wait a little longer. Unloading the bees took her about half an hour. Gramps had said to put them in the shade and feed them, but to wait till evening to rehive them. So that's what she did.

This afternoon, Gramps was nowhere around. His absence gave Amelia a sharp stab of annoyance, which persisted even though she realized it was fueled mostly by her own feeling of incompetence.

Once she had the bees unloaded, the first order of business was to feed them. Like all living creatures, they were mellower when their bellies were full.

Amelia had stocked up on corn syrup on Gramps's instructions. She hauled out one of the ten-gallon tubs she'd bought, then turned the stair-stepped crates on end, so the screened sides were level. She used a clean paintbrush to cover the mesh of each carton with syrup.

Even she could tell the difference in how the bees sounded after they got their syrup. By the time she had fed them all, the sun was westering. Amelia walked up to the house to get a drink from the pump and collect her gear. It was time to move the bees, with or without Gramps's coaching.

She'd ordered a beekeeper's veil, and gloves with elastic in the elbow-length sleeves. At Gramps's insistence, she'd also gotten a long-sleeved khaki jumpsuit and sewn elastic bands into the cuffs of the pants. He said it was cheaper than a full bee suit, and that the bees would be soothed by the light-colored, smooth fabric. Amelia suited up and went back down to the apiary.

The method used to move the bees into their hives was pretty straightforward. Each box of bees had been split off from another hive and shipped with a new queen, which rode in a separate palm-sized wooden carton inside the larger one, with a few worker attendants to care for her on the trip. The queen's carton was vented, its opening closed by a sugar plug. Once the foil cap on the plug was removed, the bees would eat the sugar away within a few days. Gramps had explained that this allowed the bees time to get used to their new queen's scent—by the time she was able to emerge from her carton, the hive would accept her instead of killing her as an invader.

Amelia pried up the cover on one of the hives and removed a couple of the foundation frames. Then she opened the first shipping crate. She removed the queen's small cage, peeled the cap off the sugar plug, then hooked the cage between two of the frames inside the hive.

Next she turned the crate over, so the feeding can dropped out. That left a four-inch hole in the box. Gramps had warned her to move slowly, so she pretended she was centering clay as she carried the crate to the open hive and shook it. Bees dropped onto the top of the frames in a thick buzzy swarm—about fifteen thousand of them—and almost immediately began crawling down between the frames of brood foundation. Amelia was sweating under the bee veil. The plastic helmet base kept slipping down over her eyes. And not a damn thing she could do about it.

Some bees remained in the open crate. She laid it in front of the hive entrance. They'd fly inside soon enough.

Already some of the other workers were clustering around the queen cage. Careful not to squash any bees, Amelia slid the frames she'd taken out back into place, then replaced the cover.

She bent down near the hive opening and gently

brushed a few explorers from her sleeve. Not one sting. So far, so good.

That was one down. Thirty-five to go.

Her stingless status didn't last long. She got popped four times that evening, three of them when a bee crawled into the crook of her arm without her noticing. She couldn't blame them—she'd defend herself, too, if someone started to squish her. The fourth one just got mad and went for her leg, stinging straight through the fabric. It felt like getting hit by a miniature nail gun, but Gramps had assured her she'd get used to it.

She worked until the light started to fade, but had to stop before all the bees were moved. Another one of Gramps's useful tidbits: Bees navigate by sunlight, and get surly when their navigational system shuts down. This was an advantage in that the bees already in their hives would likely stay put overnight, settling in to their new homes instead of taking off to look for a better spot. But it also meant she'd have to wait till tomorrow to move the rest of them.

So when the sun touched the rim of the Organs and twilight sprang up around her, Amelia nestled the last twelve boxes of bees under the tarp and turned to loading the empties back into the truck.

Then she rested on the tailgate for a moment, bone-weary, listening to the bees. They sounded a little quieter now, and their humming soothed her.

Amelia would have liked to stay put for a while, listening as she waited for the moon to brighten and the stars to come out. She'd been cleaning house for days, and before that, the dust storm had been blowing. It seemed ages since she'd been out to enjoy the clear evening air. She looked north. Above the ridge of rocks and trees along the arroyo, the pale peaks of Sierra Blanca gleamed against the dusky sky.

But with the dark came the evening chill. And there were still the goats to milk. They'd be cranky because she was late. Amelia stood up and gave a long, weary stretch.

"Hasta mañana, abejas," she said.

When she finished with the goats and got back to the house late that evening, she could feel Gramma's fretfulness even through her own exhaustion. It was a constant edge in the background, and Amelia knew she couldn't put off cleaning Michael's room much longer.

The next morning dawned a clear spring day that seemed too bright to be haunted by dark dreams. Amelia armed herself with a broom and bucket, dust rags, and vinegar water, and edged past the gallery of photographs in the hall to the door of Michael's room.

His furniture was arranged precisely as she remembered it—a sleigh bed set against the wall, next to a rush-bottomed chair so old it had been built with hand-shaped nails. A huge maple chifforobe with drawers down one side and a cupboard in the other dominated one wall. Michael had loved to squirrel his treasures away in its recesses. The steamer trunk where he'd kept his comic books still sat at the foot of the bed.

Dust lay palely over the entire room, giving it the faded look of an old sepia-toned photograph. Even the bright colors of the Spiderman curtains and bedspread looked dim and distant. The whole room seemed shrouded in layers of the past.

The last time she had stood in this room, she had been barely sixteen. Still a child herself, happily arrogant about how she intended to manage her future, serenely certain of the presence of her parents and brothers in it.

The broom clattered to the floor. Amelia let the bucket fall too as she crumpled to her knees, curving her arms around the sudden sharp hollow in her chest.

The shrouding layer of years frayed, and the last night they had spent at the ranch came back to her. The final summer of her childhood. It was as if she were watching the ghosts of those two long-lost children, still playing at their kid-brother-big-sister dynamic in some sad repeating loop: Michael in Spidey pajamas, caught reading comic books under the covers with a flashlight; the child-Amelia, a blithe sixteen in her baggy Foreigner T-shirt and fuzzy slippers, tickling him to the near edge of hysteria when he resisted her efforts to confiscate it.

"Oh, Michael," she whispered, rocking herself around the pain. Could Michael even read any more? The headline from the news clipping seemed to float in front of her eyes: *"Doctors Fear Brain Damage."*

She could almost see his sturdy body, the little-boy shock of mahogany hair, the bittersweet chocolate of his dark-lashed eyes. Or hear his voice, saying her name. "Mellie," his nickname for her. A kid-brother tease of a nickname, because of all the things she had hated about *Gone With the Wind,* she had hated the saintly, insipid character of Mellie Wilkes most.

The room remained still around her, sepia pale and silent.

She had thought she would never be strong enough to face her brother. How much did Michael remember of that night? Did he know that what had happened to him was her fault? Gramps may have forgiven her. He might have absolved her of blame for her deadly mistakes and her years of cowardice.

Had Michael?

She cleaned his room like an automaton, keeping her movements careful and steady so they wouldn't jar the ache in her chest. She laundered his curtains and his bed linens, scrubbed his windows and walls, dusted his bed and his chifforobe and his trunk and swept his floor.

When she opened the closet door to sweep inside, she found a floor-to-ceiling thicket of brown paper bags. They were all sizes, from lunch bag to grocery bag, their tops folded neatly down and clamped shut with black spring clips. The closet exuded a wild, faintly sour smell.

Cautiously, Amelia lifted one of the bags from the intricate tangle. It was very light, and rustled as she moved it. On the front, Gramps had written in pencil, "Red Curl-Top—12 oz." With her other hand, she extracted a larger bag from the nest. This one said, "Blue-stem, Pastura—10 lb." She jiggled the sack a little, listening to the dry whisper of the contents. It was like a promise.

She had found Gramps's seed store.

Around one o'clock, she made herself a sack lunch of sandwiches and a couple of Mary's winter apples and drove up the wash to the Folly. Or rather, Spencer Reed's hay field. He still had a week before his lease expired.

But she needed to spend some time there anyway. Amelia parked at the foot of the ridge and clambered up the rocks. The tract was billowing with the heavy stalks of mature oats, lush in the April sunshine. Beautiful, much as she hated to admit it. She settled down on a big boulder to eat her lunch, staring out over the fields and letting the new-honey sunlight soak into her shoulders. She had another long shift in the bee yard ahead of her this evening.

Gramps had been absent since the second week of the dust storm. Or maybe she had only missed seeing him because she had spent so much of her own time indoors. She kept glancing around, expecting him to turn up.

Amelia munched an apple, enjoying the crunch and the tart spurt of the juice, and stretched her legs out in the sunshine. It weighted the fabric of her jeans with heat, and she arched her back and yawned deeply. For the first time in weeks, the stored tension in her shoulders was draining away.

She leaned against a second slab of rock and lapsed into a drowse. She had no idea how long she had been nestled there when a shadow fell across her legs.

The pulse of fear sucked every bit of released tension back into her body. Amelia jerked her legs back from the shadow and scrambled to a squatting position against the boulders.

Spencer Reed was standing over her with a shotgun.

"The lease isn't up yet," he said.

With her back flat to the rocks, Amelia dragged in a breath. "Didn't say it was."

His little black crow-eyes were sharp with animosity. "You come to gloat? I don't hold with that."

Amelia pushed herself up from the rocks to face him. "No," she said. "I came here because I love this place. That's the plain truth, Reed, though I don't expect you to understand it."

He turned his head to look out over the field, showing her a seamed cheek. "I like it fine, myself. It's good rich land, with plenty of water. It's a shameful waste to let it sit with nothing but a bunch of weeds on it."

"Matter of opinion," Amelia said. She leaned down and gathered up the remnants of her lunch, stuffing them back in the paper sack.

"Don't let the bastard run you off, Melia," Gramps said, his voice high and sharp. "This is our place, not his."

She stood up. "I've got goats to—" she started to say, but Reed was staring straight at Gramps, white-lipped. "Mr. Reed?" Amelia said.

The muscle in his jaw twitched, and he turned away and started to scramble down the ridge.

"Good riddance, you bastard," Gramps said clearly, and Reed's shoulders tensed. "Righteous S.O.B. He never swears, did you know that, Melia? He's so uptight he can't even cuss."

Amelia waited until Reed got to the other side of the arroyo before she answered. "He could see you," she said. "Hear you, too."

"Not like you can," Gramps said. "But he can probably hear me better'n he can see me." He laughed. "Spooked him proper, didn't I?"

"Why?" Amelia demanded. "I mean, how come Reed can see you? Nobody else has."

But he was already gone.

Amelia looked at the field for a moment, waiting, just in case Gramps reappeared. Then she picked her way down the rocky slope to the truck and headed back.

She would work in the garden until time to hive the rest of the bees.

She was trying to rig a small subrogated drip system for the garden out of PVC pipe scavenged from the tractor shed when she heard the truck. Amelia stripped off her hat and went to draw herself a cup of water from the old hand pump. The water chilled the tin cup that hung beside the pump, chilled her teeth as she drank. She splashed the last of it over her face to cut the sweat, then walked around the side of the house and looked up the road. Burk's Jeep had turned in the gate and was headed toward the house, trailing a spume of yellowish dust.

Amelia's gut got tight. More mail?

She wiped her face with her sleeve and put her hat back on. Overhead, the leaves of the cottonwoods shone translucent in the sunshine, half-furled twists of new green.

Burk pulled up near the base of the trees, stopping far enough away that the trailing dust didn't drift over her. His arm jerked as he set the brake. When he stepped out, she saw that he wasn't in uniform and he wasn't holding a letter.

His khaki shirt and pants had faded to the color of the road dust, the same sandy color as the ranch house. But then, everything here took on the color of the desert after a while. He removed his hat and held it in front of him in one big sunburned hand. "Afternoon, Ms. Rawlins."

Men in the south had such good manners, especially out here in the country. "Mr. Burkhalter," she said. She angled her own hat down to shade her eyes.

He cleared his throat. "Got your bees home all right?"

Seeing him made her uncomfortable, after she had told him more than she'd intended to yesterday. "Yes, thanks."

"Goats still keeping you busy?"

"The goats are fine, too," Amelia said. She

propped herself against one of the fat cottonwoods. "What brings you out this way today?"

He stared at his hat for a minute, as if he could see something important in its band. Then he looked up and met her eyes straight. "Ms. Rawlins—"

She waited. Her fingers were digging into the rough bark behind her.

He lowered his voice. "You've met Caroline Garrity, got the place just across the road—"

"Yes?"

"Well. Caroline Garrity—her husband left about a year ago, so it's just her and her son now."

Amelia nodded.

"She's having a hard time," he said. "Money trouble—all kinds of trouble, really." He cleared his throat and went on. "They kept some goats, but all of them took sick and died a couple of months back. What with that, and her business falling off, and the way some folks act—well it's a tough time. The boy wants to do a summer FFA project, and the Granberds have offered him a pair of their best Nubian stock—nursing kids, you know. But since his goats died, he doesn't have a way to bottle-raise the kids."

"You saying you actually found me a buyer for my extra goat's milk?"

"Well, not exactly. Since you were saying—well, I thought he could maybe work a trade with you. A barter for the surplus milk."

She was surprised. It was unexpected, someone asking her for something. Ever since she got here, it seemed like that shoe had been on the other foot.

"I guess we could work something out," she said. "What kind of trade were you thinking of? Who'd pick up the milk?"

"Well, I'd swing by—"

"You're going to a lot of trouble . . ." A thought struck her, and Amelia chuckled. "You got a special interest there or something?" Then she watched in astonishment as brick red color climbed his tanned cheeks. He looked so embarrassed that she felt bad for teasing him.

"Just helping out," he muttered, then gave a little come-along signal with one hand and called, "Mark."

A skinny kid about twelve years old unfolded himself from the back of the jeep and jumped out. She hadn't even seen him back there. Maybe because he was bare-chested and already very brown. He was wearing baggy faded jeans and scuffed boots. His body had the emerging angularity of early adolescence: lean with a hint of sinew, but without the full-fledged musculature of a grown man.

She had vague memories of her brother Daniel being this age. But not Michael. He'd only been nine the last time she saw him.

"Well, like I was saying, Mark'll be doing an FFA project this summer," Burk said. "We figured he'd come do chores for you, do the milking, whatever you like. Morning and evening chores till school lets out, then full-time in the summer. His mom wants him back at suppertime, so I figured I could swing by on my route and pick him and the milk up every afternoon."

"I thought you ran this part of your route in the mornings," Amelia said.

Burk shrugged.

The boy spoke for the first time. "It'd be just for the summer, ma'am. The kids can go on solid food pretty quick."

She glanced at him and saw that his eyes were the color of bitter chocolate. Why was she even considering this?

"What about the beehives?" Amelia said sharply. "They're dangerous—I can't have strangers messing around them."

The boy looked at Burk.

"Mark's responsible," Burk said, laying a hand on the boy's shoulder. "He does a lot of work at his mother's place. Knows better than to bother anything you tell him not to, Ms. Rawlins. Least of all your bees. You have my word on that."

Mark looked back at her, eyes half resentful, half beseeching. Like Michael's eyes in her dreams.

"Mom—I mean—my mother's been real worried

about college money, ma'am. This is a good chance. See, if I do a good job on my projects now, I'll have a better chance at an FFA scholarship later on."

Amelia remembered the note of pride in Caroline's voice when she'd talked about Mark. College money must matter a lot. "I'll think about it," she said abruptly. Her fingers flexed as she thought of having mornings free for the clay. With someone to do the milking, she might even manage to get started on her kiln. But if the boy were here, she'd be responsible for him.

Might be smarter to keep her distance.

"Thing is, it's a pressing question, Ms. Rawlins," Burk said. "The Granberds will give him the stock, but the youngsters have to handle the project themselves to get credit. If he can't work out a way to bottle-raise the goats, he'll have to figure out something else to do."

Not ready to commit, she gestured toward the house. "Care to come inside and have something to drink?"

Burk and the boy were standing side by side, watching her. "Well," Burk said after a minute. "Guess it depends on whether that's a yes or a no."

She arched her neck and looked up into the waxy blue depths of the sky. No rain today. The real rainy season didn't come until midsummer. Even if the skies clouded up this afternoon, it would only be for show. Any rain that fell from those clouds would probably evaporate before it hit the ground.

From a distance, in the clear desert air, you could see the smudged violet curtains formed by the falling drops. But it was just a mirage, a joke the rain god liked to play. What folks here called a ghost rain.

No guarantees that there would be enough rain for the garden or the prairie. But then, she had learned the hard way that the world didn't offer any guarantees. No promises there would be enough to go around. Rain, the land, the milk Burk wanted her to swap—it all came down to the same thing in the end. Life. There wasn't enough life, and you couldn't change that.

All you could do was even out the portions a little.

Amelia ran her fingers lightly over her left sleeve. Through the cloth, she could feel the rippled skin of the brand. Just even things out a little, that's all anyone could do.

She looked at the boy, still watching her steadily with those dark eyes. Watching her as if she were as powerful and capricious as a rain god. As if she held his fate in her hands.

"It's a yes," she said.

Chapter Eight

Paul Boucher's attackers were brought to trial on August 20, 1983. The trial lasted seven weeks and was a vigorous contest between the city's prosecutors and the nationally known trial attorney retained by the organization to defend its members.

The jury deliberations lasted nine days. Three of the attackers—including the driver and the members who had used spiked two-by-fours to batter Paul—were convicted of manslaughter and sentenced to prison terms ranging from two to four years. The other four were convicted of malicious assault; they received fines and suspended sentences.

The site of Boucher's beating had become a shrine: A mural appeared on the alley wall; a profusion of white candles in tall glass cylinders burned before it; and a collection of crosses, fresh flowers, jazz records, and small fossils littered the pavement.

The evening that the verdict was announced, hundreds of Montrose residents made a spontaneous pilgrimage to the shrine. Many of them had never met Boucher, though some had known him well. A number of musicians came to pay their respects.

Mournful blues drifted through the streets of the district all through that night.

—MOLLY CATES, "Blood Relatives,"
Lone Star Monthly, April 1986

New Mexico

Amelia worked in the garden until the sun went down, digging a series of trenches to bury the PVC pipe. Having underground irrigation was important out here, where the humidity usually stayed under ten percent.

The house was dark by the time she came in, exhausted and dirty. She went to the kitchen sink and was scrubbing her hands and face when the phone rang.

"Shoot." She snatched up a cup towel to blot her eyes, and picked up the phone. "Hello?"

"A-me-li-a." The voice was very deep, and he drew her name out into four separate syllables. Just the way he said it made her pulse jump.

"Who is that?" she asked sharply.

"A-me-li-a. We're going to get you." There was noise in the background—loud music and the sound of people laughing. A bar?

"Who *is* this?" Her voice cracked.

"I'm warning you, we're coming. Some night when you're asleep—" It sounded as if he'd cupped a hand around the mouthpiece now. The background noise dimmed, and his words sounded even breathier and more menacing. "Better get out while you still can."

She heard the click as he hung up, then the hum of an open line. She couldn't seem to get her breath. After a moment, the off-hook signal blared, and Amelia cradled the receiver.

She'd immersed herself in the work of the ranch, staying busy to avoid thinking about the threats, and had managed to convince herself that whoever was behind them had given up once she changed the locks.

What a fool.

She turned on the outside floods, grabbed a flashlight, and went across to the workshop. The windmill hummed overhead, and the cottonwoods tossed, casting shadows everywhere. Amelia hadn't lived in a city for years, but right then she would have given almost anything for a streetlight.

Once inside, with the shop lights on, it only took her a minute to find some three-quarter-inch screws. She ran back to the house.

She didn't go to bed until she'd put screws in every window frame in the house, and wedged a couple of two-by-fours under the door handles. That should keep the doors from opening even if the locks were broken.

She heard wing-beats. Amelia looked up and saw a dark bird circling the house, nothing more than a shadow, a darker blot against the dusky sky. The black shape circled three times, in three sweeping beats of its enormous wings; then it folded them and coasted down to land. Its shadow loomed over the house.

Hunched beside the barn, its beak nestled against its chest, the bird's body became the crouched shape of the windmill. Gleaming blades began to spin in silhouette against the occluded sky.

Her terror was wholesale, consuming all thought—she fled toward the mountains. It was only after the whine of the blades rose behind her that she knew she should have run for the truck.

Her legs churned desperately, but she gained no ground. She looked back as the whine surged higher.

It was almost on top of her. Then the spinning blades of the windmill mutated into the bent ax blades of an enormous swastika. It spun, gathering speed with each circuit, until the blades sliced screams from the air.

That's when she saw Michael. He stood, blank and frozen, directly in the path of the spinning blades.

She screamed—or tried to—as she dived toward him.

She couldn't reach him. As she fell, dust swirled in her face, stirred by the spinning blades overhead. They sounded like enormous heartbeats, like the throb of helicopters.

Something hot dripped on her back. She brushed at her shoulder.

Her palm came away coated in blood.

She woke screaming, with the image of the deadly swastika dripping above her, the sticky heat of phantom blood still on her hand.

There was no sleeping after that. Amelia rose in the remote stillness of the early morning, dressed, and made a large pot of coffee. The weather was still turning cold at night, so she built up the fire—she was running low on wood again—and sat in the big armchair with the afghan around her for warmth. She drank three cups of coffee before her teeth stopped chattering.

In the dream, she had known Michael instantly, without confusion. But once awake, she realized that the boy who was slashed apart by the spinning swastika had looked like Mark Garrity—older, the hair a much lighter shade of brown, the face narrower and more adult.

Amelia subsided against the back of the chair, awash in weariness. How could Frank Burkhalter have suggested that the boy come to the ranch every day? Burk knew she'd been getting threats. And she—how could she have agreed to it?

She gulped at the steaming coffee, glad when the liquid scalded her mouth. Such a minor pain was almost a comfort in comparison to the feelings the dream had stirred.

Those dark brown eyes of Mark's had been her undoing. The eyes and his awkward dignity. She had never stood a chance against it, and Burk must have expected that. It was why he'd brought Mark along with him. Well, her good sense might have been dulled for a while, but the dream had honed it.

Having the boy work at the ranch was too dangerous. She couldn't risk it.

It was Sunday morning, but still far too early for the church bells to ring. The coffee in her cup suddenly tasted bitter. Amelia set it aside and curled into a knot to wait for dawn.

*   *   *

She had made a second pot of coffee and was trying to motivate herself to fix some breakfast when Mark tapped softly on the kitchen door. Amelia glanced at the clock. A quarter to five.

Mark blinked in the electric lights when she let him in. Cool desert air followed him, mingling the smells of piñon and wood smoke with the cozy house smells of cinnamon and coffee. She was glad to see that he was dressed more warmly today, wearing a chambray shirt, a denim jacket, and an age-softened Stetson that was too big for him. Once indoors, he removed it.

"Morning, ma'am," he said. His voice cracked, and he cleared his throat. "Sorry to come so early on a Sunday, but I know goats like to be milked the same time every day, and—Well, during the week, the school bus comes at seven-thirty—but I sure don't want to put you out any."

"It doesn't matter," Amelia said. "Have a seat." She emptied her cup at the sink and refilled it. "Want some coffee?"

He hesitated. "Thank you, ma'am."

She shoved a chair out for him before filling a second mug and setting milk and sugar on the table.

He added sugar and lots of milk, sipped cautiously, then poured in more milk—just to cool the coffee off, she realized—and drank eagerly. She wondered if he was hungry.

"Look—" she began, just as he started to say something, too. "Go ahead," she told him.

He took a deep breath. "Ma'am, I noticed you're running low on wood. Thought I might chop you some more—we've got cutting privileges on Mr. Wickten's place up near Cloudcroft. After I take care of the goats and other chores, I mean."

She didn't know what to say.

When she didn't answer, he went on anxiously, "You'd have to drive me up there, but I can do the cutting. Mr. Wickten lets me use the chain saw—he knows

I'm careful. Later on, I can cut it down to stove size for you."

She drank some coffee, then set the cup down with a clunk. "Look—I appreciate the offer. You'd be a big help around here, but I've been thinking it over, and it's just not going to work."

"I'm sure sorry, ma'am—didn't mean to get out of line. Whatever chores you'd rather I do, that's fine with me. I just noticed the wood was low and thought—"

"No," Amelia said, and he stopped, watching her seriously. She was having a hard time meeting those brown eyes. "It's not that." She paused for a breath. "It's just not going to work out, you being over here. I've decided it's too risky."

Mark set down his coffee cup, carefully aligning the handle with the edge of the table. "You think I'm too young to be trusted." His voice was bleak.

"Not at all—it's nothing to do with you—"

"I see." He stood up and pushed his chair neatly into place. "You've heard bad things about my mother, and now you don't want anything to do with us."

The look in his dark eyes hit her hard. They could have been Michael's eyes, after the kids at school had tormented him because of Mom's politics.

Amelia jumped up. "No," she said forcefully, "that's not it."

He was turning to go, his shoulders rigid.

She caught the sleeve of his jean jacket and held on. The fabric was cool and stiff under her fingers.

"Mark," she said. It was the first time she'd called him by name. "I've been getting threats."

He looked at her, still not speaking. Angrily she gave his jacket a tug.

"*Death* threats," she said. "Don't you see? I can't take a chance on getting you hurt."

His face tightened, then went blank. "Like I don't get threats all the time."

Amelia let him go. "What? Who from?"

He twitched his jacket higher up on his shoulders and turned his face away.

"What kind of threats? Does your mom know?"

He jerked around. "No. And I don't want her to. She's got enough to worry about."

"What's going on, Mark?" Her head was starting to ache. She rubbed at her forehead.

He shrugged. "Just other guys trying to pound me. Nothing too bad."

She figured it was miles worse than he was letting on. "Why are they after you?"

He shook his head, and she knew he wouldn't say any more. At least not right now.

"I'm sorry, Mark," she said. "Really sorry. But I just don't think it's safe for you to work over here. That doesn't mean you can't have the milk for your baby goats—"

"Can't take it unless I do the chores for you," he said immediately, and turned to go.

"Wait—"

Fifteen minutes later, they still hadn't sorted it out. Mark Garrity was the stubbornest twelve-year-old she'd ever met. He refused outright to take the milk as a gift. He wouldn't even sit down again unless she agreed to honor their original deal.

Amelia's head hurt from arguing with him. And her stomach was grumbling about too much caffeine and no breakfast. She got up and turned on the oven and the front burner of the stove.

She took two pans of yeast biscuits she'd made up the night before from the fridge and put them in to bake. As she started cracking eggs into a bowl, she thought about what terrible financial shape she'd be in if Mary and Willy hadn't gone out of their way to help her. And they'd done it in a way that respected her pride. Didn't Mark deserve the same respect?

He was standing by the door like he was about to bolt.

"Breakfast in a sec," she said.

His narrow face went even more rigid. "Thank you, ma'am, but I've had mine, so if you'll just show me the chores—"

"Never knew a guy your age who couldn't eat two breakfasts. Pour yourself a glass of milk."

He stood there at the far end of the table and looked at his boots. Then he lifted his chin—a mannerism she already recognized. "Much obliged, ma'am, but I can't take charity from you. I've got to earn the kids' milk and do the project myself."

Amelia poured eggs into the heated skillet. "Too much here for just me—and I don't care for eating alone." It was true.

She stirred the eggs, then quickly turned them onto a platter and brought them to the table. He remained standing next to it. Stubborn kid. She *had* agreed to the swap, but it wouldn't be right to put him in danger.

Gramma's voice whispered, *"He'll be fine here, you'll see. And a promise is a promise, Melia."*

Gramma was right; it didn't feel good to go back on her promise to help.

Amelia set the eggs down. "You'll have to come after the sun is up and be gone by dark," she said, "for safety's sake. And you can't stay on the place alone. If I have to leave for any reason—run an errand or whatever—you'll come along or go home. Got that?"

He eyed her sideways for a second, started to say something, then closed his mouth and sat down.

"And I'll have to talk to your mother about it," she added. "No deal unless she gives her okay."

He thought about that. "She will."

Amelia doubted it, but didn't say so. She pulled the biscuits from the oven and set one pan directly on the kitchen table. She remembered her grandmother doing that, this same battered tin pie plate on this same scarred tabletop. Something about the memory made her feel safer.

"Right," she said, and pried a couple of biscuits out of the pan for him with her knife. "Preserves in that jar there."

Outside, the sun was rising over the mountains along the eastern rim of the basin, spilling rose and gold into the night-blue sky. The air was crisp, just on the cold side.

They walked over to the goat pen. She had built it out from the back of the tractor shed. Their pen was a square lean-to with an overhang on one side, which allowed fresh air in while protecting the animals from the worst of the wind. At the back was a fully enclosed space she used as a milking room.

"How many goats you got?" the boy asked.

"Two. Both nannies," Amelia told him.

The goats were mixed-blood. Brown-and-whites, nothing fancy, though their Roman noses were evidence of a little Nubian ancestry. But they'd proved to be good milkers, which was all she cared about.

The two goats skittered out of the shed when they heard her voice, hooves clicking as they trotted across the enclosure to the fence. Both of them propped their front hooves up on the gate, butting at each other for position.

"Cut it out," Amelia said to them. "You don't want to get stuck in the fence, do you?"

"Goats are kinda dumb that way," Mark said. "Always climbing on things." He slipped the wire loop latch off the fence post and eased the gate back. As he did, he caught the near goat's front legs and lowered it to the ground. The second goat bounced down as Amelia followed him into the enclosure.

He was rubbing the first goat under the chin, making her go slant-eyed with pleasure. "What're their names?"

"That one's Margot Kidder and the other one's Lois Lane."

Mark laughed so loud he startled Margot. She jerked away from him and snorted before trotting over to the milking room door. Amelia was absurdly pleased that he liked her silly play on names.

"Looks like she knows the drill," he said, indicating Margot with a wave. She was parked in front of the milking room, bleating, her stub of a tail twitching eagerly.

"Yeah. I usually milk a little earlier—she wants her breakfast."

She walked Mark through the routine as she milked and fed Margot. Then Amelia watched him as he did the same for Lois. He made no mistakes, although he did start to confuse the wash bucket with the milk pail. She stopped him and pointed out the piece of electrical tape marking the handle of the wash bucket. "The disinfectant would make the milk taste pretty strange."

"Yes, ma'am, it sure would," he said, and switched buckets.

After he finished milking, she helped him filter the contents of his bucket into the big milk can. She told him, "We need to start the milk cooling right away. Then we can come back and do the shed."

They'd gotten nearly a gallon. The half-full can made an awkward load, but Mark refused to let Amelia carry it. Next she took him to the tractor shed side of the building, where the rake and hay were stored, so he could clean out the nannies' shed and lay fresh bedding for them.

"Then I put the old bedding in the compost pile," she told him, and he nodded. He was sweating a little from loading fresh hay on the wheelbarrow, although the morning was still cool.

When she had tried to break off their agreement that morning, he'd said, "You think I'm too young." Amelia knew she should leave him to do his chores by himself. She didn't want to reinforce his feeling that she didn't trust him. But it worried her to leave him alone out here, even in broad daylight.

"I'll look out for him," Gramps said. She turned around and found him standing next to her. "Get on back to that contraption you've been working on in the garden."

Amelia smiled. Gramps's hair was ruffled up, as if by the wind, although the air was still this morning. He was watching Mark closely, his eyes crinkled up. He looked happy.

"Thanks, Gramps," she said softly. "Come on up to the house when you're done," she called to Mark.

Knowing Gramps was keeping an eye on him reassured her; she went back to her irrigation system feeling calmer.

Burk's Jeep turned in at the ranch gate around five-thirty that afternoon. Caroline Garrity was with him.

Tucker bounded down from the Jeep before it came to a full stop and loped over to her for an ear-scratching. Amelia obliged him, laughing at the blissful tongue-lolled expression on the dog's face.

Mark set his rake aside and watched them curiously. "He sure likes you," he said.

"No accounting for taste," Amelia said. She leaned down to give Tucker's chest a few thumps. "Say hello to him, Mark."

"Hey, Tucker," Mark said, and snapped his fingers.

Amelia stood up. Tucker gave her fingers a couple of licks, then ambled over to collect a little ear-scratching from Mark.

"You're an embarrassment to me, you know that?" Burk said to the dog as he and Caroline came up. Amelia liked the way he looked out of uniform, wearing jeans and a crimson T-shirt. They made him seem younger. He removed his straw cowboy hat and smiled at her. "No manners at all."

"Oh, he's got perfectly good manners," Amelia said.

"Just not using them, is that what you're saying?" Burk's smile widened. "Next thing you know, he'll be begging for scraps, looking at you like he hasn't been fed for a month."

"Enterprising," Amelia said. "I like that in a dog." She and Caroline exchanged hellos, then watched Mark flail around on the ground laughing while Tucker licked his face.

"Dogs are disgusting, loathsome creatures," Caroline said to her son, rolling her eyes. "How can you let him lick you like that? Do you *know* where that mouth has been?"

Burk looked down at Tucker and asked him softly, "Are you a disgusting, loathsome creature? Your Auntie Caroline says you are, yes, she does."

Amelia covered her mouth, trying not to laugh. Caroline grinned and went on, "Why would anyone have a dog? They eat excrement. They vomit it back up and eat it again—and you *feed* this animal, Burk. You encourage him to hang around my impressionable young son."

"Your son better get that wheelbarrow put away before I make a real impression on him," Burk said. Mark laughed and scrambled up.

Tucker rolled over and abased himself in front of Caroline. He cocked his ears and gave his tail a tentative wag.

"See, now. You've gone and hurt his feelings," Burk said.

Caroline was unimpressed. "Why don't you get a nice iguana, instead, Burk? They're neat and clean and affectionate, keep the bug population under control. And they never do *that* sort of nauseating stuff." She waved a hand at Tucker, who had started slurpily licking his privates.

Burk looked at her thoughtfully for a moment, then said, completely deadpan, "It would be hard to love something with no eyelids."

Amelia started laughing helplessly. Caroline was laughing, too.

Burk just watched them, smiling a little. As they were winding down, he reached over and fondled Tucker's ears. "Don't worry, Tuck," he said consolingly, "I like you better than some lidless lizard."

That set the two women off again. Amelia couldn't remember the last time she'd laughed like this. Not since before Jeff had died, that's for sure.

She gasped for breath, then managed to say, "You know what your problem is here, Burk? You're too conventional. When it comes to pets, you've got no imagination."

"When it comes to pets, maybe so." He gave her

a frankly admiring look. "Have I mentioned that you've got *nice* eyelids?"

Still chuckling but a little rattled, Amelia said, "I'd better get the milk," and escaped indoors.

In the kitchen, she wrapped the second pan of biscuits in a clean cloth and put them in the basket Caroline had brought the chamomile tea in. She thought for a second, then added a jar of plum preserves. Mark had seemed to like them. Then she poured a quart of milk into her stoneware jug before taking the basket and the milk can out to Burk's Jeep.

Burk and Caroline were still in the garden. Tucker had settled into a lion sprawl beside the pump. He lay there panting, ears up, and watched Mark fasten the door to the shed.

Burk glanced at her as she walked up. "How's everything going out here, Amelia? Doing okay?"

"Doing fine," she said, not meeting his eyes. She ought to tell Caroline Garrity about the threats now, but found she was reluctant to bring up the subject in front of Burk. And with Mark around—this just wasn't a good time.

Burk waited, as if expecting her to say more. "I've been kind of worried about those letters you got." His voice was very quiet, and much more serious now.

She looked away. "Yeah, well, so have I."

He paused for a few seconds, then said, "Look— Spence Reed came into the post office yesterday afternoon. He was saying you'd canceled his lease to work that parcel of land at the mouth of the canyon."

"News travels fast."

"He's pretty ticked off. Reed's a good man, even if I don't always agree with him. I don't think he's the type to hold a grudge, but—" He broke off. "Look, the last thing you need right now is a feud with one of your neighbors."

"That's for sure," Caroline said.

"Don't worry," Amelia said. "I don't have time for feuds."

Caroline gave a short laugh that had an edge to it. "Who does?"

Burk glanced at Caroline, hesitated, then said to Amelia. "If you'd like to talk to the sheriff about those letters—"

"No," Amelia said.

"I'd be glad to go along—or talk to him myself—"

"No, thanks," she said. Her tone was sharper than she'd intended.

Caroline turned away. Burk shook his head, looking troubled.

Mark walked up then, back from the tractor shed, and Amelia said, "The milk's cooling down nicely, but you might want to pour it into jars when you get home."

"Yes, ma'am," he said.

"And the can has to be sterilized before we can use it again."

"I'll take care of it, ma'am," Mark said. "And I'll be sure to bring it with me tomorrow."

She hesitated. "It's awkward to carry all that way if you're walking."

"I'll use a knapsack," he said. "No problem."

He's like a little adult, she thought. *He's trying so hard*.

Caroline and Burk exchanged a look, then Caroline said, "Okay, Mark. Why don't you round up Tucker and get in the Jeep? Burk'll be ready to go in a minute."

"Yes, ma'am." Mark gave a sharp whistle between his teeth. Tucker ambled over and Caroline herded them both toward the Jeep.

Burk turned sharply toward Amelia, and she flinched.

"Sorry," he said, watching her. "Didn't mean to startle you."

Embarrassed, she said, "Just a little jumpy, I guess."

He set his hat back on his head. "At least consider telling the sheriff about those letters."

She didn't answer.

After a few seconds, he pulled a folded white index card out of his shirt pocket. "Here's my phone number. If you won't call the sheriff, at least call me if—if you have any trouble."

"It's kind of you," she said. Her lips felt stiff.

He looked at her. "You won't call, will you? Well, then, I'll check in with you. And you keep this number, just in case you need something."

He tucked the card in her hand and closed her fingers around it. His callused fingertips were surprisingly gentle. He gave her hand a final squeeze before he turned away.

She watched until the Jeep had pulled out and the dust it raised had settled again. The place seemed much too quiet now. She unfolded the card. Inside, his name and phone number were neatly inked in black, draftsman-style print.

Amelia put in another half hour in the garden, but went inside around sunset. She washed up carefully and changed her shirt, then drove over to see Caroline Garrity.

It was dusk when Amelia pulled up at the Garritys' place. Long cool shadows slanted across the basin from the Organ Mountains, reaching toward the old house. Up close, it looked in even worse need of paint, but the garden was incredible. An herb border was already flourishing, and climbing roses made a lattice of green branches across the chain-link fence.

Caroline Garrity opened the front door before Amelia could knock. She seemed surprised but pleased at the unexpected visit. "Amelia! Good to see you—come on in."

"Sorry to just drop by like this. I—is Burk here right now?" She hadn't seen his Jeep, but wanted to make sure.

Caroline led the way to a big kitchen that stretched the width of the farmhouse, where she motioned Amelia to a seat at the table. "Actually, he took Mark into town for a hamburger. Would you care for some herb tea?"

"Is—excuse me, but—do you and Burk—I mean, does he live here?"

Caroline laughed, a low, warm ripple of sound. "Lord, no. Burk and I are old college buddies. He's Mark's godfather, and since Ken—Mark's dad—left, Burk kind of tries to fill the gap." She took the chair next to Amelia.

Amelia could feel herself flushing. "Sorry. That was nosy." She glanced around the kitchen. The table was beautiful—Shaker style in solid maple—and the walls were freshly painted a creamy yellow, but the floor tiles were scarred and cracked. Bundles of drying herbs hung from the ceiling beams, and there were beakers of green goop on the tiled counter.

"Not at all. To tell the truth, I'm glad to see Burk taking an interest in *you*—it's been more than eight years since his divorce." She grinned suddenly. "Is that why you came? To make sure he wasn't involved with someone else?"

Amelia leaned her forehead into her hand, raking at her hair with her fingers. It would have been funny if it hadn't been so embarrassing. "I—it just popped out. Pure curiosity, I guess. I actually need to talk to you about something else."

"You sound kind of upset. What's the problem?" Caroline's beautiful voice sounded less fluid now.

Amelia took a quick breath. "I'm worried about having Mark work over at my place. I've gotten some threats—"

Caroline touched Amelia's hand; from her, the gesture seemed completely natural. "Yes, Burk said he's been worried about you. It must be awful. Those letters you were talking about earlier?"

"That and—and a phone call." Amelia drew back. "It's—I'm—I came because I'm worried about Mark working for me. It's nothing against him, I can already see he's a terrific worker. But I can't risk him getting hurt because of my problems—"

"No, of course you couldn't. How about filling me in a little more on what's involved?" She sounded sympathetic.

Amelia tried to think how a normal person would answer. Someone who hadn't seen her family murdered. "There've been two letters. One of them had a—a news clipping about my family."

"Your family?"

Amelia's hands were shaking. She never talked about this. "They—" She swallowed. "They were murdered. Years ago."

"How terrible for you. I'm so sorry."

Amelia looked away. "There was a—a note that said something like too bad I wasn't killed, too. And—and then I got the phone call."

"You must be terrified," Caroline said. "How serious do you think they are? I mean, is this just malicious mischief, or do you think someone really means you harm?"

"I—I can't help but take it seriously."

"Right. Of course you have to. A dumb question."

Amelia noticed that the skin around Caroline's eyes looked drawn.

Caroline said, "Of course you can't ignore something that might be dangerous. Trouble is, we're—Mark is struggling with a lot of things right now—" She hesitated. "Did you tell him about the threats?"

"I tried to," Amelia said. "He acted like it was no big deal—" She broke off, remembering his bitter initial response—that she thought he was too young. "The last thing I meant was to question his abilities. He's a wonderful kid, and I'm glad for the help. I'm just worried about his safety. I don't—I can't be responsible for him getting hurt."

"He's been touchy since his dad left," Caroline said. "Thinks he has to be the man of the family now. It's so silly—he's only twelve years old, for heaven's sake."

Amelia remembered the ground rules she'd laid down with Mark. "They—whoever sent the letters—all talk about coming for me at night, so I told Mark he had to leave before dark. And that he can't stay on the place by himself, ever."

"That sounds sensible. I appreciate it."

"But if you don't want him over there at all, I'd understand. Completely."

Caroline's mouth firmed. "I'll think things over, and then talk with Mark about this when he gets back," she said. "I usually try to let him make his own decisions, or at least have some say in them."

Amelia swallowed. "But what if whoever is doing this comes after me, and Mark gets in the way?"

There was a brief pause. Then Caroline said quietly, "I'm not saying it doesn't worry me. But I'm just as worried about—other stuff. Mark's emotional health—well, he's been shaky lately. And this FFA project means the world to him."

Amelia tried to gather her thoughts. This conversation sure wasn't going the way she'd expected.

Independence had been thrust on her when she was a teenager, and she'd responded by fighting desperately for self-sufficiency. She had been determined never to rely on anyone else again. But for years she'd lived with the constant fear that some well-meaning adult would realize who she was and make a phone call. One call that would put an end to all her hard-won autonomy.

The choices she'd made might not have been perfect, but at least she'd had the chance to make them herself. Did Mark feel the same way?

"And—" Caroline hesitated. "What about you?" Her voice was as gentle as ever, but when she went on, she sounded very firm, "Have you let the sheriff know about this yet?"

"It's—I'd better go." Amelia stood abruptly.

But Caroline caught her hand, and pressed it. She stood up, meeting Amelia's eyes. "I can tell talking about this isn't easy for you," she said, "but I'd like to help. I may not be much of a friend, but I'll do whatever I can. Just remember that, okay?"

Mark arrived even earlier the next morning, ready to go to work. He brought with him a housewarming gift from his mother—a box of seedlings for the garden. Amelia took it as Caroline's blessing for Mark's working here.

He left right after he milked the goats, it being a school day. It was also the first of May, which meant Reed's lease on the Folly had expired at midnight. Amelia needed to replant it as soon as possible, so the grasses would get a good start. The runoff from the snow melting up-mountain would give the prairie an added boost if she got the seed in the ground soon.

Amelia opened up the shed and pulled the tarps off Gramps's tractor—a single-plow John Deere, older than she was. It took her a couple of hours to get it ready to go.

Driving the tractor was like riding a half-broke horse with a bad gait; she jounced and rattled on the seat. And handling the huge steering wheel was an uncomfortable stretch. She decided to take the tractor up the wash by the stream before attaching the planter. She wanted to make sure she could maneuver it up the narrow ungraded road to the Folly before she had the extra weight to unbalance things.

A swirl of canyon wrens wheeled overhead as she inched past their territory along the creek. She couldn't watch them; driving the tractor took all her concentration. As she began the climb toward the Folly, the tractor's balance seemed precarious. The worst part was the last narrow scrape of road between the mountain and the cliff along the western edge of the Folly that separated it from the rest of the ranch. The road was very steep; she had a bad moment when she thought the tractor wouldn't make the turn, but she managed to wrestle it around.

She had told Atkinson to have Reed disc his crop stubble under, and he had done it. Seeing the Folly stripped completely bare was worse than seeing it planted in hay had been.

Amelia pulled the tractor up onto the plateau, cut the engine, and slid off the seat. The naked earth was a rich rusty brown, and when she stooped to gather a handful of it, the soil crumbled loose between her fingers.

Fine land. She should have been able to put the planter on the tractor and reseed the prairie right now.

Except that Reed had run his furrows straight downhill from the mountain—a pattern designed to sluice the soil straight off the edge of the cliff. Any seed she planted would be washed away before it could sprout.

The son of a bitch. She was going to have to replow before she could plant.

The three-pronged plow for the tractor weighed several hundred pounds. Gramps had positioned it in the shed so the tractor could be backed up to it and the plow levered on, but it was still a struggle.

Persistence eventually turned the trick, though it was more like her thirtieth try than the third that did it. She got the tractor and plow up onto the prairie around two o'clock, and spent the rest of the afternoon lightly discing the soil, carving long gentle curves that followed the line of the escarpment.

It was tougher than she remembered from her days on the cooperative in Navasota. The plow had a tendency to dig into the ground or skip. Once it caught on a buried root, and nearly flipped the tractor over backwards. Amelia got the hang of instantly throttling down any time she felt resistance from the plow. But then she ended up creeping across the ten-acre tract like a snail. Dusty, miserably slow work. By four-thirty, she was more than ready to call it a day.

She engaged the lift that retracted the plow, and headed back toward the ranch house. At the rate she was going, it would take the better part of another day to finish plowing.

And then she still had to plant.

Mark was already in the goat pen, spreading fresh bedding for Margot and Lois.

"Why are you so early?" Amelia said. "You

know you're not supposed to be over here when I'm not around."

Mark didn't say anything right away. She could almost see him counting to ten before he answered her.

"Sorry," he said after a minute. "My kids were born today. Burk's going to run me up to the Granberds' to get them. Just wanted to be sure I got Lois and Margot taken care of first."

"I didn't mean to snap at you. But I promised your mother you wouldn't be here by yourself."

"It's not like I was all alone—I could see you up there on the tractor."

She perched on the edge of the goats' manger. It felt good to get out of the sun, and she lifted her hat off so the breeze could cool her sweaty hair. "I hate driving a tractor. It's hard and it's boring—the worst combination there is."

"You fixing to plant that field you got back from Spencer Reed? What're you putting in up there?"

"Native grass. My grandfather had a restored prairie there before Reed plowed it up. I'm going to put it to rights."

"We had a talk at FFA a couple of months back about how with the right kinds of planting and grazing, this can be great grass country."

"That's right. Gramps always says the grass here was stirrup high before the cattle ranchers moved in and grazed it to desert. But sometimes he exaggerates."

"You talk about him like he's just around the corner," Mark said. He finished spreading the fresh layer of bedding for the animals and came over to sit next to her. He picked up a piece of scrap wood from under the manger, pulled a pearl-handled pocketknife out of his jeans, and started to whittle. "Instead of like he's been dead for ages."

"I guess I do," Amelia said. "Maybe because it makes him seem closer."

Mark wasn't much of a whittler, and his knife wasn't well suited for the work. He tended to dig the blade too deep into the wood. Amelia had done enough sculpting to know that was one of the most common mistakes, but she didn't say anything.

"What are you making?" she asked after a minute.

He glanced up, and that was another common mistake. When he put pressure on the deeply embedded knife blade, it snapped like a twig.

"Oh, damn," she said. But when she saw the look on his face, she grabbed for his hands. "Did you cut yourself?"

Mark jerked away from her. "No!"

She saw that he had tears in his eyes. She couldn't stand it when people cried.

"Mark, what is it?" The words came out harsher than she meant them to.

He had turned away, and was looking out toward where the sun was turning bloody above the smoky purple ridges of the Organs. In profile, his face looked older. "My dad gave me this knife," he said. His voice broke a little.

Remorse dropped over her like a net. Amelia found herself putting an arm around his shoulders. "I'm so sorry," she said. "Here, keep the steel. You can save up your money and have it mended."

He sat very still. "You think so?"

"I know so," Amelia said. "It'll cost something, but you're going to make a bundle off those kids you're raising. Now c'mon—let's go get us a glass of tea before Burk picks you up."

The next day, inching the tractor along the Folly's contours was even worse. Mostly because she got up onto the plateau earlier, and had the whole day to spend on the tractor.

It took her until after five to get the rest of the ten acres plowed, but Mark wasn't anywhere around when she pulled the tractor back into its shed. Probably having a hard time tearing himself away from his new babies at home.

Amelia got herself a drink from the pump. She

sloshed water on her face and throat, opening the top snaps of her shirt and unsnapping the cuffs to pump some over her wrists. The creak of the pump and the rush of the water masked the sound of footsteps, so she was taken unawares when Mark called her name.

She jerked around. He was still twenty feet away. Amelia put her back to him while she yanked the sleeve back over her left arm and fastened the cuff.

"What's the matter?" Mark asked as he came up next to her.

"Not a thing," she said. "You just caught me washing up. Been out on the tractor all afternoon."

He watched as she pulled the other sleeve down and snapped it. "Sorry I'm late—had to go home and feed my kids first. Sure will be glad when school's out. I've got lots to do." His narrow face was very serious. This was one boy who wasn't daydreaming about summer pleasures.

"You've worked hard over here, Mark," she said. "If you need to back off a little till the kids are bigger, it's no big deal. You're more than earning their keep, you know."

"I can handle it," he said stiffly and headed down toward the goat pen, moving fast.

Amelia let him go, too tired to try to argue him out of his misconstruction of what she'd said. But after drinking another cup of cold water, she followed him down to the enclosure and refilled the goats' manger with hay, raked off the soiled top layer of their bedding in the shed, then spread a light blanket of fresh straw over the old. By the time Mark finished milking, the rest of the evening stock chores were done.

When he started to protest that she was doing his work for him, she just grinned.

"I've got ulterior motives," she said. "Have you ever connected a seed drill to a tractor?"

Mark did his level best to help her disconnect the plow so they could hook up the seed drill. But the truth was, neither of them really had enough mass to handle the heavy attachment.

Amelia wasn't looking forward to spending as long to unhook the plow as it had taken to connect it, so she was relieved when Burk showed up to get Mark.

Tucker tracked them to the shed, and Burk followed him in. "What's up?"

Amelia quit straining to raise the prongs of the plow up off the tractor's tail. "Trying to swap this plow out for a seed drill. You got a minute to help?"

"Sure." He was wearing walking shorts again, and his legs were starting to get tanned under the permanent sunburn—kind of a pale gold overlaid with bronze. He came over next to the plow. "Mark, you ready to yank those pins out?"

"You bet."

Amelia glanced at Mark, but for once he didn't seem to feel insulted. Maybe because Burk was so matter-of-fact about helping.

Burk lifted the plow easily. He was stronger than he looked. Nice broad shoulders, and arms with good musculature—defined, but not too bulky. "Amelia, you pull the tractor out after we unhook the other side, okay?"

She climbed onto the tractor and started it up. The engine racket was twice as loud inside the shed; she turned around in the seat so she'd know when he was ready.

Burk lifted the second prong. His shirt came untucked in the front, showing dark hair and taut stomach muscles. Mark pounced on the plow pins. Burk was still holding the attachment up, and she was just sitting there staring at him. He gave her a nod, and she collected her wits and pulled the tractor out.

When she turned around again, she saw that Burk had aligned the plow carefully on the cinder blocks to make it easier to reattach next time.

He glanced up and yelled over the din from the tractor, "Which attachment you want now?"

Amelia pointed out the seed drill, then started angling the tractor back to it. She got the tail aimed straight in and cut the engine. By the time she'd jumped down, Burk and Mark already had the drill hooked up.

"Thanks," she said. "I've been dreading this. Getting the plow hooked up was a real struggle."

Mark said, "I bet," then whistled to Tucker and ran outside.

Burk was frowning. "You did it by yourself?"

"You see anyone else around here?"

But he was shaking his head at her. "Jesus. Why didn't you just call me? Wrestling with stuff like that alone is crazy."

She shrugged and started toward the shed door. "I can't be calling for help every time I turn around."

"Amelia."

She turned back reluctantly. He was tucking in his shirt, smoothing the blue cloth along the plane of his stomach.

"Don't take chances. Having a plow fall on you could kill you. We all need help now and then—just call me next time."

When she didn't say anything, he asked. "Will you?" He looked dead serious, his gray eyes intent and watchful.

Amelia nodded. "Okay, Burk. And—thanks for the hand."

He held his out to her. After a second's hesitation, she took it.

"Any time," he said, and smiled.

She was able to begin planting as soon as it was light the next morning, starting with the basic seed varieties Gramps had stockpiled the most of: blue grama and little bluestem.

The first twenty minutes or so of planting were uneventful, almost pleasant. The early morning air was still cool, the day bright and sweet. After two days of driving it, Amelia had grown accustomed to the tractor's huge rumbling voice and bone-jarring ride. Cutting neat lines of seeding rows across the furrows was gratifying and somewhat hypnotic. She was actually restoring the Folly, just as she'd promised.

The sun had gone from cinnamon to a deep honey color when the planting rig gave a deep chug, and the regular thunk of the seed drill biting into loose earth stopped.

Having learned from the past few days, Amelia immediately cut the throttle on the tractor, then set the brake and retracted the planter.

It didn't take long to locate the trouble. The seed Gramps had harvested himself hadn't been hulled or polished the way commercial seed generally was. It was coarse with chaff, and had jammed the narrow line that fed into the drill.

She used a bit of old wire to unjam the feeder line. When she started it back up again, it worked perfectly.

For about fifteen minutes. Then it jammed again.

She ended up spending two more days planting roughly a third of the Folly, climbing down at least every half-hour to unclog the seed bit.

The job was so miserable that it was almost a relief when she ran out of seed from Gramps's cache. Until she could get some commercial seed to plant the remaining six acres with, the rest of the great restoration would have to wait.

Chapter Nine

In early October of 1983, citing the newly opened Montrose Police Substation and city-wide budget considerations, Chief Hiram Williamson announced the plainclothes foot patrol program had served its purpose and was being discontinued. Three days later, Mayor Rawlins-Caswell smiled for the news cameras as, despite narrow majorities, her gay rights and antihate ordinances were adopted by the Houston City Council.

On October 14, 1983, at the urging of her influential brother-in-law, veteran U.S. senator Robert Caswell, Marian Rawlins-Caswell announced for the Texas governor's race.

Senator Caswell flew to Houston for the announcement, which was made from the lobby of the Warwick Hotel, where the senator kept a suite of rooms. The *Patriot's* subsequent editorial speculated that, with the mayor's combination of old-money Democratic connections and tough-on-crime, diehard liberal political savvy, she would handily unseat the mush-mouthed good ol' boy of a Republican incumbent.

Reaction to her candidacy from the gay community was ebullient. Reaction from the Christian Right, the KKK, and several neo-Nazi groups was vitriolic. Mayor Rawlins-Caswell began receiving threatening mail. In response, *the city police instituted a round-the-clock guard on her home in River Oaks.*

—MOLLY CATES, "Blood Relatives,"
Lone Star Monthly, April 1986

New Mexico

Amelia was doing the breakfast dishes early Saturday morning when the phone rang. She hesitated, reluctant to answer it, but it might be Mark's mother. She wouldn't want to worry Caroline.

Her heart thumped when she heard the man's voice, but settled down when he said, "Amelia? Nick Atkinson here. How are you doing?"

Amelia had her shoulder hunched to keep the receiver against her ear while she finished drying her hands. "Okay—I've started replanting, anyway. What can I do for you?"

Nick didn't miss a beat. "Come to dinner with me tomorrow night. I thought we could drive up to the Inn of the Mountain Gods, maybe go dancing afterward."

This time he took her off guard, and Amelia hesitated before answering. The prospect of not having to spend another night alone at the ranch was appealing, but she'd get back late, and the place would have been empty all evening.

Besides, what would she wear? No. He was just too upscale.

"Thanks anyway," she said. "Can't make it tomorrow."

"Damn, Amelia. I wish you'd think about it. I worry about you, being alone out there all the time."

"Thanks for the invitation. Another time, Nick."

He sounded disappointed but accepted her turndown with as much grace as he did everything else.

After she got off the phone, Amelia went down to the milking room where Mark was. Margot had already been milked and turned out; she trotted over to butt at Amelia's thigh. Amelia flicked her on the nose. "Cut it out. That's a bad habit."

Margot backed off, shaking her head so vigorously that her ears flapped loudly against her jaw. Her expression of combined embarrassment and disgust was funny.

Amelia opened the door to the milking room. Mark looked up as she came in. Lois was already licking the bottom of her feed bin, and Mark was stripping her udder, the last stage of milking.

"Nearly half a gallon from her just this morning," Mark said. "She may not have the greatest personality, but she's an awfully good milker."

Amelia scratched along Lois's jaw. "Not going to win any Miss Congeniality contests, is she? But you're right about her yield. How're your bottle babies doing?"

His face lit up. "They've grown a lot just since last week! The county agent stopped by last night and says they're doing real well."

"That's great news," Amelia said. "You must be taking real good care of them."

He picked up the milk pail and took it to the counter. "Just doing what I'm supposed to," he said.

Amelia came over to hold the milk can steady while he screened the milk into it.

"Come on, let's get this iced down and make a run to town," she said, once he'd finished pouring. "I've got some errands to do. I want to price some firebrick."

"What's it for?" He was gathering up the pail, screen, and squirt cup to be washed and sterilized.

"A kiln," Amelia said. "For my pottery."

Mark glanced at her, but didn't say anything.

"Hey," she said. "Don't look at me like that. Sooner or later, I'll come up with something that'll sell."

She wasn't as certain as she sounded, but the truth was, she didn't really have a choice about potting. If she didn't get some clay time in soon, she'd go crazy. Shaping clay—working it with her hands—had always dimmed the fear. The only thing she could count on for oblivion.

They carried the milk and equipment up to the house. After Mark had washed up, Amelia herded him out to the truck. Once on the road, he asked what errands she was going to do.

"Gas up, price brick and pipe fittings for the kiln, check on some seed arrangements," she said.

After a minute, he looked over at her. "You won't get rid of the bees, will you? If you start doing pottery?"

"Not a chance. I've already signed nine pollinating contracts for this season."

"Good." He jiggled happily in his seat. "They're way cool."

They didn't talk much on the drive into town, but it was a comfortable silence. Somewhere in the past week, she and Mark had become friends. Realizing that troubled her a little, but she brushed it away. Nothing wrong with being neighborly.

They hit the outskirts of Tamarisco, and she turned into the lot at Peterson's Feed & Seed. Amelia stepped out of the truck and made sure her wallet was in her back pocket. "You coming?" she said to Mark.

His face was turned away from her, and he was looking at the weathered sign with its green and brown lettering.

"Mark?" she said again.

He scrunched down in the seat, still not looking at her, and said, "I'll just wait here. If you don't mind, ma'am."

That wasn't like him, and Amelia hesitated. "Well, okay," she said. "Back in a few minutes."

Another truck pulled in next to theirs and a sandy-haired man got out of it and went into the store. As she followed the man inside, Amelia noticed that a boy who looked a little older than Mark had stayed behind in the other truck.

There were half a dozen customers in the store, but none of them were in line at the counter except the man who had come in just ahead of her. Amelia waited behind him as he placed an order for five hundred pounds of sorghum and a June delivery of alfalfa seed.

The air in the store smelled thickly sweet. She found it oppressive.

Before the man finished with his delivery arrangements, the door behind them opened. Mark came over to stand at Amelia's elbow. His face had a tense set to it, and she put a hand on his shoulder. She was afraid he would be embarrassed, but she felt him relax. Had that kid in the other truck hassled him?

"Won't take long," she said softly. The sandy-haired man concluded his business at the counter and turned away. When he saw Mark, his mouth tightened.

Peterson wasn't at the counter, and Amelia was relieved. The clerk nodded when she said Mr. Peterson had told her they would special-order some seed for her, and took down the specs. A hundred pounds of blue grama and sixty of little bluestem. All she cared about this year was getting some staple grasses established. She could add variety later on.

She was handing over the address of Gramps's seed supplier when Mac Peterson came out of an office to one side.

He walked straight over to where they were standing, but to Amelia's surprise, he only nodded at her before turning his attention to Mark.

She still had her hand on Mark's shoulder; his muscles tightened under her fingers.

"Why, if it isn't young Mark. How are you, son?"

"Fine, sir." Mark's voice was almost inaudible.

"You catchin' a ride into town with Miz Rawlins?" Peterson went on. He leaned across the counter so his face was nearly level with Mark's.

Mark hesitated, and Amelia answered for him. "Mark's been helping me out at the ranch," she said. "Taking care of the goats and chores like that. Sort of a summer job."

"Why, that's fine, fine," Peterson said. "But if you want a real job, Mark, you should come work for me. I could use an extra hand right now—pay you minimum wage, just like the high school boys."

Mark seemed to shrink. "Thank you, sir," he

said after a minute, "but I'm already obligated to Ms. Rawlins."

Peterson straightened. His pale blue eyes looked milky in the dim light of the store. "Well, if you say so. Seems to me like Miz Rawlins would understand if you got a better offer, but you suit yourself, young man."

"Yes, sir."

The clerk had finished writing up Amelia's receipt, he handed it to her and said, "That total is four hundred eighty-five dollars, plus whatever the supplier charges for shipping, ma'am."

"You just put that on the Rawlins account," Peterson said. "Don't be bothering Miz Rawlins with it."

"Thanks, Mr. Peterson," she said, "but actually, this should be billed to Nick Atkinson at the Tamarisco Savings and Loan with a note that it's for native grass seed." She scrawled the address on an Ortho notepad that lay on the counter and pushed it toward the clerk. "We'd best be getting on with our errands."

Peterson nodded to her. Then he leaned toward Mark again. "The offer's open. Call me if you change your mind, young man."

"Sir." Mark's answer was barely audible.

Amelia stepped back, drawing him with her. "Thanks again, Mr. Peterson. You'll call me when the seed arrives?"

"Why, sure. We'll deliver it, if you like."

"Just give me a call," she said. "I'll decide about delivery when it gets here."

"Have a nice day," the clerk said, as they turned to go.

Reaching the door felt like an escape. Once outside, Amelia drew in a deep breath before they got into the truck. "That place bugs me," she said as they buckled themselves in.

Mark didn't answer. After a few seconds, she went on. "You seemed pretty uptight in there. You okay?" She put the truck in gear and pulled onto the highway. She still had to gas up, but her interest in pricing pipe fittings had evaporated.

Mark shook his hair back out of his face. Without looking at her, he said, "Peterson hates my mom. I don't know why he was asking me to work for him. It was weird. Skunky. He's the reason everybody—" He broke off.

"Everybody what?"

He sucked in a breath, then released it. "Hates us, I guess. I wouldn't've come along if I'd known you were going there."

A ripple of guilt ran through her. She abruptly remembered the first time she'd come to the store: *Peterson leaning across the counter and saying, "—tell you about the new folks took over the Veracruz place— woman's a butcher."*

"I'm sorry," she told Mark. "I didn't think about it ahead of time."

Mark looked at her. His bangs had already fallen into his eyes again. "Did you know?"

She hesitated. "He said something about your mom last time I came in, but—" She shook her head. "I didn't really think about it. One of the workers came over and said he's gotten kind of strange since his son died—and I was upset anyway and I just put it out of my mind."

Mark was still watching her. "What were you upset about?"

Cut straight to the heart of things, don't you? Amelia thought. "I—there were some men in the store, and they were standing . . ." She realized she couldn't explain it to him, not really. "Something happened— nothing important—but it reminded me of—of a bad time in the past. I—got rattled and left, and then I just pushed the whole thing out of my mind." Amelia guided the truck along the road, following the broken white line automatically. "I'm really sorry, Mark."

"It's okay," he said.

It was quiet for a while. Maybe he wasn't blaming her, but she felt that her answer had been inadequate. The only problem was that she didn't know how to explain it any better.

"Is that how you handle things that bug you?" he asked after a minute. "Just not think about them?"

The question was unexpected. "I never thought about it," she said, hoping to make him laugh.

He didn't even notice. He was chewing his lip.

She considered. "I guess it is how I handle things."

"Does it work?" he said.

She managed a smile. "Not very well. Maybe I should try something else. What do you do when something's bothering you?"

"I just—I don't know. Try to work through it on my own, mostly. Before my dad—well, we used to talk things out sometimes. But I try not to bother my mom with stuff. She already worries too much."

Amelia thought about Caroline Garrity. "Your mom strikes me as someone who could handle just about anything."

"Yeah, she's great. But she's got enough to deal with."

Amelia remembered feeling the same way about her own mother. That's why it had meant so much when Mama had taken her shopping for her prom dress. Their conversation had covered a lot of ground that day, from the trivial to the serious. What colors would be most becoming, how Amelia should wear her hair with a certain neckline. How her parents met, the sacrifices people made for a political career. Remembering the day now, Amelia could almost picture what her life would have been like if her mother hadn't been killed.

The taste of blood and burning was suddenly strong in her mouth, and instantly she shut away the memories again. The sour metallic tang was so overpowering that she had to roll down the window and breathe in gulps to keep from getting sick.

She held her thoughts to the mechanics of driving: the sound of the truck's motor, the gritty feel of the steering wheel under her hands. By the time they reached the gas station, the sharp, ugly taste in her mouth had faded.

Mark stayed in the truck while she pumped and paid; for once, Jorge Valdez's cheerful chatter didn't help her mood.

She and Mark made the trip back to the ranch in silence. This time it wasn't an easy one.

As soon as they got back to the ranch, Mark went to the goat pen to wash down the milking room and spread fresh bedding for Margot and Lois.

She fixed them grilled cheese sandwiches and home fries for lunch. Mark ate well, but didn't say much, and excused himself to go back to the goats right after they finished.

Amelia spent the afternoon working on the subrogated drip system for the vegetable garden. When she was ready to test it, she called Mark to come help by turning the feed from the pump off and on for her while she checked the water flow to different parts of the garden.

He helped her until time for the evening milking, but his mood was still subdued. Amelia blamed herself for taking him to Peterson's. When he went back to the goat pen, she went inside and started making bread, something she always found soothing.

She was kneading the dough when Burk came to the kitchen door—which she'd left open—and tapped.

"I thought I'd get the milk can," he said. "When it's full, it's really too heavy for Mark, but he doesn't like me to help."

"I don't think he's done with the evening milking yet." Amelia turned the dough into an oiled bowl and washed her hands. "Got time for a cup of coffee?" she asked him.

"Sure," he said. "Got an early start this morning."

"Have a seat." She poured two cups and brought them to the table. "Milk or sugar?"

"Just black," he said, taking the chair next to hers.

She sat down. He sipped his coffee and waited.

"When we went into town earlier—"

"Yeah?"

"I went by Peterson's feed store. He's special-ordering some seed for me."

Burk grimaced. "Uh-oh. Should've warned you. What'd he say to the boy?"

"Nothing, really. He just offered Mark a job. But—"

"A job? That doesn't sound so bad. Better than I would've expected, anyway. Although Mark's too young really to work a regular job—he won't turn thirteen for another couple of weeks."

"Well, he was real upset," she said. "He told me Peterson's the reason everybody hates him. And his mother. He said he didn't know why Peterson offered him a job, either. That it was weird and—and skunky."

Burk didn't say anything for a minute. "Well, he's got a point. Mac's been pretty hateful to them."

"What's going on? Why would anybody hate Caroline? She seems so kind—"

"That's just it," Burk said. "She's too kind. Peterson's only son was in a riding accident late last year. A bad one—he didn't make it. Caroline tried to help him, even though she could tell it was pretty well hopeless. Guess Mac blames her for not saving the boy."

"It's a damn shame all the way around—Rich Peterson was a fine young man."

Amelia looked out the kitchen window. Mark had come up to the yard and was having a round of rough-and-tumble with Tucker.

"As good a kid as Mark?"

"Older. But yeah."

"Then why's Peterson taking his son's death out on a kid?"

"I know it doesn't really make sense." Burk pushed a hand through his dark hair, which was tangled around his ears again. "Truth is, I doubt Mac knows why he's acting this way. Maybe because underneath he blames himself. That's hard to face."

Amelia leaned back. This she could understand. "It's hard to forgive yourself when someone dies and it's your fault."

His eyebrows went up. "I didn't say it was Mac's fault. People die all the time. Mostly it's nobody's fault."

"Not always."

"I guess not. But that's how it was with Rich. An accident, and a damn shame. He was smarter'n a whip and way too serious—he and Mark had that much in common." He paused, then added, "Amelia—"

"Mark doesn't look exactly serious right now," she said quickly, pointing out the window.

The seedlings Caroline Garrity had sent her were still in a box on the windowsill, which was blocking his view of the yard. Burk came around behind her chair so he could see. "Look at that thoughtless little cuss, spoiling my dog. Between the pair of you, he'll ruin it for sure."

"Tucker likes us," she said.

Abruptly, he squatted down next to her and took her hand. "So do I," he said. His hand was warm on hers. "And I'm worried about you. Caroline says those letters were death threats. And that you've gotten phone calls. Think they're from the same person?"

He'd startled her, but she wasn't scared of him. She studied his eyes. Frank Burkhalter was a kind person. She could just tell him. He wouldn't blame her. He would say it wasn't her fault her family had been killed. That she wasn't to blame for her kid brother having brain damage.

"I'd like to help," he said.

She could just say it, she thought. Open her mouth and say, *"It's this hate group called the Wolfen."*

But then he would want to know why she was their target—and the past wasn't something she had the strength to look at head-on. Not now. Just thinking about her mother earlier had practically made her sick.

She pulled away and stood up. "I can't talk about it."

"And I can't make you." He rose, not looking self-conscious at all. "But if you need help—or change your mind—"

"I appreciate that." She was relieved when Mark burst into the kitchen then. His cheeks were red with

exertion, and he smelled of goats and dog and the outdoors. Any lingering trouble from the encounter with Peterson seemed to have blown over.

"Hey, Burk," he said. "You ready to go? Didn't
mean to keep you waiting. Just let me get the milk poured
into the milk can, and I'll be done."

"No hurry. I've been having a cup of coffee with
your boss." He picked up his cup and set it in the sink.
"Thanks, Amelia."

"Any time," she said.

Mark was surveying the box of seedlings on her
windowsill. "We need to get these in the ground," he
said. "I better help you in the garden tomorrow after I
milk. Okay?"

"Such a deal," Amelia said. She brushed his hair
back out of his eyes. "You think I'm going to turn it
down? I'm no fool."

Burk's gaze met hers over Mark's head, and the
look on his face made her uncomfortable. *Don't be so
sure about that,* she thought. *Fools come in many guises.*

That night, a car pulled up by the gate around
nine o'clock. Amelia was reading in the living room when
she heard the engine slow and then stop. She got up right
away and went to the window by the kitchen door to see
who it was.

The moon had risen, so she could make out the
big station wagon parked by the gate. Caroline Garrity's
car.

Within a few minutes, Caroline had reached the
cottonwoods beside the house.

Amelia unlocked the kitchen door and opened it.
"Evening."

"Hi, Amelia. Sorry to drop by without calling,
but I wanted to talk to you while Mark wasn't around.
Got a minute?"

"Sure, come on in. Would you like some coffee?
It's a fresh pot."

"No, thanks anyway. But I'd love a glass of water." Caroline settled herself at the kitchen table.

Amelia brought her ice water in one of Gramma's cut-glass tumblers, then poured herself a cup of coffee and sat down too. "Having second thoughts about Mark being over here?"

Caroline took a long drink of her water, then shook her head. Wisps of dark hair were escaping from her bun, curling around her face. "No. Not that I haven't been worrying about both of you. But it's—I wanted to talk to you about Mac Peterson."

"I'm so sorry about taking Mark over there to-day—I should have realized. I can't blame you for being upset about it—"

"Oh, no. It's nothing like that," Caroline said. "Look, I'm just going to say this. I'm pretty much an outcast around here. Mac Peterson isn't the only one around here who thinks it's my fault his son died."

"Burk doesn't," Amelia said.

Caroline gave her a wry smile. "He's an old friend. Of course he gives me the benefit of the doubt. But the last thing you need is to get tarred with the same brush as me—I should have told you about it the first day I came by—"

"No, you shouldn't," Amelia interrupted. "It's none of my business."

"It's your business if it drags you into my mess. I'm really sorry, Amelia. I know I should've warned you. I guess I just wanted a friend too much—I couldn't bring myself to do what I knew was right." She gave an apologetic smile, and her eyes crinkled in that particular way that made her look like Amelia's mother

Amelia could feel her resistance to getting close to this woman crumbling like a sandbank. "You weren't afraid to get dragged into *my* mess," Amelia said. "Or if you were, you didn't let it stop you."

Caroline tucked a strand of hair back behind her ear. "Ken always said I had a way of diving straight into the thick of every crisis that came along. Guess he got tired of it after a while."

The phone rang. Amelia hesitated before she got up to answer it, worried it might be another threatening call. But it would look too strange not to answer it while

Caroline was here—and it might even be Mark calling for his mother.

"Excuse me," she said to Caroline. "Hello?"

"Amelia? It's Burk. Everything okay there?"

"Uh—fine, thanks." She glanced over her shoulder, wondering if Caroline could hear his voice.

"Mark was saying you're in the market for some brick for a kiln. You found any yet?"

It took her a second to switch tracks. "Oh—well, nothing so far, but—"

"One of my remodel customers has decided to tear out a fireplace big enough to roast a bear in. There's almost three cubes of brick to be had for salvage. You interested?"

"Well, sure. You said—a remodel customer?"

"I do construction work on the side, mostly restorations of old houses. But this job is a straight remodel, up in Ruidoso. Can you use the brick?"

"It's firebrick?"

"You bet," he said. "In good shape, too."

"Then—yes. Thanks. Thanks a lot, Burk." It was starting to sink in. She was going to have a kiln again.

"Glad to help." He sounded pleased with himself. "Got a pencil? I'll give you directions. The only thing is, you should pick it up soon."

"Tomorrow soon enough?"

He laughed. "Tomorrow's great."

After she got off the phone, Caroline gave her an interested look. "So—did he ask you out?"

Amelia stared at her, shocked. "What? No—he—he just called about having some brick for a kiln I want to build. A remodeling job he's got?"

Caroline nodded. "He does a lot of design and restoration work on the side. Did he tell you he'd almost finished his degree in architecture?"

Amelia had gone past shock to embarrassment. This was what she got for that time when she'd asked if Caroline and Burk were involved. If she expressed the least bit of curiosity now, it would just reinforce Caroline's belief that Amelia was attracted to the man. But she *was* curious, dammit. "I didn't know he did anything except deliver mail." That sounded pretty neutral. "But he dropped out before he finished?"

"Sort of. His dad died, and money was really tight," Caroline said. "And there were his two younger brothers to worry about, so he didn't finish his last year. Went to work for the post office instead of founding the new style of architecture he was always talking about. And then he and Shellie—his ex—got married . . . Maybe he'll tell you all about it sometime." She grinned, clearly aware she was only heightening Amelia's curiosity, and just as clearly enjoying it. "*After* he gets around to asking you out."

That was too much for Amelia. "No way. I mean, I like Burk, but I'm not—I don't want to get involved with him. With *anyone*. Not right now." She'd had too many bad relationships in the rough years after her parents were killed. When she finally realized that sex wasn't love, she'd quit trying. And having just lost Jeff made this a bad time to try again.

Caroline raised her eyebrows. "If you say so. But for what it's worth, I'm pretty sure he's interested."

This was getting out of hand. Amelia changed the subject. "Is it okay for Mark to come with me to collect the brick tomorrow? Up to Ruidoso?"

"Sure. He loves going to job sites with Burk." She stood up and gave Amelia a smile with extra twinkle in it. "Bet you will, too. Just try not to break his heart, okay? I better get back—don't like leaving Mark alone for too long."

Amelia got up to walk her out, and Caroline gave her an unexpected hug. She smelled faintly of verbena.

"Thanks for understanding about all this," Caroline said, her voice serious again. She went quickly out the door, leaving Amelia standing there without any idea what to think.

She had a hard time falling asleep that night. For once, it wasn't fear that kept her awake.

*   *   *

The next morning came soft and pure and sudden, in a dawn like golden lightning that didn't fade. It found Amelia shivering by the kitchen door, getting wood for the stove.

During the day, the weather was so warm you'd think the season had turned completely, but the dawn light still reflected like a blush from the snow on Sierra Blanca. Amelia could remember summers when the grandmother mountain had kept her white shawl until July.

Amelia breathed in the sharp desert air, sweetened with pine and moisture from the mountain. Her teeth were chattering when she went indoors and built up a small fire, just enough to take the chill off the house. Once she had it going, she took a shower and washed her hair. It was curling almost to her shoulders now, and tended to tangle badly. She jerked a comb through it irritably, then swabbed steam from the narrow bathroom mirror with a damp towel and examined her reflection.

Her face looked narrower, her skin more tanned than when she had first come here. Her hair had streaked from the sun and, even damp, looked more blond than brown now. Amelia pulled on her clothes, then went hunting for the scissors.

She found them in Gramma's sewing kit in the linen closet—the same small silver scissors she remembered her grandmother using when she was a child, with the delicate line of scrollwork along the handles. Amelia turned them in her hand, remembering these scissors and Gramps's pocketknife, the one with the pearl handle. Not exactly like the one Mark's father had given him, but similar. And Burk had mentioned Mark's birthday was coming up—she'd have to look for that pocketknife.

Her hair was curly but not too curly, so cutting it was fairly simple. She pulled the comb through until it was about four inches from her scalp and snipped off everything that stuck out on the other side. The haircut took about ten minutes. She was sweeping up the spilled cuttings when Mark knocked at the kitchen door.

She let him in and, before he even said good

morning, asked if he wanted to go with her to pick up the bricks for her kiln.

The drive up through the mountains was pure pleasure. She was getting used to mountain driving again, no longer unnerved by the switchbacks and tunnels and unexpected hairpin turns of Highway 82, which led to Cloudcroft. The temperature in the basin had been in the seventies, but by the time they reached Cloudcroft—topping ten thousand feet—the air was crisp and cool, somewhere in the high forties. Isolated banks of old snow remained in shaded spots, although the sun was shining brightly. It was warm inside the truck, and they traveled in silence. *We're like a couple of lizards,* Amelia thought, *so sun-drunk we don't even want to blink.*

At the crest of the mountain, they turned north, winding their way through Mescalero's lush valleys and forests, the pastures filled with glossy horses and white-faced cattle.

She noticed oncoming cars with clumps of muddy snow clinging to the fenders and ski racks on top.

"You know, I've never done any skiing," Amelia said. "Seems kind of a waste. I mean, here's a major ski area, practically in our backyard—"

Mark was grinning. "There's a missile range in our backyard, too, but that doesn't mean we have to do something with it."

"You got a smart mouth, you know that?" she said. "Okay, here we go." She slowed as they reached the Ruidoso city limits. The main street had a resortish look to it: upscale shops right next to convenience stores, all backed by large clusters of condos. She checked the directions Burk had given her and made a right turn, then a left.

They were immediately in a residential area, one where the homes were large and impressive. The yards were plush with tall pines and evergreen shrubs, frosted with softened clumps of snow.

"Help me watch for sixteen-oh-four," she told

Mark. She didn't know if the house number would be visible, since the place was being remodeled.

He spotted the place first. "There it is."

A fleet of pickup trucks and a Dumpster blocked the front of the house. Amelia spotted a metal yard sign that read "Tucker Construction, Historic Renovation and Remodeling," with a phone number underneath.

"Yep, this is the one," she said. She pulled the truck to the side of the road farther up the hill.

Mark came along with her without any hesitation this time.

An Hispanic man about twenty years old was pounding a loose surveyor's stake back into the ground along the property line.

"Hi," Amelia said. "I'm looking for—"

The man shrugged, and said, *"Lo siento, señora. No hablo inglés."*

"Está bien," Amelia said. *"¿Dónde está el jefe, por favor?"*

He pointed toward the open garage of the house. *"Por allá,"* he said, then called, *"¡Señor Burk! Una señora quiere hablar contigo."*

"Gracias." She walked toward the garage.

Burk came out carrying a thick slab of yellow pine with dovetail joints carved in one end. He was stripped to the waist in spite of the chilly weather. Tiny curls of wood clung to his skin and tangled in the dark hair on his chest. She thought the smell of fresh-cut wood was sexier than any cologne.

"Glad you found the place okay," he said. "Hey, you cut your hair. It looks great. It's curlier when it's short."

She'd forgotten about cutting it. "Oh—it was getting in my eyes." *Was* he interested in her? Or was Caroline matchmaking?

"Where's Tucker?" Mark asked.

Burk gave him a playful poke in the ribs. "He picked up a nail in his paw last time I brought him out here—he's staying home till it heals." He turned to Amelia. "C'mon. The brick's back here."

He showed her to the side yard, where there was

a large tumble of oversized brick. "We were careful pulling the fireplace down," he said. He laid the piece of lumber aside, and picked up one of the pale yellowish bricks. "They should be in good shape."

Amelia stooped to examine the bricks. Firebrick all right, most of it soft—the more porous kind of brick she needed for the interior of the kiln. And there looked to be enough hard brick to insulate the outside. She was already sketching kiln dimensions in her head.

"So, can you use it?" Burk asked. He sounded anxious.

"It's perfect," she said. She looked up and met his eyes. "Really. Thank you."

She turned to Mark, who had trailed after them. "I'm just going to pull the truck up. Wait here, okay?"

Burk said, "Loading these by hand'll take a while. Shame they're not banded. And that truck of yours probably can't haul but about a third of them—too much weight for the engine."

"Yeah. I figured I'd end up making several trips."

"Oh, no. No need to do that. We're going to knock off here in an hour or so. I'll have the guys load the rest of the brick on my flatbed. I can come by your place on the way home and drop it off."

"That's too much trouble—and you're already giving me the brick—"

He smiled at her. Wood curls were caught in his hair and eyebrows, too, like shavings of pale gold frost. She had to fight the urge to brush them off. "My pleasure, Amelia. Go ahead and get started—I'll see you down at your place before long."

Someone called to him from the house then, and he picked up the piece of lumber and walked away, the muscles in his back standing out as he steadied the board on his shoulder. He might be thin, but he had great shoulders.

Amelia looked after him for a moment, then went for the truck. It took some cautious maneuvering, but she was able to ease it into the side yard and back it up to the brick pile. Burk sent two helpers named Guillermo and José over to load. Neither of them spoke much

English, but her Spanish was good enough to get by. Mark stacked the bricks in the bed of the truck while she, Guillermo, and José used a wheelbarrow to shift them from the pile. As they worked, she took a rough count. She was going to get that walk-in kiln she wanted, as big as the one she and Jeff had built a few years back.

Loading her truck took all four of them the better part of an hour. When they were done, Amelia thanked Burk's helpers, then looked over the neat basket-weave stack of brick Mark had made, layered three deep in the bed of the pickup.

Burk was up on the roof now, where he and one of his men were framing in the gables of a new addition. She called another thank-you to him before getting in the truck. He glanced down and waved to her, smiling.

"We'll have to take it slow going downhill with this load," she said, easing the truck carefully back out of the yard.

"Yeah?" Mark said. "Think we might need the runaway truck ramp?"

She finished negotiating the curb, then glanced at him. "Hope on, hope ever."

He grinned. "Hey, I didn't know you could speak Spanish."

"I grew up speaking Spanish," she said.

"How come?" Mark said.

"Well." She pulled out onto the main street cautiously, shifting gently to ease the strain on the old truck's transmission. "My father taught Spanish literature at Rice. He always used to read to us in Spanish when we were kids."

It was an old pain, buried under a twelve-year accumulation of scar tissue, but she couldn't talk about him without seeing his face slack and waxen, a spill of blood blackening his chin. Her stomach was already starting to tighten.

So she was glad when Mark said, "I like to read, too—did you ever read *The Outsiders*? It's so cool—"

They talked books all the way down the mountain. Amelia was feeling so good, she stopped in Alamogordo and treated to burgers before they headed back to the ranch.

As they rounded the last curve to home, Mark yelled, "Look out!"

Amelia had already seen the goats and hit the brakes as hard as she dared with this heavy load. Lois and Margot scampered off down the road, their hooves clicking on the pavement.

"How the hell did they get out?"

"I—I don't know," Mark said. "I closed the gate to their pen, I swear it."

She pulled the truck over and got it stopped. She tried to speak more calmly. "Of course you did. C'mon, let's get them back in the pen before someone runs them over."

It was easier said than done. The goats had moved farther along the roadside, to a spot where the barbed wire fence jogged inward around a pile of boulders. The goats were apparently enjoying their freedom; they dodged nimbly when Amelia approached. Mark tried to get behind Lois and head her off, but she made a quick jump up onto the rocks, while Margot squeezed between the fence and the boulders and scooted away.

Mark circled around to herd Margot back closer to the gate. She bounced out into the middle of the road again. Lois bleated and scrambled higher up the rock pile. Amelia took a few steps back and signaled to Mark. He edged closer to Margot. She danced along the road toward Amelia, then darted off to the other side just as Amelia made a grab for her.

"This isn't going to work," Amelia said. "Why don't you keep them off the road while I go get their harnesses, okay?"

"Sure," Mark said. "Or I can go get the stuff if you want."

"Nah. I can take the truck—it'll be quicker." She went quickly, glancing behind her once to see Mark shoo Margot back toward the rocks.

She opened the main gate and drove straight to

the goat pen. She was hurrying as she came around the back end of the pickup, and the twisted bumper that stuck out clipped her knee. The bladelike piece of metal sliced straight through her jeans.

Amelia swore, then forgot about it. She didn't have time for Band-Aids right now. The goat pen gate was swinging slightly in the wind. She took a moment to check the latch and saw it was undamaged. The goats' harness was in its usual spot in the milking room, but as she glanced around, Amelia had the feeling something was out of place. She hesitated, then took the harnesses and tethers down and ran back toward the road. They could look things over later.

When she got back out to the road, Burk was there. He and Mark were standing calmly by a Supercab truck that had been converted to a flatbed. It was loaded with her brick, and Lois and Margot were tethered to it with nylon line. Tucker was sprawled by the front bumper. The two guys were wearing identical, self-satisfied grins.

"Fast work," she said, laughing. "Thanks."

Burk smiled at her. He was wearing a T-shirt now, and his eyes were shaded by the brim of a cowboy hat. She thought their expression didn't quite match his smile.

"No problem," he said. "Everything okay back there?"

"Sure," Amelia said. Tucker ambled over then, but before she could scratch his ears, Lois turned and butted at him. Tucker gave a startled *whoof* and belly-crawled under the truck.

Mark burst into laughter. Amelia glanced at Burk. His mouth was still curved in a faint smile, but all he said was, "Tit for tat, Tucker."

She handed one of the harnesses to Mark. "Okay. Let's go." She slipped the other harness on Lois and removed the nylon line. Burk took it and tossed it into the truck cab.

Mark headed through the gate of the ranch, leading Margot. Amelia turned to follow him, but Burk stepped in front of her.

"Hang on, there—you're bleeding."

She glanced down. The sliced denim above her knee was red. "Caught it on the bumper of the truck is all," she said. "Just being clumsy—it's nothing serious."

"If you say so. Mark's sure he left the goats shut in their pen. How'd they get out?"

"Don't know. When I got there, the gate was open."

"What about the latch? Can they open it?"

"They never have before," she said. "And not for lack of trying."

He was frowning. "Mark's worried you'll think he wasn't careful with the gate, but he swears he shut it."

"He's been real responsible," she assured him, "and the goats are fine. Everything's okay."

"Yeah, but—"

"But what?" she asked when he didn't go on.

He pulled his hat off and smoothed a hand over his tangled hair. "Never mind. Go ahead. I'll bring the truck through and close the gate."

She and Mark got the goats settled back in their enclosure and checked the latch on the gate. It seemed to hold fine. They were turning back toward the house when Amelia hesitated.

"Notice anything funny inside? When you were putting the harness away?" she asked.

Mark glanced back, eyes narrowed against the afternoon sun, then shook his head.

His straight brown hair was in his eyes again, and the sun struck veins of pure gold in it. Amelia wished she had a camera.

"Want me to go back and look again?" he said.

"It's okay. Probably just my overactive imagination. And Burk's waiting for you—I'll handle the evening milking tonight. In fact, I'll cover the evening chores from now on—you've been putting in more hours than a few gallons of milk is worth."

They headed for the house. After a few seconds,

Mark said, "I really did latch the gate, Amelia." He peered up at her through the shaggy bangs.

She couldn't resist brushing them back. "I'm sure you did," she said. "Don't worry."

The worst part was that she *was* sure he'd shut it. Which meant someone or something had come along after they left and opened it again.

She invited Burk in for coffee, and sent Mark to play catch with Tucker. Amelia was plugging in the coffeepot when the phone rang.

She hesitated, reluctant to answer it. "Excuse me. Hello?"

"Hi, Amelia," Nick Atkinson said. His voice had a resonant quality, even over the phone. "How are you?"

"Fine, thanks. I've got company right now—" She figured he was going to ask her out again, and didn't want Burk listening to her turning him down.

"Well, I won't keep you. But I'm afraid we've got a problem. Apparently, you've changed the locks to the gate and house?"

That took her by surprise. "How'd you know?"

"Remember," Atkinson said mildly, "as trustee, I'm supposed to have a set of keys."

She did tend to forget about his being the trustee. After all, this was her home. She fought back a surge of annoyance. It wasn't in her best interest to antagonize Nick Atkinson. "Sorry," she said. "I didn't think about that."

Burk was watching her. "Everything okay?" he asked quietly.

She nodded. Atkinson was talking again.

"Sorry to be such a stickler," Nick said, "but I do have to have access to the place—I'm supposed to inspect it at least once a month."

He sounded so apologetic, Amelia's annoyance faded. She said, "I just didn't trust locks that umpteen other caretakers have had the keys—"

"Hey, I understand completely. No big deal. But could you drop off a duplicate set next time you're in town?"

"Sure," Amelia said. "Next chance I get."

"Good," Nick said. She could tell he was smiling. "At least this way I'll get to see you again."

"Who was that?" Burk asked, after she'd hung up.

The coffee was done perking. She pulled down a couple of mugs and poured. "Atkinson—my grandfather's trustee—he was calling to ask for a set of keys. I changed the locks out here without telling him."

Burk sat down next to her and laid his hat on the table before taking a sip of coffee. "Nick Atkinson, from the savings and loan? What business is it of his? Mr. Rawlins left this place to you outright, didn't he?"

"Yes. But . . ." She drank some coffee, enjoying its scalding temperature. "You see, I haven't actually dissolved the trust my grandfather set up."

"Trust?" Burk went on, "Like I said, I always had the impression that he meant to leave it to you outright."

"He did. The trust was just to—to hold the ranch until I—till I came home. I'll have to get an extra set of keys cut and drop them off at his office tomorrow."

"You know your own business best."

"Wait a minute," she said. "Do you think Nick—Nick Atkinson—was out here while we were gone? And left the gate open?"

Burk gave her a level look. "Why would your banker bother your goats?"

She got up and brought the coffeepot to the table. "He's not my banker, he's my grandfather's," she said, refilling their cups. "Okay, so he's not the type to dirty his handmade shoes in a stock pen. It's a silly idea—"

Burk smiled. "You could always ask him."

Amelia thought about it, then shook her head. "No, I'll just take him the keys. I'll have to settle things eventually—but I've got bigger worries right now. Like making a go of this bee business, so I can pay Mary Zuniga and her cousin back."

His hat was lying on the table. He adjusted its position, then looked up and met her eyes. "That's important to you."

"Of course," she said, surprised.

"Maybe it comes from living in a small town," he said, "but most folks around here are pretty used to helping each other out. It's no big thing to lend a hand now and then. After all, what goes around comes around."

"I had to learn to stand on my own two feet pretty early. Guess it got to be a habit."

"Self-sufficiency is all well and good, but I've learned that sometimes our habits hold us back," he said.

She shrugged, uncomfortable with the turn the conversation had taken.

"Well, I better run Mark home now, before Caroline sends out a search party." He paused, a thoughtful expression on his face. "Then again, maybe she's been reading 'The Ransom of Red Chief,' and will make me pay before she takes him back."

Amelia laughed. "Always a possibility. Burk—I can't tell you how much I appreciate your giving me the brick. Not to mention hauling it down here."

"My pleasure," he said. He smiled and added, "I forgot all about the brick on my truck, though—and I'm pretty well whipped. How about I swing by tomorrow evening after work? Okay if we unload it then instead?"

"Whenever suits you," she said. "I'm lucky to be getting it delivered."

"Remember that when we're lugging bricks around at midnight tomorrow," he said wryly, and she laughed again.

But then Burk was always making her laugh. No wonder she enjoyed having him around. He put the milk can in the truck while she rounded up the boy and the dog. Burk waved to her before he pulled away.

The place seemed way too quiet after the sound of the truck's engine faded. She called to Gramps, but got no answer.

Amelia walked down to the goat pen to check on things. Everything was fine. Margot and Lois were having a little siesta in the shade.

"Resting up after your adventure?" she said.

Lois blinked lazily a couple of times, but neither of the animals moved.

The goats had the right idea—right now, a siesta would be wonderful. But she didn't have the excuse of having put in a full morning of carpentry work, and there were bricks to unload.

She searched every drawer and cupboard in the house that night—even in Michael's old room—looking for Gramps's pearl-handled knife. She couldn't find it. Maybe she could buy a similar one in town, but it would have to be used for her to afford it. She decided to ask Mr. Valdez who in town carried knives.

Then she fell into bed exhausted. Her back ached and her hands burned with scratches from handling so much brick, even though she'd worn work gloves. In spite of her weariness, she slept fitfully.

The windmill whisked outside her window in a continuous grumble. She dreamed that she lay on the floorboards of a van, listening to rough-voiced men argue. She strained to understand—what they were saying was important—but she could make no sense of their words.

When she woke, panicked, the mutter of their voices seemed to continue for a moment, somewhere above her head.

"Who's there?" she cried out.

Silence. *Nothing but a dream,* she told herself.

Or ghosts, muttering to each other in the dark.

Chapter Ten

Halloween in Montrose has always been a crush. The streets become thronged with cars and pedestrians, and temporary "No Left Turn" signs are installed on Shepherd Drive and Westheimer Boulevard. The wait to get into area clubs and restaurants rarely runs under an hour and can swell to three or four at the most popular venues.

In the mid-eighties, drinking, drugging, and screwing formed a continuous backdrop to life in Montrose, and were never more extravagant than during the Halloween weekend.

To imagine a Montrose Halloween in those years, picture Mardi Gras without parades or krewes. The event was instead given its distinct flavor by tiny sugar-candy skulls, chains of tissue-paper skeletons, and hordes of outrageously dressed transvestites: equal parts Dia de los Muertos and Rocky Horror.

In 1983, the Halloween weekend unfolded into an electrifying, madly campy, pheromone-powered Monster Mash. Mayor Rawlins-Caswell's campaign committee planned a major political fund-raiser for Friday night at Numbers, one of the most popular clubs in the district. The ultraconservative Houston Record *was not amused.*

—MOLLY CATES, "Blood Relatives,"
Lone Star Monthly, April 1986

New Mexico

When she woke the next morning, Gramps's pocketknife was on the small cherry-wood table beside her bed. Amelia picked it up and smoothed the handle with her thumb. "Thanks, Gramma," she said softly. She found some tissue paper and wrapped it up before Mark arrived. She would give it to him for his birthday.

It was a Monday. When Mark got there, Amelia decided to walk down to the goat pen with him. Whatever subtle difference she'd been aware of in the milking room yesterday was still nagging at her, even though she hadn't been able to put her finger on precisely what it was.

Mark was acting a little stiff, and she realized he was offended, thinking she didn't trust him anymore.

"Mark," she said, as the lights came on in the milking room. "Remember I thought I noticed something different in here yesterday? I only came down here with you to try to figure out what it was. I know you take good care of the goats."

He froze with his hand on one of the harnesses and looked at her for a moment before lifting it down. His hair was hanging in his eyes, as usual. "If you say so."

Amelia's shoulders were sore from hauling brick yesterday, and she hadn't slept well. She mastered the impulse to snap at him. They could talk about this more later on, when she felt less ragged herself.

Mark went and collected Lois. As he buckled the goat into the milking stall, Amelia looked over the small milking room, trying to detect what was wrong with the picture.

She'd scrounged an old white enamel kitchen cabinet from the tractor shed to use in here. It was in its normal place, with the milking equipment stowed as usual.

The milking stand couldn't be moved; it was

bolted into the concrete slab, in case the goats got too frisky. Once they were buckled into the stand, they couldn't really make much trouble. Of course, getting them buckled in was another story.

Mark handled it well, though. Even Lois—not the good-tempered sort—had stepped docilely into the stand, and let him buckle her in. Now she was waiting for him to bring her feed. Mark went to the thirty-gallon plastic garbage bin where they stored the grain and pulled the tightly fitted cover off it.

His face scrunched. "Eew," he said. "This smells funny."

Amelia joined him at the bin. They fed the goats a grain mixture of corn, oats, wheat bran, molasses, soybean oil meal, and a little salt. Ordinarily, the mixture was moist and smelled sweet and a little yeasty.

But this morning, the contents of the bin had a distinctly metallic odor. "No kidding," Amelia said.

Mark leaned closer, his nose wrinkled up. "Does it look a little green to you?"

She took the lid from him and put it back on the container. "You're right. This is what was bugging me. See how the bin's pulled out from the corner? It was right up against the wall yesterday morning. And now something's wrong with the feed."

Mark was frowning. "You think it's some kind of mold?"

"I don't know," Amelia said. "Maybe. But it's also possible that something got put in the feed."

"You mean like sabotage? Why would anyone do that?"

"No telling. But don't feed this to the goats. I'll mix another batch up from the stores in the barn—give me fifteen minutes or so, okay? It won't make you miss the bus, will it?"

He glanced at Lois, who had realized her feed bin was empty and was already exhibiting her displeasure. "I'll turn her back out in the pen. She won't like it, but she'll get over it."

"I'll bring the fresh batch of grain as soon as I can. Go ahead and give them some hay. They'll be fine."

Amelia left the milking room and circled around to the entrance of the tractor shed. Once inside, she made a point of looking things over, but the tractor was still under its tarp, the stored bales of hay still stacked neatly against the back wall.

She measured out the contents of a tub of wheat bran, then spent a few minutes recalculating the measures for the other ingredients. As she worked, her frustration grew. How could she be sure what had happened to the grain? Replacing two hundred pounds of feed was the last thing she could afford. Maybe she was just getting paranoid. She started mixing the molasses through the bran. Mark came in to get another minibale of alfalfa hay.

"Is the stuff in here okay?" he asked.

"Seems to be."

"You going to take the old stuff to the county agent?"

Amelia was measuring salt. "What for?"

"For testing. To find out what's wrong with it."

She looked up. Mark was waiting in the doorway, his arms quivering slightly under the weight of the bale. "Oh. Yeah, maybe. Go ahead, I'll be around in a minute with their ration."

"Okay."

Amelia finished mixing the feed. Only about twenty pounds to this batch of rations—less than a week's worth of feed for the two goats. She didn't want to think what it would cost to replace the stores.

And the start-up money Mary had loaned her was nearly gone.

Burk stopped by the ranch around noon to see how the goats were. When she told him about the feed, he seconded the idea of taking a grain sample to the county agent. Amelia was noncommittal, but Burk pointed out that the feed might still be usable, which was enough to persuade her. She scooped a couple of cups of the greenish, odd-smelling mixture into a canning jar and drove to Alamogordo, to the courthouse where the county agent's office was. A guard at the front desk gave her instructions to the agent's office.

Amelia thanked him and followed the instructions, her boot heels echoing on the floor tiles. She passed a dozen people on the way. Most of them were in line outside the Department of Motor Vehicles.

The agent was younger than she expected—in his early thirties, she guessed—with thinning reddish hair and a cheerful, rounded face. He was sitting at a desk awash in folders and papers, and wore a harried expression. Amelia thought he looked relieved when she rapped on the open door.

"Morning, ma'am," he said, standing up. "Can I help you?"

"I'm Amelia Rawlins," she said.

"Jerry Garner," he said. "You must be Hector's granddaughter. Good to meet you." She shook his hand and sat down in the guest chair squeezed in front of his desk.

She pulled her backpack onto her lap and removed the jar of feed. "This grain ration looks like something's been added to it. Or maybe it's some kind of mold—I don't know enough to tell." She handed the jar across to him. "When we went out to feed the goats this morning, my—my helper noticed that it smelled funny."

Garner had screwed the lid off the jar and dumped some of the grain out into his palm. He rubbed it between his fingers, then lifted it to his nose and sniffed. "Well, I'll have it tested," he said, "but it smells like LPS to me. It's a commercial mineral supplement that lots of folks add to their grain mix. You don't use it?"

Amelia shook her head. "Here. I wrote down the grain recipe for you. Thought you'd need it." She took it out of her wallet and gave it to him.

Garner had taken a sample bag from one of the drawers. While she watched, he jotted something on the bag with a black felt-tip pen, then shook about half the grain inside. "Don't feed this until we get an answer back from Santa Fe," he said. "I'd stake my hat on it being LPS, but best not take chances."

"How long do you think it'll take?"

"Should hear within the week," he said. "You hired a new hand or something? Someone who might've meddled with your feed?"

"I thought of that. But the truth is, I only have a neighbor kid helping out on the place. And he's the one who first noticed the difference. If he'd added something, I don't think he would have turned around and pointed it out to me."

Jerry Garner was frowning at the stack of leaflets on his desk. They were sagging sideways at an acute angle now. "Keep an eye on the place, then. We don't have a lot of trouble around here, but you never know." He stood up and offered his hand. "I'll give you a call when we get the lab results."

Amelia stood up and shook hands. "Thanks."

"Any time."

She paused in the hallway outside the D.M.V. office to zip up her backpack. As she was wrestling with the zipper, someone touched her shoulder. She nearly dropped the pack when she twisted around to see who it was.

"Miss Caswell? How good to see you again."

She didn't immediately recognize his face; it was the softly accented voice that clicked things into place for her. "Señor Jarmel," she said, drawing back a step. "How are you?"

He smiled, his face creasing. "I am well, Miss Caswell. And you? You have found an outlet for your work, I trust?"

"No, you were right—no one would take it."

"How unfortunate," he said. "I hope you are continuing to search—perhaps one of the galleries in Santa Fe—"

"Well, the main thing is to make a living. A friend has helped me restart my grandfather's beekeeping business."

He was frowning. "Unfortunate," he repeated. "You have real talent. But we all do what we must." He glanced at his watch. "You must excuse me—I have an appointment."

"Of course, Señor," she said.

"I hope you will come to see me again when time permits. Good afternoon, Miss Caswell." He turned and walked toward the courthouse door.

Amelia watched him leave, then turned her thoughts to practical matters. She'd intended to replace the goats' feed while she was in Alamogordo, hoping for a better price in the larger town. But since Garner thought there was a chance it would still be safe to feed the altered grain, she decided to put off buying more. Maybe they'd hear back from Santa Fe before the fresh batch she'd mixed that morning ran out.

When she got outside, she found Nick Atkinson leaning against her truck. He saw her and straightened, smiling.

"Hi, Amelia. What are you doing in Alamogordo? When I saw your truck, I thought I'd wait a few minutes, try and catch you. How are you doing?"

"Just fine," she said. "Afraid I haven't had copies of those keys made yet, but it'll only take a few—"

"Did I give you that hard a time about it? I'm sorry. I wanted to tell you something—not give you a hard time about keys. Got a minute to have a cup of coffee with me?"

She hesitated. "Well, sure."

He took her elbow and steered her across the street to the White Sands Café. He chose a booth by the front window. His long legs didn't fit under his side of the table. To avoid tangling her feet with his, she turned sideways in the booth. Sunshine poured through the window's painted sign, falling on his face in sharp-edged shadows.

Nick held up two fingers, and the waitress brought them coffees. "Thanks, Marilyn," he said, adding a big dollop of cream to his. "Amelia, when I saw your truck in front of the courthouse, I realized I never followed up on sending you a copy of your grandfather's will. I'm so sorry to have forgotten—"

"Oh, I wasn't at the courthouse for that," she said. "Had to see the county agent about something."

"Oh. That's good. Long as it's not about a problem," he said.

She sipped her coffee. "Things are fine, thanks."

"Well, I'd heard you'd had a little trouble out there."

"What did you hear?"

He paused with his cup halfway to his mouth. "Nothing specific, really. You know how people talk. But I'd be glad to help out—you know that, don't you?"

"Nice of you," she said. This was making her uncomfortable.

He leaned toward her. "Wanted to let you know that I got a call from your uncle this week. Just routine, checking in."

Amelia set down her coffee cup. Her stomach was already knotting up. "You—you didn't say anything about me, did you?"

"No," he said slowly. "Although I probably should have. You've got me bending the rules right and left, Amelia. But you said you hadn't been in touch with him—and you seemed so nervous about talking to him—"

She could breathe again. "So you didn't say anything?"

"No. But have you considered talking to him yourself? He's such a nice man. I've been thinking of running for public office myself, actually—at the state level—and he took the time to talk to me about it. Gave me some excellent advice."

Her fingers were cold. She laced them around her cup, and tried to think. She had wondered why Nick Atkinson seemed so interested in her. Was this the reason? He wanted a political connection to her uncle? If so, he was way off base.

"I think he'd be thrilled to see you," Nick went on. "If it's a matter of airfare—I mean, if you'd rather talk to him face to face, I'd be glad to loan you—"

She shoved the coffee cup away and scrambled out of the booth, stepping on his foot in the process. "Thanks for the coffee. I'll get you those keys soon."

Nick stood, far more gracefully than she had. "Amelia—"

The bells on the café door jangled as she jerked it

open. Nick didn't follow, but she could feel him watching her as she crossed the street to the truck and made her escape.

When she got back to the ranch, she drove straight down to the honey house. She did a quick walk-through inspection of the hives, refilling the feed jars with syrup. The repetitive work calmed her, and she thought the bees were in good shape.

Finding someone to help move the hives had been one of her biggest worries, but the last time she'd stopped for gas at Mr. Valdez's little store, he'd asked her, "*¿Señora, es colmenera?*"

Amelia wasn't used to thinking of herself as a beekeeper, so she had paused before saying that yes, she was keeping bees now.

Mr. Valdez had been delighted. He introduced her to his son, Mannie, a farmer who raised specialty *chiles* in the Mesilla Valley near Las Cruces. He had come up to Tamarisco to deliver some *chile ristras*—gorgeous fat plaits of dried, dark-red chiles—for his father to sell at the store.

Mannie was interested in pollination for his second pepper crop, which he would be planting in early July. "Would you be interested in handling the pollinating for it, ma'am?" he asked politely. "My farm is certified organic, so you wouldn't have to worry anything would happen to your bees."

"You bet," she said. "I don't have any contracts for July. But I have to warn you, I haven't got anyone lined up to help me shift the hives yet."

"How are you moving the bees?" Señor Valdez put in.

"I'll be using my pickup truck. But it'll take at least two trips, so the distance I have to bring the bees is a major cost factor for me. Mannie's farm is about sixty miles from here? That'll affect the per-hive rental, I'm afraid."

Mannie had pointed to a twenty-foot flatbed truck parked outside. "Would all the hives fit on there?"

"Sure, easy," Amelia said.

"How's this sound? I'll bring my truck and help you move the hives for the whole season, however many times you need me to. And then you pollinate my pepper crop for me in exchange. What do you think?"

Amelia thought it over for about five seconds. "I think it's a great idea. I need to make the first move in four days—can you come out about six in the evening and help then?"

They had settled the details. Mr. Valdez had even offered to sell jars of her honey at his store, while Mannie said he could take honey to the farmer's market with him, too. They'd given her one of the gorgeous *chile ristras* to seal the bargain. Amelia had walked away feeling like her worries were over.

They weren't, of course.

Once she'd calmed down after hearing about Nick's phone call from her uncle, she sat in the honey house and read through the manual for the hive carrier. She wanted to be absolutely sure she knew how to use the carrying handles. A hive with two supers weighed over a hundred pounds; she didn't want to drop one.

"Wonder how much it would cost to have Mayflower move thirty-six hundred pounds of beehive?" she said aloud.

"They charge extra for hazardous wildlife," Gramps said.

She turned. He was perched on a five-gallon honey drum near the door. She had left it open; sunshine streamed through the doorway onto the floor in front of him. Surprising how noticeable the absence of a shadow was—it made the whole picture look wrong, somehow.

"How'd you move all those bees around so much?" Amelia said.

He raised his eyebrows at her. "Used to rent an old vegetable hauler for the season. Plus I hired help."

"Weren't your helpers afraid of getting stung?"

"Well, I always kept the hives closed up nice and snug," he said. "And there's always guys up from Juarez who want work bad. I paid a good wage."

Her mother would have disapproved. She would

have said Gramps was taking unfair advantage of the illegals. Her position on immigration had been one of the things the right-wingers had screamed about—

Amelia shoved the memories away and took the carrier handles out to a hive. The center opened out and fit down over the hive, then attached to the narrow hive handles on either side.

"Gramps—"

He had squatted down next to a stack of old hive frames and was examining them. "Yeah?"

"Atkinson knew I'd changed the locks out here. Did you—" She hesitated. "Have you seen him out here lately? By the goat pen, maybe?"

"Nah, haven't seen him around since right after you got here. But it's none of his business if you change the locks."

"Well—he's the trustee and has some say right now. Till things are settled. Have you noticed anyone messing with the goats?"

"Don't see why it's not settled," Gramps said. He had his head cocked as he checked the brood comb. "Shoot. You got mouse damage on some of these, Melia. You'll have to replace 'em."

"We don't need any more, do we? The hives are all set up."

"You'll want to split off some colonies sometime in June, else you'll get swarms."

"So I have to wire in more of that foundation wax?" she said. "Now there's something to look forward to."

He grinned. "You're the one who was so fired-up about beekeeping. This is just part of the job."

"You're an inspiration to me, you know that?"

Gramps drifted over and leaned against the truck. "You haven't been up to the Folly in a while."

"No, sir." She moved around the hive.

"You go and forget about it, Melia?"

"No, sir," she repeated. She looked up, steeling herself against the reproof she expected to see in his eyes. He was gazing toward the Folly with a wistful expression. "I'm sorry, Gramps. I'll finish planting—soon as the seed comes."

He was still watching the distance.

"Gramps? Remember the time I came out here on spring break when I was nine? You and Gramma picked me up at the airport in El Paso." It had been the first time she'd ever flown by herself. Seeing their faces in the crowd after that solo flight had been the real home-coming.

"Course I remember," he said.

"You wanted me to come grass hunting with you the next day, and I wanted to help Gramma in the garden. She was giving her roses their spring feeding."

He didn't say anything, but she could tell he was listening.

"You got your feelings hurt and went by yourself," she said.

"Your grandmother fussed at me about that later. Said you needed to be close to home for a day or so, after taking the plane out by yourself."

"That's right," Amelia said. "I did. Then you and I went out together on the third day, and found a stand of red-grass putting up shoots over by the railroad easement." She rocked back on her heels. "The Folly's important to me, too, Gramps. Taking care of this ranch—everything about it matters to me."

He looked at her then. "Guess I'm forgetting how much work this place is. I know you've got a lot on your hands." He flexed his big fingers. "Wish I could be more help."

"I wouldn't be making it without you. Any tips on how this contraption works?"

"Why don't you and your helper practice a few times," Gramps suggested. "Get a feel for it—you'll need to raise them nice and smooth to reduce the strain on the hive. You've never seen such a mess as a hive coming apart in the middle of a move."

"Now there's a cheery picture." She was really dreading the first transfer. She put the carrier back inside and locked up.

"You'll do fine," he said. "You're entitled to a little beginner's luck."

"Hope whoever's in charge of luck agrees with you."

They heard the truck at the same time. The trees lining the wash blocked her view of the ranch road from the highway. Amelia jumped into the bed of her pickup to get a better look, but couldn't see over the trees. She'd left the gate unlocked for Burk, but it was early for him to be here.

A shiny white Supercab pulled into the dirt circle between the outbuildings and stopped next to the tractor shed. Mac Peterson got out. When he saw Amelia, he waved.

She walked up to meet him. The sun was westering, warm on her face, and she tugged her hat lower over her eyes.

"Afternoon, Miz Rawlins," he called. "Your seed came in."

"That's fast." She felt more awkward than ever with him now, knowing he'd given the Garritys such a hard time.

"Yes'm. They were quick about shipping it. Called out here couple a times, but got no answer. So I just brought it along."

She nodded. "Been working outside most of the day."

"Well. Probably need you an answering machine, ma'am." Sunlight gleamed on his silver hair as he glanced around. "Place is looking good."

"Thank you," she said. She walked around to the bed of his truck. It was piled with twenty-pound burlap seed sacks. Amelia picked the first one up. The seed shifted inside the bag as she held it, nestling against her.

"Young Mark around?" Peterson asked. "Or we going to have to unload all this ourselves?"

"Afraid we're on our own," she said, slinging the bag to her shoulder. She balanced it there as she unhooked her keys from her beltloop and opened the doors to the shed. The lights came on as she went in, and she put the seed bag on a big table Gramps always used for laying out engine parts when he worked on equipment. Keeping it up off the floor might delay trouble with insects and mice. If she was lucky.

Peterson came in with a bag over each shoulder, and Amelia went back out to get another. She didn't try to match him; she settled for taking one bag at a time. He might be in his fifties, but he hauled these things every day. They got the hundred and sixty pounds of seed unloaded in under five minutes.

Neither of them said much as they worked, but as they were stacking the last few sacks, Peterson asked, "So Mark isn't working over here anymore? That job offer I made him is still open."

She hated people asking her questions. Her instinct was to stonewall him. But he'd gone out of his way to help her.

"He works mostly mornings," she said. "I'll let him know you're still interested." She went out into the sunshine, glad of its brilliance, and waited by the door until Peterson followed. She fastened the padlock carefully and checked to be sure it had caught.

Then she shook hands with him. "Thank you for bringing this out, sir. And for handling the order for me."

"Anytime, Miz Rawlins," he said. He climbed back into the big white truck, put it in gear, and gave a wave out the window as he pulled away.

Amelia watched until the truck was off the property, then headed back to the honey house. Gramps was gone when she got there.

She finished up with the bees a little before sundown. Evening shadows pooled across the ranch, and the air chilled. As she walked up toward the house, Burk pulled in at the ranch gate and jumped out to open it. He had brought the rest of her brick.

Just thinking about unloading it made her shoulders hurt. But she waved to him, then went to the pump to get herself a drink of water. It tasted terrific.

Burk pulled into the space between the house

and the outbuildings slowly, barely stirring the dust. "Where we going to put this?" he called to her.

She pointed to the space to one side of the workshop where she'd stacked the first load of brick. She wanted the kiln fairly close to the workshop, but far enough away to let the heat radiate away from the building.

Burk backed the flatbed right up to the stack and cut the engine. "You might want to turn on the outside lights," he said as he got out. He had on a faded green T-shirt the color of sage. It made his gray eyes look almost blue. " 'Fraid this is going to take a while."

Amelia glanced at the mountain of brick on the flatbed. "No kidding," she said.

The two of them worked well together, as if they'd been doing it for years. Amelia got an old plank from the workshop, and they used it to scoot a few lines of stacked brick up to the edge of the truck bed at a time. Made it easier to load the brick straight from the truck to the wheelbarrow.

Burk took care of pushing the wheelbarrow over to the other pile; loaded, it was heavy and unwieldy, and he was better able to muscle it around. They dumped the brick, then Amelia stacked it while Burk started reloading the wheelbarrow.

They worked steadily without setting a burnout pace. After an hour and a half, Amelia realized she was getting shaky. It was way past her suppertime.

"Are you hungry?" she asked him, stripping off her work gloves. "I'm famished."

"Starved," he said.

"Let's take a break and have something to eat. Come on in."

They took turns washing up at the kitchen sink, then Amelia pulled sandwich fixings out of the fridge and put them on the table. "Sorry—nothing fancy tonight."

Burk was already slicing cheese and didn't bother to answer. He handed her a piece, then ate one himself. They had thick ham sandwiches dripping with mustard, washed down with some of Mary's cider. Amelia couldn't remember the last time food had tasted this good; she ate every crumb.

She took an apple from the bowl on the table. Burk was making another sandwich. He assembled it with a precision she found both absurd and charming: the mustard spread exactly to the edges of the bread, mayo over, lettuce between the bread and the tomato slices, then the ham and cheese.

"There's nothing better than homegrown tomatoes," he said, adding another slab. "I've just been having terrible luck with mine the last couple of years. First I lost 'em to a late frost, then last year the greenworms got 'em."

"Gardening's never a sure thing." Amelia munched another bite of apple.

"Got ten plants started, and they're covered with little green dots, but no yield yet. If I don't get me a good crop this year, I'm going to sacrifice a goat in the backyard."

Amelia started to laugh and a bit of apple went down her windpipe. She was choking and laughing at the same time. Burk gave her a thump between the shoulder blades, looking contrite. "You okay?"

She wiped her eyes and caught her breath. "I'll live—to warn Mark about keeping his kids out of your way."

He grinned and went back to constructing his sandwich. "Tell me about this kiln," he said, as he cut the sandwich in two. She'd never seen one divided so evenly. "Have you got a design you'll be working from?"

She got up to fetch her copy of Rhodes from the living room. "Kind of a smorgasbord of plans, actually. I'll use some of these plans for dimensions and stuff, but Jeff and I built a great kiln a few years ago and—"

"Jeff?" He had set down his sandwich and was watching her intently.

"Jeff Crawford, the potter I was working for before I came here," she said. "He died the end of January."

The skin around Burk's eyes relaxed. "I'm sorry,

Amelia. It's just—I'm realizing I don't know much about you."

"Not much to know," she said. She flipped to the plan for a sprung-arch kiln that was most similar to the one she and Jeff had built. "This is the design I like best, but I'm worried about the height of the chimney—see here? The book says it needs to be two and half times as tall as the kiln. I want to be able to stand up inside, so we're talking a fourteen-foot chimney."

Burk turned the book toward him. His hand was big and graceful, with long spatulate fingers, sprinkled with hair that gleamed gold against the pale bronze of his skin. "Well, he's right about the volume, but you don't have to do it all with height. You could make the chimney broader—say four by three—and make up the volume that way, instead. Here, let me do the calculation for you. What are the kiln dimensions?"

She told him. He pulled a small notebook and a fine black felt-tip pen from his hip pocket and jotted down some numbers. Then, as she watched, he turned the page and deftly sketched the kiln, as neat an architectural rendering as any in the book, each dimension clearly marked.

"Here you go," he said, pointing to the sketch with his pen, "if you have a chimney four feet wide and three feet deep, it only has to be eight feet tall. Still plenty of displacement for the size of the kiln." He tore the page from his notebook and handed it to her, then went back to his sandwich.

She studied the page, delighted by the way he'd suggested the brick walls with a few lines, and the neat curve of the center arch. The drawing made the kiln seem real.

He had left his notebook lying next to his plate. Amelia glanced over at the drawing beneath the page he'd torn off.

"What's this?" she asked him. "A project you're working on?"

He looked, and flushed. "Just a sketch of the Santa Clara Pueblo."

"Why?" She turned the notebook toward her for

a better look as he reached over to point. Their hands brushed, and she drew back.

"See the line?" he said, tracing the outer wall of the pueblo. "It's one of the purest I've ever seen—almost organic."

She smiled at him. "Lovely."

"Are you laughing at me?" he said. "Caroline does—says it's nuts for a grown man to get excited over old buildings."

Amelia leaned back in her chair. "Nah. I get jazzed about things like that, too—I'm always looking for good shapes to use in my pottery. And opening a kiln after it's fired gets me as wild as a six-year-old on Christmas morning."

"I get like that when I'm looking at wood," he admitted. "Hardwoods for furniture and cabinets, especially. And paint—I like looking at paint colors, too." He took a big bite of sandwich and chewed vigorously.

"I go on binges over colors myself," she said. "Like cobalt blue. I love it so much, sometimes I just want to pop my eyeballs out and soak 'em in it, so everything I look at would be saturated in blue."

Burk swallowed and wiped a speck of mustard from the corner of his mouth. "Guess it's a good thing you've got such fine eyelids—to keep 'em in place," he said.

It was unexpected, so it took her a second to start laughing. "I never knew anyone with an eyelid fetish before," she said.

He smiled at her, studying her features. "Well, it's not *just* the eyelids," he said reflectively. "It's the eyelids with those big brown eyes. Curly brown hair shot with gold highlights doesn't hurt either."

"You are nuts," she said.

He just kept smiling.

"Ready to haul some more brick?" she asked quickly.

He said, "Sure," and tossed the last bite of sandwich into his mouth as he got up.

During the hour and a half it took them to unload the rest of the brick, she kept the conversation on his remodeling business. He told her that the restorations—especially of historic adobe structures—were his first love, but that he took other jobs when he couldn't get restoration work.

"Why do you work for the post office? Wouldn't you rather do the other full-time?"

He shrugged. "Sure, but it's not very steady. Besides, the job gives me enough income to buy old houses myself and fix them up. I've done three so far—they're paying a little at a time for the place I'm building for myself. You'll have to come see it when you get a chance."

They pulled the last brick off the truck about eight-thirty. Amelia's hands and shoulders burned and ached, and even Burk looked exhausted, but the pile of firebrick next to the workshop was impressive. They were leaning against the back end of the flatbed; Amelia wasn't sure she could move.

"I can't thank you enough," she said. "For everything. This means a lot to me." The wind gusted and blew her hair forward.

He smiled and smoothed the hair back from her eyes with one finger. "Glad to do it."

She could feel the heat of his hand against her cheek, though he wasn't quite touching her. He hesitated, and for a second, she wondered if he would try to kiss her.

Well, if he did, she was too tired to duck.

He let his hand drop. "Guess I better head home before Tucker gets mad and starts rearranging the furniture. See you tomorrow."

"See you," she echoed. Her face felt exposed without his hand to warm it.

He climbed into the truck and started it up. Over the rumble of the engine, he called, "I'll lock the gate on my way out." He pulled away.

The truck paused on the other side of the gate, and she saw him go back to close it. She waved to him, even though she knew he probably wasn't watching her. When his headlights disappeared around the bend in the road, the night seemed much darker.

Amelia had thought she was too tired to move, but suddenly she was restless. She walked around to the front of the house with some thought of checking on Gramma's rose garden. She had fallen into the habit of using the kitchen door almost exclusively, and out of sight had meant out of mind. She felt a pang of remorse over neglecting her grandmother's roses. The bushes were leggy and overgrown, the beds overrun with weeds. She would have to make time to prune the roses and work the beds.

Amelia stretched her arms above her head and arched her back, which ached badly. How would she have managed without Burk's help? And Mark's. He was not only taking care of the goats every morning, he had pitched in on lots of other chores. She really ought to pay him in cash, not just in free milk.

Cool night air flowed across the desert. Amelia sucked in several deep breaths. The air smelled sweeter now that the acacias and desert sage had started blooming. The basin was poised on the tip of full spring. Any moment it would tilt over the edge and drown them in sweetness.

Maybe tomorrow she could get out the cultivator and do a little work on the rose beds, work a little potash into the soil.

The floodlights from the patio slashed shadows across the face of the house, straight-edged and harsh. She hadn't turned on the front porch light earlier. Amelia wiped her boots on the front mat before unlocking the door. The sharp shadow cast by the eaves obscured the mark drawn on the door until she pulled it open, into the light.

She saw it then: a white sign chalked on the glossy pine-green paint of the door. For an instant it looked Dali-esque, like a melted windmill. Then her mind clicked into gear, and she saw it for what it was—a swastika.

Whoever had done this had taken their time. The edges were cleanly marked, and the inside of the symbol had been carefully chalked in—a thick white mask over the dark paint of the door.

Amelia's fingers went numb, and she released the doorknob. A wind came sharply up off the desert and butted the door back into the darkness. But now that she knew the mark was there, she could see it, even in the shadows. Behind the house, the windmill hummed.

Her body was trembling. Suddenly chilled, she rubbed her hands up and down her arms. Her mind was blank, emptied of anything but shock and fast-building fear.

She had no idea how long the mark had been there.

Chapter Eleven

Quietly, Chief Williamson planned for a high number of foot patrols in anticipation of the Halloween weekend. Staffing at the new substation was tripled. Rumors of a major hate campaign planned by area reactionaries reached his office. After making private and forceful expressions of concern to the mayor, he received her authorization to purchase M-16 rifles for issue to the riot squad. The squad was temporarily transferred to the Montrose substation and placed on continuous alert for the weekend, ready to move quickly to quell any altercations.

A loose affiliation of the KKK and several paramilitary groups planned to stage effigy-burnings on Montrose street corners on the Friday and Saturday nights before Halloween. A number of their dummies wore curly blond wigs, and were readily recognizable as the mayor.

—MOLLY CATES, "Blood Relatives," *Lone Star Monthly*, April 1986

New Mexico

It was difficult for her to go through the door into the unlit house, but she did it. Once inside, she pushed the braces under the door handles and made a quick circuit, turning on lights and checking all the windows. They were secure, the screws she'd put in the frames undisturbed. She ended up back in the living room, where she stood still and looked around, trying to sense whether they'd been inside.

Birds were chittering softly in the cottonwoods, their small night sounds, and the windmill droned. It only emphasized the stillness inside the house.

She was accustomed to being alone here, but it suddenly seemed such a precarious thing. She felt like a foolish duck, settling down to make an easy target of herself.

She went into the kitchen. The card Burk had given her with his number on it was still stuck between the phone and the wall, but he wouldn't be home yet. Amelia looked at it, the neat vertical lettering on a white index card. Black, straight. Not slashed blue printing. Lots of people used white index cards. But when she looked at this card, all she could see were the words on another card that had surrendered so reluctantly to flames: *TIME TO FINISH THE JOB.*

She was scared stiff. Most of the time, she kept busy and managed to blot out the past that stalked her. But for some reason, not knowing when the mark had been chalked on her door brought everything back with a vengeance. Early morning, dreaming safe in her bed one minute and the next—

She grabbed the phone. Mary's phone number was listed in the High Rolls section of the phone book. Amelia hesitated, listening to the windmill for an instant, then dialed the number. Mary would be glad to put her up.

Somewhere between the third and fourth rings, she changed her mind and hung up. Mary could offer her a safe place to stay for the night, or even a week, but eventually Amelia would have to come back to the ranch by herself.

She had only two choices: to make a go of things here, or cut and run. And if she stayed, she wasn't going to shift the risk to her friends.

Her past, her decision. Her risk. That's the way it had to be.

She took a sponge and a bottle of spray cleaner from under the sink and went to scrub down the front door.

Her dreams were restless again that night, vague and threatening at the same time. When she woke from one in a startled sweat, she remembered trying to talk to Papa, who stood with his back to her and refused to answer. She kept begging him to talk to her. But when he finally turned, his face was gone.

Amelia piled the extra pillows up against the headboard and leaned against it, hunching the covers—and Gramma's quilt—up around her. She had shut the blinds tightly, so no moon shone through to silver the room. The darkness was dense, almost solid. Amelia found it comforting in a way.

She didn't especially want to see the ghosts who were attending her tonight.

She waited for daylight, then rose, showered, and dressed. Mark arrived as she was drinking her second cup of coffee. She had no appetite that morning, but made breakfast for them both anyway. Then she forced herself to eat, treating the food like medicine.

As he was scraping the breakfast dishes and stacking them in the sink, Mark asked if she'd found out anything from the county agent.

Amelia poured herself another cup of coffee. "He thinks the additive is something called LPS—it's used in grain feeds pretty often. He sent a sample to Santa Fe to have it tested. We'll know for sure in about a week. Meantime, we'll use the new mix."

"And if we run out?" There was anxiety in his voice.

She squeezed his shoulder. "We buy more feed. It'll be okay, Mark."

He nodded, but didn't look at her. "I better get to work."

"I'll walk down with you," Amelia said. She set the freshly poured coffee aside.

"Why?" he asked. "Don't you trust me?"

"Of course I do," she said. "You've been doing more around here than I ever expected. I don't know how I'd have managed without you. But there was—" She broke off. "I had another threat yesterday."

"Another letter?"

"Not this time. I just want to make sure everything's okay down there, all right?"

He seemed to accept that, and they walked outside together. The early morning air had a hint of moisture in it, which kept things cooler. The cottonwoods were fully leafed out now, a glimmering green against the dawn sky.

When they reached the goat pen, everything looked normal. The place seemed quiet, but Amelia went inside with him anyway. She checked over the goat shed and the milking room, satisfying herself that nothing was out of place.

Mark was settling Margot into the milking stand.

"I'm going down to the honey house," she told him. "Stay clear—just holler if you need me for something."

"I was thinking—" He broke off.

"Yes?"

He finished latching the stand around Margot's neck and scooped her grain ration into the bin to keep her quiet. Then he reached into his pocket and pulled out something that gleamed silver. He handed it to Amelia.

It was a nickel-plated whistle strung on a length of dark blue ribbon.

"I know you don't want me to bother you when you're with the bees," he said. "But what if you have trouble and you're down there all by yourself? If you have this, you can blow on it, and I'll know to go for help."

Amelia looked at his earnest young face. Those deep brown eyes, which had seemed so familiar at first, no longer reminded her of Michael. Now they were Mark's eyes, distinct from her memories of her brother.

She looked at the whistle in her hand. "I don't know what to say. Thank you, Mark."

"You'll wear it?" he asked.

She slipped the ribbon around her neck. "I sure will." After a brief hesitation, she blurted, "But what about you? What if you have trouble up here and I can't hear you?"

He dipped a hand inside the neckline of his flannel shirt and pulled out a whistle identical to the one he'd given her. "Got one, too," he said.

Her relief was out of proportion, she knew that. A couple of whistles were no real protection. But the truth was, she was tired of being scared.

She brushed his cheek with the back of her fingers.

"Thanks, Mark," she said again, then turned and headed for the honey house.

Gramps had told her she had to inspect all the hives before she attempted to move them. That meant smoking the hives to sedate the bees, pulling the frames out to check them for disease or insect damage, then strapping the hives up with nylon harnesses so they wouldn't separate when they were moved.

The hives were relatively quiet that morning, which was clear and still. The small striped bees darted in and out of the hives, down near the ground, catching the sunlight on their gold-and-brown fur. Like hundreds of tiny exotic teddy bears with wings. The wild sweet tang of honey was noticeable in the cool morning air.

The methodical work with the bees kept her calm, in spite of the chalked swastika she'd discovered the night before.

It took her a day to get all the hives ready for the move; she spent the next two replanting the rest of the Folly. The commercial seed wasn't as rough as Gramps's stores had been, so the drill jammed less frequently. And the earlier planting was already up, faint green fuzz along the lower third of the field.

Around three o'clock in the afternoon, she finished planting and went back to the house to cool off. Mannie was coming that evening to help her move the bees up to Mrs. Braun's place, and Amelia needed a second wind for that. Once the sun went down and all the field bees returned to the hive, she'd have to block the hive entrances to keep them inside. But that wouldn't take long.

Mannie and she were going to move them near sundown, so the bees could settle in overnight. That way they'd be less likely to abandon the hive when they found themselves somewhere else tomorrow morning.

In the dry desert heat, the old-fashioned evaporative cooler in the ranch house worked like a charm: Indoors, the air was almost too cold, its higher moisture content as refreshing as a dip in spring water.

Amelia poured herself a glass of iced tea and crushed some mint leaves from the garden in it. She had just settled down at the kitchen table and taken a long drink when the phone rang. Calls still made her nervous; she answered cautiously.

"Ms. Rawlins?" a man's voice said.

"Yes."

"Glad I caught you this time. This is Jerry Garner, over at the county agent's office? Got the results back from Santa Fe on that grain sample you brought in."

"That was quick. So is it safe to use the feed?"

"I asked them to fax me the results. And the answer's yes and no. The additive is LPS all right. Added to your mix, it's upped the salt content fairly high, but the grain isn't contaminated, strictly speaking. But I thought I remembered something about LPS and goats, so I checked on it—"

Amelia heard the sound of papers being riffled. "Yes?"

"Here it is. 'The feeding of Liquid Protein Supplement is contraindicated for goat stock, due to the high concentration of urea.' If you feed this mix, you could end up with a dead goat. It'd be okay for cattle, though."

"I don't raise cattle," Amelia snapped.

"No, ma'am. Sorry—but I thought you might swap it out to someone who does. In fact, I talked to Spence Reed about it. He'd be willing to buy it from you at a discount."

At a discount. Amelia couldn't control the flash of rage she felt. Reed was far better off than she was, and if he could use the grain, why not pay her what it was worth?

"Thanks for the suggestion," she managed to say, "and for your help, Mr. Garner."

"Any time," he said cheerfully. "That's why we're here."

She stood there after hanging the receiver back on its hook. Someone had put something in her goats' feed that could have killed them. But poisoning her goats didn't make any sense. If the Wolfen had wanted to terrorize her by killing her goats, she would have found their mutilated carcasses on the patio. Could Reed have done this to pay her back for canceling his lease on the Folly?

Either way, where was she going to come up with the cash for more feed before she got paid for her first pollination contract? Her caretaker's stipend came next week, but it wasn't enough. And she had to buy gas and groceries. No matter how she added up the figures, they wouldn't balance.

As much as she hated the idea, it looked like she was either going to have to sell the grain to Reed for less than it had cost her, or ask Mac Peterson to give her replacement feed on credit.

Mannie came around six with his big flatbed pickup, right on schedule. Amelia was blocking the hive entrances with strips of folded window screen, which she stapled to the hive body. No sense taking chances with the screens coming loose.

Using the Katz carrier handles, she and Mannie

were able to get all the hives loaded in about an hour and half. Mannie hummed a little as they worked, seeming unperturbed by the prospect of ferrying a truckload of bees up a mountainside.

Once they finished loading, Amelia helped him strap a cargo net over the hives.

"That it? Ready to go?" he asked her.

"Sure. I'll follow you. You know Mrs. Braun's place?"

"Yeah, I remember where it is. Once we get there, you'll need to show me where to park, so we're close to the place you want to set these guys up."

He got in the truck and started it idling to warm the glow-plugs. She walked back up the hill and got in the pickup, ready to follow him.

That first trip up-mountain with the bees was a hair-raiser; Amelia found herself watching Mannie's cargo—her livelihood—for signs of shifting or loose bees. She had moments of pure panic when she pictured smashed hives and hundreds of thousands of furious bees swarming the highway. It all seemed such a precarious enterprise. But Mannie handled his truck smoothly and, when they got to Mrs. Braun's, backed it deftly into the narrow space between the apple trees.

This high on the mountain, they had about an hour of sun left, which they put to good use. They were able to get all thirty-six hives unloaded before it got too dark to see.

Mannie put the carrier handles into Amelia's pickup, stowed his cargo net, and gave her a wave before pulling away. Amelia planned to leave the hives strapped together for the pollinating season, to keep from having to re-lash them each time they were moved. All that remained was for her to unblock the hive entrances. She removed the staples and pulled out the folded screen and replaced it with a strip of wood that narrowed the hive entrance without blocking it entirely. This way the bees could move in and out freely to pollinate, but couldn't all leave at once. She didn't want them to swarm.

Mrs. Braun came out as she was finishing up, and said she'd almost forgotten to pay her.

"Pay me?" Being new to the business, Amelia had agreed to take payment after the services were rendered.

"Oh, I know the contract says pay ten percent for moving expenses now and the rest after they do the pollinating. But your grandfather always done a good job for me, and why do I want to write two checks?" She was scribbling the amount. "I still make it to Rawlins Apiary?"

"Uh—actually, ma'am, if you could make it to 'Amy Castle.'"

Mrs. Braun blinked at her, her blue eyes magnified owlishly by thick glasses. "Amy Castle?"

"Yes, ma'am. I'm a potter—it's my professional name." Who was she kidding? She hadn't finished a pot since she got here.

"Oh," Mrs. Braun said. "What your bank account says."

Amelia didn't have a bank account, but she didn't correct Mrs. Braun, just thanked her for the payment and assured her she'd come back in a couple of days to make sure the hives were doing a proper job.

"That'll be fine, dear. But what about the bear fence?"

"Bear fence?"

"Yes, you know, dear. The electric fence Mr. Rawlins always put up. We get lots of black bear up here, and he always was very careful with the fence. Bears, they'll smash all your beehives just like that," she said, snapping her fingers.

Amelia thanked her for the reminder and said she'd go bring the fence up now. She climbed into the pickup, bone-weary and thoroughly irritated with Gramps. How could he have forgotten to mention something so important to her?

It took her forty-five minutes to get home and locate the electric fence—stored in the tractor shed instead of the honey house—and twenty minutes to get back up the mountain to the orchard. She'd had to pirate the tractor's battery to power the fence.

She finished setting up the four-foot electrified

fence sometime after eleven, working in the weakening illumination of her truck's headlights. Then she got to push-start the truck—shoving it downhill and scrambling into the driver's seat—because she'd drained its battery.

Once she popped the clutch and the engine caught, she pulled onto Highway 82, and headed for home. Not the most efficient day's work she'd ever done.

Amelia rolled down the window and let the cool piney air rush in to clear her head. The moon was up, and the world was a study in black and silver.

She was beat, so she was taking the curves slowly. When someone pulled out of the turnout just below the tunnel and came up fast behind her with their brights on, she pulled to the right, almost onto the shoulder, so the other vehicle could pass.

She thought it must be a pickup truck or some kind of four-wheel-drive because the headlights were high enough to blaze into the cab of her truck. The reflection from her rearview mirror was blinding her, so she twisted it up to face the ceiling, and slowed down a little more.

The truck was right behind her, making no effort to pass.

She was starting to wave the other truck by when it slammed into her.

Her truck veered onto the soft shoulder—she grabbed the wheel with both hands and stomped on the brake. They were coming up on a steep left-hand curve. The warning reflectors on the guardrail glowed like animal eyes in her headlights.

Amelia yanked the truck back onto the road and accelerated into the turn, trying to gain traction.

The other truck hit her again as she rounded the turn. Harder this time.

She clung to the steering wheel and tried to hold the truck on the road. The other truck jabbed her again from behind, and she felt the right tires drift onto the gravel.

Then she was riding the guardrail, watching a shower of sparks from her right fender spray into the emptiness on the other side of the rail. The blackness below the road seemed to go on forever.

Amelia pulled the wheel around slowly, terrified that if she turned too hard, the back of the truck would spin out and she'd go over. By inches, she hauled the left wheels back on pavement. The fountain of sparks stopped. Then her right wheels were back on the highway.

What could she do? Her teeth were chattering. She clenched her jaw and tried to think.

The road held straight for half a mile below this turn, she knew that. There was a big dip up ahead, impossible to see past, but the road didn't curve on the other side of the drop.

She put the truck across the yellow line and punched the accelerator.

She'd taken him by surprise. She fumbled the rearview mirror back into position, squinting against the glare of his high beams. He was two car lengths behind her and dropping back.

Amelia pushed the truck harder. She needed to be well ahead when she went up the rise. That twisted bumper of hers might be a blessing in disguise. If he hadn't already rammed it flat again.

The dip was coming up. Amelia tried to watch the mirror for the truck behind her and keep an eye on the road ahead, too. If someone was coming up the mountain here, she was screwed.

The glare from his brights made it impossible to tell if there was a glow up ahead. He wasn't risking her middle-of-the-road course; he was squarely in the right-hand lane. And he was gaining on her. She held her breath as she topped the crest.

The road was clear.

She yanked the truck over to the right lane and down-shifted, slamming it into second gear. Couldn't risk him seeing the flash of her brake lights.

The truck jerked, and the sound of the transmission rose to a piercing whine. She checked the speedometer—the truck had slowed to about thirty-five.

When the other truck came over the rise behind her, it didn't have a prayer of stopping in time.

The glare from his headlights made her eyes blur, but she aimed as best she could, getting all the way to the right so her twisted bumper blade was lined up with the center of his radiator.

The impact snapped her head back. Then the two trucks separated with a jerk and a metallic screech, and she was thrown forward. The old plastic of the steering wheel cracked clean through under her fierce grip, and the pickup went into full skid for a few terrifying seconds. Amelia grabbed another part of the wheel.

Slowly, she fought the old beast under control. Her palm was slick with blood where the broken edge of the steering wheel had cut her.

But the headlights in her rearview mirror weren't as blinding. Amelia braked lightly and looked back.

The other truck was an enclosed one, or had a camper cab that was painted a dark color. It was slewed half off the road, with steam pouring out from under the hood.

Amelia blotted her palm on her blue jeans and let out her breath. Then she took a tighter hold on what was left of the wheel, and hightailed it down the mountain.

She was shaking so hard that she had trouble steering. It didn't help that her right hand was still oozing blood, and the right headlight was canted off at a crazy angle. Its beam bounced jaggedly off the cliff faces or speared out into black space. Seeing light in unexpected places rattled her. She kept thinking they were coming up behind her again.

Her first instinct was to head for Alamogordo and drive straight to the sheriff's office. But Nick Atkinson's persuasive voice came back to her: *"—got a call from your uncle—"*

She'd disabled their truck, at least temporarily. But what if they came after her again? She should have gone back after their truck was stalled and rammed them over the edge herself. The rotten sons of bitches.

What a bunch of cowards, trying to run her off the mountain like that. *And they nearly did it.*

The fury rose up in her chest again, hot and wild, and her shaking intensified. She wanted them to die, she wanted to murder them herself—she was going to get a gun—a great big shotgun—

Amelia sank back against the truck seat and slowed down. Was she insane? Hadn't she learned a damn thing? The last time she'd yielded to rage and fought back, her family had died. She'd killed them.

All except Michael. Him she'd only left brain-dead.

She was as bad as they were. Worse, because she'd murdered her own family. Who was going to end up dead because of her this time? Mark? His mother?

Burk?

She could barely breathe.

His phone number was in her kitchen, right over the phone. It was late. He'd be home, probably asleep. She could call him.

And he would come. She knew he would. He would get dressed and drive straight over to her place, and he would comfort her—he would sleep on her couch in case they came after her again—he might even bring a gun—

No. Burk was a sensible man. What he'd do was bring the sheriff. Make her tell the sheriff everything.

This is how it happens, she thought. *You start caring and draw him close to you—and he dies for it.*

Normal people were so naive. They thought the police could keep you safe. Make everything all better. Well, twenty-four-hour police protection hadn't kept her family alive.

Amelia shuddered, and her hand slid painfully across the gap in the steering wheel. Then, up ahead, she saw the sign of a small country gas station. The interior lights were out, but there was a floodlight mounted on the outside wall above the familiar blue Mountain Bell phone sign. Maybe calling the sheriff was the sensible thing to do—Burk would say it was.

She braked hard and pulled into the lot, already checking the road behind her for headlights. Nothing.

The bare expanse of wall looked too exposed. She couldn't imagine standing there, away from the truck, even for the two minutes it would take to make a call.

She pulled the wheel around, wincing, and cut a donut to bring the truck alongside the phone stall. Did she have any change? Maybe she didn't need any for an emergency call. She put the truck in neutral, cranked the window down and leaned out to lift the receiver. She could barely reach the phone dial with her right hand.

Dialing 911 left red smears on the metal buttons.

"Nine-one-one," a tinny voice said in her ear. "What is the nature of your emergency?"

"I—someone—" Amelia gulped for breath and started over. "I need to report a hit-and-run." Good. That sounded sensible.

"Do you need an ambulance?" the voice asked.

"N-no—"

"Please hold while I connect you." More ringing.

It was a man who answered this time. "Sheriff's office, Deputy Clark speaking."

She tried to steady her voice. "I need to report a hit-and-run."

"Do you need an ambulance, ma'am?"

"No," she said. "But someone just tried to run me off the mountain near High Rolls. On—on Highway 82, just below the tunnel."

"Yes, ma'am. Could I have your name, please?"

"What difference does it make? Someone just tried to kill me—"

"Yes, ma'am, but I do need your name. For the report."

"I don't care about any report," Amelia said frantically. "I want someone to catch the guy who tried to shove my truck off the side of the mountain!"

"Do you have reason to believe someone is trying to hurt you, ma'am?" His tone held a note of suspicion. "Please give me your name."

Her teeth were chattering again; she clenched her

jaw to make it stop. "Of course I have a reason—some-one just tried to *run me off the road*. The last time he hit me, his truck was damaged—it was stalled out—right down from High Rolls, on that straight strip below the tunnel."

"You're sure it's a man, ma'am? Been having trouble with a boyfriend or your ex-husband?"

She was furious. "No! It's just more likely to be a man—but why don't you send someone to check? He's probably still sitting there! Can't you match the paint scrapings from my truck if he hit me?"

"Possibly, ma'am, but I can't collect any evidence from your vehicle if I don't know who you are. And we can't do much to help if you won't tell us why you think someone's after you. Now, if you'll give me your name—"

Headlights appeared in her rearview mirror. Amelia hung up and jammed the gearshift into first. But the approaching lights were from a car, not a truck. It passed the gas station without slowing down.

The steering wheel was slick with her blood. She gripped it tightly and pulled the truck over to the road.

At the edge of the parking lot, she hesitated. She couldn't face driving back up the mountain to Mary's. And going home would be crazy—what if others were there waiting for her?

Amelia headed for the Crossroads. Caroline would help.

There was one light on at the Garritys' place, soft and yellow at the back of the house. The kitchen?

Amelia cut the truck's engine and lights and coasted to a stop in front of the house. Now that she was here, she was having second thoughts. Hadn't she said all along that she wasn't going to embroil them in her problems?

The delicious green smell of Caroline's garden drifted through the open window of the truck. Amelia's hand throbbed. She pressed the base of her palm hard against her jeans, trying to stop the bleeding. Trying to decide what to do.

There was a flicker of movement from the darkened porch. Caroline rose from a rocking chair and came over to the truck.

"Amelia?" she said softly. "What's wrong?"

No deciding after that. Caroline swept her inside to the kitchen as soon as she got a look at the blood. She kept her voice hushed, so as not to wake Mark, but insisted on stitching the cut. It was a nasty gash, a deep ragged slice in the meaty part of Amelia's palm, near the wrist.

"It doesn't need stitches," Amelia said.

Caroline gave her a level look. "It's on your *hand*," she said, "where even small cuts need stitching, because they get tugged around so much. Now sit down and hold still."

She washed out the wound and carefully pieced the jaggedly torn flesh back together. Amelia watched because it helped her keep her mind off worse things— like headlights bearing down on her from behind—

Caroline stitched inside the cut with one kind of thread, then closed the wound with a darker, sturdier type. She worked with steady precision, and didn't ask questions until she was done.

Then she neatly bandaged the cut with gauze and tape, and washed up at the kitchen sink before making a pot of tea.

"Have you eaten lately?" she asked as she set a steaming mug of reddish tea in front of Amelia.

Amelia shook her head. "No, but I don't want anything."

"You will," Caroline said. "After the tea settles your stomach. Drink up." She pulled a jar from the refrigerator and poured its contents into a pan. "Vegetable soup. It'll make you feel better."

Amelia nodded, too exhausted to argue, and sipped her tea. Raspberry and mint.

Caroline adjusted the flame under the pan, then

came back to the table and sat down. "You going to tell me what happened?"

"It—I was coming back from setting the hives up for my first pollinating job—"

"I thought Mannie was helping you with that."

"He was, but he'd—I'd forgotten the electric fence, so he went on. By the time I finished setting up, it was late, and there was no one much on the road."

Caroline nodded. "Okay."

"Just below the tunnel—you know where the turnout is?—somebody came up fast behind me. I tried to get out of his way, but he rammed me up against the rail." Amelia took a gulp of tea, shivering in spite of its warmth. "I thought I was going over."

Caroline laid her hand lightly on Amelia's wrist, above the bandage. "But you didn't."

"No. I got away. I think the last impact damaged his truck—he was stalled on the side of the road, last I saw. But when I called the sheriff's office, they wouldn't *do* anything about it unless I gave them my name—"

"You told them where it happened?"

Amelia nodded.

"They'll send someone to check it out, then," she said. "We'll call tomorrow and see what they found." She got up and stirred the soup, then poured it into a bowl and brought it to the table.

It smelled wonderful and tasted better. Amelia found herself swallowing the last spoonful before she even realized she was eating.

"Come on," Caroline said. "I've made up the bed in the spare room for you." She handed Amelia some aspirin and a glass of water, then helped her get ready for bed, providing a nightshirt, a new toothbrush, clean towels.

Amelia was stumbling with exhaustion by the time she had washed up and changed. It was a relief to crawl into the borrowed bed. Caroline gathered up her bloodstained jeans and shirt. "I'll wash these so you'll have something clean to wear tomorrow. Get some sleep."

As Caroline turned out the light, Amelia remembered to ask, "You won't say anything about this to anyone, will you?"

Her friend paused, backlit in the doorway. Then she said, "Not if you don't want me to. Now sleep."

Amelia dreamed of Michael.

Not the Michael she remembered. Michael the vegetable. A withered body with her brother's face, lying in a hospital bed surrounded by tubes, the only sound the hiss of the machine that breathed for him. His dark eyes were wide open in the dimness, but they showed no expression at all.

His eyes were as blank as his mind.

Chapter Twelve

> On Saturday, October 26, 1983, at approximately 10:15 P.M., a young skinhead emerged from a van parked at the corner of Westheimer and Kirby. As he began preparations to immolate a dummy dressed as a drag queen, a nineteen-year-old leather boy waiting for entrance to the Rip-Cord Club apparently mistook the neo-Nazi's jackboots, khaki uniform, and paramilitary insignia for one of the "dominant" costumes that were common in his own sexual subculture. Suggestively presenting his buttocks, he told the skinhead to "Bring that riding crop over here and stick it where it can do some real good." Witnesses later reported that he also called the skinhead "Sweetface."

> —MOLLY CATES, "Blood Relatives," *Lone Star Monthly*, April 1986

New Mexico

She woke before dawn the next morning, in spite of her exhaustion. She felt like she *had* been run off the mountain—and been rolled all the way to the bottom. Her back and arms and neck ached, and the cut on her palm throbbed.

As she eased out of bed, she groaned. Caroline heard her and came to the door, already dressed. She took one look at Amelia and said, "You need a long hot shower and some aspirin. When you're done, I'll check that cut." She wrapped Amelia's hand in a plastic bag before she left her alone in the bathroom.

The hot water felt good. After twenty minutes in the shower, Amelia felt less like all her joints had rusted solid. Her jeans and shirt, freshly laundered, hung from the clothes hook on the bathroom door. Amelia dressed and went out to the kitchen, but Caroline wasn't there. They needed to talk before Mark got up—if he heard about last night's attack, it wouldn't be long before Burk had the whole story. That was the last thing Amelia wanted.

She checked through the front part of the house. While she was in the living room, she glanced out the front window and saw Caroline standing by the front of the truck with the door open. Amelia went outside to join her.

Caroline had scrubbed the blood off the seat and steering wheel, and was carefully wrapping the wheel with adhesive tape.

"You didn't have to do this," Amelia said, dismayed. Caroline had already done so much for her.

"Well, you asked me not to say anything about what happened, so I figured you didn't want Mark to know. Just clearing away the evidence."

"I shouldn't have come here," Amelia said. "It's not fair to involve you in my problems." She scrubbed at her eyes. "I've got to call the sheriff's office—but I don't want them to trace the call here—"

"Don't be silly," she said. "What are friends for? And I already figured out that we ought to call from my office in town." Caroline finished wrapping the wheel and snipped off the end of the adhesive. She shoved the roll in her pocket and closed the door of the truck, then put an arm around Amelia's shoulders and gave her a gentle squeeze. "Now, let's have breakfast and decide what to do next. I've been thinking about it, and I'll bet we can catch this guy."

Mark came to the table as they were finishing a breakfast of granola with fresh peaches. When he expressed surprise at seeing Amelia, his mother said, "She cut herself moving the bees yesterday, and came over to get stitched up."

"How many stitches?" was his first question.

Caroline smiled at Amelia. "My son, the ghoul," she said. "Nine. Four inside and five outside."

"You'll have a cool scar," Mark said knowledgeably. "Is there orange juice?"

Amelia was relieved to get over this particular hurdle so lightly. Caroline disagreed with Amelia's decision to keep the incident from Burk—she thought they should enlist his help to track the culprit down—but had promised not to say anything to him about it, either.

It hadn't been easy to explain why she was so determined not to tell Burk. Her certainty that he would get hurt—misjudge the danger, and try to protect her when he couldn't—wasn't exactly rational. At least Caroline didn't think so. But Amelia's resistance to telling him anything more about her history was so deep-seated that Caroline didn't press the issue.

At least Amelia had finally come up with a way to keep Mark off the ranch.

"I've been thinking," she said to him as he poured himself a bowl of cereal, "about the goat's feed getting tampered with. It wasn't poisoned exactly, but the stuff that was added to it is bad for goats, and might even have killed them."

"Yeah?" he said around a mouthful of granola.

Caroline served herb tea instead of coffee; Amelia took a sip, longing for her usual morning brew. "So I was wondering if you'd mind keeping the goats over here for me for a while. Just till everything settles down at my place. I'd swing by every other day or so for my part of the milk, and this way you could spend more time with your kids."

He stopped in midchew, eyeing her suspiciously.

"But if it's too much trouble for you—"

"No trouble," he said. "Just have to partition the pen, so the babies have their own."

"A playpen?" Caroline said.

Mark rolled his eyes. "She's hopeless," he told

Amelia. "It means I'd be later coming over every day to help with the other chores—the garden and stuff. You wouldn't mind?"

"Of course not. The goats are the main thing." She paused, glanced at Caroline, then added, "You've been doing an awful lot at the ranch, Mark. I feel guilty that you're working so hard when I can't pay you. Maybe we should just leave it at taking care of the goats."

"No way," he said. "Mom won't let me stay out here by myself during the summer anyway—if I don't come to your place, I have to go to the office with *her*."

"A fate worse than death, you see," Caroline said dryly.

Amelia turned to Caroline, troubled. "But under the circumstances—"

"It'll be all right during the day," Caroline said. "You'll take good care of Amelia, won't you, Mark?"

"You betcha."

Amelia only wished she could be as certain of taking care of him. She hesitated, still watching the two of them. How could she have risked forming friendships? She had known better.

"C'mon," Caroline said. "Let's get this show on the road."

Everything at the ranch was calm, except for the goats. They were madder than fire about their morning milking being late. Mark decided to milk them and feed them here before trying to move them. Caroline said she wanted to watch an expert at work, which made him roll his eyes, but he didn't object. Amelia went to make sure the house was secure. It was; nothing was out of place at all.

While Mark and Caroline were still inside the milking room, she made a circuit of the truck, taking inventory of the damage. The front right fender had a deep gouge where the paint was completely stripped. Looking at it brought an image of sparks showering into a black void.

The housing of the headlight on that side had been creased too. She'd have to get that fixed before the truck would pass inspection. At least the current sticker didn't expire until January. The rear bumper was in bad shape; the twisted part had most of the chrome scraped off now, and the rest looked like a piece of aluminum foil that had been crumpled up and opened out again. A mess.

Caroline had pieced the broken steering wheel back together and taped it, but the adhesive tape she'd used was meant for people, not plastic. Amelia got a roll of duct tape from the workshop and rewrapped the entire wheel. That should hold it, at least for a while. Then she tried to open the tailgate, and found it was jammed. Great.

If they were going to take the goats over to the Garritys' place in the truck, she needed to get the tailgate working. Her back and arms ached from being thrown around last night; all she really wanted to do was stretch out on the grass and rest. Amelia got a heavy screwdriver from her tool kit and went to work on the catch that had jammed.

By the time Mark and Caroline finished in the goat shed, she had it working. The catch was stiff and not exactly pretty to look at, but it would serve.

She started to go help Mark with the goats, but Caroline stopped her by saying, "Let me see that bandage. What have you been doing? You're not supposed to use that hand much for a day or so, remember?"

Mark was efficient about putting the goats on their tethers and coaxing them into the bed of the truck. "I'll ride over with 'em so they don't jump out," he said.

He *was* a pro. He had Margot and Lois settled in their new home by nine o'clock that morning.

Caroline had called Burk from Amelia's house and asked him to meet them at her office in half an hour. "I'm invoking your godfatherly responsibilities today," she told him firmly. "Amelia and I want to do some shopping, so you're taking Mark." She listened for a second, laughed, then said, "Sure. Okay, see you there. Bye."

Amelia cocked an eyebrow. "As easy as that?"

"Sure," Caroline said. "All I had to do was promise him he could have dinner with us afterward."

"Your cooking must be quite an incentive," Amelia said, teasing Mark. He made a face at her.

"Oh, it's not my cooking—it's the company," Caroline said with a grin. "I promised him you'd come too."

Caroline's office was a small converted storefront off the main street in Tamarisco. Nothing fancy, but the plaster walls inside had been freshly painted a crisp blue, and the tile floors shone with polish. Burk got there the same time they did, and came inside with them.

"I thought you were going shopping," he said. "Why are we here?"

"A little paperwork to clear up first," Caroline said airily.

"You're up to something. I can always—" Burk caught sight of Amelia's bandage and broke off, scowling. "What happened to your hand?" He came over to her and cradled her hand in both of his.

Caroline answered smoothly. "She cut it last night—she was moving beehives, remember? But she had the good sense to come and let me fix her up. She's fine."

Amelia noticed she hadn't lied—just made it sound like the accident happened while working with the hives.

"*Nine* stitches," Mark said, with evident relish.

Burk gave a short whistle. "A lot. You sure you're okay?"

"Fine," Amelia said, and turned away. She didn't want him asking too many questions. It wasn't safe.

Caroline went on briskly, "So, you guys want to treat us to dinner here in town later? Or are you going to make us cook for you after a whole strenuous day of shopping?"

They arranged to meet back at the office around six, then Caroline told Burk and Mark to hie themselves off "and do guy stuff."

As soon as she had shooed Burk and Mark out, Caroline phoned the sheriff's office. "Deputy Clark, please," she said. "Oh, I see—well, who could I talk to about an accident report he took last night? Okay, thanks." She covered the mouthpiece and told Amelia, "They're transferring me.

"Hello. This is Caroline Cook," she said, her tone crisp and professional. "A friend of mine reported a hit-and-run last night on Highway Eighty-two. The truck that hit her stalled afterward, but she was afraid to stop—thought the guy might be drunk or something. I wanted to check back with you, see what y'all found out about it. Sure, I'll hold."

Amelia watched her in astonishment. "You should have been a detective," she whispered. "Cook?"

"My maiden name." Then Caroline held up her hand. "Yes? I see. Did you check the area thoroughly? Uh-huh. Okay. Yes, I understand. Thanks for your time, Officer." She hung up, shaking her head. "They sent a car up as soon as they could, but there were no stalled vehicles on that part of the road. The reporting officer noted some skid marks, but couldn't find anything else."

"The guy must have gotten a tow truck before they got there," Amelia said glumly.

"Right—so let's start by calling towing companies." Caroline flipped open the yellow pages. "Towing—towing—'See Wrecker Service'—God forbid they should put it the first place you look. Okay, here we are. I'll take A through L, and you take M through Z." She tore two pages out of the book and handed one of them to Amelia.

Amelia glanced at the list. There were at least thirty listings in her section alone. "Do you really think they'll tell us anything?"

"Only one way to find out," Caroline said, and picked up the phone. "C'mon—there's a second line over there."

Amelia quickly discovered that Caroline had a genuine talent for blarney. Her friend came up with a plausible sounding story about a message on her answering machine from her brother-in-law that had come in around eleven o'clock the night before. "He was having trouble with his truck, right below High Rolls," Caroline would say. "Oh, I don't know—one of those camper trucks. I haven't been able to reach him since he called, and I've been worried. Did you tow any trucks from that area last night?"

Most of them answered her question, and only a few bothered to ask for the imaginary brother-in-law's name. But none of the towing companies either of them talked to had gotten a call from the High Rolls area the night before.

"How else could he have gotten the truck off the road so fast?" Caroline asked.

"Maybe the damage wasn't as bad as I thought," Amelia said. "Or maybe he called a friend, and they came and pulled him. Or some garage that only tows its own customers."

"You think we ought to try calling all the repair places too?" Caroline said, wrinkling her forehead.

"No." Amelia stood up, winced at her sore muscles, and stretched cautiously. "I think we ought go up there and look around."

Amelia was glad not to be driving. She didn't ever want to drive on this mountain again. And Caroline's old station wagon had softer springs than the truck—easier on her bruises.

The drive from Tamarisco only took about fifteen minutes. She watched the road closely, and pointed out the spot to Caroline when they reached the straightaway.

"It was along here," she said.

"Let's go on up to the turnout and park, then walk down," Caroline said. "He hit you more than once, right?"

"That's right."

Caroline pulled off and parked behind a white minivan. A bunch of tourists were standing around taking pictures of the mountains, but they didn't pay any attention to Caroline and Amelia. The two of them kept to the shoulder as they walked downhill, cautious of the traffic whipping past on their left.

"Where'd he hit you the first time?" Caroline asked. The wind off the canyon tugged at her dark hair, loosening the knot.

Amelia hesitated. "Along here, I think. Just before the big curve." They looked around and found some skid marks that might have been from her truck. Or they might have been from some other car skidding down the steep road.

"Nothing here," Caroline said. They walked on.

At the first big curve, Amelia saw a long streak of blue paint on the guardrail. The metal had buckled, and the row of reflectors along the top were smashed.

"Good thing it didn't give," Caroline said as she inspected it and the cliff below.

Amelia glanced around the road instead. She didn't particularly want to look at the drop in daylight. But there was nothing to show for the collision except a few skid marks and the damaged railing.

She left Caroline and walked on down to where he'd hit her the last time. The place where she'd *forced* him to hit her. The skid marks here were long and distinct—he'd braked for all he was worth. An instinctive reaction, she figured, since he couldn't have known what she was trying to do. Shattered red plastic littered the road—probably from one of his hazard lights. Then the skid marks jagged sideways and off onto the shoulder. A few feet farther on, Amelia found a smudge of bright green antifreeze in the gravel.

"This is the spot all right," Caroline said, coming up to where the skid marks jagged. "Now what?"

"Look around, I guess," Amelia said. Seeing the traces of last night's encounter scared her all over again. What was the point of coming up here? It had been a crazy idea. They weren't going to find anything anyway.

"What's that?" Caroline said.

Amelia looked where she was pointing. Something silver was caught in the branch of a pine tree just down the hillside from the point of impact. Caroline was already balanced against a sapling, reaching for it. Amelia ran over and grabbed her shirttail to steady her.

"Got it," Caroline said. They climbed back onto the shoulder to examine her find. It was silver-coated plastic—the nameplate from the front of a truck—and it said, "Explorer." There were flakes of dark green paint stuck to the back.

They spent the rest of the afternoon on the phone to auto repair shops all around the basin, asking if their fictitious brother-in-law had brought his Explorer there for repairs.

One mechanic laughed in Amelia's ear. "Who could tell? You know how many Explorers I see in a week? Forget it, lady."

"I get the feeling we're no better off than we were before we found out what kind of truck it was," Amelia said after that call. It was almost six; Burk and Mark would be back soon.

"Of course we are—how many dark green Explorers can there be around here?"

Amelia grimaced. "I don't know—a thousand? Two thousand?"

Caroline gave a reluctant laugh. "Okay, so a lot. Still, at least we know what we're looking for. I'm going to stay on it, okay? Things are pretty dull around here during office hours lately—I might as well put the time to good use."

Amelia said, "You've been terrific about all this, but you've got to be careful, Caroline. I should never have dragged you into it—"

"No more of that. Did you mark all the shops you got an answer from? Okay, I'll do the rest tomorrow. Now, let's get Burk to buy us supper—I'm in the mood for some *chiles rellenos*."

Amelia felt ridiculously shy about going to dinner with Burk and the Garritys. They drove into Alamogordo to the buffet at the Lamplighter, which Caroline assured her had *"chiles rellenos* to die for."

Mark insisted on riding over with Burk in the Jeep, and Amelia rode with Caroline. Once at the restaurant, Mark kept up a steady stream of chatter about the remodel job in Ruidoso—he and Burk had spent most of the day at the site. To hear him talk, he'd loved every minute of it. The hardest-working kid in the county.

Burk insisted on carrying her plate through the buffet for her. She was touched and mildly embarrassed. "My hand is fine," she said, but he ignored it, busy loading her plate with *frijoles refritos, arroz con chiles y mies,* a blue-corn *tamal, chile con queso,* and the restaurant's vaunted *chiles rellenos.*

The food was wonderful, and Burk and the Garritys were so comfortable together that Amelia began to relax, too. She was having some trouble managing both knife and fork, though, and couldn't cut her *chile relleno.*

Burk noticed immediately. "Here, let me help," he said. He took the knife and fork from her and cut the stuffed poblano pepper into neat, bite-sized pieces. He was as precise about cutting her food as he had been about building a sandwich, his hands graceful and quick.

But his solicitousness embarrassed her all over again. She hardly said a word during the rest of the meal, and avoided his eyes.

"You seem tired," Burk said eventually. "Maybe I'd better run you home."

"My truck's at Caroline's place," she said quickly. "I have to pick it up." The idea of driving it back to the ranch by herself after dark gave her the shudders, but she preferred that to having him with her. Easier to face it alone—risking herself was less frightening than risking him.

She avoided asking herself why. One thing experience had taught her: Sometimes life ran smoother when you didn't examine things too closely.

He was reluctant to let it go, but Caroline intervened and settled it. Amelia rode back to the house with her.

Chapter Thirteen

Five members of the neo-Nazi group (known as "The Wolfen") piled out of the van and surrounded the young man. They forced him to the ground and began kicking and stomping him. Gay customers waiting to enter the club—which catered to a rough trade crowd—intervened violently.

Within seconds, the disturbance had spread into the street. The skinheads were vastly outnumbered. As one Rip-Cord patron later put it, "This time the bastards found out what it's like to get the shit stomped out of them."

—MOLLY CATES, "Blood Relatives,"
Lone Star Monthly, April 1986

New Mexico

Going back to the ranch proved anticlimactic. The place was as peaceful as a park, not a leaf out of place. Amelia moved around the house tidying up, restless even though she was tired. It bothered her that spending one night away at Caroline's could reveal how solitary—how *lonely*—her life here was. She stalked through the living room, straightening cushions.

She was angry—at herself for being scared and lonesome without other people around—at the Wolfen for continuing to hound her after all these years. Furious at Burk and the Garritys for making her care about them. She didn't want any more hostages to fortune.

Amelia thumped one of the armchair cushions into shape, wincing at the twinge in her right hand. "Enough sulking," she said, and went to bed.

The next day, she was jittery and on edge. Mark didn't come over early, because he was taking care of the goats at his place. And for the first time in weeks, Amelia didn't have pressing chores with the bees. Just when she most needed to distract herself, she was caught up. Only momentarily—she'd have more chores with the hives soon—but there was nothing she had to do right this second. Oh, she hadn't fixed the mailbox yet—and the house certainly could have stood a little cleaning. But the main work was covered.

When she found herself listing everything she could remember about the driver of the Explorer for the fifth time, she knew she had to find something else to occupy her mind. Immersing herself in work was the only way she'd survived all these years, and with any luck, it could still quiet the incessant fears.

Amelia went over to the workshop and unlocked it. The air inside was stuffy, so she propped the door open with a rock. The trench she'd started digging for the kiln's foundation lay about four yards west of the workshop. The edges of the trench had weathered, and the pile of firebrick behind it looked ragged. But the outline where the slab was supposed to go was clear.

Moving slowly because she was stiff, she gathered up string and chalk powder to mark lines with, scrap wood to use for braces, and plywood for the concrete forms.

Time to get to work. She had a kiln to build.

It took her three days to dig the foundation and build the forms for the slab, which was going to be ten feet square. She could have done it faster if it weren't for the cut on her hand and the other aftereffects of being rear-ended.

Mark spent his days at the ranch, in spite of her ploy with moving the goats. She was worried about that, but the place seemed to be perfectly safe, especially in the daytime.

He helped a lot, and was excited by the building project, not minding the hard work in full summer heat.

Amelia was pouring a big slab because she wanted a fair-sized apron around the kiln itself. A sprung-arch kiln needed to have a roughly cubical interior space with a nice shallow curved roof so it would heat evenly. This kiln would be about five by five by five inside, and—even at her top production speed—she should be able to fire a couple of weeks' worth of pots at once.

They set the poles for the canopy in the ground on a Monday, then poured the slab on Tuesday. Pouring was a big production; Mark relished every second of it. After they got the cement poured and smoothed, Amelia let him carve his initials in the corner. Then she covered the slab with a tarp to slow down the drying time, so it wouldn't crack in the desert heat.

After forbidding Mark to come to the ranch while she was gone (on pain of permanent banishment), she spent the next morning up at Mrs. Braun's, checking the hives. They were strong and collecting well, and Mrs. Braun was pleased with the service. Amelia swapped out the battery on the electric fence—which seemed to have kept the bears out of the hives just fine—had a cup of coffee with Mrs. Braun, then drove home. She couldn't stop herself from searching the rearview mirror all the way down the mountain, but this time no one followed her. The worst part of all this was never knowing what direction the danger would come from.

She swung by the Garritys' place to check on Mark. He was occupied playing with his kids. She walked up without him noticing her.

The kids were appealing little creatures, dainty and playful, with strong Roman noses and silky brown coats. It tickled Amelia to see how certain they were that

Mark was their mother; they butted at the bottle when he fed them and followed him around the pen crying when he didn't pay attention to them. He had named them Wednesday and Morticia.

"Everything okay in the nursery?" she asked.

He looked up at her and grinned. "Fine, except when I let them out earlier, Wednesday tried to climb the tractor again. It's like Mount Everest or something for her—if it's there, she's got to try."

"Sir Edmund would have been proud," she assured him. "I'm going to work in the studio today—you might as well stay here."

"Forget it," he said. "If I let you get in there by yourself, you'll never come out again." He'd taken on Jeff's old practice of reminding her about mealtimes, and wasn't above using drastic measures when necessary. The day before, it had taken a blast on his nickel-plated whistle from outside the workshop door to dislodge her from the studio. "Besides, I've got some stuff to do in the garden."

Amelia shrugged. She'd learned that direct opposition didn't work with Mark. "Suit yourself." He settled the kids, double-checked the latches on the goat pen, then scrambled into the truck to ride over with her.

Having him in the truck with her still made her nervous—despite Caroline's best efforts, they hadn't located an Explorer with a damaged front end. But at least this was a short trip; and Mark would have thought she was crazy if she'd asked him to walk.

She stopped outside the workshop, and told him, "I'll leave the door open. Holler if you need help with anything."

He nodded. Within minutes, he was dotting mineral oil on the tassels of the corn in the garden—a preventive for corn worms he'd learned about in FFA and wanted to try.

When she opened the studio door, it was as if a curtain dropped between her and the outside world. A blessing: Once she was in the studio, her problems shrank. She just had to decide which of two projects to work on. The first was the more compelling—a large sculpture that was as exhilarating as it was disturbing—but the second was far more practical.

Amelia looked at the draped sculpture, and promised herself she could put some time in on it after she got ten more honey pots thrown, and had altered the ones she'd done the day before. But as soon as she got her fingers into the luscious elasticity of the white stoneware clay, she forgot her reluctance.

Gramps had warned her that she'd have to do the first big honey extraction within a few weeks. As fast as her hives had built up this year, he was predicting a good honey harvest. When he mentioned ordering containers so she could sell the honey retail, it had sparked an idea.

For weeks she'd been watching the bees take the slightly textured foundation wax and build on it, creating frame after frame of pure white honeycomb bursting with honey. Each individual cell was a perfect hexagon—a shape the bees produced naturally—with a slightly domed wax cap.

Honey pots were one of a potter's common bread-and-butter items. But Amelia had never seen a honey pot that improved on the natural storage cell the bees themselves used. She was fascinated by the regularity of the shape and the translucent quality of the white beeswax, which let the golden color of the honey show through when she held a frame up to the sunlight.

At first she had thought six-sided cylinders would have to be hand-built, which would have made them too labor-intensive to be of any commercial use. But she'd been playing with her design for several days and now thought she had a solution. The afternoon before, she'd thrown a dozen cylindrical jars about six inches in diameter and about five and a half inches tall, and had left the walls of each pot an inch and a half thick.

This morning, she had pilfered Gramma's apple corer from the kitchen. Now that yesterday's pots were leather-hard, she used the corer to lightly score the top of each pot, marking the circular lip into six even sections. Then she took a wire loop and sliced straight down the side of the pot between each set of marks, changing each rounded section into one side of a hexagon. When she finished, she examined the result critically. The points of the hexagon were thicker than the walls of her pots usually were, but they could still be fired safely.

She threw a set of shallow domed lids, which she would alter the same way when they had dried enough to handle. The basic design delighted her. She would use a vanadium stain to give the pots a golden tint, and once they were finished with the glaze Jeff had always called "opal," she hoped to capture the look of honeycomb—that golden color under a creamy, translucent surface. Now all she needed to do was decide on what shape she wanted the handle of the lids to be. . . .

Amelia pinched off a quarter-pound knob of damp clay and started modeling a bee.

Mark had to call her for lunch four times.

She came out of the studio late the following afternoon to find Burk sitting on a stack of brick outside the door. Apparently he'd been waiting for her for some time.

"What are you working on?" he said.

Amelia had a momentary flare of guilt because he looked so hot and patient, sitting there. The feeling beguiled her into answering his question, which she normally wouldn't have done. "A sculpture."

His brows lifted a little. "Can I see?"

She hesitated. "It's not finished." Since the incident on the mountain, she'd tried to keep her distance from Burk. It had been ridiculous for her to think there could ever be anything between them.

But he kept watching her expectantly, not unlike the way Tucker watched her when he was hoping she might scratch his ears.

Amelia opened the door to the studio, and the lights flickered back on inside. Burk rose and edged past her. He stood inside the door, waiting respectfully for her to come and show him her work. He glanced at the honey pots drying on the shelves, but didn't stare. Being polite. Amelia was glad; she wasn't satisfied with the shape of the lid handles yet.

The sculpture was draped in damp towels to keep the clay from hardening before she finished modeling it. Here in the desert, she had to moisten the towels every day; in North Carolina, they would have stayed damp for a week.

Amelia went to the long table that had been built to hold Gramps's radial-arm saw. She had sealed the saw's cover with duct tape to keep clay dust out. She was using the table for her hand-building projects because it was the right height for her to work at standing up. She hesitated a moment before pulling the damp towels away from the sculpture.

This was the part of her occupation she had always hated most: the moment when others looked at what she'd made, and judged it.

This piece was formed from an earthy brown stoneware with lots of grog in it, giving the clay a gritty texture. She had used over a hundred pounds of clay; the sculpture was more than two feet tall, and nearly four feet from one end to the other. A model of the mountain range east of the ranch. The ridges of the chain stretched down onto the basin—the flat base of the sculpture— where the creek and miniatures of the house and ranch buildings showed.

The mountains were realistically carved, and their silhouette was very familiar. But this piece was not strictly representational: The wrinkled dinosaur-skin of the cliffs had faces carved into it. Four very familiar faces.

Amelia looked at them, and wondered what they were thinking. Their expressions were impossible for her to read. The ridges of the mountain chain formed their arms, which reached down toward the house. She couldn't tell whether the hands were straining toward the house to shelter it or to crush it.

Maybe the people trapped in her mountain hadn't decided yet.

"Wow," Burk said softly. He angled his head

sideways and sighted up along the ridge. "It's huge. How are you going to fire it?"

"Once the carving is done, I'll hollow out the back," she said, "so it isn't too thick anywhere. It should fire okay." She hoped so, anyway.

"I didn't realize you sculpted."

"Don't do a lot of it." This was making her uncomfortable.

He looked at her. "It's very good."

"Thanks."

He brushed at some clay dust on the canvas-covered workbench. "I noticed earlier that your truck's front fender is all banged up. What happened, Amelia?"

She shrugged. "A little fender-bender."

"Does it have anything to do with how you hurt your hand?"

"What difference does it make?" she said irritably. "You're not my keeper, Burk."

He was watching her, his gray eyes steady and thoughtful. "No. But I am your friend. Why does it bother you so much that I'm concerned about you?"

She started to cover the sculpture, but he stopped her with a touch on the arm.

"Are you going to glaze it?" A safer subject. And he sounded interested, not like he was making small talk.

"I'll use some washes—iron oxide at least, in the crevices, to emphasize the shadows. But I want the texture of the clay-body to show." She eyed the piece critically. "I need to take some pictures of it—to check the shapes—before I decide for sure. You wouldn't happen to have a camera, would you?"

"At home I do—you mean a thirty-five millimeter, right? I could bring it out tomorrow. The only one I've got with me here is a Polaroid."

"A Polaroid would be great. I won't have to wait to get film developed. Mind if I take a couple of shots?"

"Not at all—it's in the Jeep. Let me get it." He went out, and came back right away with the camera. "Film's already in it. Take as many as you want."

She had to step back to get the entire piece in

frame. She snapped one photo and waited for the image to form before taking another.

Burk picked up the pictures as she snapped one more. "These help you check the shapes? You can't just look at it?"

"Photographs isolate the image more. Maybe it's only me, but a photo helps me see what's really there instead of what's in my head."

"I guess I see what you mean." He glanced from the picture to the sculpture. "Either way, it's impressive."

She handed the camera back to him. "Thanks."

It wasn't until long after he was gone that she stopped to ask herself why he was carrying a Polaroid camera around with him.

Once the slab had cured, Amelia installed angle-iron braces for the kiln floor. The kiln would require stabilizers because the firebrick would be stacked loose, without mortar. With Mark's help, she laid a double layer of hard firebrick on the slab to form the floor of the kiln, then began the laborious process of building the exterior walls.

The hypnotic rhythm of laying brick did nothing to blunt its difficulty—Amelia decided masonry work could be summed up in two words: *grueling* and *painful*. Although she always wore work gloves, her hands were constantly covered with scratches, nicks, and bruises. And her wrists and elbows were one huge ache from repeating the same motions over and over. Brick on top of brick on top of brick, every third row a soldier row with all the bricks turned sideways for strength, then back to the original pattern. It seemed like the job would go on forever. Amelia wasn't sure her knees and wrists would survive it.

She didn't remember it being so bad the last time she had built a kiln, but Jeff had been there to help her then. Mark was a trooper, constantly replenishing the stack of brick she worked from, shifting hundreds of them from the big pile at the back of the slab. He seemed as anxious to get it finished as she was; she'd shown him how to make a pinch pot earlier this week, and he was already pestering her to teach him to use the wheel.

Grueling and painful the masonry work may have been, but it was also worthwhile. Her kiln was gradually taking shape. And, in spite of her anxiety about the attempt on the mountain, she was holding onto her sanity just fine.

The work on the kiln consumed her completely. That was a godsend in most ways, but a week and a half went by before Amelia realized how long it had been since she'd seen Gramps. Or checked on the Folly. She decided to knock off work on the kiln a little early one afternoon, and pay the prairie a visit. Her back was stiff, but her knees no longer complained as much; the walls of the kiln were high enough now that she could work on them standing up. Amelia considered that real progress.

They'd had a smattering of rain over the past couple of weeks, and the grasses seemed to be thriving. Although she couldn't look at the prairie without remembering her miserable week on the tractor, seeing results was gratifying.

She'd been there only about five minutes when Gramps turned up. "Did a good job, for a beginner," he said.

Amelia turned and smiled at him. "I had expert advice. Is it my imagination, or is that section close to the ravine raggeder than the rest? Did I miss seeding it good there?"

He glanced over, then laughed. "You planted fine. The elk've been down for a little chow is all. Freeloaders."

"Elk? Really?" Amelia decided she'd have to come back up here one evening around sunset and watch for them.

He nodded. "They forage down here every summer, especially once the rains come and the grass gets good and thick." Then he looked sharply out toward the north edge of the Folly, and his expression changed.

"What the hell are those?"

Amelia looked where he was pointing. At first, she saw nothing unusual. Then the wind lifted and she noticed the narrow red plastic strips fluttering from a line of wooden stakes. The stakes started down on the flats of Spencer Reed's property, ran across the ridge to enclose a large section of the Folly, then stitched uphill toward the top of the canyon.

"Surveyor's stakes," she said slowly. "Gramps . . . he's had a surveyor out here."

They looked at each other.

"Are you sure we have clear title?" she asked.

She was moving slowly as she walked back up the wash twenty minutes later. Her first impulse had been to drive straight over to Reed's place and confront him about the stakes. Gramps had wanted her to just pull the damned things up. Amelia was clinging to her temper, but barely. She wanted to consider—form some plan— before she approached Reed. Since returning to the ranch, it seemed every time she turned around, she was facing a new problem.

Maybe coming back here had been a mistake. It might have worked if she'd come home while Gramps was still alive—it might have actually meant something then. But now . . . Amelia rubbed at her forehead, trying to ease the ache behind her eyes. She had left it too late. What good was she doing now?

Gramps was long dead; she was dreaming his presence here because she was so desperate for his forgiveness. And the Folly—she had finally gotten the lease canceled and replanted the prairie, and now Reed was plotting some fresh way to take it from her.

Her mother had always said that there were some battles you couldn't win, and that you should pick your fights accordingly. Amelia was realizing that, in returning to the ranch, she may have picked the wrong fight.

This one might be more than she could handle.

She bottomed out that night. For the first time in many weeks, she thought seriously about packing up again and taking off. Amelia lay in bed with her eyes open and enumerated all the reasons that staying here was pointless and dangerous. She'd had threats—letters, the phone call, the mark on her door—and somebody had tried to run her off a mountain. God only knew what was next. She had held on, not bolted. But she knew she couldn't face losing the Folly.

The moon rose, and Amelia still hadn't decided what to do.

When she gave up hope of sleeping and went to the open bedroom window, the desert reached in and touched her. The night sky looked like the one that had watched the beginning of the world: an arch of lapis with runnels of moon spilling down it like a waterfall of light.

No matter what was going wrong here, she could no longer imagine living anywhere else. Out past the stucco wall and the garden, the sturdy shape of the kiln showed distinct in the moonlight.

It was more than half finished now, the brick walls almost four feet high. Another week and she'd be done. Then all she had to do was save up enough money to have a plumber run the gas line from the propane tank and install the burners. She had bought them the week before with the last of Mrs. Braun's pollinating fee. Mark had been frustrated when she'd explained that she didn't know enough about pipe fitting to safely lay the gas lines herself; he was eager to fire some of the pots he'd made. They weren't done with the kiln yet, but they were getting close.

And grass was growing on Gramps's prairie again, knee deep in places. Amelia stretched her arms high and yawned.

How could coming home have been a mistake?

Once school had let out, Amelia insisted that Mark take weekends off—it didn't seem fair to let the kid work as hard as he was inclined to, not when she couldn't really pay him in anything except goat's milk. She was planning to assign several cases of honey to be sold in his name—at least it would give him a little starter for his college fund.

So she was surprised to see him poke his nose around the screen door as she was eating her breakfast the next morning.

"Aren't you going to work on the kiln today?" he said. "It's seven-thirty already."

Amelia laughed. "Give me a break, would you? I worked in the studio before I had breakfast this morning. You want some?"

"No, thanks. Mom made blueberry pancakes." He was having a hard time holding still, she noticed. Every few seconds, he twisted around in the doorway and looked out toward the highway.

"What's up?" Amelia said. "You've got the day off, remember?"

"We're almost done with the kiln, right? All it needs is a roof and to have the burners put in?"

"We're getting there," she agreed.

Then she heard someone turn in at the gate. She looked at Mark, who had a key to the padlock now. "Did you unlock the gate this morning?"

He was grinning as he jiggled from one foot to the other. "Yeah, but don't worry."

Amelia set down her fork and went to the door. Mark stepped aside, then darted off toward the ranch road, waving.

Burk's Jeep pulled up by the cottonwoods, and two men got out. For a second, Amelia couldn't tell which was Burk—then she saw that the man on the passenger side was a little taller. He lifted a large toolbox out of the back of the Jeep, and the two of them came over to the patio.

"Morning, Amelia," Burk said. "Like you to meet my brother, Dave. Dave, this is Amelia Rawlins."

Dave smiled at her shyly and mumbled something that might have been a hello.

Amelia leaned over to shake hands. Dave had to switch the tool kit to his left hand before he could shake. His hair wasn't as dark as Burk's, more of a sandy brown.

"What's up, you guys?" she asked, looking at Burk and Mark. The look they exchanged seemed conspiratorial.

"Mark says your kiln's being held up because you're waiting on getting a gas line run out to it? Dave's just in town for the weekend, but he works for the gas company in El Paso. We figured he could put in your pipe for you while we help get the roof on—get you squared away a little quicker."

"You—" Amelia had been caught completely flat-footed. She'd had no idea they were planning something like this. She tried again. "You're going to—"

Dave Burkhalter gave her a shy grin and spoke up. "Guess it's what you'd call a kiln-raising, ma'am."

Mary Zuniga turned up a half hour later. Mark had called her about the kiln-raising too. She gave Amelia a big hug, and said she wouldn't have missed this for anything.

Mary proved to be better than any of them at fitting the bricks into an arch shape for the roof. They had laid a base of Kaowool and galvanized steel on the ground, raised the edges in an inverted arch, then started laying brick on it from the center out. Mary suggested using some wet fire-clay as mortar for the arch, which helped steady the bricks. Plus, once the kiln was fired, the clay would harden and make the arch more substantial.

By midmorning, Burk had the kiln walls to full height and had moved on to the chimney stack, and Dave had run the pipe from the propane tank and was working on stepping the pipe-size down to increase the pressure flow to the burners. He assured her he'd get the burners themselves in before sunset. Mary and Amelia were nearly finished laying the arch bricks.

Amelia excused herself to fix them all a jug of iced tea. While she was in the kitchen, she checked the freezer and pulled out three chickens, and some venison sausage and two racks of pork ribs that Jorge Valdez had given her the week before. Mr. Valdez had tried to give her a dressed *cabrito* too, but she couldn't have eaten it, not after watching Mark with his baby goats.

Before she carried the tea out to her friends, she stacked some piñon kindling in the big built-in grill on the patio and started a fire. She still had some of Mary's apple wood left, which would make nice slow-burning coals, and she got a bucket of water from the pump to soak some mesquite and piñon chunks in. The soaked chips would add a nice smoky flavor to the fire later.

Dave was tightening a connector when she brought the tea out. He took off his hat and pulled his T-shirt up to wipe his face before giving her a shy smile as he took the glass she offered him. He was as sunburned as his brother.

"This is real good of you," she said. "Taking your Saturday to do this for a stranger."

"My pleasure, ma'am," he said. "And any friend of Burk's is no stranger."

Mary and Burk were discussing the best method of getting the heavy arch up and installed on top of the kiln, and Mark was carefully laying out bricks for Amelia to use in forming the flue and internal kiln fixtures.

Amelia brought the tray over and set it on a stack of brick. "Ready for a break?"

They smiled at her and took the glasses she offered, but didn't stop discussing the logistics of getting the arch installed.

"I figured we would set the beams for the canopy first," Amelia put in after a few minutes of waiting for them to wind down, "and hook the pulley up there. Then we can use the Jeep to lift the arch up."

Mary and Burk looked at each other and burst into laughter. "Sounds like you got it all worked out," Mary said. She took a big gulp of iced tea. "Ahh. That's good."

"Sure is," Burk said. He looked relaxed and pleased with himself.

"Well—I wanted to invite you all to stay for supper," Amelia said. "To celebrate. A barbecue. The folks back in North Carolina thought I was a pretty good barbecuer."

Burk smiled at her. His brown hair was damp with sweat and tangling around his ears as usual. "You seem to be pretty good at everything."

Around one o'clock, Caroline drove up. She got out of the car and gave Amelia a big hug.

"I closed the office for the afternoon," she said. "Couldn't miss this." She'd brought a hamper of cold fried chicken, fruit salad, and a birthday cake.

When she saw the cake, Amelia quietly asked Burk if today was Mark's birthday.

"Yesterday," he said. "He told Caroline no party, but she thought he wouldn't mind having a cake here."

Amelia felt rotten that she hadn't kept better track of when Mark's birthday fell. And why hadn't Caroline said anything?

Everyone came in and sat around the kitchen table for a long picnic lunch, letting the worst heat of the day pass. Mark refused to let them sing happy birthday, but seemed to enjoy the cake. While the others were having seconds, she went and got the tissue-wrapped pocketknife from her bedroom.

She called Mark into the living room so she could give it to him privately.

He ripped the tissue paper open and stared at the pocketknife. The mother-of-pearl handle gleamed in his palm.

"I know it's not the same as having your own back," she told him, "but this belonged to my Gramps. I think he'd like you to have it, to use till you can get your own fixed."

He thanked her, but seemed subdued. She could have kicked herself for not giving it to him yesterday.

While the others chatted, Amelia started a vat of pinto beans and put new potatoes on to boil before taking the ribs and cut-up chicken out to lay them on the grill. She had good low coals by then, and the wood chips were nice and wet, providing lots of smoke for the meat.

She started basting the ribs with a sauce of melted butter, garlic, pepper, lemon juice, and Worcestershire sauce.

The barbecue smelled wonderful, and reminded her strongly of summer Sundays in Cooperton, where barbecuing had been a ritual. As she was turning the meat and basting it again, Burk came out onto the patio. They were in the shade of the house here, but the heat from the grill was high. Sweat gleamed along his cheekbones as soon as he came over.

"Smells great," he said.

"I was just thinking the same thing, if I do say it myself. Haven't had barbecue in quite a while."

He settled himself on the stucco wall and watched her baste the chicken. "You were in North Carolina before you came here?"

"That's right." Amelia's hair blew into her eyes and she pushed it back.

"You worked as a potter there?"

She set the pot of sauce at the edge of the grill, then closed the lid. She didn't need to add any wood yet.

He was still watching her, waiting for an answer.

"Yes," she said.

"What brought you back here? To the ranch?" Burk asked. "It'd been quite a while, right?"

Usually she hated questions, but with Burk it was different. He'd been helping her out one way or another since the day they met. And then what he'd done today—well. He and Mark had knocked themselves out to see that she got her kiln finished.

"When the man I was working for up there died," she said, "I was going to have to move on anyway. Coming here seemed like the best choice."

"Are you sorry you did? What with the threats and all—"

Amelia looked up at the Sacramentos. The sky above them was a hot, clear blue. The nearer slopes were wrinkled brown rock and olive green scrub, but the farther peaks were a smoky blue-violet. Breathtaking. The smell of piñon from the fire was sharp and sweet. But the soft hum of her friends' voices from the kitchen was the sweetest thing of all.

"No," she said. "I love it here."

A wind lifted suddenly. Burk pointed behind her, out toward the basin. "Look—got a dust storm brewing out on White Sands."

She turned and looked. In the brilliant afternoon sunshine, the swirling white sand was forming shapes along the horizon.

"People will say the White Lady's walking again," Burk said.

She glanced back at him. "White Lady?"

"The Bride of White Sands," he said. "Legend goes that she was traveling by wagon from El Paso to Tamarisco to be married. Her lover was supposed to meet her near the pass to guide her across the desert, but he never came. She got caught in a dust storm, and was lost in the Sands and died. When the moon is bright, she still walks the Sands in her wedding dress, searching for him and crying."

"Oh—*la Llorona*," Amelia said.

"What's that?"

"*La Llorona*," she repeated. "It means 'the Weeper.' It's this Mexican folktale about a ghost-woman dressed all in white who was betrayed by her lover. She walks and weeps—usually she's searching for her lost children, but there are different versions. Sounds like this is one."

He smiled. "So you're also a folklorist? *Is* there anything you aren't good at, Amelia?"

She laughed. "Most things. I don't know much folklore—just bits I picked up from my dad. And I'd never cut it as a tractor driver. Or a socialite."

"Oh, you're a terrific hostess," he said. He came over to her and stood very close. She imagined she could feel his heat, distinct from the heat of the barbecue pit.

Uh-oh, she thought, *now it's coming. That's what I get for letting my guard down—*

He pulled a bandana out of his pocket and offered it to her.

She took it, but looked at him, puzzled.

"You've got barbecue sauce on your cheek," he

said. He gave her a teasing smile, then went back into the house.

Amelia swabbed at her face, her emotions jumbled. It annoyed her to realize that the dominant one was disappointment.

Chapter Fourteen

Crowded streets delayed police response to the riot. By the time the riot squad arrived at the scene, two of the neo-Nazis—who had remained in the group's van—had taken matters into their own hands. They climbed onto the roof of their vehicle and began firing Uzis over the heads of the crowd attacking their companions.

According to reports, one of the neo-Nazis was struck by a flying brick, sending a burst from his automatic rifle wide. The burst struck a riot squad officer in the chest. The rest of the riot squad interpreted this as hostile fire; the two neo-Nazis were killed instantly by return fire from the squad's new M-16's.

The five surviving skinheads and fourteen gays—including the leather boy who initiated the incident—were hospitalized as a result of the Rip-Cord Riot. The police officer shot by the skinheads was treated and released, having suffered severe bruising on his chest from the impact of the bullets stopped by his Kevlar vest.

Late that night, a blue Norther swept through Texas, dropping temperatures into the low forties in a matter of minutes.

—MOLLY CATES, "Blood Relatives,"
Lone Star Monthly, April 1986

New Mexico

The moon lifted her head above the eastern mountains late that evening, near ten o'clock. That first spill of moonlight across the desert was always breathtaking. The field grasses and clumps of sage took on an otherworldly look; even the air tasted different after the moon rose, as if some mysterious substance had been added.

The world was so wide here that the cradle of mountain ranges surrounding the basin didn't narrow the sky. It went on forever, cool cobalt, glimmering with starry light.

Amelia sat on the adobe wall that surrounded the patio. This morning, she hadn't asked herself why she was inviting Burk and the others for supper. It was a habit of hospitality, some residual that remained, buried under years of solitude. A seed of her grandmother's ways, still resting, dormant, under all the years of separateness and silence, patiently waiting for the right conditions of temperature and soil to put out shoots. Amelia could not explain the presence of that seed, not after all these years, not after the events those years had carried.

She kicked her feet against the wall. The long day of finishing and loading the kiln—in between entertaining guests and cooking—must account for her restlessness. That, or the worry about the surveyor's stakes on the Folly.

She was tired enough to sleep for a week, so why couldn't she settle down?

It had been months since she loaded a kiln; it had taken her from late afternoon to well into the evening. And she hadn't even had a full load of pots.

But once she had the kiln entrance bricked up, and held the long flame of the lighter in the stream of gas from the new burners . . . the burst of blue flame was a perfect match for the burst of joy in her chest. Burk, Dave, Caroline, Mary, and Mark had broken into spontaneous applause as the first burner caught, and that had boosted her own delight.

They'd left over an hour ago. She looked toward the kiln, at the faint blue glow that shone from the burner holes on this side, about a foot and a half from the ground. The jets were turned very low, just enough to start preheating the kiln and its contents. She would let it soak that way overnight, and then in the morning—

Amelia stretched, grinning madly. In the morning, she would turn the gas up, and the flames would rise, burning higher and hotter, transforming the fragile greenware to bisqueware. Sturdier, but still porous. Thirsty and ready to drink up glaze before being returned to the fire for a final transformation.

Until the kiln had cooled for half a day, and it was safe to unbrick the opening, she wouldn't know how her pots had fared. Any flaws in structure or air bubbles trapped in the clay would cause a pot to bleb or even explode, sometimes taking its neighbors with it. She hoped she hadn't lost her touch.

Amelia stood and stretched her arms overhead again, stretched until the shoulder joints popped. There was no resisting the desert tonight. The itch wasn't going to go away.

She unhooked her canteen from the nail by the kitchen door, and filled it. She screwed down the top, then turned to choose her direction.

Not the Folly. She wanted no reminders of worrisome things like surveyor's stakes. She chose the open desert of the unfenced federal lands to the southeast.

Amelia slung the canteen around her neck and shoulder, letting its canvas-webbed weight rest against her hip, and stepped out sharply.

A wind came off the mountain, smelling of water spiced with the resinous greenness of pines. In Houston, rain had always smelled of steamy cement and rotting vegetation. She remembered the stink of the bayou and felt sick. But the air off the mountain was cool and fresh, blowing the old memories away.

It took a quarter of an hour to reach the south edge of the property. She eased herself through the fence and into the desert, her boots making a soft crunch in the packed dirt and gravel of the surface. She picked her way around creosote bushes, watching for runoff channels.

The only sound was the wind in the brush. Her restlessness was easing as she walked. Being out here comforted her, the way it had when she was a child and her grandfather walked beside her. However separated from her past she felt, her life and the things she cared about had been shaped by her family. Her habits were formed from theirs as well: whether offering food to a guest or walking the desert for pleasure, her impulses sprang from those same roots. The realization was both reassuring and unsettling.

The moon was well above the mountains now, pouring itself over the world like a bottomless jug of milk. An owl hooted overhead, and she saw its dark shadow skim the plain ahead of her. The sound made her step falter; in folktales, hearing an owl portended death.

She followed the fleeting shadow with her eyes. When it struck something boxy and flat, the shadow careened off at an oblique angle and scattered on the wind. Amelia was left staring at a string of abandoned boxcars.

She shivered. The owl swooped overhead again, traveling the other direction now. Back toward home.

As she turned to follow the owl, she saw several pairs of headlights moving along the ranch road toward her house. An instant later, she saw the flames.

It took her a few seconds to comprehend what she was seeing, a few more to pinpoint the fire. Her first thought was that the kiln's gas lines had leaked. But it looked like the corner of the field along the northeast perimeter of her place was burning. Not near the house, thank God. But the west wind was pushing the flames straight up the ridge toward the Folly. Amelia was running before she thought about it, hollering as she weaved around brush and rocks. The canteen banged against her hip.

"Damn it, damnation—" She caught her foot on

an exposed root and took a tumble that wrenched her shoulder and left her palms scraped raw. She rolled to her feet and went on, slowing a little for the rougher stretches after that.

The flames were easy to see, even from where she was, a couple of miles away. They licked and swirled over the land in an eerie dance, like some demonic presence come to claim her prairie as a sacrifice.

Amelia tripped again, and swore. After that, she kept her eyes on the ground, looking up only to take an occasional bearing on the fire. She could hear men's voices now, and see figures beside the flames, beating at them. She picked up the pace again.

Later, she was never certain how long it took her to reach the perimeter of the ranch, ten minutes, maybe, or fifteen. Time was stretched and sharp, and afterward she remembered only fragments of those minutes, like so many snapshots: the shape of the flames, and the men outlined against them like dancers; the hissing of the fire, and the sporadic bursts of white noise as it ate her land. In between bursts, it was oddly quiet. She had no trouble hearing the clang of shovels and the men's shouted instructions.

She flung herself across the fence. Her shirt sleeve caught on the barbed wire and ripped open, leaving her scar showing. She fumbled with the snap and got her arm covered again, still racing toward the fire.

It had already spread. Smoke was pouring up from it in great oil black clouds. When the wind gusted, the smoke scorched her throat and eyes. There were maybe a dozen people along the fire line, using shovels to fight the flames. She couldn't see anyone with hoses— where were the fire trucks?

A tall man wearing a fire helmet threw down his shovel and grabbed her.

She flinched from the pressure on her wrenched shoulder.

"Amelia!" he shouted. "Where have you *been?*"

The hardness of his hands made time stop moving in jerks and start running in sequence again. Her mind snapped into clarity, and she realized the man was

Burk. The helmet shadowed his face, making it hard to read his expression.

"Where *were* you?" he yelled, shaking her. "I thought whoever set this got you—"

She pulled away from him, and rubbed her sore shoulder. "Took a walk," she said, breathing hard from her run. "Where's the fire truck? Dammit, it's spreading toward the Folly—" She looked toward the front edge of the fire, where the flames leaped twenty feet in the air, spiraling gouts of orange and yellow. A cloud of smoke and sparks spilled across the sky, so dense that the moon disappeared. "I've got to go—"

"No—stay here. We've got the brush trucks out now—they can handle it. So you were gone? You didn't see who started this?"

Amelia shook her head. "The kiln—"

"It's fine. Checked it while I was looking for you."

The fire was racing east while she watched, sending hundreds of sparks soaring gracefully ahead to land like a constellation of fireflies in the grass. Gramps's prairie was already catching in half a dozen places. "The Folly—I've got to do something—"

"The brush trucks will knock it down. Don't worry!" He grabbed his shovel and ran back to the fire line.

Amelia scanned the area. The brush trucks Burk was talking about were big four-wheel-drive pickups equipped with water tanks. Two of them had joined the fight, the drivers coming at the fire line from either side, while men on the back of the trucks worked the hoses in a circular motion, knocking down the flames. With every burst of spray, clouds of steam rose into the sky, mingling with the smoke.

Once the water reduced the flames, the people on foot pushed in to scrape at the burning grass and brush, breaking it up or smothering the fire with shovelfuls of dirt.

As she watched, one of the brush trucks ran dry. The driver backed away from the fire, turned in a tight arc, and headed toward the ranch road, where a big semi rig—the water tanker—was parked. The flames on that side of the fire line immediately surged higher, a rippling curtain of yellow silk, brilliant against the darkness.

Amelia glanced around and spotted a pile of shovels. She seized one and ran toward the Folly. No one was on that side of the fire line, even though sparks were settling and flaring to life there. But before she could get to the prairie, somebody caught her hard by the arm. It was Spencer Reed.

"You can't get ahead of the fire," he shouted. "You got to stay in the black, or you'll get burned!"

"But that's my prairie up there! The grass hasn't seeded yet!"

He shook his head. "Grass isn't worth getting killed over, lady! With this wind, that fire can move faster than you can. You stay behind it, where it's got nothing left to burn. Try to narrow the line—squeeze it toward the middle." He pointed to where the men with shovels were beating at the fire.

Now she could see the pattern—they were flanking the flames and working in toward the center.

"See?" He pulled off his helmet and put it on her head. "Stay in the black, or I'll call the sheriff to come and take you off the property till the fire's out, you hear?"

"You son of a bitch!" she yelled. But he was already gone, over to help couple the supply line from the tanker to the second brush truck, which had also come in for a refill.

She shouldn't waste time arguing anyway. She intercepted the first brush truck, heading back from retanking, and waved it down. The driver had his window open—it wasn't anyone she knew. "The prairie—" she pointed to the small fires that were starting to catch uphill. "It's a restoration—can you get some water up there?"

"Do what we can," he said, putting the truck in gear and pulling away.

Amelia joined in and started shoveling, staying behind the burn as Reed had ordered. The brush truck edged partway up the ridge and arced some water onto the Folly. They got the small fires there out, but new sparks landed and started burning as soon as they headed back to the main fire line. The Folly was protected from the dry desert wind, so at least the fire was spreading more slowly there.

She watched the men around her, and tried to imitate the way they worked their shovels. Occasionally, the wind would eddy back, dousing all of them with sparks and smoke, but that didn't stop them from doing the hot, backbreaking work. When the brush trucks went for another refill, the volunteers fell back for a breather, only moving to stamp out sparks that fell nearby. Amelia remembered her canteen. She unscrewed the cap, drank gratefully, and passed the rest around.

When the trucks came back, everyone turned to again. Under the renewed onslaught, the fire line began to narrow. It had been almost a quarter of a mile wide when she got back to the ranch; now they'd cut it down to a couple of hundred yards.

Then the wind shifted and the air on her face cooled a little. As she watched, the fire line dipped and turned toward the creek. Now the flames were running parallel to the ranch house, instead of away from it.

"Shit," one of the men working near her said.

She recognized the voice and looked over at him. It was Mac Peterson. There were at least twenty-five or thirty people out here now. "Won't the water stop it?" she asked.

"That little creek won't slow it down a bit," Peterson said. "And once trees and brush get to burning good, it's damn hard to put 'em out."

The fire reached a juniper tree that stood out a ways from the water. She expected it to take time for the wood to catch fire. Instead, the entire tree exploded. It looked like it had been hit by lightning.

"Jesus!" Peterson ran toward the new fire line. Amelia was right behind him.

The brush trucks swung around and attacked from a new angle, but the fire was burning hotter and steadier now, feasting on the denser fuel provided by the trees. Then three more brush trucks, another tanker, and about twenty more people arrived, backup from other volunteer departments in the area.

At some point, several of the other departments brought out sandwiches, water jugs, and hot coffee. The fire crew took breaks in shifts. Amelia didn't intend to stop, but Burk saw her and sent her back, saying she needed to at least have a drink to keep from getting dehydrated. The coffee smelled so good, she had a cup. It tasted even better, and she decided to grab a sandwich too. Peanut butter and grape jelly. She ate it as she made her way back to the fire line, where the volunteers were finally getting the upper hand.

Once she saw that the fire by the creek was coming under control, Amelia went to the brush truck crew she'd talked to the first time. They let her climb in, then crossed the creek and drove up the wash to the Folly. More than half the field was already gone, but the wind was beginning to drop.

One of the fire fighters showed her how to operate the nozzles and told her to use a circular fog pattern. Then he took her shovel and jumped down to work the ground. Amelia was grateful. She hadn't stopped for work gloves, and her hands were covered with blisters—burns from the showering sparks and pressure blisters from the shovel work. And it was a relief to do something that really made headway against the flames. With the water directly on it, they had the smaller fire on the Folly knocked down in about ten minutes.

"Go back on down, ma'am," the driver told her. "We'll do a rollover with the sprayer up here, make sure all the sparks are out. But you'll have lots to take care of down there."

She thanked them, looked once around the Folly, then walked back down the wash. The new grass had barely begun to establish itself before being burned off. It hadn't seeded yet. Where was she going to find the strength to start all over?

This time, the desert had no answer for her.

The smoke was fading into the night sky, and the moon was clear again. Amelia could not remember ever being wearier than she was at that moment. It took everything she had to set one boot in front of the other.

Down by the creek, things were in the cleanup stage. Many of the volunteers were packing up to go home, while a few of the later arrivals stirred the ashes and made certain the fire would stay out. Amelia made the rounds, thanking as many of the fire fighters as she could. They waved her off with tired grins and jokes about calling her to come out with them next time. Dave Burkhalter was there, too. When she thanked him, he gave her the same shy smile he had earlier when she'd tried to tell him how grateful she was for his work on the kiln. She looked around especially for Mac Peterson, wanting to ask him about reorders on the grass seed, but she didn't see him before Burk came and found her.

"How're you holding up?"

"Okay," she said. "Considering. How did you all get here so fast? I'd only been gone about a half hour when I saw the fire, and you were here before I made it back."

"A bunch of the volunteers were over at Spencer's playing cards," he said. "Dave and I stopped off there on our way home. Then Mac Peterson went out on the porch for a smoke and saw the fire. If you'd been looking in this direction, you would have seen it, too—it was like a beacon. Good thing, really. With the wind, if it had gotten much more of a start on us, we'd have never gotten it under control this fast."

"This was fast?" Amelia felt as if she'd been fighting fire for days. She lifted Burk's wrist and checked his watch. It was ten till eleven. The fire had only burned for a little over an hour.

"Mr. Reed needs to talk to you. He sent me to find you," Burk said. His tone was flat and definite.

She didn't like being summoned. Especially not by Spencer Reed. Amelia glanced at the people around her. Everyone was grimy-faced, muddy, and clearly exhausted. They had knocked themselves out to help her, a stranger. As much as she hated Reed, she had to admit he and his crew had done right by her.

"Where is he?" she said.

"He's up by the ranch road, where this thing started," Burk said. "C'mon."

She followed him. Most of the fence posts along the ranch road had burned out, leaving a sagging tangle of barbed wire behind. Add replacing the fence to the unending list of chores—and expenses—for the ranch. Maybe Atkinson would pay for someone else to come and fix the fence. That's if he didn't try to blame the fire on her, and kick her off the place entirely.

Spencer Reed looked as tired and dirty as everyone else. In contrast to the other volunteers' cheerful weariness, his mouth was set in grim lines. He was holding some chunks of burned wood, and he didn't bother to greet her.

"Where were you when this thing started?" There was an accusatory note in his hoarse voice that made her jaw get tight.

Her shoulder ached from her fall earlier, and she was starting to notice the scrapes from her exertions on the fire line. The combined effect made her want to rip into Reed. A flat-out fight would feel good right now: A little adrenaline would defer the exhaustion that was gaining on her.

But she owed him. "Took a walk," she said.

"It's foolish for you to live on this place alone. I won't even talk about the crazy way you run it, wasting some of the best arable land in the basin. I'm just saying living alone out here is foolhardy. But to hie off into the desert—alone, at night. Now that's downright suicidal."

"Well, if it is," she said, "it's no concern of yours. On the contrary, me getting myself killed would be good news, wouldn't it? You could start raising oats on my land again." She remembered the surveyor's stakes. "Or have you got something more profitable planned this time?"

"I leased that plot," he said. "And I didn't come out here and work like a dog to keep this place from burning just to get kicked in the teeth. Do you know how this fire got started?"

Her uneasiness suddenly flared. Amelia cleared her throat. "No." She needed to cough, but stifled it.

Reed held up the charred wood, which she had assumed were burned fence posts. There were notches cut in them, and he fitted the pieces together into an X.

"Ma'am, why would somebody burn a cross on your land?"

All around them, volunteers were getting into their trucks and pulling away. Mac Peterson walked up with two of them, and Amelia raised a hand in greeting. Reed's blunt question and the aftermath of her adrenaline high had leached every ounce of strength from her spine. She felt like a rag baby that had been washed too many times.

Reed was still waiting for an answer from her. It went against the grain to lie to anyone, even Spencer Reed, but she needed time to sort this out. She shook her head.

Burk started to say something, but she put her hand on his arm, and he shut up.

"Well, it was arson, plain enough," Reed said. He pitched the charred cross back on the ground. "It'll be the sheriff's job to figure out the who and the why, but all's I can say is you best be careful."

All the fear and worry of the past months crested abruptly, and Amelia's self-control snapped. "Is that a threat? Because, if it is—"

Burk put a hand on her shoulder—the sore one—and said firmly, "You're out of line, Amelia. Mr. Reed's just expressing some neighborly concern. What happened here is no joke—whoever did this meant business."

She looked at him, astonished. His voice was quiet as always, but his soft, country way of talking had disappeared. His words sounded crisp and definite, and they hit her like a dash of ice water in the face.

"And Mr. Reed's right about solo walks in the desert not being real bright." He turned to Reed. "Come on, sir. I'll run you home now."

Burk was angry at her.

"Much obliged," Reed said. He cast a look at

Amelia, but didn't say anything more before following Burk to the jeep, where Dave was waiting.

Mac Peterson cleared his throat. " 'Scuse me, Miz Rawlins. That's my truck right there."

She was still struggling with the idea of Burk's anger—and her own reaction to it. She was crushed, and it stunned her. When had his opinion become so important?

"Oh, sorry." She moved out of Peterson's way, and he opened the door and got behind the wheel.

"Lucky for you a bunch of us were all together, Miz Rawlins," he said. "Out here, grass fire'll spread faster than chicken pox in a grade school." He took a cigar stub from his shirt pocket, stuck it in his mouth, and chewed on the end of it.

"You're right," she said. "I was damn lucky. Thanks for smoking that cigar, Mr. Peterson."

"Anytime, Miz Rawlins," he said and gave her a grin. "Long as you explain it to Clara for me." He touched two fingers to his helmet and pulled out.

He was the last of the fire fighters to leave. Amelia walked inside, beyond exhaustion, in a state of floating alertness. She stripped in the bathroom and left her smoke-soaked clothes on the floor. Then she went to bed and drew the old quilt up around her. But her hair reeked of the smoke, too; the smell made her nervous. What if whoever had set the fire decided to try again?

The window beside her bed faced south. She pulled up the sash of the wooden blinds so she could see the fields. The moon was still up, and, after a few minutes, her eyes adjusted. Everything was quiet. Still . . .

Amelia unhooked the window latch and cranked it open. Fresh air would help mask the sickening smoky smell in her hair. And she would hear if the arsonist came back. She curled up in the middle of the bed with her head beside the window, nesting in the thick folds of the quilt, and went to sleep.

Fear blew in through the open window, invading her dreams.

*   *   *

She woke in an iced sweat, shivering and sick in the aftermath of her dream. She had been back in Houston, in the hands of the Wolfen again.

The dream never failed to astonish her. She did not try to remember the events of that night. But in her dream, each detail was so perfectly etched; indelible, undeniably real. The smell of burned flesh and urine. The look in Michael's eyes when they dragged him into the kitchen, the shattering echo of the gun.

Blood on the cabinets. The look in Michael's eyes.

Chapter Fifteen

Houston police clamped a curfew on Montrose immediately after the riot. An uneasy peace descended.

No more incidents occurred. Chief Williamson confided to the mayor that the lack of retaliation by extremist groups had him worried. Preoccupied with campaign issues, she discounted his concerns, believing that tempers had cooled with the weather.

By the third week of November, even Williamson began to relax. When the mayor requested that the police surveillance of her home be downgraded so as to be less intrusive, the chief agreed. He gave orders to reduce the guard to a single pair of patrol officers in a cruiser parked near the street on the mayor's circular drive, almost out of sight of the house.

—MOLLY CATES, "Blood Relatives,"
Lone Star Monthly, April 1986

New Mexico

Although Amelia felt as if she'd scarcely slept, she woke abruptly, just ahead of the dawn. She knew the time; she felt it, in the utter stillness of the air and the land. There is a time when the whole world rests: all the creatures of the night gone to ground, not even the earliest of birds yet risen. Even they waited for the sun to come closer before they ventured out of their nests.

Amelia left hers. Something had wakened her.

She pulled on drawstring pants and a sweatshirt, shoved her feet into moccasins, and went quietly out the front door.

Outside, it was cool; she smelled water and ash on the wind, the aftermath of the fire in the night. But she could sense no movement on the ranch.

Rather than risk the creaking wooden gate, she slipped through the arch on the west side of the courtyard, a decorative open window ornamented with a carved and painted Santa Fe cross suspended on chains. The high grass outside the yard whispered cautions around her feet as she eased up to the corner of the adobe wall and looked around.

Nothing.

The outbuildings were neat and silent. The furor of last night had been erased, except for churned-up ruts along the lane and the charred barrenness of the northeast field. She held herself completely still, until even her heart beat softly, and strained to hear whatever disturbance in the natural rhythm of the ranch had woken her.

There was no one on the place. Not a leaf, not a blade of grass stirred except as it should.

So what had woken her?

Amelia went around to the cottonwood tree and seated herself on the bench beneath it, to watch.

The sun came up over the Sacramentos, a god in the sky, huge and sudden above her, heralded with streamers of saffron and crimson and rose. A desert lark sang accompaniment to the spectacle, and Amelia waited.

As the sun left the cradle of the mountains, she saw the shape of a car along one side of the ranch road. Then two figures came around it, dark shadows outlined in gold, one tall, one a little shorter. They walked along the edge of the lane slowly, pausing at one point to pick something up. Small bursts of dust puffed under their feet and drifted out behind them in a faint gilded haze.

Amelia stood up, still watching them. She was

certain they couldn't see her in the shadow of the cotton-wood.

The figures resolved themselves from shadow and highlight to those of two men. Sun gleamed on the hair of the shorter one, glancing off the coffee-dark strands. He turned his head, and she saw his profile.

Amelia let her breath stream all the way out. It was Burk. She walked down to meet him.

Burk must have seen her coming, because when she got within hailing distance, he turned. "Morning. This is Ted Brady, the sheriff's chief deputy. Ted, this is Amelia Rawlins." He didn't look directly at her as he made the introduction, which she found disconcerting.

The deputy was a big man, well over six feet and burly. He touched his hat. "How do, ma'am? Hope we didn't disturb you. Wanted to collect evidence soon's it got light." He glanced at a form he was holding, and said, "Owner of record is listed here as the Estate of Hector Nathaniel Rawlins? So you don't actually own this place?"

Burk glanced at her, but didn't say anything.

"I'm the beneficiary of the trust the estate set up," she explained. "I haven't been back in the area long, but my grandfather left the ranch to me."

"I see." Brady pushed his hat back on his head, revealing a band of pink, moist flesh across his forehead. "I've taken up some of the burned material here where the fire started, and we'll send that off to the lab for analysis, check it for accelerants and so forth. Why don't you tell me where you were when the fire started? Burk here says he thinks it got going good around ten-forty?"

"I'm not sure about the exact time. I was sitting on my patio a little before ten last night," she said. "Just watching the moon come up, you know, and—and I de-cided to take a walk."

"You see anybody around the place as you were walking around? Notice any vehicles or anything that seemed suspicious?"

"I didn't walk this direction," she said. "I went southeast, out into the desert a little way. So I didn't really see the fire start. I walked for maybe thirty minutes, and it wasn't till I turned around to head back toward the house that I saw the fire."

"I see," Brady said. He doubtless thought she was batty, hiking in the desert at night, but then he probably dealt with people's oddities every day. "Well, you got a mess of tire tracks out here, and footprints all over the place."

"Most of those are probably from the fire crew," Burk put in. "We parked along this road and brought the brush trucks and other apparatus right through here."

"So the gate was open when you all got here?" Brady asked.

Burk looked startled. "Why—yeah, now that you mention, it was."

"Miz Rawlins?" Brady said. "You in the habit of keeping your gate open?"

"No," she said. "It's got a padlock, and I always use it, especially at night. Burk and some friends were out to supper yesterday, but Mary Zuniga said she'd make sure the gate was locked after her when she left. I'm sure she did."

"You might want to check," Brady suggested. "Just so's we know. But there's no lock on the gate now—just the regular latch. Maybe whoever did this cut your padlock off to get in."

"Maybe so," Amelia murmured. It gave her a sinking feeling that she hadn't checked the gate last night after the fire. She'd watched everybody drive out, and never thought about it.

"Well, it looks like you had some bad business out here, ma'am. Burning a cross—that's got an ugly feeling. Any idea who'd want to do something like that? You got any enemies, people who'd like to see you in a bad way?"

"Sorry," Amelia said. "No idea."

Burk spoke up then, his voice sharp. "Amelia, you have to tell Ted about the threats you've been getting."

She couldn't believe he was forcing her hand this way. Why? And he sounded so abrupt. Was it because he was still angry at her over what she'd said to Spencer Reed?

"Threats?" Brady squinted up at the sun, which was well clear of the mountains now and was already turning hot.

The sunlight was burning the blisters on Amelia's hands, and she stuck them in her pockets. She should have put something on the burns last night. "I've gotten a couple of threatening letters. Burk—Mr. Burkhalter looked into it for me."

Brady pulled a notebook from his shirt pocket and flipped it open. "How many letters exactly? And when was this, ma'am?"

She thought about it, trying to remember. The weeks had blurred together. Had she really been here for three months?

"The first one came the last week of March," Burk said. "Postmarked the twenty-third. The second came about three weeks ago, postmarked June fourth. I'll bring the envelopes by your office later if you like."

"That'll be useful. What about the letters? What kind of threats were they exactly? You still have 'em, Miz Rawlins?"

She swallowed. "I burned them."

Brady shook his head. "That's a shame, ma'am. Why didn't you call us about it before this?"

"Didn't think they were really serious," she said.

Brady gave her a searching look. "But you asked Burk here to look into 'em, you say?"

"He offered," she said.

Brady let it go. "What kind of threats were they, ma'am?"

She tried to think of a way to answer without explaining about the Wolfen. The last thing she wanted to do right now was bring up her past.

"She told Caroline Garrity they were death threats," Burk said, "but I never saw the letters, just the envelopes."

"Death threats? And you didn't think they were serious?" The chief deputy shook his head again.

"Didn't want to waste your time," she said.

Burk looked at her, his mouth grim.

Brady said, "Do you have anyone staying here with you, ma'am? I think you ought to have somebody around for the next little while. Our people'll try to check by, but we're spread pretty thin. And, truth is, arson's one of the hardest laws to prove. You have to prove intent, so it's hard to get a conviction." He fished in his shirt pocket for a business card and handed it to her. "Call me if you see anything suspicious, or get any more of these letters."

He touched the brim of his hat and walked back to his car.

She half expected Burk to go with the deputy, but he took a step toward her. "Why didn't you ask for police protection? This is *crazy*."

"What's crazy is thinking some hick deputy would make any difference," she snapped. "You have no idea what's involved."

He looked at her. "That's right. I don't. Because you haven't told me a damn thing about what's going on."

"What business is it of yours, anyway?"

He turned his face toward the road and said nothing.

Instantly, she regretted the sharp response. Nerves—and her habitual secretiveness—had made her cruel. He didn't deserve that.

After a moment, she cleared her throat. "How about some coffee?"

"No, thanks." As the deputy's car pulled away, she saw Burk's Jeep parked behind it. Burk gave a short sharp whistle, and Tucker bounded out of the back. He raced up to them and stopped, his whole back end wagging.

Relieved that Burk wasn't planning to leave yet, she squatted down and hugged the dog. "Hey, Tucker! Long time no see! How you been, boy?"

He licked her face and gave a bark that nearly deafened her. She rolled him over and scratched his belly.

"I'm going to be pulling double shifts for the next few weeks," Burk said. "Driving a parcel truck and covering an extra in-town route. Rotten timing, since it means I won't be able to check in with you as often. Not that it sounds like you mind."

She looked up at that. "Burk—"

He went on as if she hadn't said anything. "I'll be getting home pretty late, and thought Tucker could stay out here with you for a while. He can't ride in the parcel truck with me like he can in the Jeep. And I figured he'd be some use to you. He's a pretty good watchdog, even if you wouldn't think it to look at him right now."

Tucker had his eyes half shut and was squirming on his back in the dust while she scratched his chest. Amelia kept watching the dog, and didn't answer right away.

After a while, she said, "What if he gets homesick and runs off?" She knew how much Burk loved his dog, and wasn't sure she wanted the responsibility of taking care of Tucker. "There're rattlers out here."

"There are rattlers all over, Amelia," Burk said. "He's got enough sense to leave snakes alone. And he won't run off. He likes it here."

She looked up then. The sun was behind him, striking bluish sparks off his hair; she couldn't see his face clearly. "I wouldn't want to be responsible for something happening to him, Burk," she said.

"God damn it," he said, pronouncing each syllable distinctly. "You won't take risks with anyone else's safety—not even Tucker's—but you won't do a damn thing to improve your own chances, will you? What is it with you, Amelia? Some kind of goddamned death wish?"

She stood up. Tucker rolled over, and his ears came alert.

"Don't you swear at me," she said. "Or take that tone. All I want is to be let alone. Just because I'm not willing to put other people in danger doesn't mean I want to die."

Tucker sat up, still watching Burk intently.

Burk sighed, then said to Tucker, "You'll take care of her, won't you, boy? Even if she is stubborn. Bite the baddies. Yes, you'll bite 'em, because you're a *good* dog." He rubbed his knuckles between Tucker's eyes, then lightly tugged on his ears.

Tucker barked once, sharply.

"Is that a yes?" Amelia said.

Burk looked up from the dog, his expression strained. "I can't help worrying about you, Amelia. I want to keep you safe, and I don't know how."

"Of course you do," she said, trying for a light tone. "Tucker's going to bite the baddies for me."

"Tucker's just a dog, Amelia. But at least he'll be some protection."

"I think he's insulted," she said.

Burk's face relaxed. "Oh, he knows he's not a people." He gave Tucker a tap under the chin. "He might try to fool you into thinking he doesn't, but if you look at him hard, he'll get off the couch and go back where he belongs. Won't you, boy?"

She had noticed the way Burk handled his dog from the first time they'd met, and she was touched that he would trust her to take care of Tucker. The responsibility still made her anxious, but she had to admit she'd be glad of the company.

"Well, okay," she said. "If he'll keep off the furniture, I guess he can stay."

Burk had come prepared. He brought a big plastic garbage can full of dog food up onto the patio for her and handed over a dog brush and a spare flea collar. Then he brought Tucker's supper dish and water bucket.

"He just gets one full bowl of food a day, don't let him fool you. Mark'll probably feed him for you, if you don't want to bother with it," Burk said. "I don't want this to be a hassle."

Tucker was leaned up against Amelia's leg. She liked the sturdy warmth of him there. "Don't worry," she said. "We'll get along fine. I'll take good care of him, Burk."

"I know you will," he said.

"What about you? Won't you miss him?"

He gave her a look that was amused and direct.

"I'm planning on visiting as often as I can. This is what you might call a joint custody arrangement."

Her cheeks got hot.

"You may not want coffee," she said, "but it's getting past breakfast time for me. Come on in while I fix us some, okay?"

He gave her a warm knowing smile. He had opened his mouth to answer when Mark came pounding across the field behind him.

"Holy shit!" Mark shouted. "Mom wasn't kidding—there really *was* a fire here! Why didn't you *call* me?"

Before she started breakfast, Amelia turned the kiln burners up. Because she had been preheating the kiln and its contents since last night, she was able to turn it right up to firing heat, instead of stepping up the heat in stages. Preheating used a little more fuel, but was easier on the kiln and the pots. Not to mention the potter.

In spite of last night's fire, seeing the kiln actually functioning gave her a lift. At least she could work again.

Burk ran Mark back to the Garrity's place to feed and milk the goats while Amelia fixed breakfast. When the two of them got back, Amelia invited Burk to stay and eat with them.

"Thanks, but I'm running late—Dave and I are going to finish out that remodel job before he goes back to El Paso. But I'll stop by later, just to check on you and make sure Tucker's settling in okay, not giving you any trouble. Right, boy?" He leaned down to give Tucker's ears a rub.

Tucker panted cheerfully, seeming completely unperturbed when Burk went to the door.

"Plan on having supper while you're here," she told him. "Still got some ribs and chicken from—from last night." It seemed like a week since the barbecue, but it had only been yesterday evening.

"Now that's an offer I can't refuse." He gave Mark a wink. "I might be a little late, though. So don't let this guy eat it all before I get here."

Apparently, Mark wasn't in the mood for kidding. "The way things are going, I won't get the chance," he said. "Supper'll be ready, and no one will even *call* me."

Amelia and Burk exchanged a look at Mark's aggrieved tone, but neither said anything. Burk waved and went on his way, and Amelia served breakfast: *migas*—a Mexican egg dish—and refried beans. They smelled spicy and wonderful as she spooned them from the pan. She was ravenous.

Mark only picked at his food, which wasn't like him. He loved her *migas*. She didn't pester him about it, just left him to brood. She had plenty to think about, herself—like how to make sure whoever had set the fire didn't come back.

After the breakfast dishes were scraped, rinsed, and stacked in the sink, she and Mark went outside.

"What are we going to work on today? Garden stuff?"

"You're staying over here today? Your day off, remember."

He made a face. "Mom got called into the office, and didn't want me to stay home alone. She said she was going to call you."

"Oh. She must've called while I was outside talking to the deputy. You're welcome here any time, you know that. You want to stay in and read?"

"That's okay. I'll help with whatever you're doing."

"Well, but—I've got to get that metal roof installed over the kiln."

"I can help with that—I helped Burk build a carport last summer."

"Thanks, Mark, but I've only got the one ladder. Besides, no taking chances, remember? I don't want you getting hurt."

"Oh, right. I forgot. I'm just a baby, and you're my babysitter."

"Mark! You know—"

But he stomped off toward the garden, ignoring her. She decided to let him sweat the mad out, and turned her attention to getting the rest of the canopy kit laid out next to the kiln.

His mood didn't seem any better when they broke for lunch. Tucker was lying in a shady spot on the patio where the bricks were cool, looking perfectly at home.

Amelia went inside and dished tuna salad onto a couple of early tomatoes, then pulled out some crackers and a crock of soft goat-cheese. Mark poured them each a glass of iced tea. He ate his meal this time, but didn't say a word, even when she asked him directly what else he'd gotten for his birthday.

After enduring ten minutes of sulky silence, Amelia said, "Look, why don't you tell me what's bothering you, instead of giving me the cold shoulder?"

"I can't believe you didn't call me last night," he burst out. "I could've helped fight the fire. Maybe saved some of the prairie!"

Amelia set down her fork. "Mark, the only ones fighting that fire last night were the fire crew. And I didn't exactly have time to stop and make phone calls."

"*You* fought the fire, and you're not part of the crew—Burk told me so. Everybody acts like I'm useless—like I'm just a stupid kid, good for nothing. I'm sick of it!"

"For heaven's sake, Mark," she said. "Nobody thinks you're useless, especially not me. I'd be nowhere close to having that kiln finished without you. But you aren't grown up yet."

He slammed his hand on the table. "See what I mean? You're treating me like I'm just some jerk kid!"

"Somebody set the fire last night deliberately," she said quietly. Surely that would make him understand.

"So what? I could've still helped put it out."

"They set a fire that could have burned out everyone along this road, if it had gotten a little more wind. People could have been killed, but whoever did this didn't care about that. You hear me, Mark? *They didn't care if people got hurt.* Do you really want to tangle with somebody like that? I don't. Truth is, I probably shouldn't have ever let you work here—it isn't safe."

"*You're* still here—you could've gone to stay with your friend who has the orchard, but you didn't. If it's okay for you, how come it isn't okay for me?"

Amelia's head was pounding. She leaned her forehead into her hand, massaging the temple with her thumb. "You think *I* want to mess with this guy—or this—whoever it is? That's nuts. I wish they'd go away and leave me the hell alone."

"If you're so scared, then why don't you just leave?" he yelled at her. "Everybody else does!"

She snapped, "Maybe I will!"

He jumped up and kicked his chair back against the wall. "You don't care about me—none of you! You're all just a bunch of jerks!"

Amelia was out of her chair, already horrified at what she'd said to him. "Mark—wait—"

He slammed out the screen door and left it banging.

Amelia raced after him, but his next words stopped her dead.

"I hate you," he shouted back at her. His face was filled with anguished betrayal, and for an instant, all she could see was *Michael's* face—his rage and pain and hatred of her for what she'd done to him. Tucker leaped up, barking excitedly.

"I hate you!" Mark shouted again, half sobbing now, and something inside Amelia whispered, *Of course you do*.

He pounded off across the fields while she watched, appalled at what she had done.

The last glimpse she had of him was the back of a faded blue T-shirt, with Tucker's square blond head bobbing along beside it.

The explosive argument had taken her by complete surprise. She knew Mark was prickly about being treated as an adult, but she'd had no idea how deep the matter ran.

Life was so damned complicated.

She considered calling the Garritys' house, but had no idea what else to say to Mark, even if he was there. She decided to call Caroline at the office instead. That way she would know Mark had taken off. She could probably calm him down better than Amelia could, anyway.

Caroline was pleasant, her warm voice cheerful and matter-of-fact as they talked about it.

"He's pretty angry at his father right now," she told Amelia. "He didn't even send a card or call on Mark's birthday."

"He forgot?"

"Yes. He hasn't called for months, and Mark is pretty upset. Anyhow, I don't think the problem's really got anything to do with what you said to him. He's just touchy right now."

"I can't help worrying about it," Amelia said. "Last thing I meant to do was upset him."

"Hey, I know that. But he'll work through this. I'll run by the house and pick him up—our deal was that if he's not working at your place, he stays here with me. He'll hate that, and maybe he'll think twice next time about running out on you."

"That's not why I called you. It's his day off, anyway."

"But he promised me he'd stay with you today. Besides, if he's angry at his father for not being reliable, the last thing he needs to do is be undependable himself. An afternoon at the clinic won't kill him. And I'll make sure he calls you tonight if he's not going to be there tomorrow, okay?"

"Sure," Amelia said. The thought that Mark might not come back at all gave her a hollow feeling. But that was pure selfishness. Hadn't she just made a big deal of him keeping the goats at his place because it wasn't safe around here? "Oh, by the way, Tucker took off after Mark—I'm glad he's got the dog with him—but I'll need to run by and pick him up before suppertime. Will you give me a call when you get home?"

"I'll go you one better—we'll drop Tucker off on our way back to the house this evening, okay?"

"More than okay. Thanks, Caroline."

"I should be thanking you," Caroline said. "For everything. Bye, now."

Amelia hung up the phone and looked out the window at the kiln. The afternoon was brilliantly blue and hot, without any breeze at all. She had the evaporative cooler running inside, so the house was temptingly cool and fresh. The perfect time for a siesta. But she wanted the canopy finished. Once she had that done, her studio was complete, and she could spend every moment not required by the bees—or the Folly or the garden or the goats—on potting.

Every spare moment. Right.

Still. She pulled her work gloves back on and checked the electric screwdriver that she would be using to tighten the canopy's locking nuts. Installing the roof section shouldn't take more than an hour, according to the kit instructions. That meant a minimum of two, of course, but what the hell.

The heat outside was intense, and she broke into an instant head-to-toe sweat. She carried Gramps's twenty-foot metal ladder from where it was leaning against the workshop over to the kiln. Then she paused to remove the kiln's eyehole brick from its loosely blocked doorway to check the cones. Even in full sunlight, the summer heat was nothing compared to the blast furnace inside the kiln. She squinted against the searing red light inside.

Since this was a bisque firing, she was only taking the kiln up to cone six. Her clay was high-fire, and wouldn't mature until it reached cone ten—about 3200 degrees. But she didn't want the clay to mature and become impermeable yet. It needed to remain slightly porous, so the glazes would soak in and form a bond with the clay when the pots were refired. The pyrometric cones had slumped, though the warning cone hadn't completely sagged down over the pat of clay she'd poked them into. Amelia decided to turn off the kiln now, rather than risk getting caught up in the canopy installation and letting it overfire. She hoped the honey pots had come through intact. She could hardly wait to see how they glazed.

The new nozzles Dave had installed turned easily under her hand, but even with them turned off, the kiln radiated heat. She was sweating profusely as she set the swivel-mounted rubber feet of the ladder firmly in the ground next to the foundation, and leaned the top against the central beam that formed the peak of the roof, about fourteen feet off the ground.

She went into the workshop and brought out Gramps's block-and-tackle set. Without Burk and Dave around—or even Mark—she'd have to use the pulley to get the bulky metal sheets up on the grid. She laid the pulley in the dust and climbed up to look for the best spot to fix it to the beam.

When her head reached roof level, she paused, shading her eyes to look out across the property. From up here, the devastation left by last night's fire was obvious. The northeast section was a greasy black; it looked like a street crew had rolled over it, pouring tar. She'd lost nearly twenty trees along the creek. The Folly was only half visible beyond the ridge, but a third of that was burnt-out stubble.

Looking at it made her head hurt, and she could have wept. Gramps must be so disappointed.

"Come on," she said. "Get a grip. Crying never solved anything."

She needed to keep her mind on one task at a time. This kiln was almost finished, and right now she could use a success. She shifted her weight slightly on the ladder as she turned back to the canopy, and suffered an instant of vertigo. The heat must be getting to her. But then things steadied again. She gripped the sides of the ladder as she stepped up two more rungs, bringing her knees level with the beam as she prepared to climb onto the canopy grid.

The dizziness returned, and she tried to steady herself on the ladder again. But the ladder wasn't helping this time. A moment later, she realized that she hadn't simply lost her balance. The ladder was tilting under her.

She still thought she would recover—that the ladder would stabilize—because the tilt was so gradual. It was also inexorable, listing farther and farther sideways. When she realized her balance point was beyond retrieving, she grabbed for the beam.

It didn't seem possible that she should miss, that the ladder could have slipped so far from the roof. That she could be so high up with nothing beneath her.

Amelia hung there for the space of a heartbeat, grasping at air, inches from the roof.

Sunlight glanced from the aluminum ladder as it toppled, and, feet still tangled in the rungs, she fell.

Chapter Sixteen

During November, the mayor's campaign schedule was hectic in the extreme. Longing for some time with her family, she planned a quiet Thanksgiving at home.

Her eldest son, Daniel, returned from his sophomore year at Stanford for the long weekend. Senator Caswell had hoped to join them for the holiday, but last-minute negotiations on an important subcommittee matter kept him in D.C.

The Wolfen launched their retaliatory strike in the early morning darkness of Friday, November 29, minutes after the regular shift change for the officers guarding the house.

According to the coroner's report, the strike occurred before the Caswell family's Thanksgiving dinner was fully digested.

—MOLLY CATES, "Blood Relatives," *Lone Star Monthly*, April 1986

New Mexico

She was lying on the ground with her face in the dirt. Dust was in her mouth. When she tried to lift her head and spit it out, pain knifed through her head. Moving made her even dizzier, so she stopped. Then, very carefully, gritting her teeth against the pain, she turned her head to the side and rested her cheek in the dust. It had a velvety texture, and was still warm from the afternoon sun. But the sun was long gone, and she was cold.

Everything hurt, especially along her left side. And she was thirsty. The dust was so dry. She remembered jumbled vegetation and the gleam of the bayou below her—but there was nothing growing here, and she couldn't smell the water.

She tried to look for it, but when she raised her head, pain stabbed behind her eyes. The world dimmed, and she slid away.

There were voices, but she refused to open her eyes. It was dark, dark and cold. There was nothing left to wake up to, and she rejected consciousness. For some reason, her mind chose to function anyway.

"How long since she fell?" A woman's voice, low and clear.

"I found her just before I called you—a little after sunset, I guess. When I came out to check in on her and Tucker. No telling when she fell."

"Mark left around two, so she could've been here awhile." Firm, gentle hands examined her. "Her pulse is shaky, and she's chilled. Those ribs may be broken—"

"What about her leg?"

"Can't tell without X rays."

Fingers pressed on her eyelids and light flashed at her eyes. Amelia flinched away from the light, moaning.

"Her pupils are reactive."

"She's coming around, isn't she?" the man said. He sounded relieved.

"Amelia?" the woman said. "Can you hear me? What hurts?"

"—everything—" Amelia said.

A gentle hand smoothed her forehead. "I know," the woman said, and gave a soft chuckle. "Hang on, angel. Can you wiggle the toes on your right foot for me?"

Amelia complied.

"Great, that's great. Now, which leg am I touching?"

"Right," Amelia managed to say. Breathing was torture.

"Wonderful. It's going to be rough for a while, and then you'll feel better. Everything's going to be fine." She added, lower, "We have to stabilize her neck and back before we can move her. Why don't you call for the ambulance—they're better equipped, and that way we won't have to move her more than once. I want her transported straight to Sierra Medical in El Paso—the Alamogordo hospital doesn't have a CT scanner."

Amelia opened her eyes, squinting against the pain and the glare of headlights flooding the area. *Was it their van? Had they come back for her?* No—Digger had said it was the House van. And the House people were safe, Digger had promised. He said it was okay.

She groped for the woman's arm. "No hospital," she said. Something in her chest stabbed every time she moved. It hurt like hell. But she couldn't go to the hospital. They would be looking for her.

The woman touched her cheek. "You've had a bad fall, angel. Hospital's the best place for you."

"No," Amelia said, as loud as she could with a shallow breath. "No hospital."

"Can't you take care of her?" the man said.

"I shouldn't, dammit. You *know* I shouldn't—"

"She's scared to go to the hospital," the man said quietly.

"So what? I'm scared of the dentist, but I go!"

Amelia gasped for a breath and ground out, "—They'll be watching the hospital—"

The man looked over at the woman. "She may have a reason, Caroline."

"It would be wrong to take a chance—"

"Sounds to me like she knows what she wants—and what she doesn't want," he pointed out. "I know you're just thinking about what's best for her—but if they take her to the hospital and she refuses to be admitted, they won't treat her, anyway."

"*—No hospital,*" Amelia said.

The woman hesitated. "Okay. We can take her to the clinic and see. But I *have* to have a backboard and some way to stabilize that leg."

"I'll get some plywood from the workshop," the man said. "You've got adhesive tape, right? We'll make one." He unhooked Amelia's ring of keys from her belt loop, and she heard them jingle. Then the soft ringing receded, growing fainter and fainter, until there was no sound at all.

The next time she woke, she was on the X ray table.

"You already took the X rays," she told them. It upset her that things she remembered having already happened were happening again. Her ribs tore at her with each breath. "I remember it. Why are you doing it again?"

"Calm down, angel," the woman said. "We had to take several. But we're almost done."

That wasn't what Amelia had meant. Besides, the X ray room looked wrong in the bright wash of artificial light. The walls were pale blue instead of white, and the table she was lying on was in the wrong spot.

"Don't worry," the woman said. She had gentle eyes. Her hair was dark, and she wore it pinned up. She looked familiar. One of the nurses at the House?

A man spoke from the other side of the table, and Amelia turned her head. It hurt to move, and her eyes watered.

"That's a good sign—that she's awake again. Isn't it?" he said. It was Frank Burkhalter.

"What are you doing here?" Amelia asked him. "You weren't here before."

"I helped Caroline bring you in, don't you remember?"

"She seems disoriented," Caroline said. "She really needs to be in the hospital."

"No!" Amelia said. She tried to struggle up, but the stab of her ribs was excruciating. "They'll be watching—hospital—promise—"

Burk slid an arm under her shoulders and eased her back down on the table. "It's okay, no hospital." He said something in a low voice to the woman.

Amelia tried to listen, but her head hurt so much . . . She drifted in and out for a while. Small snatches of talk came clear for her, and she was aware when the woman cut off her jeans to work on her leg. But things blurred together.

Amelia spiraled back in when the woman—Caroline—was winding gauze around her leg.

"—Simple fracture, no misalignment," she was saying. "The leg should be fine. And far as I can tell, her neck and spine aren't damaged. But I'd feel better if I had a radiologist around to check the films."

She had such a beautiful voice. In spite of her anxious tone, listening to her talk was soothing.

"What about the concussion?" Burk said.

"She needs a CT scan." Caroline started applying plaster to the gauze on Amelia's lower leg. "Her B.P. and pulse are stable, and she's rousable. But we can't be sure there's no subdural hematoma till she goes for a scan."

The plaster was cold against her leg, and Amelia shivered.

Caroline looked up at her and smiled. "Need a blanket?"

Amelia shook her head. With the movement, dizziness and nausea swamped her. The room was swimming around her again, and the light was forming distorted stars around Caroline's head. She closed her eyes for a moment.

Then Caroline came around, wiping her hands on a towel. She touched her wrist to Amelia's forehead. "Just lie still, okay?" Then she said to Burk, "I'm going to put a light tape on those ribs so she can rest better. Let me wash my hands."

Amelia lay still and tried to breathe gently.

"Can you help me lift her?" Caroline was back, pulling open the snaps on Amelia's cuffs.

It hurt to have them move her, but Amelia didn't

protest. She was confused about the long-sleeved shirt. Hadn't she been wearing a T-shirt?

"Right side first," Caroline said crisply. "Then we can ease it over this arm, where the worst damage is."

They were shifting her again. Amelia closed her eyes and let the pain wash through her. She'd learned not to resist it; that only made it worse. The best way was to just let the waves come through. If you did that, you could breathe a little in between, in the troughs.

"Oh, my God," Caroline said. Her lovely voice sounded stripped and shaken.

Burk's breath hissed between his teeth. She remembered this too—that she had been hurt worse than they realized.

"Did you know about this?" Caroline said. She clasped Amelia's wrist.

Amelia opened her eyes with an effort. Burk was shaking his head. His face was chalk white.

Dizzy and more confused than ever, she looked at Caroline.

Caroline lifted Amelia's arm slightly, careful not to jar her ribs, drawing her forearm completely out of shadow. The twisted shiny flesh of the scar was stark under the harsh fluorescents.

Ugly, Amelia thought. *It's so ugly.* The darkness was spiraling in on her again.

"What happened to her?" Caroline demanded.

Later on, Caroline woke her and told her they were taking her home.

Amelia was bewildered. Weren't they already at the House? But her head ached fiercely, and her chest felt hot and throbby, so she let it go. The ride—in the back of a station wagon—made everything ache more, especially her head and ribs. But she drowsed for all except the worst bumps and turns.

She woke when Burk picked her up, because it hurt. Where had they brought her? She tried to look. All she could see were the branches of tall trees moving against the sky overhead.

"Is this the House?" she said. "What if they're watching?"

"Shhh. Nobody's watching," Caroline assured her.

She sounded so certain that Amelia quit struggling to see, and lay still again.

She was in bed when things drifted back into focus. Caroline stood beside her, switching a lamp on the nightstand down to a lower setting. She turned her head toward the door and said something about calling Sally to let her know she wouldn't make it back tonight.

"Thanks for doing this," Burk said. "I'll stay and spell you."

Caroline moved away from the bed, and the two of them stood silhouetted in the light from the hall.

"You really don't have to," she said. "I'll catch naps between times. Like doing my residency all over again."

Burk hesitated. "Just in case," he said, and then added something Amelia didn't catch.

"If you think so," she said. "I need to find more blankets. And a comfortable chair."

"Let me do that," he said and turned to go.

"Where's Brother Paco?" Amelia asked them. Her voice was insubstantial because it hurt so much to talk. "He brought me here—where'd he go?"

"She's really confused," he said. He sounded worried.

"Quite a knock on the noggin you took, sweetie," Caroline said, coming back to the bed. "Everything's fine. You just rest now, okay?" She smoothed the covers. "You warm enough?"

"Yes," Amelia whispered.

"I'm going to sit here with you. Close your eyes now."

Amelia did as she was told. The last thing she was aware of was Caroline's hand gently stroking her hair.

*   *   *

Later, Caroline woke her. "Amelia? Can you wake up and talk to me just a little? We need to make sure you're not sleeping too well here."

The pain in her head was sharper. "—What time—" she asked.

"What time is it? Oh, a little after two," Caroline said. She sounded as calm and kind as ever, but she looked tired. "How do you feel?"

Amelia tried to moisten her lips with her tongue, but her mouth was parched. "Thirsty," she whispered.

Caroline smiled at her. "How about a washcloth for your mouth?"

Amelia pulled in a cautious breath. "Sounds good—"

"Hang on. I'll be right back."

Amelia closed her eyes while she waited. Caroline brought a damp cloth and helped Amelia wipe her mouth.

"No drink?" Amelia said.

"Not yet." Caroline took the cloth and set it in a saucer on the nightstand. "You can have a drink tomorrow. Need anything else? Okay. Rest, then."

Amelia went back to sleep.

Caroline woke her several times, letting her use the cloth and soothing her headache with a cool hand on her forehead. Caroline spoke to her, too, but the words seemed unimportant. All that mattered was the reassurance they offered: that Amelia was safe. Amelia had no idea how much time passed between drowsing and these brief awakenings; each time, she slipped easily back into sleep.

Too easily, maybe. But she was grateful for the consuming emptiness: For now, no dreams came to trouble her.

She was in a room that seemed familiar, though she couldn't place it exactly. She wasn't in the clinic at the House. Maybe one of the bedrooms nearby, where the doctors and Brother Paco could keep an eye on her. She ached all over, and the pain in her head stabbed every time she shifted against the pillows, but the agony in her arm was gone. She must be getting better.

The room had wooden shutters instead of curtains, and they covered the bottom three quarters of the window. Above the shutters, rectangles of ghostly sky showed: the paled colorlessness that precedes dawn.

Amelia was queasy, her chest tight. She was such a fool; she should never have let them bring her here. No place was safe. Not from the Wolfen. Every time she closed her eyes, she was swamped by the frozen images of their handiwork: the dim yellowed light, the white cupboards splintered and smeared, the limp bodies laced with dark, wet holes.

Hadn't Spider warned Mama that they would know every move she made? Finding Amelia would be a cakewalk for them. She wished she had fallen all the way into the bayou and drowned. Saved them the trouble of coming after her.

Someone gave a little tap at the door, then pushed it open. Amelia gasped, but it was only the woman doctor who had been taking care of her. She was carrying a tray.

"I'm glad you're awake," she said. "I was getting tired of waking you up. How do you feel?"

Amelia couldn't admit how scared she was without explaining why. "Okay." Talking hurt her ribs. She lifted the covers, which hurt worse. There was a cast on her leg that encased her foot and calf, ending just above the knee. Had her leg been broken? That didn't seem right. But her toes were puffy, and the leg ached. She had nothing on except her underwear and the tape on her ribs.

She pulled the covers over her and tried scooting back against the headboard. When she shifted position, it felt like someone had hit her in the ribs with a broadsword, but she managed to sit up. The pain in her side was just this side of unbearable.

"Finished with the inventory?" the woman said from the doorway. "What's the verdict?"

Amelia didn't risk taking a fresh breath. "Need a shower."

"You must be doing better, if you're thinking about cleaning up." She looked different today. After a minute, Amelia realized why—she had taken her hair down. It made her look younger. "Do you know where you are?" the woman asked.

The question made Amelia uncertain. She glanced around the room, trying not to move her head too much. "The House?" Then she noticed the photograph on the nightstand—a picture of her mother, the one taken at her graduation from law school, when she was seven months pregnant with Amelia's older brother Daniel. Amelia sagged against the headboard and closed her eyes.

She was at the ranch, Gramps's ranch. The events she had been reliving with such dread were almost thirteen years in the past.

"Which house would that be?" Caroline asked.

"You're Caroline—Caroline Garrity," Amelia said, still not opening her eyes. "This is my grandfather's ranch."

"You seemed confused about that before. Thank God you're tracking a little better this morning." Amelia heard her set the tray down. "Think you could eat a little something? I fixed you hot tea and some Cream of Wheat."

"I hate that stuff—"

"Well, it's not the world's most exciting breakfast, but it's soft—easy to eat—and will warm you up."

Amelia didn't answer, but she opened her eyes.

"How about some tea?" Caroline brought the mug over and sat down carefully on the edge of the bed.

The bergamot scent of Earl Grey reached Amelia. It reminded her of home. Her mother's standard remedy. Remembering magnified the ache in her chest.

"I added some honey." Caroline offered the tea. "And it's not too hot."

Amelia sipped. Warmth spread through her, easing the tightness in her chest and stomach. She drank until Caroline said, "Okay, that's enough for now. I don't want you to fill up on tea. Let's try some cereal."

She traded the mug for the bowl and stirred the Cream of Wheat before spooning up a bite for Amelia. The stuff didn't taste as bad as she'd expected. Caroline had added honey and fresh milk, and the warmth of it was nice. Caroline fed her slowly, letting her take her time between bites. Amelia managed to eat about a third of it, but the whole time, her gaze kept straying to the photograph of her mother.

Caroline offered the tea again, and Amelia drank the rest, even though it was lukewarm now. She felt better for having eaten, and better yet when Caroline brought a bedpan. After Amelia relieved herself, Caroline washed her face and helped her brush her teeth. By the time they were done, golden light was streaming through the top of the windows. The sky beyond the panes had brightened to a clear summer blue.

Caroline came back and sat on the edge of the bed. "You need to rest, I know," Caroline said. "But I have to tell you something first. Since I'm treating you for something pretty serious, you have a right to know that there have been—questions raised—about my fitness to practice."

"That's right—Mac Peterson said—" Amelia broke off. The bleak look that had come into Caroline's eyes made her heart twist.

"His son died last year," Caroline said. "Mr. Peterson believes I'm responsible." She hesitated for a few seconds, and cleared her throat before going on. "And he may be right."

Amelia didn't know what to say.

"I was absolved of liability by a board of inquiry, but Mr. Peterson attributes that to the A.M.A.'s 'buddy system.' If he only knew—they'd get rid of osteopaths altogether if they had the chance."

"What is osteopathy, exactly?"

Caroline said, "Our training is different—and emphasizes prevention. And we sometimes use nontraditional treatments like acupuncture and Chinese herbalism. So you can see why we're not exactly the darlings of the A.M.A." She was turning the empty mug around and around in her hand. "And why Mr. Peterson thinks I'm a butcher who killed his son."

Amelia didn't think she could bear to hear about death just now—anyone's death. "You've taken good care of me. I feel fine." That was stretching the truth some, but she knew she wasn't dying. She remembered what dying felt like, and this wasn't even close.

Caroline glanced down and didn't answer immediately. The room had gradually brightened, and now the light from the windows illuminated one side of her face, emphasizing the hollows under her cheeks and the shadows under her eyes.

"You have a right to know what happened," Caroline said. "I probably should have told you before now." She took a deep breath. "Rich was working for me last summer—he was interested in medicine, you see. His father—disapproved of the arrangement. He wanted Rich to work at the feed store."

"But if he was thinking about medical school—" Amelia was curious in spite of herself.

"He wasn't thinking about medical school. Rich had decided he didn't want the pressure—said he had too much pressure on him already. So I—I encouraged him to consider other careers in the field. Nursing, or a tech of some sort—radiology, maybe—" Her hands moved restlessly in her lap. "There were lots of options."

"And Mr. Peterson hated it."

"He was furious when Rich told him he'd decided on nursing school. He and Rich fought—they were always fighting, but apparently this time was worse. Rich called me—said he hated the constant pressure from his father. Said he couldn't stand it anymore. I thought he was just blowing off steam. The way kids that age do, you know."

She sat quietly for a moment, then went on. "He took off on a half-trained horse of his father's—trying to prove himself, I guess. The horse went wild and tried to go through a metal-barred fence with him." She swallowed hard. "The animal had to be destroyed."

"And Rich?"

"Skull fracture, spinal and internal injuries—it was terrible. The horse fell on him." She pressed a fist to her mouth.

Amelia stayed quiet, and after a minute or two, Caroline went on. "One of his friends called me and the ambulance. I helped stabilize him, then had the techs take him to Sierra Medical in El Paso." A tear slipped down Caroline's face and trembled next to her mouth until she abruptly wiped it off, like someone swatting a gnat.

Amelia looked away. She hated it when people cried.

"Anyway. Rich died during transport. Mr. Peterson is convinced that if I hadn't interfered—if they'd taken his son to the hospital here, he would've been okay."

"But if the medical board doesn't think . . ."

Caroline blotted another tear with the back of her hand. "With injuries that severe, there was never much hope. But when someone you love dies, it's tough to accept that there was nothing anyone could do. You want to believe that somebody's to blame—that something could have been done to prevent it." She took a shaky breath. "Even if it means blaming yourself, you want to believe somebody was in control."

Amelia didn't want to think about death or guilt or Mac Peterson's son. Her headache was worse, and the room was suddenly much too warm. She pushed the blankets off her legs. Caroline glanced around, and Amelia adjusted the sheet to be sure it covered her forearm.

The skin around Caroline's eyes tightened, and there was suddenly something bitter in the set of her mouth.

"What's wrong?" Amelia said.

Caroline looked like she was about to cry some more. She took a deep breath. "That's the other thing we have to talk about. Burk thinks the threats you've been getting—that they have something to do with the scar on your arm."

Reflexively, Amelia covered the scar with her hand, even though the sheet already hid it. Beneath her fingertips, the surface flesh was slightly roughened, the indented areas smooth and tight. She could trace each line of the mark from memory.

"Your grandfather told Burk your mother—he said she was killed by a hate group," Caroline said softly.

Amelia's stomach clenched. She never talked about this. Not to anyone. No one had ever connected her with the story, not once in all these years—

No one except Brother Paco. And he hadn't forced the issue. He'd left it for her to decide who she was going to be: Amelia Caswell or Amy Castle.

"Old Mr. Rawlins never talked about it much, but after Burk found out about the threats you've been getting, he started putting things together. Are you in some danger? You kept saying, 'They'll be watching the hospital.'"

"I—" Amelia broke off. She didn't know what it was safe to say. There was so much she couldn't tell.

"Who's watching? Does it have something to do with what happened to you?" Caroline's voice dropped. "Those scars aren't new. How long ago . . . ?"

Amelia swallowed. "Twelve years. Thirteen in November."

Caroline's face was anguished. "So you were—how old? When it happened?"

"Sixteen," Amelia said. The word came out hoarse and strained.

"My God," Caroline Garrity said. Her eyes were brilliant with tears. Gently, she drew Amelia's arm out from under the sheet. Her fingers were light and steady on Amelia's wrist, as if she were measuring the pulse that fluttered rapidly there. "You were just a kid. How could anyone do something like this to you? These scars—they're from third-degree burns." Her voice broke on the last word.

Amelia jerked her arm away and rolled to her side, facing the wall. Moving was agonizing, but it hurt less than talking about this would.

After a moment, Caroline laid a hand on her shoulder. "Amelia, the last thing I want is to upset you. But Burk and I are so worried. This is dangerous. Do you

feel well enough to talk to the sheriff? After this accident—"

"I don't want to talk about it." Amelia's throat
was tight, and her eyes were burning. Why didn't people
understand there was no point in raking up the past? It
was dead and gone. Gone to dust.

"Isn't it time you talked to *someone?* No one
should have to deal with something like this alone,
Amelia. No one."

She *couldn't* talk about any of it. If she even
thought too much about it, she would cry. And there
were too many tears stored up inside her, enough tears to
last forever. So many they would wash her away if she
ever let them loose.

Besides, crying never solved anything. Did it?

She must have spoken out loud without realizing
it, because Caroline hugged her. "It's okay, angel. If anyone ever deserved a good cry, it's you. God, you weren't
much older than Mark is!"

That hit Amelia like one of Spider's bullets. She
couldn't manage an answer. Had it really been that long
ago? In her heart, it felt like the whole thing had happened last night—the chatter of gunfire, the hiss of a gas
flame—

Too many things were swirling in her head, making it ache. Too much—how could she make sense of it
all?

Then her gaze fell on the picture of her mother
on Gramps's nightstand. Mama's smile was like a sun-
burst. She always said it was one of the happiest moments of her life. The dimple in her cheek—no wonder
Caroline had reminded her of her mother. Caroline had
her mother's smile.

That picture had been taken when she was only
twenty-seven. Younger than Amelia was now. It didn't
seem possible that her mother would never smile like that
again. That she was dead and gone. Dust.

Amelia Caswell laid her head on Caroline's
shoulder and wept.

Chapter Seventeen

Houston, November 29, 1983, 3:07 A.M.

Amelia was dreaming of slow-dancing with one of Daniel's friends when they jerked her from bed. Their hands were rough and hard on her sleep-soft flesh. She couldn't see them at all in the dark.

It was like being attacked by the phantom monsters that had inhabited her childhood nightmares. The terror of it harkened back to those nightmares: It came on her instant and entire. She shrieked at the top of her lungs. And, as in a nightmare, no matter how hard she screamed, she couldn't seem to make any sound.

One of them grabbed her by the arms, hard enough to cut off her circulation, and she realized this was no dream. He shook her, then shoved her head back so another of them could slap a piece of duct tape over her mouth. There were two of them, only two, she thought. She was clammy with sweat and shivering at the same time, and she couldn't hear anything. It was as if all the sound in the world had been shut off.

They dragged her out of the bedroom and downstairs to the kitchen.

They hadn't turned on the overhead lights, only the single bulb mounted under the vent over the stove. Its light was frail and yellowed, like old silk, and spilled weakly across the utility island and kitchen chairs, corrupting the familiar room with shadows.

Awkward shapes that she hadn't identified abruptly resolved into her parents and older brother, their mouths taped and their hands bound behind them.

They were sitting on the floor, propped up against the cabinets like life-sized rag dolls. Her father was in the middle, with her mother and Daniel on either side. Their eyes were closed.

Three men wearing black jumpsuits, gloves, and hoods stood over them. All three were big, with the pumped-up look of weight lifters. Each had a sub-machine gun hung from a shoulder strap, held casually in firing position. Their black-gloved hands were on the triggers, and the guns pointed directly at her family. The hooded faces turned toward Amelia, and she shrank back, suddenly conscious of how little of her was covered by the T-shirt she slept in.

The men holding Amelia twisted her arms when she moved, and she moaned behind the tape. She thought she saw her mother's eyes flicker at the faint sound. Another hooded man—slighter than the others—entered the kitchen, pulling Michael with him. Her little brother's face was bone white, his eyes like stark midnight above the rectangle of duct tape. The strip was so wide it covered his whole chin.

"You checked the entire house?" one of the men standing over her parents said. His voice was muffled by the hood, but otherwise it sounded normal. Like anyone's voice.

Michael's guard nodded.

The man beside her parents pulled a walkie-talkie from his belt and said into it, "Target secured." Then he leaned down and nudged her mother's jaw with the barrel of his submachine gun.

Amelia's throat clamped shut.

"Open your eyes, Madame Mayor," he said. "No use playing possum. We've gone to considerable trouble to arrange this little demonstration, and we don't want you to miss a second of it."

Her mother opened her eyes. Even in the weak light, their expression showed clear. Rage and anguish. No fear. Mama never showed fear. It was against her principles.

"Get the shears," the talker said to one of

Amelia's guards. He glanced at her, and she saw his eyes glitter behind the holes in the black fabric.

Amelia tried to breathe, forgetting the tape, and she choked. The first man's hold on her arm tightened. The other one released her other arm and moved out from behind her. He went to a drab canvas carryall that lay on the kitchen island across from Daniel. Her older brother's face wasn't mottled by shadows, she realized. It was darkened by bruises. He was limp against the cabinet. Unconscious.

This isn't real, Amelia thought.

The man pulled a big pair of utility scissors and a set of electric shears out of the bag. His hood turned toward the leader. "Do the girl first?"

The leader nodded and nudged at her mother with his boot. "You watching, Madame Mayor? Pay attention."

The man who was holding Amelia shifted his grip to her upper arms, twisting. The pressure bent her forward, and he shoved her over to the island. The second man set the scissors and shears on the counter next to Amelia. He grabbed her hair in one hand and yanked. Her eyes watered from the pain. The man behind her squeezed harder on her arms.

The second one picked up the scissors and started chopping her hair off next to the scalp. Each cut pulled painfully. Tears spilled down her face as she listened to the crunching sound of the scissors hacking at her hair. The long brown-blond locks dropped to the floor, where they curled gracefully around his boots.

"Jeez, she's got more hair than a gorilla."

The scissors scraped through another twist of hair. Amelia's nose was dripping, making her struggle to breathe. She tried to duck her head and wipe her face on her shoulder, but the man tightened his grip and forced her to be still. He was cutting close to her ears now, and the scrunching sound of the scissors was louder.

Her entire body was shaking. How could this be happening? Where were the police who were supposed to be guarding the house? What about the burglar alarm?

The man forced her head lower. As he moved,

she got a whiff of his sour body odor and gagged. Her mouth flooded with saliva. For a second, she thought she would vomit. With her mouth taped, she could choke to death. She breathed shallowly and fought the nausea under control.

The spill of hair on the floor was inches deep now. The man doing the cutting kicked at it impatiently before he shoved her head down and made one last cut.

"Jeez," he said. "Took for-fuckin'-ever."

Amelia blinked. Tears and mucus dripped in dark spots on the curls at her feet. He wasn't pushing on her head any more. Quickly, she swabbed her face on her shoulder.

"Just get on with it." That was the leader's voice.

"Gimme a minute," the man in front of her snapped. "Gotta plug the goddamn thing in."

The man behind Amelia spoke for the first time. "Watch it, Jag. Attitude." He pushed Amelia closer to the counter.

"Don't look away, Your Honor," the leader said. "This is the best part."

Jag had the shears plugged in. He clicked them on, and they buzzed in his hand. He grabbed her by the face this time, gloved fingers digging into the flesh over her jaw. He was more proficient with the shears than with the scissors, and zipped them across her head. They tugged at some of the longer pieces of hair, making her eyes water again, but it was over fast. Her scalp felt naked and cold.

The man holding her arms shoved her down against the island so she was facing her parents, then angled the gun slung over his shoulder at her. Amelia's hands were numb and tingling from having her arms held so tight. She flexed her hands, rubbed her arms, as if to reclaim them. Cautiously, she touched her head. Nothing but stubble.

Jag gestured with the shears, and Michael's guard hauled him over. Michael looked terrified. Seeing that, she started to cry again.

Jag didn't bother with the scissors this time, just used the clippers to shave Michael's head. It was shocking to watch the thick swatches of silky dark hair fall away from his pale scalp. The job was done in seconds. His naked head and stricken eyes made him look like a concentration camp child. The guard pushed him down by the island next to Amelia, and she hugged him. Michael clung to her, his teeth chattering.

Across from them, their mother shifted position, and the leader squatted down in front of her. "You took two of ours," he said. "Now you see how easy it would be for us to take two of yours. See? We've made skinheads out of them. So maybe you should change your faggot-loving attitude. Maybe you should drop out of the governor's race. What do you think, Your Honor?"

Her mother was watching him carefully, but she couldn't answer. They hadn't untaped her mouth. Amelia realized they must be part of that neo-Nazi group—the Wolfen—the skinheads who started the riot in Montrose. The police had killed two of them.

"You going to drop out of the race, Madame Faggot-Lover Mayor?"

Mama nodded vigorously. The leader of the skinheads stood up. "You know what, Your Honor? I don't believe you. I don't think you're convinced yet." He jerked the muzzle of his gun at one of his men. "Get the buckle out."

Amelia had no idea what he meant, but something in his tone made her terror spike again. Her legs and arms went numb.

The leader picked up his walkie-talkie again. "Spider to Hook—we're still conducting business. How's it look from your end?"

"All clear, Spider," a squawky voice said. "H.P.D. is sleeping like a big baby, and you're right on schedule."

"Roger. Spider out."

One of them clumped over to where Amelia was huddled. She didn't look up at him, just squeezed Michael closer and stared blankly at the pair of black boots beside her. A few strands of hair were tangled in the laces of the Doc Martens. It was the one they called Jag.

He leaned over her head, and she heard the unmistakable pop of a gas burner lighting. She couldn't stop herself from looking up.

Jag was standing over her, his gun strung behind his shoulder with its barrel pointing up. He'd traded in the clippers for a pair of vise-grips with insulated handles. Pinched in the grips was an elaborate belt buckle with a high-relief design: a wolf's head superimposed on a swastika.

He adjusted the gas flame and laid the buckle in it.

A line of ice water ran up the veins of Amelia's arms, and pooled in her chest. There was no going back, she thought dully. Whatever happened was going to last forever. She tried to swallow, but her mouth was suddenly too dry.

The leader leaned over her mother and used the barrel of his gun to lift her mother's chin. "You don't look so sure about this sudden decision of yours, Your Honor. Maybe you'll find this part of our demonstration more convincing."

He stepped to one side and gestured with his gun. Two of his men came, jerked Michael away from her, and dragged Amelia along the floor, away from the island. The one who'd held her arms earlier followed, and they surrounded her, a half-circle of shadows looming above her.

Two of them pinned her legs and sat on them, the other knelt on her right arm and leaned on her forehead. The floor pressed up against her, but she was too numb to struggle. The fourth man—the skinny one—pulled her left arm out from her body and knelt across her wrist.

Then Jag brought the buckle and, without any fanfare, stuck the glowing metal against her left forearm.

The pain was so terrible that her nerve endings couldn't track it as pain. It was something else, something worse. Something unnameable. She screamed, twisted, bucked—or tried to—but the tape was over her mouth and the men had her pinned. The sizzle of the buckle on her skin was louder than her muffled screams.

She kept waiting to black out from the pain—praying to. She didn't.

Her awareness narrowed to the line of fire that ran from her forearm to her chest, narrowed until the pain became her universe. Agony was everything.

Then, with a faint shock, she popped away, outside of that universe of pain.

She was floating up near the ceiling somewhere, watching men with black hoods brand a hairless girl. Watching as a yellow spill of urine spread out from under the girl's long black T-shirt, and the men on her legs jumped back. Watching as a smaller figure—also hairless—launched itself against the back of the man kneeling on the girl's right arm. Watching as the man backhanded the child so viciously that the shaved head slammed into the clean white cabinets and left a long red smear on them as it slid to the floor.

Still watching as the legs of the middle captive convulsed, watching as he flung himself sideways across the floor to kick the torturer with the vise-grips. Watching as the man standing over the captives took one step forward and swung the butt of his machine gun against the prisoner's temple, smashing him into an inert lump.

And then her view faltered, shrank—sank—

Jag ducked backward, pulling the buckle away from her, but the pain didn't stop. Her forearm was on fire—she could feel the burning all the way down to the bone. There was blood in her mouth where she'd bitten herself. She had to swallow it or choke, so she swallowed, then nearly vomited. Without considering, she fumbled with the tape over her mouth and ripped it off. A lot of the skin of her lips came with it—a new fire—on her mouth this time. Blood leaked down her chin, but at least she could breathe. The muscles of her chest ached with a sick pulsing feeling.

All the men had moved away from her at some point. She rolled to her right side and curled around the sickness. Her legs were sticky. The stench of burnt meat mingled with the smell of urine.

One of the black-hooded figures bent over her, and she flinched, sending waves of pain through her arm and shoulder. It was the thin one, Michael's guard. He pressed something carefully against her arm.

She hadn't thought the pain could be worse, but the touch was like being branded all over again. Then she realized he was applying an ice compress packed in a kitchen cloth, tying it around her arm. After a few seconds, the ice began to blunt the edge of the agony.

Amelia lay still and tried to breathe shallowly. If she didn't move, she might be able to endure this.

There were voices, but she shut them out. She thought of nothing but drawing this one breath, of keeping the movement of her rib cage smooth. She concentrated on not jarring the arm, not breathing too fast, doing nothing to intensify the roiling nausea in her gut.

It was the smell that brought her back, the renewed stink of burnt meat and hot metal. She lifted her head, slowly, and blinked. Her eyes were feeding her brain only dim light and blurred shapes. Slowly, she got things into focus.

Spider stood across from her, his hand resting comfortably on the trigger of the submachine gun suspended from his shoulder. Even with the hood hiding his face, he looked relaxed and confident. He gestured with the gun, and two of his men hauled her father's limp form back up and propped it against the cabinets.

"Convinced yet, faggot-lover?" He nudged her mother with his boot. "We know everything about you, Mayor. We have people everywhere—we'll know every move you make, every word, every *thought*. We know that pinko brother-in-law of yours was supposed to be here this weekend, but got held up by committee work. We know you invited your dear old dad for Thanksgiving, but he said no because he doesn't like to leave his place in New Mexico. We know where everyone you care about is *at any moment*. So don't think you can say one thing and then turn around and do something else. We'll know. And we'll strike."

Tears were pouring down her mother's face. Seeing her mother cry petrified Amelia. The only time she had ever known her mother to weep was the night Gramma died. Was Papa dying? Michael? Was *she*?

Something moved at the edge of her vision. Carefully, Amelia turned her head. Jag had the vise-grips in his hand again. He was approaching Michael, who had been pinned by two of the others. The puddle of blood behind his head spread like a dark and terrible halo.

Amelia dragged herself up to a sitting position against the island.

"No." The word was a croak, and talking was enough to make shadows swim at the edge of her vision. "Don't! He's—just a kid. Please!" Her lips split again as she spoke, spilling fresh blood on her chest and chin. The pain from the branding was displaced now, boring holes in the bones of her upper arm. She grabbed the edge of the counter with her good hand and struggled to her feet. She wavered there, leaning heavily on the island.

The two men holding Michael looked at her. Behind the masking black cloth, she was certain they were blank-eyed as demons, expressionless and indifferent.

"Don't—hurt—him." The words rasped her throat, tore her mouth.

Jag laughed at her.

The skinny one stepped in front of Michael, facing the leader. "He's just a kid, Spider."

"And how old were Smack and Hammer?" Spider said. His gloved hand was taut on the grip of his gun. He lifted it, flexing his fingers, and took a step closer to Amelia. "This bunch of faggot-lovers didn't stop to ask how old *our* boys were, did they?"

Jag laughed again and brandished the smoking belt-buckle. "I just got it to cooking heat," he said. "Can't let all that work go to waste." He waved it in Amelia's direction. "You want I should do your other arm instead?"

She recoiled against the island.

"No?" Jag said. "Don't love li'l brother *that* much, huh?" He took a step closer. "But the arm's too easy. You already know what that's like. This time, think I'll do your *face*—" He jabbed at her with the smoldering buckle.

Time twisted. She could see the blackened scum of her own skin on the surface of the buckle, smell the death on it, feel its heat sharp on her cheek as it came toward her. His mask loomed closer, and he laughed.

It was the laugh that propelled her away from the island, the laughter with its note of cruel pleasure. Pure rage blazed through her, and she lunged for the vise-grips, twisting her head to one side to avoid the buckle. She grabbed his hand with both of hers and shoved the buckle straight at his eyes, throwing all her weight behind it.

Jag gave ground with her weight, letting the force of her lunge propel the buckle back as he ducked to one side. But Spider was close behind him—closer than he must have realized—and the brand connected solidly with Spider's gun arm.

Spider's bellow was drowned in the chattering thunder of the submachine gun's burst. In the enclosed space of the kitchen, the sound exploded—immense echoing thwacks that made Amelia's head ring.

Time was still strange. It seemed that she heard the burst of gunfire before she saw the punch of the bullets that sketched a connect-the-dots line across their bodies. But she knew that wasn't right. She knew the sound came *after* the explosive plops that marked the bullets' entry into flesh—leaving the dark wet hole where her mother's left eye had been, a splotch in her shoulder—then in Pop's chest, another, lower—then Daniel's chest and belly.

Their bodies jerked, convulsed, sighed, lay still. Sprawled there, in a heartbeat they became no more than spilled flesh, ruined housings.

The crisp white paint of the cupboards was splintered and bloodied behind their slumped bodies, as if it had been wounded, too. The buckle had fallen to the floor next to her mother's pale bare foot. Amelia watched as the vinyl tile bubbled, blackened, and warped under the hot metal.

That's what they've done to me, she thought.

Then Spider was on her, swinging his gun, clubbing her across the cheek with it. Was the barrel still hot, or was that her imagination? She went down without resisting, hardly noticing this new pain.

"YOU—STUPID—BITCH—" He was shrieking, out of control.

Footsteps rang along the sidewalk next to the kitchen, and the door burst open. "I heard shots—"

Another man in a hood. It was one of them, not a rescuer. *But there's no one left to rescue, anyway.*

Spider turned on the newcomer. "What are you doing here? You're supposed to be guarding the cops—get back out there and do it!"

"But the shots—" The man looked at the bodies sprawled across the floor, and sucked air. "Oh, God—you said no killing! You said—"

"Shut up!" Spider shouted. He kicked at Amelia where she lay. "We didn't shoot them—this stupid bitch did."

Jag was laughing again. "Their own daughter did 'em. A regular Lizzie Borden, ain't she?"

"Shut up!" Spider yelled again.

A crackle of static burst from his walkie-talkie. "Hook to Spider—come in, Spider. You're snagged—units on their way. Get out!"

"Shit!" Spider waved the submachine gun at his men. "Get the bag, come on. Grab the kids—we'll need hostages."

More static from the walkie-talkie. "Spider, do you read? Cut line!"

He snatched at the radio. "Yeah, I got it. Now shut the fuck up!"

Jag grabbed the buckle—still pinched in the vise-grips—and stuffed it into the canvas bag. Two of the men grabbed Amelia and dragged her toward the kitchen door. She managed a look back to where Michael lay. The puddle of blood was bigger now. The skinny one had raised Michael's head. All Amelia could see was blood, dark and glassy, masking his pale scalp.

"Too late—this one's dead," the skinny man said. "Caught a ricochet." He laid Michael's head back down on the floor gently.

"The girl'll do," Spider said. "We can scrag her later. Now scramble!"

No one left to rescue, Amelia thought again. *No one at all.*

Things got blurry then. They dumped her on the floor of a van that was parked on the circular drive out front, shoved her down on top of wire cutters and rounds of spare ammunition, the tools of their trade. Heavy boots connected with her more than once as they piled into the seats. She didn't really feel the blows. Maybe she had managed to fall away from her body again; maybe a semiconsciousness had finally claimed her.

She didn't brace herself; she let the motion of the van slam her around as it cornered, slowed, and lurched forward again. The skinheads were talking—sometimes yelling—at each other, but she didn't try to make sense of what they were saying. Very little penetrated the haze of shock.

Then a loud thumping noise built up around them, a beat that matched her pulse. She couldn't identify it until one of the skinheads said, "Shit! They've sent out the chopper!"

Lights flashed off to their right.

Spider's voice answered. "We're under the trees, no lights. Slow down—that's it. Slower."

The *WHUMP-whump-whump* faded again.

"There's the turn." Spider sounded sharp and controlled again. The van lurched, throwing her against the feet of the men in the middle seat. Boots stomped over her, the van door slammed open, and cold air splashed over her like a bucket of water. She heard another engine cough, then catch, before the van lurched off again, its side door still latched open.

Sirens were wailing in the distance.

"One more stop, and we can ditch the van," Spider said.

"What about the girl?"

"Once we're clear—"

I'm dead, Amelia thought. It was a pleasant thought. *Mama, Papa, Daniel, Michael—Michael—everyone's dead. I should be dead, too.*

The sirens drew closer.

"There's the park road—just up there on the left—take that." Spider's voice was taut and crisp.

"It dead-ends in the bayou," somebody protested.

"I know what I'm doing."

"Right. That's why there's a chopper and half the H.P.D. on our butts."

"Shut up and turn. We'll ditch the van there and cut across—the car's just down Memorial."

"What about the girl?"

"Do her and dump her with the van," Spider said.

The van lurched to the left, flinging Amelia toward the open door. Her bare feet slid across the sill.

One of the skinheads leaned down and grabbed her shoulders.

"No point," he said. "She's already kicked. Shock, prob'ly."

The van swung left again, sharply, and the man heaved her through the open door.

The ground was farther away than it should have been. She fell through darkness, hearing sirens—landed on a steep slope, skidded, rolled—glimpsed the bayou's sheen below her. The tangle of vines and brush was chill and sharp against her bare skin as she pitched wildly down the embankment, and with every impact, pain shattered more of her, chopped more parts away, and she thought gratefully *I'm dead, I'm dead, I'm dead—*

And then, finally—blissfully—blackness came for her, and she was.

Death, like everyone else, abandoned her.

There were voices, but she refused to open her eyes. It was light, though, she could tell even without looking. A thin gray iceberg of a day. There was nothing left to wake up to. She rejected consciousness, didn't want to understand the voices, but her mind chose to function anyway.

"She's gone and pissed herself," one of them said clearly.

"You would, too, Digger, if you was hurt as bad as that. Ain't seen someone beat up this bad since I left home."

"What's that thing wrapped on her arm for?"

"Bandage, fool, can't you see the blood? Listen, you stay and watch her. I'll go get the dude from the House van. They got doctors and everything there. They fix her up."

"Then I won't get no gimmes from the van!"

"I told you, gonna bring the man over here. You prob'ly get extra for helping out, Digger."

"That dude ain't coming all the way down here just 'cause you say so."

"Digger, you know the House always help kids that's hurt. Who else gonna take care of her, after her folks beat her that bad? You just stay put till I get back, hear?"

"Shit," Digger said. He said it softly, under his breath.

Silence. She waited, but nobody said anything more. She opened her eyes. It took a few seconds to get things into focus, and even then, the world kept blurring on her.

But she could see well enough to tell that a kid with a bright red mohawk was kneeling a few feet away, watching her. He was maybe fourteen, and emaciated, bones sharp under his skin. He had a blue tattoo on his cheek and two rings in his nose.

"Hey," he said, looking at her. "You awake now? You okay?"

She closed her eyes again.

He coughed, a loose ragged sound. "Guess you got hurt pretty bad. But it'll be okay. Sandi's bringing the House guy. They'll fix you up."

She didn't believe him. No one could fix her.

"Hey," he said softly. "What's your name?"

Her lips cracked when she moved her mouth. "Amelia Caswell," she tried to say. It was a scant, husky whisper.

"Amy? Amy Castle? That's real pretty," he said.

A new voice said, "It sure is. How're you doing, Amy?"

She raised her eyelids, an enormous effort. Darkness swirled at the edge of her vision, narrowing the thin gray day into a tunnel in front of her. A chubby, balding man in a blue polo shirt was bending over her. He began lightly touching her legs, moving her joints. His touch was impersonal, careful; his face kind. There was no shock in his eyes as he looked at her, only a sad, terrible certainty.

"I'm going to pick you up now, Amy," he said. "It's going to hurt, but I have to take you somewhere safe. Okay?"

"No—hospital—" She clutched his arm with her good hand, and choked out again, "No hospital." They would be watching.

The kind eyes grew even sadder. "No, no hospital. We have a private clinic—that's where we'll take you. To a safe place. Okay, Amy?"

She managed a faint nod, no more, before the darkness spiraled into a knot and blanked out the world.

New Mexico

Cool damp air swept across the basin as steep cloud banks the color of charcoal piled against the flanks of the mountain. Lightning exploded, thunder cracked and trembled across the desert, and a life-giving torrent poured from the sky.

Caroline had rocked her as she cried. She had listened to the whole hideous story and absolved her. Amelia was not to blame for what had happened to her family. Caroline had said so.

The sweet wild smell of rain in the desert flowed through Amelia's open window like a benediction, a balm to her aching throat and burning eyes.

The rainy season had begun.

Part 3

LA LLORONA-
MIDSUMMER

Ruin hath taught me thus to ruminate,—
That Time will come and take my love away.
This thought is as a death, which cannot choose
But weep to have that which it fears to lose.

—William Shakespeare,
Sonnet 64

Chapter Eighteen

New Mexico

Amelia's arms and shoulders ached. She was already sweating with the effort of crutching her way along on the uneven ground between the garden and the kiln. The strain was aggravated by the fierce rash developing under her arms, where the padded tops of the crutches tended to chafe.

She paused and looked up into the crayon blue sky. In a few hours, clouds would roll in and pile up against the Sacramentos like a flock of panicked sheep. This time of year, it rained every afternoon, big crackling thunderstorms that drenched the desert with raindrops the size of quarters.

The rains came every year at this season and, during that season, usually fell each day between one and five. It was as if the land's precarious balance between thirst and death wrenched pity from the rain god. Not enough to swell the basin's portion of rain, but enough to settle the god's erratic impulses. Enough to bring constancy to the basin's meager allotment.

With the advent of the rainy season, the basin was blooming, and her bees were thriving on the bloom. Mannie had brought his young cousin Roberto up to help move the hives twice already. Stuck on crutches like this, Amelia couldn't do much more than supervise. She'd wielded the smoker; checked the moving straps on the hives and replaced the folded screens to keep the bees inside, but she couldn't help shift the boxes.

Mannie and Roberto had done all of that, positioning them carefully in the areas she'd selected, first in

Mary's orchard, then in Steve Navarro's pistachio grove. Roberto had even set up the bear fence for her.

It went against the grain to rely on others as much as she'd had to over the past month. First on Caroline to take care of her while she was recovering, now on Mark and the Valdez cousins to take care of the goats and bees. And Caroline had been giving her rides everywhere because she couldn't drive the truck's stick shift with her leg in a cast. Amelia didn't like the arrangement one bit—it seemed too risky—but Caroline and the others had insisted on sticking close since her fall.

About the only thing she was still managing to do on her own was work in the studio. She'd even had to have Mark help load the kiln yesterday—which he'd done happily. He still felt guilty about running off and leaving her the day she'd fallen, even though she and Burk had both explained that it wasn't his fault. Burk showed him that the screws holding the ladder's swiveling rubber feet on had been loosened, deliberately destabilizing it, but Mark persisted in blaming himself for not being around to help her.

The ladder *had* been tampered with, though. That was something that still had all of them edgy. Since they'd used the ladder the day before her fall without any trouble, it was pretty clear that someone had deliberately sabotaged it the night of the fire. Unfortunately, that didn't narrow the field of suspects much; half the county had turned out to fight the fire.

Caroline had taken over picking Mark up in the evenings, since Burk was working double shifts right now at the post office. Amelia missed seeing him more than she cared to admit, and she had worried that Tucker might feel abandoned. But Tucker seemed to be perfectly content to stay at the ranch. Apparently the dog was more secure than she was.

Mark was here all day during the week. Caroline kept her office open till five-thirty, so she usually didn't make it by to pick him up until after six. As a result, the three of them had fallen into the habit of having supper together almost every night. Cooking was something

Amelia could still handle; it felt good to do something for her friends in return for their help.

Amelia maneuvered carefully around to the kiln's bricked-up entrance. Leaning mostly on the left crutch, she managed to put on the heavy asbestos gauntlet and a pair of safety goggles, then leaned forward to remove the eyehole brick so she could check the cones. As she bent forward, the loose right crutch slipped out from under her arm and skittered several feet down the dirt path.

Amelia swore. She was sick of gimping around. Everything was five times harder to do on crutches, and she hated being unable to drive. At this rate, she'd never keep up with the honey flow. Caroline said it would be at least another three weeks before the cast came off, maybe longer if Amelia didn't start eating better.

She let the strayed crutch lie there while she hopped closer to the kiln and got herself balanced. Cautiously, she removed the eyehole brick and checked the cones. They were slumped, but not full over yet. Farther inside, stacked neatly on the kiln shelves, she could see some of the honey pots. They were glowing gold-red, like dishes from Hell. Gorgeous. But she wouldn't be able to tell how the glaze had turned out until the pots cooled.

She got the brick fitted back into its niche and pulled off the gauntlet and goggles. But when she tried to move away from the kiln, the rubber tip of her remaining crutch caught a bit of gravel and skidded. She wavered for an instant, then went down sideways, scraping her elbow along the edge of the concrete slab.

Mark came around the corner of the tractor shed in time to see her fall. He dumped the basket of vegetables he was carrying and raced over to her.

"You okay? Did you hurt yourself?" He got down next to her, eased her up, and brushed at the dust on the back of her T-shirt.

"Nothing hurt but your pride," Gramps said. He was standing behind Mark, watching her.

"Easy for you to say," Amelia shot back.

"Huh?" Mark had turned to gather up the crutches.

"Sorry, just talking to myself," Amelia said. "Thanks, Mark."

"Are you okay?" He handed her the first crutch, let her get it set, then pulled her to her feet before giving her the second one.

He was getting good at this, Amelia noted sourly. "Nothing hurt but my pride," she said, and Gramps laughed.

"What about your arm?" Mark asked. "You're bleeding."

"It's just a scrape." She wiggled the crutches. Even her hands were sore from holding onto the grips. "You think I'm going to thank you for reclaiming these for me? Instruments of torture."

His expression lightened. "Don't you hate 'em? When I broke my ankle playing softball, the crutches hurt worse than my foot did. Does the cast itch?"

"Worse than a zillion mosquito bites," she said.

"Sometimes you can scratch down inside it with a straw or something."

"Thanks for the tip. You better get your harvest inside now, though."

"Oh, yeah." He ran back to where he'd dropped the basket, snagged it, and trotted toward the house. Watching him move made her feel even more sluggish. And it was too damn hot. But if she was going to have enough honey to fill her pots, she needed to get to work in the honey house.

She hadn't worked with the honey extracting equipment since she was a teenager, and the prospect made her nervous. But Gramps was here now, although lately she hadn't seen much of him.

"You going to help me figure out that extracting contraption?" she asked him.

"You bet," he said. "How many supers you got?"

"Mannie and I pulled four full ones when we moved the bees off Mary's place," she said, as she crutched her way cautiously around the kiln, turning the burners off. If she was going down to the honey house, she wouldn't want to hobble all the way back up here to turn them off later, and the built-up heat would probably take the pots to a full cone ten anyway. "Mannie says they're real heavy."

"Good. That means you got you a good honey flow. How're the bees handling the moves? Had any queen killing?"

Sometimes a hive killed its queen when the bees got distressed by too many moves.

"Not that I could see. We lost a hive to fire ants, but Steve Navarro gave me some cinder blocks to get the rest up off the ground, so I think they'll be okay. Only thing I'm worried about is splitting some of the bigger hives before they swarm. I've never split one before."

Gramps nodded. "We'll get you through it. Let's worry about the extraction first, though."

It was a stickier, messier business than she'd ever dreamed. Amelia didn't remember it being so much work when she was a kid, but then it was always easier to watch someone else do something than to do it yourself.

She used a hive tool to separate the frames—the bees had built small burr combs along the top of the frames, so they stuck together. Then she pried the first frame up from the super and pulled it out. This was fresh honeycomb, built on new foundation, so the wax comb was translucent and creamy. The frame was heavy, and when she held it up to the light, she could see the cells glowing golden with honey.

As kids, she and Michael had uncapped honeycomb for Gramps, but she couldn't remember much about it. Gramps had to show her how to balance a frame full of honeycomb on end against a narrow strip of board laid across the tank of the capping melter. She had the electric uncapping knife plugged in; it took only a minute or two to heat up.

"Take a nice deep cut," he told her. "Don't try to save the comb—the bees'll build that back up in no time. You need to make sure all the cells get uncapped on your first pass to be efficient."

The trick was to use the wooden sides of the frame to guide the heated knife blade through the wax comb. Gooey clumps of wax cappings and honey fell into the melter, and she flipped the frame over and made another cut on the other side. It worried her at first how much honey was draining into the uncapping melter, but Gramps said the melter would separate the honey from the melted wax, and showed her the tube that ran from the uncapper to the big fifty-five-gallon storage drum.

As soon as she had the comb on both sides of the frame uncapped, he showed her how to load the opened frame into the big stainless steel extractor. "The upper edge of the frame always goes to the outside," he said. "The bees build the comb on an upward slant, see? They don't want their honey running out on the ground when they open a cell. This way, when you start the extractor spinning, the honey flows out along that slant. You'll be able to see it accumulating along the sides of the extractor. Now do another one."

Amelia had thirty-six frames to uncap and extract. The extractor was a good-sized one, and could hold twelve frames at once. It took her an hour to uncap the first dozen frames and load them in the extractor. By the end of that hour, her wrist ached from plying the electric knife, and there were hundreds of honeybees in the house. They were crawling across spilled cappings on the concrete floor, exploring the untouched supers, and getting in Amelia's hair—literally.

"Where'd all these bees come from?" she asked Gramps, brushing one off her arm. "The hives are all fifteen miles from here, at the pistachio grove." No stinging yet, but there were bees *everywhere*. She knew these weren't her bees.

He laughed. "I've had bees in this yard for thirty years, girl, and a few of 'em have taken off on their own. There's probably more than one hive in the trees down there by the creek. You start uncapping honey, they're going to come find it."

Amelia blew gently at a bee that was buzzing around her face. "Right," she said.

Working on crutches, it took her all afternoon to uncap and extract the four supers of honeycomb. She was exhausted, sticky, and sick of the smell of honey by the end of it—and this was only a fraction of the honey she expected to harvest this season.

But Gramps had nodded approvingly when she checked the storage barrel at the end of the afternoon. Honey was up to the ten gallon mark.

"That's about thirty pounds to the super," he said. "Not bad for your first season. Not bad at all."

Amelia was thinking that Caroline Garrity would have made a terrific chauffeur as she got settled in the passenger seat of the old station wagon the next afternoon. Caroline had moved the seat back before Amelia sat down to make sure she had enough room for the bulky cast, and had brought an extra cushion for her back. It helped; her hip and lower back ached all the time from the weight of the cast.

Burk had come out for the afternoon to bathe and dip Tucker, who had picked up some ticks, and Mark had elected to stay and help. Not an exciting agenda, but Amelia wished she were staying, too. She hadn't seen Burk much lately. He said it was because he was pulling double shifts at the post office, but she worried that it was because he was still angry with her for losing her temper at Spencer Reed.

He had his shirt off and was sudsing one very mournful-looking yellow lab. Mark was holding the flea shampoo and talking consolingly to Tucker as Caroline pulled out of the yard. Amelia watched them in the side mirror, thinking she probably looked as miserable as Tucker did. She was apprehensive about her plans for the afternoon—delivering pots of honey as thank-you gifts. And apologizing to Reed.

"I really appreciate your driving me around today," Amelia said. "I know it's an imposition—"

"After all you've done for Mark? You've got to be kidding. He's so much happier these days." Caroline bounced into the driver's seat and cranked the ignition key. A grinding sound came from under the hood, and she made a face. After a minute or so, the engine caught. "Starter trouble," she said darkly. "Just what I need."

"Combustion engines are sentient," Amelia said as they crept along the rutted ranch road. "They know when you're tapped out, and time their ailments accordingly." Then she looked around for some wood to knock on; the truck was about the only thing that hadn't given her trouble lately. Of course, she thought, that was probably only because she hadn't been able to drive it since she broke her leg.

Caroline stopped at the gate and jumped out to open it.

It was frustrating not to be able to even drive the car through for her. Amelia had to sit there and wait while Caroline did it all.

"How long did you say till the cast comes off?" she asked when Caroline had the gate closed behind them.

"Not till the X rays come back clean," Caroline said. She put the elderly wagon in gear and pulled carefully out onto the road. "A few weeks. Although at the rate things are going, we may have to take you to Alamogordo to get the pictures."

Amelia looked at her, realizing that something was wrong—something more than usual. "What is it?" she asked quietly.

Caroline shot her a glance. "Shows, huh? Sorry for the gloom-spreading. I went in to Tamarisco yesterday to renew the commercial note on my office equipment—the X ray machine and the centrifuge—all that expensive, essential stuff."

"And?"

Caroline shook her head. "Here I've been scraping like crazy—even dipping into our dwindling savings—to make those note payments on time, and now . . ."

"Now . . . what?" Amelia said.

"The loan officer at the S and L says they won't renew the note."

"But if you've been making the payments—"

"Apparently it's nothing to do with my credit or my payment record. They just aren't making loans, even standard renewals. Which is just hunky-dory for them, but what the heck am I supposed to do? I don't have twenty thousand dollars lying around, and the note comes due in thirty days."

Amelia wondered if Mac Peterson was on the board of the savings and loan, but she didn't say anything about it to Caroline. "Can't you go to the bank in Alamogordo and get them to pick up the note?"

"Last year I could have, sure. When my practice was doing well and I could show them a positive cash flow. But not only is the equipment ten months older now, my balance sheet is for shit." She glanced over at Amelia, then said, "Look, don't sweat it. The practice is a goner anyway. I've just been kidding myself, thinking I could weather all this bad talk."

"You're a terrific doctor," Amelia said. "People around here are lucky to have you. Eventually they'll realize that." She wished she could help financially. But Caroline had even refused to accept payment for Amelia's medical care.

"I wish." Caroline made the turn at the Crossroads, and headed up the hill toward High Rolls. "Look, I hate to bring it up when you've already done so much for us—"

"Hang on a minute," Amelia said. "Who was taking care of me around the clock for a week after I fell? And now here's Mark doing all the stock work and even taking care of my garden—"

Caroline dismissed that with a wave. "What are neighbors for? Anyone else would've done the same."

"No one else did."

Caroline grinned at her. "Well, they didn't need to, did they? We were already on the scene."

"Seriously, Caroline. How can I help?"

Caroline took a deep breath. "I'm thinking of taking a part-time job at a twenty-four-hour clinic in Las Cruces. I'd be pulling three twelve-hour shifts a week, from noon to midnight. The money—we really need the money. But I don't want to leave Mark on his own out here at night. With the drive back, there's no way I'd be home before one-thirty or two in the morning, but if I say anything about being worried about it, he'll—"

"—be insulted," Amelia finished for her. "But he shouldn't be at my house at night, Caroline. You know that."

"I know—I was just thinking if he has your number and can call you—you're so much closer than Burk is—"

"You got it. If push came to shove, I could manage to drive the truck, I guess."

"Well, the job won't start for a couple of weeks. With any luck, your cast'll be off by then. I appreciate it, Amelia."

"What are friends for?" Amelia said, quoting Caroline.

Caroline reached over and squeezed her hand. "I don't know what we would've done without you. I'm awfully glad you came home."

Tears welled up unexpectedly, and Amelia sniffed. "Oh, damn it."

Since the accident, she had several times found herself unexpectedly overcome by tears. Caroline said it was perfectly normal, that Amelia would need a little time to metabolize so much grief.

"Tissues in the glove box," Caroline said. She was always matter-of-fact about the tears; she said crying was a healthy person's response to pain.

Her attitude made Amelia a little less self-conscious, but she wasn't accustomed to crying easily. For the first time as an adult, she had someone she could talk to freely, without guarding every word she said. She wasn't really used to that yet, either.

Caroline had tried to get Amelia to talk to Burk about what had happened to her family. So far, she hadn't been able to. Her feelings about him and about her life were in a terrible tangle. Until she felt a little more certain of her future, she didn't think she could unravel them.

She picked up one of the honey pots from the seat next to her, wrapped in a brown paper bag. She had eventually settled on a simple drawer-pull style knob for the lid, embossed with a bee. She'd used the same die-stamp to emboss a bee on the front panel of the hexagon, too. The honey-colored titanium wash was concentrated in the crevices of the pattern, making the bee an even darker gold under the creamy overglaze.

After filling the pots with honey and sealing the lids with beeswax, she had tied a wooden honey spool alongside the knob of the lid with a few strands of dried grass. She examined the effect critically. "You really think she'll like it?"

Caroline rolled her eyes. "Trust me," she said. "She's got good taste, doesn't she? These are gorgeous. I've got mine right in the middle of the dining room table, place of honor."

Her prediction proved accurate. Mary was delighted with the gift, and assured Amelia that Willy would like his just as much. She invited Amelia and Caroline up onto the deck for a glass of cider, and they ended up talking for over an hour, catching up on how the summer tourist trade was going and Mary's plans for planting five acres in cherry trees next fall.

"I've sold seven hundred dollars worth of cider, applesauce, and apple butter already this month," Mary said. She kept the roadside stand open for the summer, even though it wasn't apple season yet. "And every other person who stopped wanted to know if I had cherry cider like they got at Jackson's, up the hill. It'll take a few years to get any kind of crop, but I've already ordered the cherry trees."

"Let me know when you plan to start planting," Amelia said. "We'll come help."

"Count on it." Mary stood up and stared off to the northwest, shading her eyes. "That's the first one I've seen this year."

Amelia struggled up with her crutches and looked where Mary was pointing. A smoky purple thunderhead about six miles deep had built up over the basin, and the storm was moving fast across the desert toward Sierra Blanca. The air was so clear that, even from here, she could see the dark lines of the falling rain under the storm clouds.

"First storm?" Amelia asked, surprised. They'd had afternoon showers every day for a week.

Mary was still watching the storm. "First *walking* rain," she said. "See how fast it's moving? And how the rain slanting down looks like legs, just walking along the ground?"

Amelia looked closer, fascinated. Sure enough, she could see stovepipe legs of rain, walking across the basin floor. "Wish I had some binoculars."

Caroline cleared her throat. "Well, if we're going to make it into town before the gallery closes, we'd better hit the road before that storm gets here. Thanks for the cider, Mrs. Zuniga."

"Call me Mary," Mary told her, "and you come back any time."

Amelia watched the rain all the way down the mountain. By the time they reached the basin fifteen minutes later, the storm had moved into the mountains.

"The ground is barely damp," she said. "You can hardly tell it rained."

Caroline smiled. "So a walking rain waters no grass?"

Amelia looked out at the desert. The summer rains the past week had fed it, but the desert sage—which normally bloomed like crazy after a rain—was a uniform silvery green. No small purple blossoms anywhere that she could see.

"Guess not," she said.

Señor Jarmél wasn't at the gallery that afternoon. Amelia was frustrated to have made the long trek across the plaza on crutches without getting to see him. She left his pot of honey and a short note, along with one of the snapshots she'd taken of the mountain faces sculpture. Ryan—the gallery's assistant manager—said he'd see Mr. Jarmél got them when he returned.

Caroline seemed to be in a quiet mood after they left the gallery, and Amelia didn't try to force a conversation. On the drive back toward the Crossroads, she found herself turning over ideas for a title for the sculpture. That was a sign she was about finished with the piece, but she hadn't come up with a name that suited her yet.

The last stop was the one Amelia had really been dreading. It was a little before suppertime when they turned in at the gate to Reed's place, and Amelia's heart sank when she saw the big shiny green supercab parked beside the modern ranch house. She'd caught Spencer Reed at home all right. The house seemed characterless to Amelia—it was built of commercial glazed adobe—a drab brown box, without the softening effect of a stucco overcoat. The roof was coppery brown metal shaped to look like traditional Spanish tile.

"Need moral support?" Caroline asked as she pulled the station wagon up in front of the yard.

The Reeds had a suburban-style lawn around their house, which Amelia noted disdainfully was planted in St. Augustine. They must have to water like crazy. Then she caught herself. She wasn't exactly approaching this in a conciliatory spirit.

"No, thanks," she said. "I'll do better on my own."

Caroline got her situated with the crutches, handed her the pot of honey in its paper bag, and gave her an encouraging smile.

Amelia didn't smile back. She was too tense. The honey pot swung in the paper sack and knocked against the aluminum of the crutch with a clanging sound as she maneuvered up the three steps to the Reeds' narrow veranda. A rusted triangle hung beside the front door, substituting for a doorbell.

She looked it over and decided to just knock instead; she was lucky not to lose a crutch in the process. Even this late in the day, it was hot on the porch, and she was perspiring by the time Reed came to the door.

His mouth tightened when he saw her through the screen, but he was of the old school. He didn't throw her off the property outright. But neither did he invite her in. He stepped out onto the porch and said, "Yes, ma'am?"

"Hello, Mr. Reed," Amelia said. Automatically, she reached over to make sure her left cuff was snapped.

But there was no cuff; she was wearing a T-shirt. Another result of Caroline's counsel—if Amelia was going to come to terms with the past, she had to quit hiding what had happened to her.

"Yes?" Reed said again. Her gesture had drawn his attention, and he was looking at her arm.

Amelia swallowed. She wasn't used to having people stare at the scar yet. But if she was going to wear short sleeves, it was time to *get* used to it. She turned a little to give him a better view. Might as well get it over with.

Her throat was clogging up on her, so she tried to speak quickly. "I've come to apologize for cursing at you during the fire that night. We've had bad blood between us since I came to the basin, but what I said was uncalled for. I just want you to know I'm sorry for it."

He didn't move, and his mouth looked as hard as ever. What had she expected? Sympathy?

She shifted the crutch under her right arm and awkwardly thrust the paper bag at him. "I brought you a little honey by way of apology, sir."

Reed blinked several times, but he still didn't say anything.

Great, Amelia thought. *I'm going to have to hobble down these steps with him watching me, still carrying this stupid sack—*

Reed reached out and took the bag. "I'm right fond of honey," he said grudgingly.

Her eyes flooded with tears. Damn it, of all the times to come over weepy—

But Reed hadn't noticed. He'd opened the paper bag and was removing the pot from it with great care.

"Would you look at that," he said. He held the honey jar up to eye level and turned it first one way and then the other. "You made this?" His voice had a faintly disbelieving note.

"Yes, sir. I hope you enjoy the honey—and accept my apology."

He looked at her for a few seconds, a muscle along his jaw jumping in a nervous tic. "I don't hold with ugly talk."

"No, sir. And I'm sorry for it." Her palms were slick with sweat now. She took a firmer grip on the handles of her crutches. "Mr. Reed, just the day before, I'd been up on the prairie and seen a bunch of surveyor's stakes running onto my land from yours. They burned off in the fire, I guess, but at the time, I thought you were getting ready to make some kind of claim on the property. I was real upset about it. That's no excuse, but—"

Reed's eyes narrowed. "I didn't have nothing to do with that surveyor. Tossed him off my place at gunpoint, and tore up those stakes myself. That boy told me he'd been hired by Nick Atkinson, and I figured you'd put Atkinson on to do it."

Amelia was stunned, and it took her a moment to react. "You're saying *Atkinson* hired him? What for? Atkinson's trustee of my place, but he doesn't have any business surveying yours—"

"That's exactly what I told him," Reed said furiously. "And the so-and-so had the nerve to threaten me! Told me to my face my operating loans aren't going to be renewed. After I've been doing business with that savings and loan for forty years. Like my credit's no good. I've never once missed a payment. Not once in forty years."

Amelia glanced out to where Caroline was waiting in the car. "You know," she said slowly, "I wonder why they're cutting down on their lending all of a sudden."

"You're not the only one," Reed said. His mouth was puckered like he tasted something sour. "I've asked around, and lots of folks are wondering the same thing."

She remembered the stakes, running across both properties and up the ridge. "But why the surveyor? What's the point of surveying part of a property he doesn't have any control over?"

"Well, he talked some trash about having a generous offer for a lease of the mineral rights along there. I told him to forget it, and he suggested I think twice before throwing away a chance like that. That's when he told me not to look to have my loans renewed. Well, you can tell that trustee of yours that if he thinks I'm going to let some mining company tear up my land, he's got another think coming."

"A *mining* company? There's no way mining operations could be started up there, not under the terms of my grandfather's will. What kind of fool does he think I am?"

Reed gave her a sideways look. "Well, no telling, but lately he ain't making a world of sense, either. Who ever heard of mineral rights around here?"

"What was he looking to lease out mineral rights for? Did he say?"

"Turquoise and silver deposits. I think he's crazy as a bedbug, but it makes no never mind to me. Like I said, I'm not letting a bunch of—some mining crew tear up my place." He turned and looked toward the mountains to their east, then spat over the porch railing. "May not seem like much to anyone else, but I've lived here all my life. I like it just the way it is."

"I can understand that, sir." Amelia realized how long they'd been talking. "Look, I really appreciate your telling me about this, Mr. Reed. My friend's waiting for me, so I should go on now. But I'm no more interested in seeing that ridge mined than you are."

He looked at her and scowled. "If you say so," he said. "But you listen to me, young lady. Best hire you an accountant and have that trustee of yours audited. It's not my place to talk, no matter what my opinion of him is. But I'll say this to you—the lease he gave me on that patch of land you're so partial to wasn't exactly on the up-and-up."

Her mind was so busy worrying over the prospect of Atkinson leasing mineral rights to the Folly that she could hardly take in what Reed was saying. But one way or another, she was going to get some answers from Nick Atkinson. It was time to find out what the hell was going on.

"Thanks, Mr. Reed," she said. "Believe me, I will be looking into it."

Chapter Nineteen

New Mexico

On the way back to the ranch, she told Caroline what Spencer Reed had said about Atkinson.

Burk and Mark were holding batting practice in the front yard. Burk had on his green T-shirt, the one that made his eyes look blue. Tucker was lying glumly on the patio when she and Caroline drove up. He came to greet Amelia, but seemed awfully subdued.

"What on earth did you do, give him tranquilizers?" she said as she maneuvered her way out of the station wagon.

"He hates baths," Mark said.

"Sulking," Burk confirmed, "the ingrate. Considering how many ticks we got off of him—"

Amelia was fondling Tucker's ears. "Well, I'm grateful, even if he isn't. See, Tuck, now you can stay in the house with me at night."

"See how she's ruining my dog?" Burk said to Mark. "He'll never be content to sleep outside again."

Amelia ignored the teasing. "Y'all stay to supper, okay? I need some advice."

Burk raised his eyebrows. "And if we give it to you, you're saying you'll *take* it?"

That wrung a laugh from her. "No promises."

He smiled. "Never mind. Any excuse is fine with me. I like your cooking."

*   *   *

She waited until after supper to discuss things, when Mark went off to read comic books in Michael's old room. Caroline cleared the table while Burk got them more coffee. Amelia pulled an empty chair around and propped up her leg. It felt great to take the strain of the cast's weight off her thigh muscles.

Burk was interested that Atkinson had threatened Reed with not having his operating loans renewed. "You know, that's not the first I've heard about the S and L tightening its lending. Any number of folks have said the same—I wonder if the place is in trouble?" He sipped his coffee.

Amelia found herself watching his hand as he lifted the cup, the strong graceful fingers with their sprinkling of hair, bright against his tanned skin.

Then she realized Caroline was running water in the sink.

"Just leave those," Amelia told her. "I can get them later. As for Atkinson's S and L being in trouble, I haven't been around here long enough to tell. But a lot of banks are still having a hard time—"

"What about the mineral rights thing?" Caroline said, coming back to the table. "Is there any truth to it, you think?"

"Well, there's a turquoise deposit that's pretty well known, not far from Portañola," Burk said. "That's less than forty miles as the crow flies. But I thought they'd never found much high-grade stone there."

"It doesn't matter anyway," Amelia said. "No one's going to excavate up there—Gramps would hate that. Would have hated it, I mean."

"So what are you going to do?" Burk asked her. "It sounds like Atkinson is more concerned with making money than with what your grandfather wanted."

"Hire an accountant, I guess." Amelia rubbed her forehead. "Though I don't know with what. Atkinson still hasn't paid me last month's wages, and most of my pollinating money went for honey jars and kiln fittings. You wouldn't happen to know a good C.P.A. who'd do the audit and let me pay him later, do you?"

"Not me," Burk said.

"The accountant I was using retired and moved away," Caroline said. "And to tell the truth, I haven't made enough money lately to look for a new one."

"I can't just sit here while Nick Atkinson cuts deals and lets them rip up my grandfather's land. Gramps loves this place, and he's counting on me to take care of it."

"You know," Caroline said thoughtfully, "you don't need an accountant, or at least not right off. What you really need is a lawyer. Someone to take that trust away from Atkinson and get it turned over to you."

Amelia looked at her, surprised. She had gotten so set in her thinking that dissolving the trust would cause too much trouble, she hadn't even considered that alternative. But it was the obvious solution.

Word would get out, though; she had to remember that her reappearance would still be news. Atkinson would make sure it was news. Her uncle would come. Facing him wouldn't be easy.

And there was Michael.

Caroline didn't think she was responsible for what had happened, but Amelia found it hard to believe that herself. Especially when she remembered Michael's head being bashed against the cabinets. He had been trying to defend *her*—

All the reasons she had tried to sidestep dissolving the trust still held. But if she wanted a future that included the ranch, she was going to have to quit hiding from her past.

"You know," she said to Caroline. "You are absolutely right. That's exactly what I should do. But that brings me back to square one—I don't know an attorney, and I certainly don't have enough money for a retainer."

"But I *do* know an attorney," Caroline said. "A wonderful one in Alamogordo who handled my divorce for me—and he deals with trusts and wills all the time. His name is Randall Duncan, and I'd bet anything he'll let you pay him after things are settled and you have control of the property. Or on time or whatever—that's what he did for me."

Amelia leaned over and hugged her. "Bless you, Caroline."

Burk smiled. "Damn, I wish I'd thought of that."

She called the attorney first thing Monday morning. When she explained the reason she was calling and that she wasn't very mobile at the moment, he asked her a few questions. Once she gave him a rundown on her situation, he not only agreed to take her case—on the condition she could prove her claim, of course—he also promised to contact Atkinson as soon as he got a copy of her grandfather's will.

"I'll bring you a copy—I just need to get a ride into town and find a copy machine," she said.

"Don't worry about it, Ms. Caswell," he said. "I'll have my clerk pull one from the probate file at the courthouse. And he'll bring out a fee agreement for your signature. This whole thing has been handled outrageously—Atkinson's demand that you be fingerprinted, for instance. If you've got folks in the area who recognize you and are willing to say so in court, that's all that's really required. We'll have you fixed up in a jiffy."

"I can't tell you how much I appreciate this, Mr. Duncan. It's such a relief—"

"My pleasure, ma'am," he said. "In fact, I should be able to talk to Mr. Atkinson about this today, once the runner gets back from his courthouse run midafternoon. So if Mr. Atkinson calls you later, just refer him back to me."

"That'll be *my* pleasure," Amelia told him.

Amelia had a restless day, trying to get some work done in the studio and still listen for the phone. Mark said she was nervous as a long-tailed cat in a room full of rockers. Nick Atkinson never did call, but Duncan phoned her a little before five o'clock. He said that Atkinson was trying to stonewall, and that she shouldn't worry about a thing; he expected to have a full accounting of trust activity in hand no later than Wednesday, or else he'd begin proceedings to get a court order. Confronting Atkinson would have upset Amelia, but Mr. Duncan sounded like he was looking forward to it.

She was encouraged by the quick results, and would have made something special for supper to celebrate, but Caroline and Mark already had plans. They were driving over to La Luz for the monthly meeting of Mark's FFA group, which was holding a potluck supper, and Burk was working late again. So the house was quieter than usual that evening.

A little after sunset, it began to pour rain.

When the thunder started, she was glad Tucker had been dipped and was inside with her. He kept her company as she fixed herself some scrambled eggs for supper, and obliged her by eating them when she discovered she didn't have much appetite after all. His efforts to follow her as she moved around the kitchen caused some problems with her crutches, so Amelia left the dishes in the sink.

It was a relief to settle in the big armchair in the living room with a book. With her broken leg propped on the ottoman, a copy of *El Cid* that had belonged to her mother in her lap, and Tucker for company, she should have had a cozy evening.

But the wind was wild outside the house, chafing at the windmill until it sounded like a helicopter hovering over the roof. When the wind rose to a howl, and the lightning strikes intensified, Amelia closed her book and turned off the lamp. She couldn't concentrate.

She used the crutches to get to her feet, and drew the curtains back from the window. Looking at the pane was like looking at a box of black liquid. It was streaming with rain, and the night outside was so dark that Amelia could see almost nothing. She remained next to the window anyway, watching the faint back-splash of lightning playing over the mountains.

It was unusual for a storm here to last this long; usually they faded by sunset. But this was no walking rain. The storm had settled over the basin and was pouring itself out over the land. Her eyes had adjusted to the dark, and she could see the gleam of the ranch road, streaming with water.

She hoped that Caroline and Mark were all right, and that Burk was home safe. It wasn't a good night for driving.

Thunder rumbled, a deep dark sound that seemed to echo back over the basin from the mountain range. In the faint flicker of distant lightning, Amelia thought she saw something move out under the cottonwood trees.

Was there someone out there?

Or was she just jittery from the storm? Maybe all the company she'd been having had ruined her tolerance for solitude.

She stared at that section of the yard, waiting for the irregular bursts of violet light to show it more clearly.

Tucker was suddenly pressed against her knee. She had to shift her crutch to make room, but she was grateful for the solid feel of his shoulder. She was still staring off toward the cottonwood trees, struggling to decipher the denser shadows there, when he began to growl. The sound was so low that she confused it with the thunder until she felt the rumbling in his body.

The wind rose even higher, and the cottonwood trees tossed wildly. Their movement made it that much harder for her to see.

"Tucker?" she said softly. There *was* someone out there. Tucker could tell, even if she couldn't. Amelia's breath was catching in her throat, her hands clenched hard around the grips of her crutches. She leaned closer to the glass, eyes wide as she strained to see better.

A huge flash of lightning illuminated the world.

A man stood just outside the window, not three feet from her. In the instant that he was visible, Amelia saw the black hood covering his head.

There had been no movement outside the window, no shifting shadows to mask his approach. *How long had he been standing there watching her?*

If she'd had any breath at all, she would have screamed to wake the dead. But she had no breath, none.

The terror was so sharp and sudden that she nearly passed out.

Tucker's steady growl rose to a furious deep bark, and he launched himself full tilt at the window. Her crutch went flying, and she grabbed for his collar. Too late.

His muzzle hit the glass with a violent crack. The windowpane crazed.

Amelia scrabbled for his collar and tugged him back, but Tucker was barking viciously at the man outside, flinging himself toward the window. Spears of broken glass hung in the frame, quivering in the blasts of wind and rain.

She couldn't see anything out there. She couldn't tell where the man was. She couldn't even think.

What if there's more than one?

Tucker lunged at the window again, and she grappled with him.

Lightning split the sky again. The man was gone.

Tucker didn't care; he was still trying to charge the window. Abruptly, she realized that the dog would be cut to pieces on the broken glass if she didn't do something fast.

The explicit fear dimmed her wider terror. It gave her a focus: She had to get Tucker away from the window.

She threw her weight against the dog, shoving him toward the kitchen. *"Come on, Tucker—come on, come on—"*

But he was eighty pounds of furious muscle, and she was down to one crutch. She'd dropped the other somewhere by the window. Amelia leaned down and pushed against Tucker's chest.

She said his name sharply, yelled it in his ear, and he calmed a little. He was still bristling with rage; she could feel him quivering against her arm.

She had to get to the kitchen. To the phone.

How many of them are there this time? Terror sang in her blood, a wild wine. She fumbled the remaining crutch into position and got a firm grip on Tucker's collar.

"*Heel*," she told him, and hauled him around to her right side. The wrong side; dogs were trained to heel left. But with only one crutch, she couldn't cope with having him on the same side as the cast.

He barked excitedly, pulling toward the broken window. Wind whistled over the broken shards of glass and she realized her back was damp from the gusts of rain blowing through.

She listened for sounds of glass being broken out, of a screen being torn away. Nothing.

She looked around, but couldn't see anything. "Quiet, Tucker. *Quiet.*"

Maybe they had the house surrounded and were waiting for a signal to strike.

She hauled on Tucker's collar again, and this time he came to heel on her right, just as she needed him to. Using the one crutch, she lurched to the kitchen and picked up the phone.

Static hissed and crackled at her, but she got a dial tone. The glow of the numbers seemed blinding in the darkness; it was bright enough for her to read the list of emergency numbers on the wall.

She would have to let go of Tucker's collar to dial. "*Stay,*" she told him. He whined, then pulled his head around and growled low in his throat.

Her skin was like ice. How could her blood run so thin and fast when she was so cold?

She let go of his collar—*please stay, please, Tucker*—and dialed the number. Her fingers were shaking so badly that it seemed to take years.

The phone rang three times before it was answered, and the connection was terrible. The open line buzzed and sparked with static, but then she heard the dispatcher's voice say "Otero County Sheriff's Department."

Her own voice was surprisingly clear. She tried to speak loud enough to compensate for the connection without shouting. "This is Amelia Rawlins at the Rawlins Ranch out north of the Crossroads—I've been getting threats and now someone in a—a mask is trying to break into my house."

There was a long pause. The rain was drumming on the roof, and the windmill was spinning its *WHUF-whuf-whuf* overhead.

They could be all around her, and she wouldn't know.

Amelia thought, *It would be easier just to die this time.*

"Can you hear me?" she asked sharply. "Did you get that?"

The dispatcher's voice came back, abrupt and clear, "Yes, ma'am—it's just—"

"How long will it take for someone to come?"

"That's just it, ma'am. I show that two deputies were dispatched to your ranch twenty minutes ago—they should have been there by now. Maybe with the weather—"

"Twenty minutes ago? *Who called you?*"

"A Mr. Frank Burkhalter, ma'am. The deputies should be there any minute—"

She was shaking, scarcely able to hold the receiver. "Send someone else—hurry!" She hung up.

She hadn't turned on the kitchen light because she hadn't wanted to give away her location to anyone watching. Although they might have heard her talking, she hoped the storm had masked the sound.

She listened, but she couldn't hear anything except the wind and the rain. Burk had called the sheriff's department. Why? Why hadn't he called *her*? Or come out here? Was he outside somewhere? Was that why they hadn't come after her yet, because they were dealing with him first?

She scrambled over to the kitchen door and fumbled for the light switches. Had to pause for an instant and think before flipping the one on the left. The floodlights on the patio came on, casting a rusty glow through the open weave of the kitchen curtains.

Tucker was growling again, set in a ferocious stance by the back door, every hackle raised.

Amelia drew the curtain cautiously away from the wall and put her eye to the narrow opening.

At first she saw nothing but the pounding rain

and the tossed shadows of the cottonwood trees. Then two of the shadows moved again.

They were both dressed in black. It was them, the Wolfen. But then she saw that they were struggling.

One of them wasn't wearing a hood—wasn't wearing black. It only looked that way because his clothes were covered in mud.

Burk—it had to be— She didn't even think about it before she dragged the board from under the doorknob and unlocked the door. It stuck when she yanked on it— all that rain—but she jerked it open.

Tucker was gone like a shot, giving throat to a savage belling. The rising howl was like a promise of certain death.

Amelia staggered after him, half running on the cast. She was soaked to the skin instantly. Through the driving rain, she saw one of them bash the other over the head with a branch, sending him sprawling. The one still on his feet lit out down the ranch road, with Tucker on his heels.

By the time she reached him, Burk was already shaking his head and trying to sit up. He was drenched, coated in mud, and blood was spilling down his forehead.

She skidded down into the mud trying to stop, and grabbed his shoulders, shouting over the noise of the storm. "Are you okay?"

His chest was heaving.

"Are you okay?" She hadn't been this scared when she thought she was about to get rammed off the mountain. She was shaking, and starting to cry.

"Burk—"

He didn't seem to have enough breath to talk. He took her face in his hands and kissed her.

Amelia leaned into him, ignoring the mud on his clothes. His hands were steady—much steadier than hers—and his mouth tasted like rain.

Vicious barking came from the darkness up the road, mixed with the sound of screams.

Reluctantly, Amelia pulled back, then took Burk's hands and helped him up to a sitting position.

He was saying something, but she couldn't make out the words. Rain poured down her face, half blinding her. "What?" she shouted. "I can't understand."

"—Call him *off*—"

"Tucker!" she shouted. "Tucker—*come!*"

And then dazzling red and blue lights spilled along the flooded road, and she heard sirens, wailing counterpoint to the wind.

The cut on Burk's head wasn't too serious, but Amelia got him inside and called Caroline right away. They were drenched and muddy, her cast was softening, Tucker's muzzle was bloody, and rain was still blowing in the window. Once she had called Caroline, Amelia didn't know what to do first.

But the deputies followed them inside within minutes, bringing the hooded man. Seeing him up close made her start shaking all over again; she was glad that he needed help to walk.

Tucker growled when he saw the man, but she shushed him.

The man was bleeding from a deep bite on one calf. *Good for Tucker,* she thought, as she started wiping the blood off the dog's muzzle. Most of it seemed to belong to the man, thank heavens. Tucker's lunge at the window didn't seem to have resulted in anything worse than a bloody nose.

Amelia pointed one deputy to the linen closet for towels while the second deputy settled the man on the couch and told him to take off the hood.

She looked at him, wondering if she was about to see the face of her family's murderer.

The man took a blood-smeared hand away from his leg and pulled off the hood.

It was Nick Atkinson.

"My God," Amelia said. "It was *you?* Why?"

"I have every right to be here," Atkinson said to the deputy, who had begun to read him his rights. "I'm the trustee of this estate, and"—he turned to Burk—"I'm going to have that dog put down. He's a menace."

The deputy said, "You can't come skulking around in the dark in a hood and expect him to lick your face—the dog was only protecting his owner and her property."

Atkinson grimaced and gripped his leg tighter. Blood was welling between his fingers.

Amelia started to tell the deputy that Tucker wasn't really her dog, but Burk spoke first. "That's right, sir, he sure was looking after her. He's a *good* dog."

Tucker sat up and thumped his tail. Amelia hugged him.

"I'd say so," the deputy added. "He came right to her when she called. Most dogs would have just kept on chewing."

Amelia noticed that Burk was shivering. She hunted around for her second crutch, and when she found it, got up and lit the fire laid in the wood stove.

The other deputy came back with the towels and handed several to Burk before starting to fashion a pressure bandage for Atkinson's leg.

The sound of the rain outside intensified, and Amelia thought how strange this was. Ordinarily, sitting inside by a fire on a rainy night would seem cozy and secure. But the man who had just frightened her half to death was inside with her.

Caroline and Mark arrived a few minutes later, about the same time the second pair of deputies did. Mark was looking pretty wide-eyed, but he didn't say anything. He came over to where Amelia was and sat down on the floor with Tucker. The dog put his head in Mark's lap with a sigh.

One of the new deputies said, "I could get some duct tape from the car and tape up that window for you, ma'am."

"I'd be grateful," Amelia said.

Caroline started to check Burk first. When Atkinson protested, she gave him an icy look. "A head injury is potentially serious."

He said, "I demand to be taken to a hospital immediately."

The deputy who'd gotten the towels shrugged.

"Your choice, sir. Dr. Garrity will probably get to you quicker, but I'll take you if you want."

"I just said so, didn't I?"

The deputy turned him over to his newly arrived colleagues after some low-voiced conversation. They helped Atkinson to the door, and then she heard their car pull away. Amelia was glad to have him gone. Looking at his Boy Scout face after he had crept up to her window wearing a hood—she shivered.

Caroline checked Burk's pupils, swabbed the cut out, and applied a butterfly bandage.

"He should be fine," she told Amelia quietly, "but he seems chilled—how about you? You okay?"

"I'm fine. I'll fix some coffee."

"Good idea. I sure want to hear what went on here tonight."

Amelia was glad to go into the kitchen and have a few minutes to herself. Nick Atkinson had come out here to frighten her, she realized that now. He must have known enough about what had happened to her family to be able to imitate the Wolfen.

She should have been relieved to know that it was only Atkinson behind it, but the whole situation seemed so bizarre that she was having a hard time getting her bearings.

Wet, the cast was heavier than ever, and cold enough to make her bones ache. Once she had the coffee perking, she went back to the living room. The deputy was taping a piece of cardboard over the window; the room was already much warmer.

Burk looked pale and exhausted, sunk down in the armchair. His hair was slick and dark against his skull. Amelia pulled the ottoman around and sat next to him while he gave a statement to the deputy.

"We'll keep it short," the other deputy said. His nameplate said he was Officer Hoskins. "I can see you're done in."

"Ms. Rawlins started getting threatening letters right after she moved back here, back in March," Burk told him. "I've been worried about her, so I decided to find out who'd been sending the mail. I work at the post office, you know."

The coffee finished perking, and Mark brought everyone a cup. Amelia hadn't realized how badly her hands were shaking until she took the cup from him, but the hot coffee did her more good than a blood transfusion. As Burk drank his, a little color came back into his face.

"I talked the postmaster into letting me drive the parcel van for a while," Burk went on, "you know, picking up the mail in the public boxes. I was hoping I could catch whoever was mailing these threats."

Amelia looked at him, but he was watching the deputy. Those double shifts hadn't been mandatory overtime after all.

"I finally figured things out this afternoon, when Atkinson came to the box with a letter. He was acting strange—kind of shifty. And then he did this about-face and didn't mail the letter after all. I knew Amelia had contacted a lawyer this morning about having Atkinson's actions as her trustee examined, so it was all starting to fall into place. I got a couple of pictures of him with the letter—just Polaroid snaps—they're in the car. When he drove off, I followed him."

"Why didn't you call us?" the deputy asked.

"I didn't want to take a chance. At first, he just went home, which wasn't exactly suspicious," Burk explained. "If he was really the one threatening Amelia, he had to be pretty desperate. I didn't want to tip him off until we had some real evidence."

"Go on," Hoskins said.

"He left the house around seven-forty, and he was wearing that black turtleneck and jeans—well, you saw him. When I realized he was heading out this direction, I stopped at the Corner Grocery and called your office. Then I came after him."

Burk paused and drank the rest of his coffee. "Could I have another cup?" he asked Amelia.

She started to get up, but Mark beat her to it. He took her cup and refilled it, too.

"Thanks," Burk said, when Mark came back. "I

couldn't see Atkinson's car when I got out here, but I was pretty sure this was where he'd been headed. So I parked over on the main road and tried to get up to the house without being seen—I knew Amelia was alone here.

"But it was pouring rain, and I couldn't see worth a damn. And then Tucker started barking, and I heard a window break—"

He shrugged. "I tore up here, and ran smack into him. He had that hood over his head—well, you saw. So we had a little tussle, and then he brained me." He gave Amelia a tired smile, and his drawl grew exaggerated. "And if Miz Rawlins' fine dog hadn't come along, he might've got clean away."

Amelia leaned her head against the arm of the chair. She was starting to cry again, and didn't want anyone to see. Tucker came over and snuffled her ear for a second, then licked her face.

She blotted the tears off on the upholstery and sat up again to scratch his ears. "You know he's really your dog, Burk."

Burk cupped her cheek with his hand and used his thumb to wipe another tear that got away from her. "I don't know any such thing," he said, "and to look at him, neither does he. Not that I blame him—if I had the choice, I'd rather live with you, too."

This time, she kissed him.

Chapter Twenty

New Mexico

For all Nick Atkinson's denials of wrongdoing, he was arrested and arraigned on charges of arson and abuse of fiduciary trust the following week. The FBI had gotten involved as well, investigating illegal use of the U.S. mail because of the threatening letters he had sent.

The first of the letters had appeared on her nightstand overnight. Amelia remembered she hadn't burned it after all—she'd stuck it in the center drawer of Gramps's old desk. Apparently, her resident ghosts were still keeping an eye on things.

The investigating officer had gotten a warrant to search Atkinson's car, and found the unmailed letter Burk had told him about. It contained references to the cross that had been burned on her property, which had served to link Atkinson to the arson. Even more damning was the receipt for repairs to a friend's Explorer for "damage to front bumper and punctured radiator," dated the day after she had almost been run off the mountain. Amelia and Caroline hadn't been able to locate the repair shop because Atkinson had taken the truck all the way to Roswell to get it fixed.

The whole thing still seemed rather surreal to Amelia. The Wolfen had terrified her for so long that they had come to be like the bogeyman. She found it hard to accept that instead, Atkinson—Outstanding Young Businessman of the Year—had been behind all the ominous things that had happened at the ranch.

The dust hadn't completely settled yet, but it appeared that the Tamarisco Savings & Loan was in serious financial trouble. The chief deputy had told them in confidence that he suspected Atkinson of manipulating funds in several trusts in an attempt to cover up the institution's problems.

All her troubles should have been over, but it hadn't quite worked out that way. She was having a hard time believing that twelve years of dread and hiding could all be finished, just like that. Was it really safe for her to be Amelia Caswell again? Could she lead a normal life?

Maybe she was too accustomed to being afraid. But there was still the matter of the rigged ladder. Half the people in the basin had been out on her place the night of the fire. And she couldn't imagine someone as clever as Nick Atkinson setting a cross on fire and then waiting around to sabotage a ladder. It just didn't fit.

A minor detail, but it nagged at her. She should be grateful and let it go, Amelia knew that. The bee boxes were back in their own yard, at least until time for the next round of pollinating contracts later this month— melons and peppers in the Mesilla Valley around Las Cruces. For now, the honey mesquite trees and the desert sage were in constant bloom, and the bees were collecting heavily right here at home. The summer rains had also stirred new growth among the burned-out grasses, a faint green fuzz over the Folly's scars. The rest of the grass was knee deep, already seeding for its second growing season.

And—maybe the best news of all—she had an order from Willy Lachte for a gross of her honey pots. He was going to bend the rules about only native crafts in the Inn's gift shop, and carry New Mexico honey in her special pots. Plus, her display at Jorge Valdez's store had brought inquiries from other markets around the area, so she had dozens of orders for honey alone.

Everything was going so well. So why did she still have this splinter of anxiety eating away at her? Why did she feel so forlorn all the time? Mark's opinion was that worrying had become a habit with her.

Burk had caught bronchitis—Caroline blamed it on his being run-down from overwork and getting soaked the night they caught Nick Atkinson—and he was under orders to stay in bed for another week. Amelia hadn't seen him since that night.

She missed him fiercely, even though she was still uncertain of what she wanted their relationship to be. She had stopped trying to convince herself that she didn't care for him. But she still wasn't certain that it was safe to love someone again.

As always when she was frightened or confused, she turned to clay. And after some settling-down time in the studio, what she found herself shaping was a model of a pueblo. When she realized what she was making, she found a picture of the Santa Clara Pueblo in one of Gramps's books, and worked from that.

It was one of the best pieces she had ever done. She used red clay, and the shape of the pueblo came to her cleanly. After it dried, she fired it unglazed, and used small sticks to fabricate replicas of the ladders and *bodegas*.

It took her four days to finish the model. She wrapped it carefully in layers of newspaper, and put it in a canvas carryall with a jar of homemade chicken soup. Then she asked when Caroline might be able to drive her over to see Burk.

His house was up in the foothills, at the edge of a canyon, but Amelia didn't spot it until they were almost on top of it. Burk was clearly an admirer of Frank Lloyd Wright. The adobe house nestled into the canyon ridge like an unusual rock formation.

Caroline helped her maneuver up the stone walk. It led through a small enclosed garden to a pair of double doors. Caroline rang the bell, then opened the door.

"He said to go on in—I'll swing by to pick you up in an hour or so, okay? Don't let him overdo it." She gave Amelia a hug, handed her the carryall, and left.

Amelia went inside and stopped dead.

The central part of the house rose to an open cupola two stories high, and the entire back wall of the house was glass, facing out over the canyon. A hawk was circling up a thermal a few yards from the pane. The view of the ravine was breathtaking.

"Amelia?" Burk sounded hoarse. "You there?"

She turned and made her way down the hallway to her right, following the sound of his voice.

He was propped up in an oak four-poster, pale and unshaven, with a tray of medicines and a pitcher of ice water on the bedside table. She couldn't believe how good it was to see him.

He coughed. "Sorry I'm so scruffy. Caroline said she'd throw my jigsaw off the cliff if I got out of bed."

"The direst of threats," Amelia said. She crutched her way around the bed and sat down on the other side. "It's great to see you, Burk."

He smiled at her. There were smudges under his eyes, but their clear gray color was as striking as always. "Same here."

"Brought you something." She handed over the newspaper-wrapped bundle.

He coughed again, then paused for a sip of water before carefully folding back the paper.

She still liked the way the model of the pueblo looked

Apparently, so did he. "Look at that line," he said, trailing his finger up the side. "It's sensational, Amelia. Thank you."

"No, thank *you*," she said. "You've been doing nice things for me since the day we met. But tracking down Atkinson—chasing him out to the ranch—" She swallowed. "Thanks, Burk. For everything."

He took her hand. His was warm—was he still feverish? "I'd do it again." Another fit of coughing racked him, and he let go. After the coughing spell passed, he wheezed, "Maybe not right this minute, though."

He could still make her laugh, even when she didn't want to. "Sorry you're sick," she said.

He waggled his eyebrows, Groucho style. "Me, too."

She looked down, tracing the stitching on his comforter. "Caroline says I need to tell you some stuff," she said. "About my family. I haven't been able to talk about it before now. Do you feel up to hearing it?"

"Yes."

So she told him. All of it.

He listened without interruption, except to squeeze her hand during the roughest parts.

It hadn't seemed possible that words could comfort her. But what Burk said did.

He said, "I'm glad you survived."

She fixed them both some orange juice and heated up the chicken soup she'd brought. As he ate, they talked a little.

"I'm having a hard time with all this," she said. "You and me, I mean."

He slurped a spoonful of soup. "Why?"

"I feel all jumbled up. These things I've run away from for years—they're all right here now." She touched her chest. "I can't get anything straight. It still feels like everyone I love is going to die and leave me."

Burk set his mug of soup aside. "Amelia. Everyone you love *is* going to die." He lifted her hand and kissed the palm. "That doesn't stop people from loving each other and spending their whole lives together."

She looked at him, realizing that he was absolutely right.

And that it didn't make any difference. "I can't help it," she said. "I'm still scared."

Burk pressed her hand between his for a moment, then let her go. "Well, that's okay. I'm patient."

After her visit to Burk, it took Mark only a few days to persuade her to let him help with the bees.

His argument was that most of what had made her so worried about his safety was the result of Atkinson trying to run her off. Now that Atkinson was out of the picture, she should relax a little. Mark had a point, but she couldn't seem to shake her fear. Not entirely.

Right now, Mannie was putting in twelve-hour days on his place to get the second crop of his *habañero* peppers in. And Caroline had taken that part-time job, so she was making the hundred-and-forty-mile round-trip to Las Cruces three times a week, while still trying to keep the clinic open. *She* had no objection to Mark helping with the bees; she had already given them an emergency sting kit to keep in the honey house, and said she trusted Amelia to take good care of Mark.

Amelia had held out as long as she could, in hopes that Mannie would have time to help her pull more supers. And she had already promised Mark that he could help with the extraction, since it would be done in the honey house, away from the hives.

But Mark wasn't satisfied with that. Faced with the possibility of missing her honey delivery deadlines, Amelia overcame her misgivings and agreed to let him help.

"I'll do exactly what you say," Mark assured her for about the eightieth time.

She gave him a smile. "Okay, Mark. I believe you. But before we start, let's go over the rules once more."

"No sudden movements, no bright clothes," he recited. "First sign of trouble, I run. I can bring back help, but I can't stop to help you, just have to get the hell out of Dodge."

"Did I really say that?" Amelia said. What would Caroline think? Probably that Amelia was corrupting her kid.

"Sure did." He sounded smug.

"You're unbearable, you know that?"

He grinned, full of himself because he was finally getting what he wanted.

"Okay," she said. "Get the veil and gloves on while I shut Tucker in the shed, and let's get to it."

She had only one bee veil and a single pair of gauntlets, so Mark wore them. She'd been stung often enough that she was getting used to it; these days she got scarcely any swelling from a sting or two. And wearing the khaki jumpsuit seemed to work fine as protection, though getting into it with the cast on her leg had been a major struggle. Caroline had replaced the cast Amelia had ruined in the rain with an even bulkier one. Amelia suspected it was a retribution.

She made sure he had the elastic cuffs of the gloves pulled well up over his elbows, and got the bottom of the veil tucked securely under his shirt collar. He had already put thick rubber bands around his pants cuffs to keep the bees from crawling up his legs, one precaution he seemed glad to take.

They weren't used to working as a team yet, so Amelia took it slow that morning. She started by showing Mark how to stuff the smoker with dried pine needles and wood chips and light it. Then she opened four of the weaker, less active hives—ones that weren't likely to give them trouble. And she didn't hesitate to smoke the bees if they acted irritable.

When Mark got excited and bounced around too fast, a few bees went for his face. But the veil kept them from connecting, and Amelia relaxed a little.

They took only three supers from those four hives, and in one of them, the comb wasn't fully drawn out yet. Under ordinary circumstances, she would have left the partial super in place for a few more weeks; it had no more than twenty pounds of honey in it. But removing the supers from these lazy hives gave Mark a chance to get used to the action and settle down. By the time they took their lunch break, she was feeling more confident.

He asked questions about the bees all through lunch—where the wax came from, how she could tell the difference between brood cells and honey cells, how the bees knew which hive they belonged in. After fifteen minutes of answering so many questions she couldn't finish her sandwich, Amelia got up and brought him a couple of Gramps's bee books. She got to eat her lunch then.

Once they'd eaten, he suited back up. They moved on to several of the more active hives then, the ones with lots of honey stores. Amelia kept casting anxious glances at the sky. The afternoon thunderstorm was starting to build; soon the overcast would make the bees more dangerous to handle. But she needed to pull at least ten more supers to meet the order from Mr. Valdez and be able to fill the honey pots for the gift shop at the Inn.

She tried to work quickly without making mistakes: smoking the bees, checking the frames of honeycomb in the supers, and pulling off the full supers. It was almost impossible for her to lift them while using her crutches, so she laid the crutches aside at each hive and balanced most of her weight on her good leg as she worked.

Mark maneuvered the dolly, positioning it carefully behind each hive, so she could load the supers on it. He was following her instructions to the letter, scrupulously staying out of the bees' flight paths.

By the time they'd pulled six full supers, the cloud cover had darkened, and she could feel the humidity building. Amelia examined the next hive and hesitated. Bees were thick on the landing board, more returning to the hive every second. She wished Gramps were around to advise her.

She was still trying to decide whether it was safe to go ahead and rob the hive when something bright in the trees by the creek caught her eye. She turned.

Mac Peterson stood about ten feet away from them, holding a rifle. In spite of the thick heat, he was wearing a hunting cap with earflaps and a bright orange-and-yellow camouflage jumpsuit. He was weaving a little as he stood there, but the barrel of the rifle wasn't.

He held the gun under his arm with easy confidence, trained on the ground directly in front of her.

"I've come for the boy," Peterson said.

Amelia's heart kicked over like a shot rabbit.

Mark said, "You can't—"

Amelia's hand clenched on the bellows-handle of the smoker, and a big puff of smoke shot at Mark. He choked.

"How you doing, Mr. Peterson?" she said, making it sound just as cheerful as she could. "You bringing me some more seed for my prairie?"

Peterson's brow furrowed. "Uh, no—the supplier's got a back-order on that stock."

"That's a shame," Amelia said. "Sure appreciate your coming out all this way to—"

"Never guess what I got in th'mail today," Peterson said. "Never in a mill-ion years."

Amelia still had the smoker in her hand. She didn't know whether to set it down or hang on to it, in case she needed a weapon. But the smoker didn't seem like much defense against a thirty-aught-six. Her crutches lay on the ground behind the hive. Without them, she was stranded. "No, sir, I can't guess," she said.

Mark was strung taut beside her; she could feel him quivering like a greyhound at the starting gate. She set the smoker on top of the hive and took hold of his wrist.

Peterson fumbled in the pocket of his orange jumpsuit and, for the moment, wasn't watching them closely. She drew Mark closer to her, putting the hive between him and Peterson. Maybe she could distract Peterson if Mark was out of his sight.

The boy resisted, then yielded to her insistent grip on his wrist. She motioned him down, and he knelt. The top of the hive reached her midriff; not much cover, but maybe enough for Mark.

Why had she shut Tucker in the shed? The bees probably wouldn't have bothered him. She was a fool.

Peterson pulled out a crumpled white envelope. "Know what I got here?"

"No, sir," she said, "I sure don't."

"Course you don't. I got me a permit here to take two big-horn sheep. Paid two thousand dollars for this piece a paper. You know why?"

"No, sir." She could hear Mark breathing in rapid, shallow gulps. Her heart was beating a drumroll against her ribs.

" 'Cause Friday's my boy's birthday," Peterson said. "His eighteenth birthday." He looked straight at her then, and his faded blue eyes seemed to focus. They looked milky in the grayed afternoon light, as if occluded by clouds.

"Eighteen," he said softly. "I was taking my boy big-game huntin' for his birthday. Put in for these permits more'n a year ago. Didn't think about 'em since. And then today, here they are. Only thing is, Rich can' go with me." He folded the crumpled page and returned it to the envelope with exaggerated care. "Can't go on his own birthday trip. That's not right, Miz Rawlins."

His voice cracked; the anguish in it touched her through the fear that was swelling in her chest. "No, Mac," she said, "it's not right. It's never right to lose kids."

"She had no business to take my boy so far," he said. His voice grew loud and insistent. "No right! *She* took him from me—she's the one—that butcher!" He jerked the rifle up to his shoulder and leveled it at Amelia's chest.

She felt like she'd just been doused in ice water. The fear was tight inside her, making it hard to breathe. Without moving her gaze from Peterson's face, she saw the darkening clouds, the black circle-and-stem of the rifle's sighted barrel, the bees swirling outside their hive entrance in a flurry of agitation. Harsh buzzing signaled their distress.

"Mac," she said, keeping her voice low, "sometimes people die too soon. It's never right. It shouldn't happen, but it does. And no matter how it happens, we can't change it. You know hurting me won't bring Rich back."

Peterson lowered the rifle a few inches and frowned. "Didn't *want* to hurt you," he said. He sounded aggrieved. "Tried to get you outta the way with the goats first. Boy's taking care of goats—so if you got no goats, he's gotta leave. Come work for me. But your goats are fine."

Mark looked at her and started to whisper, "*He—*"

Amelia reached down and tapped a finger sharply on his helmet.

"So then I rig the ladder. Lay you up, scare you enough to get you out of the picture." He shifted the rifle and added, "After that trouble with the fire, thought sure another mishap would run you off for sure. But you still didn't go."

"*You* meddled with the ladder?"

So she'd been right—Atkinson wasn't the only

one trying to terrorize her. All this time, there had been two of them.

If Peterson had tampered with the ladder, he must have done it the night of the fire—minutes after working side-by-side with her to beat back the flames. The balloon of fear in her chest burst in a surge of outrage.

A bee dived at her face, and she ducked. She was too close to the hive entrance for safety. Amelia took a hop back. Her palms were slick with sweat, and her fingers slipped when she tried to steady herself against the hive.

Peterson stepped toward her when she moved, coming within a few feet of them. "Just wanted the boy to come work for me. It's the only fair thing, don't you see?"

"For Mark to work for you?" Amelia said, watching the rifle carefully.

She could smell the booze on him now. His eyes shimmied back and forth, and a muscle twitched beside his mouth. But his grip on the rifle was rock steady. Casually, she rested her hand on the hive and hopped sideways again, edging Mark a little farther back into concealment.

"It's only right, you can see that, can't you? She took my boy. I got no one to go huntin' with—it's her fault. So her boy—he'll come with me now. Be my son. It's only right." His voice had gone flat, and the rifle barrel tracked her with chilling precision, aimed at her heart. "An eye for an eye. A son for a son. Says so in the Bible. Get in the truck, boy."

The blank eyes and dead tone were far more terrifying than his earlier ravings. She'd been there herself once; she recognized this state. Peterson considered himself already dead.

He wanted to take Mark off somewhere with him, up mountain roads. And—if they ever made it to where he was headed—he wanted to shoot things. Maybe he hadn't admitted to himself yet who he planned to kill, but Amelia had no doubts.

There was no way she was letting him take Mark.

The white-painted hive had a light coat of dust on it. "You want to take Rich hunting," Amelia said. "For his birthday. That's real fine."

She turned sideways to hide what she was doing from Peterson, watching him the whole time. Using her fingertip, she started writing in the dust on the hive. She moved very slowly, struggling to keep her upper arm completely still.

"—Take him hunting—" Peterson said.

Carefully, Amelia sketched out *I YELL U RUN.* The letters were barely visible. Could Mark read it?

Peterson fumbled in his pocket again. "—Got th'permit today—"

Amelia gave Mark a quick look, and squeezed his shoulder. Beneath the mesh of the bee veil, his face was ashen. But when she ran her finger in a line under the word *RUN,* he nodded.

She took a breath.

"—Just want to take my boy huntin'—" Peterson mumbled.

Amelia braced herself against the white wooden frame. She had taken the moving straps off last week to simplify the honey collecting. The bees were furious—clouds of them jittered in front of the entrance. This hive had always been mean-tempered, but the bees were really stirred up today. Because the sky had grown dark, the field bees—the more aggressive ones—couldn't navigate, and had all returned to the hive. There were probably fifty thousand bees guarding it. And she had removed the hive cover and then quit smoking the bees before they were sedated. Not a good move.

Peterson was folding the hunting permit against his leg with one hand, the rifle still aimed in her direction. He seemed oblivious of the bees, even though hundreds darted around him, trying to drive him from the hive entrance. He wasn't directly in their line of flight as they exited the hive, but he was close enough now to get in their way. Loud colors provoked bees, and his orange-

and-yellow jumpsuit made a vivid target. It was only a matter of time before he got stung.

She hoped one would sting him before he worked himself up to using the rifle. It would provide an instant's distraction and allow her to brace herself better. The hive had two supers stacked above the food chamber, both of them filled with honey. The whole structure weighed close to two hundred pounds. She had to shove it over in one clean move. She couldn't afford a false start.

Peterson got the permit back in his pocket and looked up at her, leaning against the hive. "Where's the boy? Got to get on the road now. We got a long drive."

"A long drive?" Amelia said. "Where you headed?"

"The Knippa Ranch, up near Capitan," he said. "Best spot for hunting exotic game in five states—run private, you know."

If he got away with Mark—Amelia thrust the thought away.

"C'mon, boy," Peterson snapped suddenly. "I want you in the truck now. Don't you care about getting you a trophy?"

Mark looked up at her, but Amelia shook her head. She wanted to distract Peterson. "What kind of trophies you going after, Mac?" she said.

"Told you," he said. "Big-horn sheep. Permits cost me a bundle, too, so that's enough of this pussy-footing around. I see you there, boy. Get over here." He jerked the barrel of the gun, and Amelia's heart jumped.

She hopped in his direction, away from the hive. "Mac, you don't want to do this."

"You've taken up for the boy for the last time, Clara," he yelled. "I should've put a stop to it years ago—this is *it*! No son of mine's gonna be a goddamn pansy! Hanging behind a woman like a little crybaby, too chicken-shit to fire a gun! Rich, you get your ass over here right now!"

The bees buzzed around him in a frenzy, but so far he hadn't winced or slapped at a sting.

"You're right, Mac," she said. "We all need to

know how to shoot. That's a thirty-aught-six, isn't it?"
She had to do something. She hopped closer to him and
reached for the rifle barrel.

Thunder rumbled loud overhead, and a stroke of
lightning flashed in the sky behind Peterson.

"You know damn well what kind of rifle it is,"
he screamed as he jerked the gun away. "No more of
your bullshit! Just get the boy out here and—"

Out of the corner of her eye, she saw Mark jump
to his feet. She spun back toward him and nearly lost her
balance.

"I'm right here, Dad," Mark said. His voice
shook, but he came straight around the hive to Amelia's
side. "I'm ready to go."

She put her arm in front of him, trying to press
him back behind her, but he wouldn't budge.

"No—" Now *her* voice was out of control, rising
shrill and strange. *She couldn't let this happen*—

Mac Peterson blinked his cloudy blue eyes twice,
his rage suspended for an instant. He stared at Mark, and
his face suffused with fury again. "You're not my son!"
he yelled, snapping the rifle up. "You're that Garrity
woman's bastard—"

Amelia's body iced. She knew what would happen before she saw it—Peterson's big hard hands raising
the gun, aiming at Mark's chest at point-blank range, his
finger moving toward the trigger—

Amelia grabbed the barrel and yanked it up,
away from Mark, just as he flung himself to one side.

The roar was volcanic—like a physical blow to
the head. The explosive flash was so huge that for an
instant she thought she'd been struck by lightning. Her
face and eyes were on fire, and the aftershock rang and
echoed in her ears. Amelia blinked tears away, trying to
clear her vision. But the white flare in front of her didn't
go away.

She was flash-blind. But she had enough periph-
eral vision to see Mark stumble to his feet. He was okay.
Thank you, God.

Shrill intermittent ringing clamored in her ears.
Something yanked at the rifle—Peterson, trying to rip the

barrel away from her. Her fingers were numb from grip-
ping it so desperately. She couldn't let go—with this rifle,
a good marksman could drop a deer at thirty yards.

But she couldn't keep her balance for long, and
she wasn't strong enough to wrestle the gun away from
him. *She had to do something.*

Amelia shifted all her weight to her right leg,
then slammed her broken left leg around violently, guess-
ing at Peterson's position. The cast connected solidly
with his leg—she thought she'd landed the blow to his
knee. She felt him collapse, crying out as he fell.

But the shock of the blow went through her leg
like a hot wire laid along the bone, and she went down,
too. She'd lost her hold on the gun. Did Peterson still
have it?

"Run!" Amelia screamed to Mark. "Get to
cover!"

Through the echoing tinniness, she could hear
the bees. They were buzzing at fever pitch. Amelia tried
to get her bearings.

The hive entrance was to her left, bees gushing
out of it. She tried to get up to back away from it, but her
leg hurt worse than when she'd first broken it. She
couldn't move it at all. Then out of the corner of her eye,
she saw Peterson. He lay a few feet to her right, his face
twisted with pain. As she watched, he planted the rifle
butt and levered himself up.

He's going to kill Mark. Adrenaline surged
through her, and she dug her fingers into the grass and
dragged herself around behind the hive.

She was gulping air, sweating, as she hauled herself along. She had to do this right. Do it right. The leg
felt like it was on fire.

When she got around to the other side of the
hive, she took two deep breaths, then clawed halfway up
until she was balanced on her good knee. She shoved the
bad leg out to one side, and muscles pulled agonizingly.
Amelia gritted her teeth. The cast would act as a brace—
she grabbed the handle near the base of the main hive
body.

One chance. She heaved on the handle with everything she had, drawing on every bit of her strength. At first she thought she couldn't do it, then she caught the shift in the hive's center of gravity.

She shoved harder—strained—and the boxes spilled over, scattering like a pile of building blocks.

The counterforce of the throw tumbled her backward, but she heard the soggy sound as the wood frame hit flesh.

Then the gun fired again, like a slap to the head. Like thunder in her brain. *Mark!*

She was yelling his name aloud. Her voice wasn't enough to mask Peterson's screams. She glimpsed a flash of orange as he contorted, arms flailing. His face was purple.

Her own face was still burning so fiercely that she barely noticed the first sting—on her cheek. The next one was on her neck. She rolled onto her stomach and shielded her face with her arms. The bees got her anyway, nailing her ears and scalp, stinging through the khaki cloth of her jumpsuit.

It was hard to distinguish the aftershock of the rifle shot from the bees' infuriated buzzing. But the ringing in her ears was gone—and she could hear the ominous crackling of flames. The smoker—she'd forgotten about the smoker on top of the hive.

Amelia rolled away from the sound, and tried to get to her feet. But the broken leg was like water under her, and she went down. She dragged herself a few feet and dropped flat, exhausted.

She'd taken about twenty stings. Nothing compared to what must have hit Peterson—she'd dumped thousands of enraged bees over him.

He had stopped screaming; he didn't have enough breath left for that now. Like an echo chamber, her fuzzed hearing seemed to magnify sound instead of masking it. Peterson's labored breathing and the lick of spreading flames were uncannily clear.

Amelia listened without moving as the breathing grew more tortured. She knew she should try to get up—crawl away—

She was still lying there, still listening, when the

beeswax in the spilled frames caught. It went up in a lake of fire between them, the heat of it ferocious along her side.

But her blood was running with its own cold fire. This man had tried to harm Mark; she would not suffer him to live.

Amelia didn't move. Not until she heard the rasping sound of Mac Peterson's breathing slow . . . and then stop.

Chapter Twenty-one

Houston and New Mexico

Amelia sat in her living room with Ben Deisler, president of the largest bank in Alamogordo, and the interim trustee appointed by the court after Atkinson's arrest. Deisler had brought her the papers she needed to sign to dissolve the trust. It should have been an occasion of pure release for her, but just now she felt as if she'd been sitting in this room talking to officials forever.

First the deputy marshal about Peterson's attack and subsequent death, then someone from the prosecutor's office about the case against Nick Atkinson. A woman from the banking commission. The medical examiner, the coroner—an unending stream of officialdom had rolled through her living room.

Things were getting sorted out at last: Peterson's death had been ruled accidental, and it seemed she might not even have to testify at Atkinson's trial. But she hadn't been in the studio once since Peterson had driven up to the house that afternoon three weeks ago.

Thank God her ghostly guardian had been on full alert. Mark hadn't had a scratch on him, and she'd lost only two beehives to the fire, although those had burned to pathetic little piles of gray ash.

Gramps and Mark had kept her from losing the entire yard. And Spencer Reed. That ringing in her ears had been Mark, blowing his nickel-plated whistle for all he was worth. Reed had been passing the ranch on his way home and had come—with the V.F.D.'s fire extinguisher—in time to stop the flames from spreading to the other hives.

When she had commended Mark later that day for having the presence of mind to blow the whistle, he only shook his head.

"Wasn't me," he told her. "It was that old guy in the red shirt—he hollered at me to blow it."

Dopey with antihistamines and squinting out of the eye not swollen closed from bee stings, she had asked *what* old guy.

Mark had given her a funny look. "You know, the old guy. The one with the mustache who's always hanging around talking to you about the bees," he said.

Then Tucker had given a long-suffering sigh and flopped his head across her knees to express his deep offense at not being allowed on her bed just because Burk was there. Amelia told him to get used to it; Burk seemed pretty settled in.

Burk had said, "You got that right. You get into too much trouble when I leave you on your own."

But Mark had said anxiously, "You know who I mean, don't you, Amelia?"

"Sure," she assured him. "I just never realized you'd seen him before—"

Burk cut in then to tell Mark that Amelia needed to get some sleep now, and she had let the subject drop. That seemed best.

The next morning, Spence Reed had come to visit her. Although she suspected her face was still decidedly lopsided, Reed hadn't even blinked when he saw her. She expected him to give her a hard time about being such a firebug. Instead he had told her quite solemnly that there had been bad blood between the Reeds and the Rawlinses for too long.

"I'd like you to bury the hatchet with me," he said, "and let bygones be bygones."

"You saved my business for me yesterday, Mr. Reed. You have my gratitude. I'd be pleased to bury the hatchet."

He had ceremoniously shaken her hand. "I have to tell you, ma'am, what you did yesterday—" he wrestled with words for a second, then burst out with, "It's the goddamn bravest thing I ever saw."

Then he turned bright red. "Begging your pardon, ma'am."

Amelia was both touched and amused. "Thank you, sir. That means a lot, coming from you."

"I'm glad to be on terms with you, Miz Rawlins," he said, all grave dignity again.

But as he rose to leave, she couldn't resist a parting shot. "Actually, Mr. Reed, my last name is Caswell."

Reed picked up his hat, and looked pointedly at Burk, who was sitting cozily on the arm of her chair. The old man gave a crack of laughter.

"Not for long, I reckon," he said. He was still chuckling as he went out the door.

So much for trying to have the last word, Amelia thought now. Or for keeping her private life private, even though she wasn't completely certain yet herself of what direction she and Burk were headed.

His presence over the past few weeks had made all the turmoil and complications bearable. But she had been leaning on him more than was good for her. Or him. Until she was sure of what she wanted, it was unfair of her to rely on his support.

Unfair, but that didn't make her miss him any less when he wasn't around, like now.

She dragged her attention back to what Ben Deisler was trying to tell her. At least she was certain about dissolving the trust. It was time for her to face whatever doing that brought, good and bad. If her uncle couldn't forgive her for what she had done twelve years ago—well, so be it.

The prospect of seeing Michael again was more disquieting. She didn't know if she could ever forgive herself for what had happened to him. The price he had paid for trying to defend her . . .

She had wanted to graft the two halves of her life together. But before this hybrid life she was trying to create for herself could flourish, she had to cut away the part that fear had poisoned. Until she confronted her past, and relinquished it, there was no chance for a new life.

So far, the worst part of letting go was losing Gramps. She hadn't seen him once since Peterson's death. It seemed that saving the apiary from going up in flames—and her with it—had been his final action as resident ghost.

She heard an engine, and glanced out the window. Burk's Jeep was pulling up under the cottonwood trees. Deisler continued to talk as she watched. After a moment, the passenger door opened, and a new ghost got out.

All the blood in her body seemed to subside at once. She couldn't get her breath, and it took her two tries to say "Excuse me" to Mr. Deisler.

He nodded, and she went to the kitchen door. Her hands were shaking so hard she could scarcely turn the doorknob. She was limping as she walked toward the phantom. The cast had only come off yesterday.

He stood there near the cottonwood trees, and as she went toward him, she watched the breeze ripple through his straight dark hair. He was staring up at the Folly, and his face was pale.

"Daniel?" Her voice was even shakier than her hands.

He turned abruptly, and his Adam's apple moved convulsively. Then he gave her a pained smile. "Y-you don't even—know me, Mellie?"

Only one person had ever called her that. She looked sharply at his forehead. Where the wind pushed back his hair, she saw the spiderweb of scars.

It astonished her that her heart could find any blood to keep pumping; she felt so emptied. She was afraid to say his name. Terrified that if she let herself believe he was there, speaking to her, he would be snatched away again. But her lips seemed to form the word without her volition.

"Michael?" It was a breath, not even a whisper, but he heard.

"Yes, it's me, Mellie." He took a hesitant step forward. "Is it—do you—mind my coming here?"

"Mind?" She began to laugh, even as tears heated her eyes and spilled over. *"Mind? Michael!"*

There was a flicker of red plaid off under the cottonwood trees, and for an instant, she thought she saw Gramps waving to them. But her brother was right here with her, and the shimmer was already gone.

Then she was holding him, hard, noticing the faint scent of his soap, his hair silky against her cheek when he dipped his head.

His voice was strained. "I thought you stayed away because—that it was my fault—I let them—"

"Shhh," she said. "It was my fault *you* were hurt, Mike. Mike, the papers said you had—you were—"

"In a c-coma for two months. Some brain damage. But I've got a tough skull."

She reached up and smoothed the hair back from his forehead. The scar was bad. *He's so tall,* she thought. And then, fiercely: *Not strapped in some hospital bed— he's all right. Still* Michael.

After that first charged moment of reunion passed, Burk got out of the Jeep and grinned at her.

"Thanks for bringing him out," Amelia managed to say.

"Wouldn't have missed it for the world," Burk said.

Mr. Deisler had waited patiently through their greeting, but he came outside at that point and politely recalled Amelia's attention to their business.

She was relieved in a way. After twelve years, what did she say to her brother next? Then it occurred to her that Michael wasn't mentioned in Gramps's will. When she had thought him incapacitated, that hadn't seemed unfair, but now—

She turned to him. "Gramps—I'm afraid he left the ranch to me, Michael. I know how much you always loved it—"

But he was already shaking his head. "Gramps w-wanted you to have it. He wrote me and said he'd gotten a card from you, so he knew you were alive. He wanted you to have a place to c-come back to—whenever you got ready." He cleared his throat. "Till then, w-we thought you'd been k-kidnapped, M-Mellie."

Burk saved her from having to answer by cocking an eyebrow and saying, " 'Mellie'?"

She smiled. "Nickname—and only my kid brother gets away with calling me that."

Mr. Deisler gave a tactful cough.

"Where are my manners?" Amelia said. "Y'all come on inside and have some iced tea while Mr. Deisler and I finish up."

She found herself observing Michael closely, trying to discern the extent of his impairment. He walked with a limp, moving his right leg awkwardly, but seemed totally unself-conscious about it. Amelia remembered the agonies of her own physical therapy. He had needed her, and she hadn't been there for him.

The business was a welcome distraction—getting them past the awkward moments between the reunion and the rest of their lives—even though it was quickly concluded.

"I have to take these before the judge on Tuesday," Deisler said as he stacked the papers and returned them to his briefcase. "It's only a formality. In the meantime, I'll transfer this quarter's income into your personal account."

"I don't have an account," Amelia objected.

Mr. Deisler broke out of his frosty banker's mode long enough to give her a wink. "You do now. That last thing you signed was a signature card for a checking account. If you could drop by tomorrow after ten, my head cashier will have your temporary checks ready."

"Thank you," she said. "You've been so kind."

"My pleasure, Ms. Caswell." He shook her hand, then turned to shake the men's hands as well.

She walked him to the door and thanked him again. Then she took a deep breath and returned to the kitchen table, where Burk and Michael were talking in low tones.

She had told herself she was ready to face her past, and here it was. The most important part of her personal history was sitting in one of her kitchen chairs.

Amelia sat down next to him. "Tell me—"

At the same time, Michael said, "What happened—"

They each broke off, then Michael repeated, "What happened to you, Mel? The police thought you'd been taken hostage."

Her heart was pounding. "Only for a little while. They dumped me by the bayou. People from Covenant House found me. They thought—they see a lot of battered kids. They thought I was one, and I—I wanted them to. I couldn't face what had happened at—" She had meant to say, "at home," but the word wouldn't come out.

Michael was watching her closely. "I'm glad there were people to take care of you. I used to have bad d-dreams about you—hurt, all b-by yourself—"

"Me, too," she said, "about you. Still do, really. They took care of me for a few months, and then I went to live on a cooperative farm—kind of a commune and school both—in Navasota. I apprenticed to a potter there, and—and that's what I do."

"Burk told me," Michael said. "Says you're really good at it. And you've been keeping bees, too?"

She was afraid if they sidetracked into small talk, she'd be afraid to bring it up later. She didn't know how to ask gracefully, so she just said it. "How are you, Michael? I mean, what's your life been like?"

He raised both eyebrows high. Except for the pale lines of the scar on his forehead that broke up the neat furrows of skin, he looked exactly like Pop.

Amelia's heart squeezed. Then his expression changed, and he was Michael again. "Well, I've lived with Uncle Bob since—since Mama and Pop were killed. In V-Virginia, mostly, but we spend some t-time in Texas every year, too."

He hesitated. "Uncle Bob sold the house. I hope you don't mind."

Amelia tried to imagine ever going back there, and couldn't. Some parts of the past were best left buried. "No, I'm glad."

"I was in the hospital a long time after, anyway. Had to learn to w-walk all over again, and I still stutter some. But Uncle Bob got me tutors, and I made up a lot of the l-lost time. Graduated from Georgetown this spring, with honors." He grinned at her. "Poli-sci. Got accepted into their law s-school, too. I start there this fall."

She touched his shoulder, feeling shy about it. "Mike, that's wonderful. You must be so proud."

He nodded, then licked his lips. "So you never got to finish school, Mellie? Uncle Bob was wondering— that is, we were b-both hoping—you'd think about c-coming back to Washington with me. Maybe try Georgetown for your undergrad work. Uncle Bob can f-f-f—arrange that for you."

The phone rang, the first time all afternoon. Amelia answered it, glad of the interruption. It was Jorge Valdez.

"Just wanted to let you know a camera crew from Albuquerque stopped by for gas a minute ago, asking for directions to the Rawlins-*Caswell* ranch," he said.

Amelia sighed. She'd known the newshounds would be after her, once word got out she was alive. But why today of all days?

"Well, thanks for the heads-up, Señor Valdez. Burk's here—guess he and Tucker'll help me get rid of them."

Mr. Valdez laughed. "Oh, I don't think you need to worry too much—last I saw, they were headed off up the road to Three Rivers."

Amelia thanked him profusely. He was still chuckling delightedly when he hung up.

The afternoon thundershower had come and gone in its typical burst of pyrotechnics. Now sunlight sifted through the open weave of the kitchen curtains and dappled the battered surface of the table. Before she sa down, she pushed the curtains back on their brass rods, letting the last of the sun in.

Michael watched her as if he were afraid she would vanish if he glanced away. She understood the feeling. They had lost so many years.

Amelia took a breath. "I'm sorry I ran, Michael. I was scared, and I hated myself for what I did. But I was selfish—I didn't think about you or Gramps—that you might need me."

Burk was watching her with a faint smile. "She says that, but your sister's one of the most generous people I know."

She turned toward him as he spoke, placing her left arm in full sight on the kitchen table.

Michael didn't say anything.

When she glanced over at him, he was staring at her scar, his eyes shadowed. What was he thinking? He hadn't said how much he remembered of that night. Did he blame her?

It was odd, but the scar didn't seem so shameful to her anymore. Looking at it now only made her sad.

Michael reached over to trace his fingers across the ruined flesh. His touch was very light.

"I'm so s—sorry, Mellie," he said. His voice broke on her name.

He sounded so much the Michael she had known, so much her kid brother, that it seemed the most natural thing in the world to wrap him in her arms and rock him. He buried his face against her shoulder.

The strangest thing was how easily her own eyes filled with tears. She didn't try to block them. She let them pour down her face and drip on his dark hair.

Sometimes crying did solve things; she was grateful to Caroline for teaching her that.

Tucker got up from his place by the door and trotted over to nuzzle her arm. Burk reached out to scratch his ears, and Tucker settled down again, this time squarely on Amelia's feet.

"So sorry—" Michael choked out.

He turned his face against her shoulder; his tears were hot as they soaked into her shirt. She imagined she could feel the web of scars on his forehead through the damp cloth.

Somehow they would have to find their way through the maze of memories to the truth of what had happened to them. A journey that had always seemed impossible. But with Michael here, Amelia believed she could find the way.

Her brother sat up and looked at her, his eyes haunted. "I'm so sorry, Mellie."

She had a lot to make up to him.

"Me, too," she said.

"Uncle Bob wanted to drop everything and fly down with me," Michael explained later, after they'd eaten supper. He and Burk had done the dishes, and the three of them were sitting around the table with their coffee. "I asked him not to. I—it's selfish to want you all to myself, but I needed to s-see you alone first. I hope you d-don't mind."

She reached out and took his hand. "I'm glad. Too many people at once—would have been hard for me."

He nodded, then licked his lips. "Mellie, you never said if you wanted—if you would c-come back to Virginia with me." His hand tightened on hers.

Amelia started to speak, then paused, letting the possibility wash through her. Simply because she'd become accustomed to not having options didn't mean they were worthless. But there was the ranch, and Mark and Caroline. And Burk . . . She looked over at him. He had leaned forward, and his hand was tense around the coffee cup.

She shook her head. "I'll come for a visit later in the year," she said gently. "Once the bees are wintered in. But I'm a potter. And this is home."

Michael blinked several times, then stood abruptly, swinging around to stare out the windows at the mountains. The last stragglers of the afternoon rain clouds stretched thin and blue above the range, their undersides tinted pink by the fading rays of the sun.

It was getting on toward dark, and the kitchen was turning shadowy around them. Before long, she'd have to get up and turn on the lights. But just now she didn't feel like moving.

Burk was in his accustomed place on her left, relaxed now. At ease with himself and his surroundings, in spite of all this serious talk. *Right at home,* she thought.

After a pause, Michael cleared his throat. "I understand," he said. Without turning, he added, "I'd like to stay for a week or so, if that's okay with you."

Amelia was still watching Burk. A bubble of pure contentment formed around her heart and spread outward—suffusing her body, this room, then skimming out to encompass the ranch, the mountains, the brilliant evening sky.

Burk smiled at her, and, all at once, her world was in perfect balance.

"I want you to," she said.

ABOUT THE AUTHOR

SUSAN WADE is a native of Austin, Texas, where she lives with too many books and an appalling shortage of shelf space. Her short fiction has appeared in a number of national magazines and anthologies, including a series featuring adult fairy tales in the tradition of Angela Carter. She is working on a new novel called *Mourning Doves*.

THE VERY BEST IN CONTEMPORARY
WOMEN'S FICTION

SANDRA BROWN

____28951-9 Texas! Lucky $6.50/$8.99 in Canada

____28990-X Texas! Chase $6.50/$8.99

____29500-4 Texas! Sage $6.50/$8.99

____29085-1 22 Indigo Place $5.99/$6.99

____29783-X A Whole New Light $5.99/$6.99

____56768-3 Adam's Fall $5.50/$7.

____56045-X Temperatures Rising $5.99/$6.

____56274-6 Fanta C $5.50/$6.

____56278-9 Long Time Coming $5.50/$7.

____57157-5 Heaven's Price $5.50/$6.

TAMI HOA

____29534-9 Lucky's Lady $5.99/$7.50

____29053-3 Magic $5.99/$7.50

____56050-6 Sarah's Sin $5.50/$7.50

____56451-x Night Sins $5.99/$7.99

____29272-2 Still Waters $5.99/$7

____56160-X Cry Wolf $5.50/$6

____56161-8 Dark Paradise $5.99/$7

____09959-0 Guilty As Sin $21.95/$26

NORA ROBERTS

____29078-9 Genuine Lies $5.99/$6.99

____28578-5 Public Secrets $5.99/$6.99

____26461-3 Hot Ice $5.99/$6.99

____26574-1 Sacred Sins $5.99/$6.99

____27859-2 Sweet Revenge $5.99/$6

____27283-7 Brazen Virtue $5.99/$6

____29597-7 Carnal Innocence $5.99/$6

____29490-3 Divine Evil $5.99/$

DEBORAH SMI

____29107-6 Miracle $5.50/$6.50

____29092-4 Follow the Sun $4.99/$5.99

____29690-6 Blue Willow $5.99/$

____29689-2 Silk and Stone $5.99/$

____28759-1 The Beloved Woman $4.50/$5.50

- -

Ask for these books at your local bookstore or use this page to order.

Please send me the books I have checked above. I am enclosing $____(add $2.50 to co
postage and handling). Send check or money order, no cash or C.O.D.'s, please.

Name _____

Address _____

City/State/Zip _____

Send order to: Bantam Books, Dept. FN 24, 2451 S. Wolf Rd., Des Plaines, IL 60018
Allow four to six weeks for delivery.

Prices and availability subject to change without notice.   FN 24